The Year of Oceans

Sean Anderson

RIVERSONG
BOOKS

An Imprint of Sulis International
Los Angeles | London
www.sulisinternational.com

Riversong Books
An Imprint of Sulis International
Los Angeles | London
www.sulisinternational.com

Cover and book design by Sulis International, 2017.

Library of Congress Control Number: 2017963629
Paperback ISBN: 978-1-946849-17-5
eBook ISBN: 978-1-946849-16-8

For Mother

Table of Contents

February

I.

The flowers had wilted.

Dangling over a yellow pot were tulips that had long ceased to live. Petals had fallen onto the surface of the table, and the stems were bent at sharp angles. Struck by how sorrowful the scene was, Hugo sighed, walked over, and began to toss the flower remnants into the trash. As he did this, he thought that he really ought to replace the flowers with new ones. Then he realized that buying new flowers today would mean more wilting in a few days, so what was the point? Still, in his mind, it was nice and pleasant to have the pretty, aromatic display in the kitchen, if only for a little while. It was worth the trouble.

After he disposed of the last petal he walked into the bedroom. For a moment he stood in the doorway, frozen, as though he forgot why he had entered the room. Once the moment passed he went into the closet and grabbed a tie. It was light blue with white stripes. By no means was it his favorite, but it was fitting for the overcast, cool day outside. No matter the occasion, it was Hugo's way to wear a tie. If dressing up served him for forty-four years of work as an accountant, then surely it was the best way to approach the world of retirement. He found navy blue corduroy pants to wear along with a scarf and stepped out of the closet.

He looked at the bed and sighed.

With one more look at where the flowers had been, he walked to the front door of his house and stepped outside. He raised up a hand, testing to see if it was raining, and was annoyed that it was mildly misting. It was colder than he would have liked. Across the street stood rows of trees. The houses on the street were small and old. Because there were so many trees, the expanse of the sky above was minimized. Hugo looked at his feet and realized that his shoes were not been tied. Once he remedied this, he continued on his way.

Reaching into his mailbox, he was irritated to find more notices from the retirement association. He also came across a letter from his son, Adrian. He took the letters inside and put them on the coffee table. Then, he stepped back outside. As he closed the gate, he heard a voice call his name.

"Hey, Hugo!"

Turning around, he saw that it was his neighbor and good friend of over thirty years, Paul.

"Hi, Paul."

"How have you been?" Paul was short and slim, with a beard and dark-colored hair.

"Oh, fine."

It seemed as though Paul was surveying his friend carefully. "Are you sure?" he asked.

"Yes, I said what I meant," Hugo snapped back.

"Okay, well it's just that, you know, given what happened last-"

"I'm not interested in going into that," Hugo fumed. "Anyway, I must be off."

"Where are you going?"

"To purchase some flowers," Hugo said, clutching his scarf tightly.

"Well, that sounds nice. Just be sure to stay warm!"

"Yes, it is so damn cold out here," Hugo replied, "you can practically see your breath!"

"It's not so bad," Paul said. "Tell me, when will you be over to play chess again?"

"Soon."

"When is 'soon'?"

"Maybe in a week or two?"

"Okay."

"Very good," Hugo said, "Now, I must be off."

"Can't delay the rush for flowers! It's a shame it's February, or else you could just take some out of your garden. Know what I mean?"

"Yes," Hugo said, "I know precisely what you mean."

"What we should really do," said Paul, "is take a chess board up to the arboretum sometime to play. That would be nice, wouldn't it?"

"Yes, I suppose so," Hugo replied.

"Anyway, I'll see you later, my friend. Until next time!"

"Until next time."

Hugo and Paul had been friends for many years. Together, they raised their children. They were so close that they were effectively family. Hugo had many, many memories of going places with Paul and doing things together. Since they were both retired, they frequently managed to come up with the time to go on adventures. Hugo was sixty-six, and Paul was sixty-eight. Hugo felt like he could talk to Paul about virtually anything, Lately, though, there was a bit of a rift between them, for there was something that Paul wanted to talk to Hugo about, but that he remained uninterested in discussing. This topic of conversation, this situation, was something that Hugo had been grappling with, that he was struggling with. Thinking about this rift between his friend and him, he decided it was best to clear his mind and focus on the task at hand.

Hugo took a left turn onto Mason Street. Vibrant, growing, containing shops and apartments, Mason Street was the central avenue of Wedgwood, the neighborhood in North Seattle in which Hugo lived. It was here, on Mason Street, that one could find pricey housing, cheap booze, exotic food to eat, trees to admire, parks to play in, and churches to visit. It was a street that meant something different to every person who visited it. Today, as he was walking, what Mason Street signified to Hugo was flowers.

It was not a far distance to the grocery store, but then again, every walk seemed to feel like a massive trek to him. The fresh air was enjoyable to experience. He moved quickly but with intention, as he always did. Several times runners overtook and passed him, nearly knocking him over. These youngsters, who wore fancy exercise clothes and had earbuds in, were oblivious as to where they were going. Hugo was slightly annoyed but did not pay it much mind. On one occasion he saw a woman who was walking a dog. Taking several steps to the side, he was sure to be out of the range of the mutt, for he despised all dogs.

His eyes were focused on the ground. The cracks and bends in the city street demanded that Hugo was cautious of his movements. In all, it was a beautiful day, and it was difficult for him to complain. The past few days were cold and wet, so even to have just an overcast day with some mist came as a relief. He realized that he left his phone back at home, but he didn't need it, so he wasn't concerned.

Already Hugo had passed a grocery store, but he found the smell inside to be less than pleasant and the prices to be more than expensive, so he was content to walk the extra ten minutes to the Wedgwood Grocery Store. Not much longer and the store was within sight. Hugo went up, opened the door, heard the sound of the ringing bell, and went inside. He maneuvered past pastries and went towards the small but quaint floral department. Hugo saw flowers of many colors and types on display. He found it reinvigorating after all that junk food to simply breathe in and bask in the scents. Wondering what type of flower to purchase, he was unsure.

"How are we doing today?" the voice of twenty-something girl with pink streaks in her hair and a bundle of daisies in her hand called.

"Not too bad," Hugo grumbled.

"Anything I can help you find?"

"Yes, well, I'm not too sure what it is I want to pick out, so I'd let you help me if I knew how."

She chuckled. "Okay, well just let me know."

"I will."

He turned around and looked back at the rest of the store. There were only a few other people who were there shopping, moving slowly up and down the endless aisles. All at once, Hugo felt alone, confused, wondering what it was he was really doing at the store. He reminded himself that he was here to buy new flowers, that they, in fact, were a nice and pleasant thing to have, and that he would be glad that he got them. Picking up a bundle of roses, he was tempted by them. After all, there were few things in the world quite as charming as red roses. Yet the romance and passion that they evoked were more than what he was interested in on this particular day.

Then he saw some tulips on the bottom of the display. He picked them up, surveying their yellow splendor carefully, imagining how they might look in his kitchen by a guest. Then he realized that these days he never had guests over, and it seemed as though the pressure was removed from buying the "right" flowers. Sure, he previously purchased tulips, but maybe the continuity of it was a nice thing after all. With his thumb, he felt the stem and was pleased by the soft sensation.

"Sir?"

"Yes?" he turned around to look at the clerk.

"We ask that customers are careful with the flowers until a purchase has been made."

"Oh, yes, of course." He held the tulips more tightly. "I'll take these," he declared.

As he walked out of the store he was bombarded at the front entrance with all of the Valentine's Day candies that went on sale since the holiday passed. There were chocolates in heart-shaped boxes of vibrant colors. He looked over the candies, still holding onto his flowers tightly, and walked out the door.

Outside, it had warmed up a bit. Glad that he did not bring a jacket, he stepped onto Mason Street and was nearly knocked over by yet another runner.

"Excuse me," the runner said, already fifteen feet up the street and still in motion.

Hugo tried to not be irritated, but he was.

When he stepped off of Mason Street, he planted a foot incorrectly on the curb and rolled his ankle. He fell to the ground, using a hand to protect himself as he collided with the concrete. For a moment he sat there on the ground in agony, wondering how he ended up in such a situation.

"Oh, I'm so sorry, sir!" a voice called. "Do you need help?"

"No, I'm fine," he said to the passerby. But he was not able to get himself off of the ground. He shifted his feet, feeling the intense pain in his left ankle, trying to get up, but he was unsuccessful.

"Are you sure?" the man asked.

"I told you I'm fine!"

Letting go of the flowers, he used both of his hands to steady himself, putting his weight on his good foot, and then he raised himself up off the ground. The pain was hardly bearable. He stumbled with the first few steps he took, but he was capable of walking. The man who offered to help stood there, and the next moment he was gone.

Evidently, Hugo was never one to ask for help from others. To live life self-sufficiently was among his highest ideals. Even when he was weak, struggling, humiliated, he was better pleased to suffer alone than to rely on anyone else to help. Perhaps this attitude was a result of how he was raised. The Larson family valued a firm, severe orientation towards the world. No one taught Hugo how to ride a bike, and no one had ever offered to pay his way through college. A long and successful career as an accountant instilled in Hugo an appreciation for figuring out how to make sense of the world and to navigate it confidently. This was simply the way he saw things.

So he stumbled, clutching the flowers, back towards his house. It started to drizzle, but it never turned into anything in the way of significant rain. The moisture falling from above was not welcomed by Hugo, who was already frustrated enough. His experiences that day taught him that it was best to simply never leave the house, because clearly the only thing waiting for him outside was trouble. His mind kept focusing on the pain in his ankle. He was practically dragging his left foot along the pavement.

If the sun had been visible behind the steady cover of clouds, surely Hugo thought that it would have been sinking into the hills by the time he reached his house. Unlatching the gate he made his way up to the front door, lifting his injured foot above the single step at the entryway. Inside, he collapsed onto the sofa, spending a moment in pure bliss.

6

Then he got up, placed the flowers in a pot, and poured some water in to go along with it. He walked around his house, looking for something to do, but there was nothing. Eventually, he found his way back to the sofa. He reached for the remote and turned on the television. As he surfed from one channel to another he made comments in his head about how the shows signified the decline of civilization. Finally, he reached a British mystery program, one of his favorites to watch. Using what seemed to be all the strength he had left he went into the kitchen and poured himself a glass of water, bringing it back with him to the sofa once more.

For a while he watched the program, getting lost in the intricacies of the case, examining the minds of the characters. Soon it became dark outside.

There was a knock at the door. Slightly alarmed by the fact that he had a visitor, he mustered his strength to rise up off of the sofa, but he fell back down. Again he rose up, this time making it firmly to his feet. He walked over, gazing through the little hole to see that it was his son Adrian waiting outside. He unlocked the door and let him in.

Tall, lanky, with blue eyes and short brown hair, Adrian was someone who radiated a sense of messiness, of disorder. Always well-meaning, Adrian was kind but slightly foolish, typically a little bit out of touch with a given situation. Hugo, who worked hard his entire career as an accountant for a vacuum cleaner company, built an empire to hand off to his son. Great hope and promise had been placed on Adrian, who graduated from high school with decent enough grades and gone off to study photography at the Art Institute of Seattle. Yet upon graduating, Adrian had seemed to lose some of his spark when it came to his career. During his final year of school, he was working as a barista at a café in Capitol Hill named Java City, and he continued to work there full-time even as he gained his degree. Somehow, with time, dreams of working in photography dissipated, becoming replaced with coffee and taking people's orders. Now twelve years of working as a barista had passed with no new career developments. Adrian was thirty-three. All that Hugo created and garnered, it seemed, was wasted on a youth who was content to earn a small wage. It was difficult for Hugo to not feel bitter as he thought about this situation. Though he was very close to his son during Adrian's childhood, for the past twelve years Hugo was in more sporadic touch with him, occasionally writing letters, sometimes visiting, but never in intimate terms. The father and son, simply put, were not close. Adrian had no kids of his own, lived alone in central Seattle, and seemed perfectly content with the life he was living. So it was with a feeling of expectation that Hugo let his son into his home, anticipating that there would be some news to report.

"Hey, Dad!"

"Hello, hello. Come on in."

Adrian entered, removing his coat. Chill night air wafted in through the open doorway.

"How's my son?"

"Pretty good. You?"

"Not too bad." Hugo stumbled back towards the sofa, hoping that his injury was not obvious to the eye. Perhaps it just appeared to be typical aging. "What can I do for you?"

"I was in the neighborhood, running an errand, and I thought I would come by."

"Excellent." Hugo looked and saw that the unopened letter, written by Adrian, was resting in plain sight on the coffee table. In one rapid movement, he grabbed it and put it into his pocket. "As you can see," he continued, pointing at the television, "I am up to a great deal tonight."

"It's been a while, hasn't it?"

"Since I last saw you?"

Adrian nodded.

"I suppose so. I probably saw you back in January, I think," Hugo said.

"How have things been?"

Sensing that he already in a way answered this question, Hugo replied, "I have been well. I try to keep busy."

"And has everything been okay since, you know..."

"Oh yes, yes. I have been fine. I have been just fine."

"Good." Adrian appeared concerned.

"How is work?" Hugo inquired.

"It's pretty good, it has been very busy since the holidays ended."

"No surprise there. People do need their coffee."

"You don't, do you, Dad?"

"Me? You know I stopped drinking coffee twenty years ago. Never liked the way it made my stomach feel."

"That's right."

Hugo reached for the remote and turned off the television.

"I finished moving two weeks ago," Adrian continued.

"Oh, did you now?"

"Yes, it wasn't too stressful."

"You're still in..."

"Capitol Hill."

"Right. How do you like it there?"

"I like it a lot. I moved maybe ten blocks away from where I was before. The setup is much better. No roommates. All by myself in an apartment. I'm pretty close to a park, and I can walk to all sorts of things that I need."

"You know, that sounds an awful lot like where I live here," Hugo gestured with a hand.

"Yes, I suppose that's true."

"Just today I was walking. I went and got some flowers."

"Well, that sounds nice. Just up the street at that one store?"

"No, there's a small community grocery store on Mason Street that I like."

"That's a pretty far walk from here!"

"Me? I've got the time to walk."

"Have you been moving around well these days?" Adrian asked.

"Yes, never better," Hugo remarked.

"That's good." Adrian looked around the house, as though he was searching for something, and then he said, "You know, Capitol Hill is a great place to live, but it sure is changing a lot."

"Everywhere is changing a lot."

"Sure, but I mean this neighborhood is being transformed. All over the place, there are cranes and fancy condos and apartments are coming up out of the ground. There is gentrification going on, and it is getting harder and harder for people like me to live there."

"What do you mean 'people like me'?"

"You know, baristas, artists, people who work at restaurants, the wage earners. It is getting really tough to live in the neighborhood because everything is just getting more and more expensive."

"I can't say I like the direction my neighborhood is going in, either."

"Oh, Dad, Wedgwood is practically the exact same. I mean, sure you have a crane here or there, but it's nothing compared to where I live."

"Well, if it's hard for a barista to survive, then maybe it's time for the barista to become something else," Hugo said, lacking subtlety.

"The café has been doing pretty well," Adrian continued.

"Good to hear. Any chance you'll be running the place soon?"

"Maybe. You should come and visit me at work."

"Oh, you know I've been there before."

"You have, but it's been a while. I'd love to show you our new single-origin coffees. We have one from Brazil that packs a punch."

"Again, I haven't had a cup of coffee in twenty years, so why would I now?"

"I dunno, for fun?"

"I don't think so," Hugo said, smiling.

"Well, it would be really great if you came. I'm always telling my coworkers stories about you."

"The last thing I need is for strangers to know stories about me."

"Come on. It's nothing big."

Hugo waved his hand. "Fine. I think I'll try and make it to Java Sea sometime in March."

"It's Java City."

"Okay."

"March?" Adrian asked.

Hugo placed his feet on the coffee table. "I'm a busy man with places to be and people to talk to. You know this. Once you retire, it isn't so easy to get around places. Plus I don't drive these days."

"How's the car running?"

Hugo looked out the window at his blue sedan. "I wouldn't know."

"Gotcha."

"Would you like a cup of water?" Hugo asked, rising from the couch.

"No thanks. Do you have any coffee?"

"What do you think?"

"No?"

"No, I don't."

"Okay."

Once he returned from the kitchen Hugo got comfortable on the sofa again.

"Those flowers look great, Dad."

"Thanks, I picked them out myself."

"So what is it that has got you so busy?"

"What's that?"

"You said you're a busy man, so I'm wondering what keeps you busy."

"Oh, you know a little of this and a little of that."

"Like what?"

Hugo began to think. "I'm busy with lots of things," he said, "watching soccer at the bar, going swimming, playing chess with Paul, working in the garden, walking around, taking care of errands, going to the store, is that enough stuff?"

"Sure sounds like it. You ever make it downtown?"

"Downtown?"

"Yeah, you ever go around and see other parts of the city?"

Hugo gestured with a hand. "Why would I go anywhere.?I have everything I need here."

Adrian appeared unconvinced. "Oh, okay, well you know there's a lot of neat stuff to see in this city."

"Like?"

"I dunno. Beaches."

"Beaches," Hugo repeated. "Well, like I said, I have everything I need here, so I don't see myself going to a beach anytime soon."

"Okay."

There was a pause in the conversation. Hugo had a sip of his water and shuffled his position. Adrian coughed and then said, "The move was pretty exciting. But not everything in life has been that good for me."

"No?"

"Yeah, ever since...well you know, I mentioned it to you in the letter I sent you."

Hugo's eyes flashed. "Well yes of course you did."

"Sorry if I went on and on about it, it was just on my mind."

"Of course. Not a problem."

Adrian rested his head on a hand. "It's been tough, Dad."

"I know, son. That really is too bad to hear. I'm sorry." Hugo placed a hand on his son's shoulder, looking upon him with genuine compassion despite the fact that he didn't know what was the matter. He suspected he knew what his son was referring to, but he wasn't positive.

So father and son talked on for a while. Hugo must have gone through at least three cups of water, and he enjoyed the company of his son, even if he was left wondering how the crime on the mystery program was solved. When it got to be late, Hugo stumbled to the front door, hugged his son, and watched him walk towards his car. When Adrian drove off, Hugo turned off the front light and went back inside. He walked up the stairs towards his bedroom, which was agony for his ankle. Yet he saw no need to complain about his condition.

Finally, Hugo rested his head against his pillow and began to think tranquil things as he drifted off towards sleep. The last coherent thought he remembered having was remarking to himself that the tulips, indeed, looked stunning on the kitchen table.

2.

He stood in front of the mirror, surveying himself. What he was confronting were several new wrinkles that had formed just above his eyes. Trying his best not to despair, he looked at himself with a calm peacefulness that was not his character. Hugo had brown eyes that looked like coffee with cream added, a mustache, and graying, vanishing hair. It seemed that every day he spent time looking at himself in the mirror in this way, principally after taking shower. Was he vain? Spending little time dwelling on this question, he proceeded to brush his teeth.

As usual, he skipped breakfast and settled for a glass of water. He knew that a day was forming outside, as the rays of the sun were poking through the tree branches. It was his habit to rise early and go to bed late. As he sat at the table drinking water he scanned the newspaper. There was news of another terrorist attack in Europe. Feeling dismayed he turned the page quickly. He looked over the sports section and became bogged down with all the numbers. For a few minutes, he sat and did nothing. Looking down at his watch he saw that it was time to be on his way.

When he rose from the table he once more felt the sharp pain in his ankle, even though it healed a fair amount in the last few days.

Inside his closet, he found his favorite jersey, which was colored purple and red. He put it on over his dress shirt, his purple tie still visible. While he stood in the living room he gazed at the light which cascaded through the window, flooding the entire room in a splendid way. He took a step into it and then turned back towards the front door to put on his shoes. At last ready, he quickly walked down the stairs, locked the front door, and went on his way.

The bar was located on Mason Street. Fortunately, he left himself with plenty of time to make it, so he was not worried about missing any of the game. Though his ankle still hurt his gait was improved considerably. Overhead there were the bare tree branches, still evoking the death of winter. He was sure to look both left and right twice before crossing the intersection, not that there were any cars to be seen on such a quiet Sunday morning. It was yet another overcast day. Hugo had been through enough cloudy days in his long life in Seattle that he no longer thought much of them. For him, a day was simply another day. There was not much that surprised him or shook him out of the little universe he had crafted for himself, or so he thought.

There was, however, a breeze today that was considerable in strength. The cold threatened to unsettle him, but his jersey was made of a thick material, keeping him warm. There were no people out walking on the street. He looked up to see the street sign, which read Fir Street. Next, there would come Blossom Street, then Alder Street, and then Spruce Street. In his life in Wedgwood, he became more than well acquainted with the layout of the neighborhood, for he was able to name the streets without thinking for even a moment.

It was his expectation that his team would perform well today. They were playing a relatively unknown club, and there was the home-field advantage, which surely counted for something. However, the pessimistic side of Hugo continually threatened to surface, spoiling his high hopes. All year he was watching as his team defeated one opponent and then another. Never did he miss a game. It was his custom to walk to this bar, The Blue Hen, and watch his games. Always he sat in the same seat, just in the back corner. He ordered himself a Guinness and proceeded to spend the afternoon watching his team play.

There were several bars and cafes that he passed as he walked, and he began to wonder why he never went to any of these other venues to watch his team play. Then he reminded himself that The Blue Hen was the only place that actually showed soccer games in the entire neighborhood. Despite the fact that all of the businesses were open, there were no people inside of them. Hugo crossed the street, took a quick turn to the left, and entered the bar.

There was no one to be seen inside except a waiter. According to Hugo's custom, he was more than a half hour early for the game. He scrambled over to his seat, as though he feared someone else would take it at any moment. Not long after he sat down a waiter walked over and asked him what he wanted.

"A Guinness, please," he said at a loud volume.

It was pleasing to him to be left to his own in the bar. He looked around. The bar was spacious, full of many seats, with dim lighting, and it had several obscure soccer posters hanging up. There hung also a flag of Hugo's team. How had it become a soccer bar in the first place? He was not able to think about this for long before he observed the signed jerseys hanging on the wall on the other side. For a while, he looked at them as though he was meditating on them. One of the jerseys belonged to his very favorite player: Hernandez. Looking at them with gentle reverence, he felt a pride to be in the bar, ready to watch his team play. Surely, this was his church.

The waiter returned with the beer. Hugo took a sip, delighted by the hints of chocolate in the flavor, and then he looked up at the television set. There was an ad for a beer playing in the background. Hugo thought this was funny, that he was being sold a beer when he was already sitting and enjoying just such a beverage. He was not amused enough to stop feeling the skittish anxiety about his team's upcoming performance. Every week during the soccer season he came to the bar feeling nervous for his team, fearful their record would decline. He was not one for using computers, but he was careful to track how his team was doing, in turn comparing them with the other teams in the league. If he felt more motivated, he probably would have tracked the statistics from the games, channeling his inner accountant. But, rather, he was pleased to simply watch the game, to bask in the experience.

Soon the game started. The first half was relatively uneventful, with no team scoring. Several plays saw the ball nearly going in, the suspense rising as Hugo slowly got up from his chair to watch the action unfold, only for the goal to be missed. On one occasion one of the players from the other team appeared to be injured.

"Come on, get up, you performer..." Hugo muttered to himself. The sense of drama that accompanied injuries was among his least favorite aspects of the game.

So he continued to boo at the television screen as the player finally got up off the ground. Later on in the game, there was a foul that was rather blatant, an offense against one of Hugo's own players. Yet, despite the action, the first half resolved in what felt like a brief amount of time. Soon the television was back to showing advertisements for beers.

Hugo had long finished his own drink, and he was left to sit by himself, watching the advertisements. By now the bar had filled up with a few other fans of the same team, but no one was sitting by Hugo, and he felt no need to associate with them. In his daily wanderings, Hugo was pleased to evade the company of others as much as he was able to. The sound of other voices chatting was getting on his nerves as he sat there. Feeling a need to move, he rose up and walked outside of the bar, stepping into the chilled February air.

A restless walker, Hugo decided he would go up five blocks, turn around, and then come back. He did not enjoy watching the half-time commentary, listening to the point-less ramblings and speculations of some paid professionals in tacky suits. Rather, he liked to make his own meaning of the game. He didn't wish to talk to anyone else about soccer. In his mind, the half he had just witnessed was rather on the forgettable side of things. There was not a lot to be said about the performance. Simply enough, some players were playing well and others were not. But Hugo's team fortu-nately enough was known for its endurance, for its ability to emerge during the second half of games as a force to be reck-oned with. He imagined his team would have little problem in securing a victory during the second half, but he would have to wait and see.

He reached the arbitrary turn-around point. Pleased by how the day was shaping up and confident that he had time, he walked to the next street corner, passing a bakery. The scents from it were glorious to behold, and he was tempted to enter and purchase a croissant. Yet his sense of disdain for all things sweet allowed him to continue walking with little in the way of a struggle. As he reached the corner he turned around and passed by the bakery once more. He shuffled quickly past a young woman who was out taking her dog for a walk. He nearly forgot he rolled his ankle, for he was now moving with such verve and speed. The pain in his ankle did not bother him much. At home, he was sure to apply ice and go through the appropriate stretching exercises. Soon the bar was coming back into view, and he was preparing himself to reenter the mode of watching soccer.

His seat in the corner was empty. Because his father was an alcoholic, Hugo resolved that he would never drink more than one alcoholic beverage per day. It was a way for him to honor his father. For this reason, he asked for water when he sat down. Hugo looked up at the flag of his team hanging in the other corner of the bar, paying reverent attention to it, and proceeded to watch the second half of the game.

First, the other team scored. A player kicked it in from far out in the field, and miraculously the ball went in. Hugo struggled to believe it. Again and again, a replay was shown of it, driving the painful memory deeper into his consciousness. At last the game moved on. There was not much action for a while; just one failed drive after another. Then, in the seventy-eighth minute, magic happened. One of Hugo's favorite players struck the ball into the goal using his head. The play happened within the context of a corner kick. Hugo raised a righteous fist into the air in celebration. He looked around, remembering he was choosing to not associate with others, feeling glad that this was so, that he could behold the glory of a goal privately, that he could celebrate it all by himself.

But the game would not end gloriously for his team. During the eighty-sixth minute, the opposing team scored in what appeared to be a rather straightforward goal. Hugo was devastated. He banged the surface of the table and whispered a curse. When the waiter passed by he asked for another water. The final few minutes of the game transpired uneventfully, with Hugo's team making several failed attempts to tie the game back up.

A woman brought Hugo his drink.

"Who are you?" he barked.

"Me? The name is Lily."

"I was just being served by a little man who was very nice. What happened to him?"

"Drew? He's busy with another customer. It's all right," she said, sliding the water towards him. "You're in good hands."

"Am I? I wanted to be served by that Drew guy."

"Well what you've got is Lily," she said, visibly annoyed. "I'm the owner of this place."

"You are? Well, you should know I think you have a very nice little operation here. It's a great bar."

"Thank you. You know, I think I see you here each and every single weekend, but I never bothered to introduce myself, so that's what I'm doing now. We at the Blue Hen really do appreciate our regulars."

"I don't know what you mean about regulars, but I'm glad you have my soccer games on your television."

"You show up week after week. You're a loyal patron of our bar, so I wanted to thank you for that. That's all."

"You're quite welcome."

She motioned as if to turn and walk away, but stayed where she was standing, saying, "It looks like your team was less than successful today."

Hugo grunted in affirmation. He looked at Lily. She had blue eyes, long blonde hair, and appeared to be around his age. She wore a necklace comprising small pieces of rounded glass. She seemed to constantly have one of her hands on her side. "That really is too bad to hear about your team. But, as they say, there's always next time!" She said this loudly, as though she doubted Hugo's hearing ability.

"Do you watch much soccer?" he asked.

"Well, it's on a lot of the time."

"What's your favorite team?"

"Oh, I don't play favorites. I merely watch and enjoy the spectacle of it all."

"That's one way to look at it," Hugo said. "Me? I've been watching my team play since I was in high school. Back then I would sit in the living room with my dad, early in the morning, and watch them play. I remember when my dad got me my first jersey for Christmas. I swear it was the best Christmas present I ever received."

"I bet it was."

"I would watch the games with my dad and root for my team. Later on, in high school, I started to play soccer for the school team. I was a forward because I was quick and I knew how to move the ball. We weren't the best team in the district, but we were okay. I remember my senior year." Hugo's eyes were glowing. "We went 7-2 in the regular season and made it to playoffs. The big game arrived and we completely blew it. We were down 2-3. I had the ball, just seconds to go. I refused to pass to my teammates, and I took the ugliest shot you'll ever see on a soccer field. The ball completely missed the goal and we went home the losers. It took me a while to get over that one. I kept telling myself that if I had been more calm and reserved, if I passed the ball and opened up the field more, we might have had a chance of winning, but no," he took a sip of water, "it was all my fault. I remember how sad I felt watching my team play on TV after that, thinking my dreams of playing soccer in college were gone forever."

"Were they?"

"I played in college It was more casual, just some intramural stuff. But it was a lot of fun. My team even won the league championship during my junior year, and I made some great friends out of it, so I guess it wasn't all wasted."

"Sounds like it," she said. "You can drink to that."

"I will!"

"You know, it was really a pleasure to hear you tell some stories about how soccer has meant so much to you."

"It has meant a lot to me. It still does. I watch it every week."

"I know. What I am trying to say is that it inspires me a little to see someone who feels so genuinely passionate about something."

"It's no big deal. It's just what I do. You think I told you a lot of stories today? I got a million of other, better stories I could tell you about soccer. I didn't tell you about the time I learned how to do a pseudo-bicycle kick."

"No, you didn't." Now she was motioning away from Hugo's table. "I need to move and check on another table, but it was really nice to meet and chat with you, Hugo. Hopefully I'll see you again soon."

"Will you be showing the game next Sunday?" he asked. She nodded.

"Then you will be seeing me again."

He paid his bill, rose from the table, and walked towards the door of the bar, still feeling low about his team's loss, but yet also glad that he had made a new friend, someone who was interested in hearing about soccer. As he left the bar he already was looking forward to next week.

3.

"Hugo Larson?"

"Here, sir."

"Sandra Lee?"

"Here."

He was sitting several seats away from her. They exchanged eye contact briefly. Her eyes, he noticed, were green, and they were lovely to behold. He wondered what she might have thought of his own eyes. The two students looked up and watched as the teacher continued to take attendance by reading through the names.

Hugo was looking forward to the class, U.S. History Advanced Placement, and he had faith that he would perform well. As he sat and imagined the lectures about state's rights and the New Deal, he was struck by this girl, Sandra. Already he knew her name, so that element was removed from the equation. In turn, she knew his name as well. He tried to look at her in a way that was not obvious or awkward. She had black hair that went just below her shoulders. Small and petite, the heads of other students hovered over hers. Lastly and most importantly, Hugo became aware of a warmth that she emanated whenever he looked at her. Now she was turning her head to look in his direction. Reactively, he turned back to face his friend Brady, and said, "Hey, man, is this class gonna be great or what?"

"Um, I think I'll go with 'or what'!"

Not all of Hugo's friends shared his passion for history. He quite liked both English and history, where he had the opportunity to grapple with ideas and concepts head-on. True enough, he was gifted in virtually every subject matter, his grades in math and science being formidable to put it lightly. It was his intention at that point, upon graduating from high school, to go to a small private college and study something stimulating and artistic, like philosophy or literature. Hugo's own dad was a lawyer, and he stressed the importance of discipline, sacrifice, and plain-old hard work to both of his sons. Matthew, Hugo's father, further cited the importance of entering into a field, a profession that would ultimately prove to be lucrative. But Hugo paid no mind to this, instead choosing to follow after his own passions and see where they led him. For this reason, he was excited beyond belief as he sat in his seat on the first day of the school year, thinking of all that he would be learning in the months to come.

The bell rang and the students shuffled out of their seats. Quickly Hugo made his way over to Sandra.

"Hey, how's it going?" he asked.

"Doing well," she said. Her eyes still emanated warmth. "You?"

"Not too bad. Mr. Kirkpatrick sure seems like he's going to be a great teacher, don't you think?"

She nodded. "I almost didn't sign up for this class, but I'm glad I did."

"Why wouldn't you have taken the class?"

"I was just worried that my course load might be a bit on the heavy side."

"Can I see your schedule?"

She lifted up her binder, which had a printed schedule inside. Scanning across the list of classes Hugo was impressed: Calculus, Physics, Advanced Placement English Composition. Clearly, Sandra Lee was not a girl who took school lightly.

"Looks pretty good," he said, "I wonder if we have any classes together."

He unfolded a piece of paper and quickly looked over his own classes. "Looks like we both have math at the very end of the day. How neat!"

"Yes," she said, smiling, "how neat." She turned her body towards the nearby stairwell. "I actually need to be off to my next class, but it was nice to meet you. Harold was it?"

"Hugo."

"Ah, well Hugo, I will see you in Calculus. Get excited." She held her binder with enthusiasm.

The two of them turned and walked in opposite directions. Next up for him was his English class, another class he was looking forward to, because the truth was he was fondly anticipating all of his classes. He loved school. He was taught to value education. As a child, his parents read countless stories to him, often outside in the heat of the summer. Matthew proved more than capable of getting into the role demanded by the character in any story, acting out the voices with zeal. This upbringing of reading meant Hugo had had an appreciation for the pursuit of knowledge.

Hillcrest High School was a massive building, tucked away in the forests of Edmonds, Washington. Not far from Puget Sound and the peninsula, the area was rife with natural beauty. Rows of trees spread out in every direction, and captivating vistas of the water were visible from atop many of the hills in town. It was not a large town; many families knew each other, and consequently, no one's business was ever fully private. The high school truly was the central point of community to be found anywhere in the town. Many of the teachers who worked at the school graduated from Hillcrest. It was not often anyone managed to graduate from school and then leave to go to college. Such a feat was an impressive one. It was Hugo's ambition to stay in Edmonds, to use his knowledge and skills to better the community and his own family. There was a university only thirty miles away, and it could be there, possibly, that he might obtain his philosophy degree. Then, upon graduating, he would be able to serve the people closest to him. During his time as a student at this university, he pondered, he might be able to commute to and from his classes, continuing to live with his mother and his father. He had no interest in going out and exploring the larger world, but rather he hoped to become further engrained in where he already was. For Hugo, simply reading and basking in knowledge was enough of a voyage.

He entered the English classroom and had a seat. The teacher, a young woman with long brown hair, stood before the class and read through the names as all the others had. As she explained it plainly, the year would present a challenging, rigorous exercise in looking at how of some of the most central texts shaped American literature and life at large: Twain, Faulkner, and Emerson were all among the authors to be read. One project, in particular, would have students selecting a novel by an author of their choice and then completing an extensive paper on the text. This project, with its opportunity for creativity, excited Hugo. The teacher was sure to mention that the class would be a challenging one, that every year there were students who dropped out, that the test at the end of the year was extremely challenging, and that right now presented itself as a great opportunity for the less than dedicated to escaping with dignity fully intact. Hugo thought about this, and knew that his abilities and resolution were at the level necessary for the class. Simply, his passion could allow him to handle whatever was thrown his way. Throughout the lecture he took notes on his syllabus, realizing that starting next week they would begin reading *Huckleberry Finn*. He wondered to himself whether he owned a copy of the book already. Surely, in the massive library, his dad possessed, there was a copy of Twain's classic lying around.

With a look across the room, he saw that his friend George was sitting not far away. During the last few minutes of class, the teacher gave the students time to pack up their bags and get ready to go.

Hugo walked over. "How's the day going?"

"Pretty good, man."

"Cool. I met a girl, and I think she's pretty great."

George patted him on the back. "Classic Larson! What's her name?"

"Sandra Lee. But listen, you don't need to go around telling everyone you see about it. It can be just between you and me."

"Right, your secret is safe with me, buddy. Sandra Lee. Well, I wish I met a girl of my own."

"In due time. All things happen when they need to."

"Easy for you to say!"

The two friends walked into the hall and continued talking.

"So are you gonna ask her out?"

"Ask her out? I dunno."

"Come on! You said she's great."

"I did. I don't even know if she's single or not."

"There are ways to find that out," George exclaimed.

They walked down a flight of stairs and found themselves in the cafeteria, just in time for lunch.

Up to that point, Hugo possessed minimal experience with females. He had always been surrounded by friends, by guys who were ready to go on adventures, who were there to support him in any way necessary. Girls were different. It seemed as though there was a particular methodology, a way of navigating the world of girls, that was beyond the reach of Hugo's understanding. His first crush had already passed by. In seventh grade, he fell utterly and hopelessly in love with Stephanie Jensen, who through a note passed on revealed that she was not in a position to reciprocate Hugo's feelings. He was devastated, locked in his room for a week, barely able to make it to swim practice. But with time, even an injury as deep and severe as this one was able to heal, if slowly. So it was easy for Hugo to say that he had no sense of how to go about talking to a girl like Sandra, someone who so naturally knew how to move through the world. It seemed as though there was an invisible wall of awkwardness separating them, and he struggled with imagining how to scale such a wall. Still, his feelings were real and true.

At lunch, George and Hugo had a seat at a table with some of their other friends. To Hugo's astonishment, Sandra was sitting on the other end of the table with a few girls.

People began to introduce one another.

"This is Sandra," Shirley said while gesturing at her friend. "She is new here from Indiana."

"Cool," the rest of the group said.

Hugo thought about Indiana and all he knew about it, realizing to his devastation that such knowledge translated into nothing.

Shirley said, "And this is my good friend Hugo."

Hugo said hello to everyone sitting at the table. When his eyes met Sandra's, he paused for a moment, trying to say something. What, exactly, he was trying to say eluded him.

The group ate lunch and chatted. Hugo learned that Sandra was from a small town called Maskville, that she liked to run cross-country, and that she spent much of her free time reading experimental fiction. All of these things were sources of approval as far as he was concerned. He, in turn, revealed that he was on the swim team, that history was his favorite subject, and that he had spent his whole life living in Edmonds. He also shared that he never intended to go anywhere else for long in his life. They ate until the bell rang, indicating time to head to the last two classes of the day. They said goodbye and were on their way. Hugo hoped he left a good impression.

Hugo sat through his next two classes, unable to think about anything other than the fact that he wanted to be with Sandra. He wanted to take her hand and hold it in his own, to feel those warm fingers and look up and smile at her. His focus was so poor during these classes that he failed to write down the homework, and so he would have to get it from a classmate. Finally, the bell rang and the school day was finished.

The halls were teeming with students who were walking in one direction and another. The chaotic mass of students was a challenge to move through, but Hugo, being an upperclassman, was well-acquainted with it. Outside it was a sunny day. The courtyard area was spacious, with grassy fields separating the school buildings. The sun seemed to re-flect golden light off the metal beams comprising Hillcrest High School. Hugo was just walking the same route he had for years, south towards the street where his house was lo-cated. He was walking with Brady at his side. However, when the two boys saw the girl with black hair sitting on the school sign, Brady nodded and turned to move in a different direction

Hugo approached Sandra with a sense of caution. "I keep seeing you! What are you reading?" he asked.

She lowered her book and said, "Oh, just reading it for fun."

It was *To the Lighthouse* by Virginia Woolf.

"How are you liking it so far?" Hugo asked.

"It's pretty good. It's intriguing how Woolf plays around with the different perspectives of the characters. It's hard to explain. I gotta say I'm looking forward to discussing it with someone."

"Yeah, I bet it's good." Hugo turned his head to look around. "So, do you walk home?"

"No, I catch the bus from right here."

"Okay, cool. Do you mind if I sit with you? It's such a nice day."

"Please, have a seat. Do you walk home?" she asked, not looking up from her book.

"I do."

"Well, that must be nice, to be able to go home on your own time."

"Yes it is, but so is riding the bus, isn't it?"

"It can be annoying, spending your time on a crowded bus, but it's all right." She smiled.

Hugo took in a deep breath, and asked, "Are you enjoying your time here in Edmonds?"

"I am. It seems like a very nice place to live. Have you lived here long?"

"Only my whole life.

"That's neat," she said. I've spent my life moving around. My dad is in the armed forces, so we have had to move a lot. California, Indiana, and now Washington. We spent most of our time living in Indiana. I've been to many places, always on the move, and I prefer to keep it that way."

"Oh yeah?"

"Mmhmm. It's my hope to always be moving in life. I don't ever want to get stuck some place. Life is like books. There is so much you can learn from every little town you enter. Each time you go somewhere new it's like opening a new book."

"So what do you hope to learn from Edmonds?"

"Hmm, I'll have to get back to you on that one."

Then a bus came up the street and parked just in front of where Hugo and Sandra were sitting. Sandra rose from her spot, her book tucked under her arm. Hugo could see that she was already more than halfway through it. "I have to go now," she said.

"Well, it was nice to meet you today." Hugo was fumbling on his words.

"It certainly was. You seem like an all right guy. Thanks for helping me feel welcome at a new school. Kids aren't always so nice."

"I suppose not."

"And I have an answer to your question," she said.

"Okay. What is it?"

She breathed in deeply. "In Edmonds, I want to encounter the kindness of ordinary people. I want to be welcomed and in turn, welcome others. I want to figure out how to take all towns of my past and make some sense of them, to put them together on a single strand of time, if that makes sense."

"It does make sense. That seems like a great goal to have for your time here in Edmonds. Hopefully, your time here lasts a while!"

"I hope so too," she said, smiling.

The door of the bus opened. "See you tomorrow!"

"Yes, see you tomorrow."

He began to walk home. One step moved in front of the other, and he thought about how much he liked Sandra, her warm eyes, her love of literature, her sense of adventure. He imagined that he didn't want to spend much time with anyone else. He simply wanted to be with her. The school year had only just begun, so he hoped that they would have plenty of opportunities to get to know each other better. For the time being, he would have to settle for the fact that they spent one sunny afternoon together. In the time they had been together and chatted it felt as though there was an infinite number of other things still left for them to discuss. What did she think of Salinger? Joyce? What other towns in America did she plan to visit? How long did she intend to live in Edmonds? More importantly, what did she think of him? Did she enjoy talking to him, or did she just put up with it? Would she even want to talk to him again?

She said he was an all right guy. What could this have meant?

So Hugo walked, passing under the cover of trees, under a blindingly warm glow of sunlight, along the residential streets towards his home, his head full of questions, his backpack containing the textbooks that would carry him through a new year of school, a year of opportunity and hope for good things.

March

I.

It was a splendid day to be walking through the park. Though it was overcast out, and despite the fact that it was far from warm, there was an undeniable pleasantness, an aura of spring, that permeated the entire city. Winter was slowly beginning to melt away, turning to the next season. Soon the days would be longer, the nights warmer. Flowers would bloom and birds would be out chirping. The promise of what was to come lingered in the very air.

On Hugo's mind was this transition of seasons. He was thinking about the fact that, at any given moment, it was always one season or another. Time never stopped flowing. There was nothing inherently wrong with this; it was the only system he was familiar with.

"We are almost there," Paul said. In his arms, he held a long box.

The two neighbors were walking at a brisk pace through the arboretum, along a narrow dirt road that wound up hills and around trees.

"I sure hope so," Hugo muttered.

They passed a large tree. Hugo reached out his hand to touch the bark. It felt moist, as though it recently rained.

Before them was perhaps the largest hill yet. Hugo groaned.

"Now, now," Paul reassured, "it will be fine."

Bracing himself, Hugo proceeded to walk with all the strength he had. He knew that if he focused on one step at a time he would be able to do it. But already he was feeling the strain, the steady pull of gravity downward, sweat forming in his brow, his lungs panting, crying out for air. To his left, he saw Paul, also, was struggling with the hill. It was to his surprise when they reached the very top.

From where they stood they could survey the entire park and see much of the city. Lush, wild masses of trees spread out in every direction. Downtown buildings poked up above the branches' reach. Also visible were the winding trails that went all around the arboretum. Nearby there were two tables. While one was occupied, the other wasn't. Hugo stood still, as though he wasn't sure he knew what he was supposed to do next. Paul had a seat, at once putting the game together.

They lined up the pieces methodically and prepared to play. Always cautious, Hugo did not take risks in chess, contenting himself rather with establishing a more drawn-out, dramatic flow of play. So he took a pawn here, a knight there, and was sure to safeguard his queen from any attack. On the other hand, Paul was an aggressive player, looking constantly for ways to stir things up. This difference in playing style was the guarantee of a dynamic, entertaining game. Today, during this particular game, Hugo in his mind was making stupid mistakes, having lost both his bishops early on. The sense of frustration and irritation such losses gave him only led to more mistakes. It was a difficult cycle to escape. The little, unassuming smile that stretched across Paul's face when he took a piece was devastating to Hugo. They continued to play, the momentum of the game shifting one way and then the other, for quite some time. The sun was gently moving across the sky as both players lost piece after piece.

Paul said nothing, attempting to hide his smile, as he took Hugo's queen.

Hugo cursed to himself, gazing at his own, barren side of the playing field.

"It happens," Paul reasoned.

"Not that it should," Hugo grumbled, "especially when it was preventable."

"Want me to put it back?"

"No," Hugo snapped. "It's yours."

Paul looked behind him and then at his friend. "Are you okay?"

"I'm fine."

"Tell me, where did you first learn to play?"

"Oh, it was a long time ago. My father was the one who taught me."

"Did he now?"

"Yes, that's what I just said."

"How old were you?"

Hugo shrugged. "I don't really feel like having a chat."

"Okay."

"But if you really want to know," he continued, "I think I was eight or so when my father first taught me to play. 'This will be the most important game I ever teach you to play,' he had said. We had a nice, glass set. He warned me to be careful with it."

"We had a set just like that," Paul said.

"Yes, yes, and we played game after game on that set. We played for hours. Of course, he always won, at least he did for the longest while. It became my mission to defeat him, but still, I kept losing."

"Doesn't surprise me."

"But I did beat him!" Hugo moved a pawn and said, "Your move."

"You beat him?"

"I think I was twelve. It was a long game. It lasted at least two hours. We seemed to dance around each other. I would take a piece only to have him take one."

"But you won?"

"I did. I don't remember how—this was more than a few years ago," Hugo admitted. "But what I do remember is the sense of triumph, of glory that accompanied my victory. We had ice cream or something after, and I don't think anything ever tasted sweeter."

"I bet it was a real rite of passage."

"It was."

"Did you play more in high school? Surely you did."

31

Hugo was smiling. "I played against my friends all the time in high school. I can't tell you how many summer evenings I spent outside on the grass, playing."

"You grew up in Lynnwood?"

"No, in Edmonds."

"Ah."

"Anyway," Hugo continued while surveying the board, "I have always played a lot of chess. In college, I tried out for the team. But I didn't make it. I remember staying after class, in the campus union building, playing games with the chess team members. I played game after game, but I just couldn't win. These guys I played against were too good."

"I bet." Paul moved his queen across the board.

"They had strategies I couldn't even fathom. It was completely beyond me. But I kept playing. I bought special books and I practiced new moves. Every week I came back to play the chess team guys. There was one autumn when I was bogged down with accounting course work, but I still applied myself first and foremost to chess."

"Did you ever make the team?"

Hugo was looking at the board intently. He sighed. "No. I didn't make the team. I tried and I tried, but I just wasn't good enough. Simple as that."

"Well, that's okay," Paul replied.

"I suppose so. I think that, if there was one thing I could revise in my youth, one thing at all, I'd go back and make it so I was able to be on the team."

"Really?"

"Yes."

"Bet you'd get to go to a lot of new places on the team."

"You got to visit the other colleges up and down the coast. But you know what would have been the best part of being on a chess team like that?"

"What?"

Hugo breathed in deeply as he moved a pawn. "As a member of the team, you got to play so much chess. Game after game! It would have been great."

"But isn't that what you did anyway?"

"What?"

"Play a bunch of games of chess."

Hugo looked around him. "I suppose I have done precisely that."

"I mean, you've been playing almost every day as long as I've known you, which is more than three decades. We play all the time."

"I know that. What's your point?"

"My point," Paul stated, "is that in a sense, your dream of playing a lot of chess has come true. You've lived a life playing chess!"

"And what could be better?"

"Not much."

They played for a while longer still. The afternoon was passing by rapidly. The friends talked, laughed, and remembered together. For years they got together to play, and over time it became a richer and richer experience that they shared. But Hugo's thoughts kept returning to the same thing. He was wondering why he still felt a sense of loss over not making that college chess team. After all, it was such a long time ago. Part of the past, like so many other things. Was it glory and prestige that motivated him? Was there glory in being a member of a college chess team? Such questions were haunting him when Paul broke the silence.

"So..."

"So what?"

"How long has it been? Two months?"

"Oh," Hugo's facial expression changed. "I don't want to talk about that."

"You sure?"

"Yes, please change the topic."

"Okay, sorry," Paul answered.

A little while later and Paul smiled again. "Checkmate."

2.

It was just before noon and Java City was packed with people. Hugo stood by the entrance of the café, nervous, looking for Adrian among the throngs of people. Feeling people move around him, he decided to step deeper into the depths of the café. He wouldn't be staying long, he had already decided.

True to how he remembered it, the café was vibrantly colored. It featured a neon sign with the title of the café, black-white tile floors, and plenty of fixtures hanging from the ceiling that flooded the room with warm light. In fact, he was feeling so blinded by the light that he had trouble knowing where to place his feet as he stepped inside. It was not long before he bumped into someone.

"Oh, excuse me," the stranger said.

"Indeed," Hugo muttered.

In the background, he could hear the strange, alien sounds of a bustling café, the hum of espresso pouring out of the machines, the steaming of milk, the calling out of orders in a language that was distantly foreign.

Then there came the process of waiting in line.

One person placed an order and then stood over to the side. Little by little, Hugo was making his way to the front. He was unable to see if his son was working at the cash register, or if rather he was making coffee. Above his head was a massive menu, the countless drink combinations scrawled into it in elegant handwriting. It reminded him of the chalk sign he encountered when he entered the café, which possessed a snarky greeting: "Have a grande! Have a grand day!"

Thinking about it made him sick.

He looked at the display case, containing soda, pre-packaged salads, and pre-packaged sandwiches among other things. To him it was appalling, thinking that people actually purchased and consumed these things. He picked up one of the sandwiches to take a look at the price. Finding the price printed on the back, he made a face of disgust and quickly placed it back down on the display case, upside-down.

"Hello, sir."

Hugo looked up at the face of a perky, smiling youngster standing behind the cash register.

"Hi there."

"What can I get started for you today?"

"Oh, a glass of water, please."

"Sure thing. Anything else?"

"No, thank you."

"Maybe something to eat?"

"Look, sir," Hugo chided, "I told you what I want. So can I have that?"

"Yes, you may. I'll be right back."

Hugo received his water and then saw Adrian.

Standing behind the counter, holding a cup in one hand and preparing the espresso shots with the other, Adrian appeared to be a natural fully engrossed in his craft. He looked up and then down, moving swiftly, talking to one of his coworkers to verify a detail of one of the orders. He was so focused on what he was doing, on the row of cups piling up before him, that he didn't notice his father was watching him closely. Hugo observed, feeling a sense of curiosity at what his son was doing, and wondering what other professions Adrian could have been practicing instead. Perhaps he might have made a gifted nurse or a teacher. Who knew?

Hugo called his son's name softly, but in the cacophony of the café, it was quickly drowned out. Once more he said it, trying to be louder, and Adrian looked up to see him.

"Hey, Dad," he said. "You made it."

"I'm here."

"I'm so glad you're here."

"Of course I'm here. Are you ready for lunch?"

"Give me just a little bit."

Adrian continued to make drinks and hand them out for fifteen more minutes. "My lunch break is coming soon," he told his father. Hugo occupied himself with watching his son work, walking around the café, and looking at the abstract, colorful paintings that hung on the walls of the café.

Eventually, Adrian maneuvered around the side of the counter and gave Hugo a big hug, who returned it mildly.

"Where do you want to go to eat?" Hugo wondered.

"I dunno. I've only got thirty minutes."

"Is there anything close by?"

"Yes, there is. There's lots of stuff."

"Well, I'll let you pick. You lead the way," Hugo offered.

"Okay, I know a great gyro place just down the street."

They walked towards the café door. "See you later, Forest," Adrian said to the guy at the counter.

"Forest?" Hugo asked in disbelief.

Outside it was overcast but without any sign of raining soon. Hugo was still adjusting to the accelerated pace of life here in Capitol Hill. It seemed as though the street was going to burst with all the cars that were passing along it. Every minute or so another bus rolled by. On the street, there were people walking this way and that, people of all sorts of descriptions but most commonly youngsters. Just as he and Adrian passed through the front door of the café a man in a rainbow-colored cardigan, with large horn-rimmed glasses walked past them, and Hugo tried not to stare. Feeling neutral towards young people in general but certainly not supportive of how they dressed, Hugo was reorienting himself to being in this sort of neighborhood, where the strangest-looking people were observable.

"This way," Adrian said.

They walked under buildings that were taller than any found in Wedgwood. The sidewalk was narrow and the cars were making Hugo nervous. A young lady in a flannel shirt moved past them, walking a Scottish terrier. She moved as though she had no time for older people. Overhead there was a thick cover of clouds. The father and son walked past a place specializing in eastern novelties, and a thick puff of incense filled Hugo's nostrils. Next up there was a bar with a chalk sign that plainly read, "Cheap Beer". Inside, despite the early hour, there were already some tough-looking people having a good time together. Standing outside of the bar was a man on a skateboard who was smoking a cigarette. Having experienced a larger variety of smells in the last thirty seconds than in the last thirty days, Hugo simply tried to keep up with his son, who was moving quickly. They reached an intersection and Adrian looked both ways before going, even though the sign had not changed to indicate that it was safe to cross.

"Son..."

"Come on, Dad. It's fine."

Mustering all his strength, Hugo followed closely behind, fearful that a negligent driver would come soaring through the intersection.

It was not that Hugo hated the young. In a sense, he was able to closely identify with his own youthful self. He remembered, fondly, what it was like all those years ago, to have energy, ambition, and passion. As a high school student and then a college student he lived his life precisely the way he wanted to. He played chess, worked hard on his studies, and occasionally went swimming when he had had time. He even smoked one or two cigarettes of his own during this time. In short, he had no regrets about how he lived his life during his youth, beyond the inability to make the college chess team. Can't win 'em all, he thought.

But now when he looked at the young people in the world around him, he didn't see himself in them. He didn't recognize them. All he saw were people staring at phones and laptop screens, smoking, drinking, swearing, wearing ironic clothing and ironic facial hair. Hugo's generation had been united around protesting the Vietnam War, but what were these people united against? Hugo basked in the golden age of folk music and hard rock, but what did people have now other than obnoxious, primal electronic beats? It just didn't make much sense to Hugo, though he tried to comprehend it all. Yet, he admitted to himself that he likely could have tried harder to be understanding. At least he was glad that his own son didn't look or dress freakishly, as so many of the people they were passing on the street seemed to.

Nearly lost in his own thoughts, he was caught off guard when Adrian turned a corner. Hugo moved past a bald man in a leopard skin leather jacket and blue pants and caught up with his son.

"Here we are," Adrian said.

Hugo looked up at the sign, which read, "Your Own Gyro!"

"Clever," he confessed.

They stepped inside. Plenty of people were seated, talking, eating. Realizing that they were operating on a compressed time scale, the two made their way to the front counter. They both ordered standard gyros and then took a seat.

"Want anything to drink, Dad?"

"Sure."

"Want a soda?"

"A soda? That stuff will kill you. Do you have any idea how much sugar is in one of those things? They're poison."

"I get the idea." Adrian was reaching towards the water dispenser.

"Sugar is the most dangerous chemical in the universe that humans consume on a regular basis. Heart disease, obesity, diabetes, sleep problems, it's all caused by sugar."

Adrian handed him a glass of water. "I see."

"Don't ever get me started on sugar," Hugo finished, his countenance proud.

"I won't."

"So how are things?"

"They're good," Adrian replied, sipping his water. "Work is work"

"Not much changes, does it?"

"Not really. Every day you walk in and there's a row of cups. You get through the row of cups, and then it's time to go. That's pretty much how it works."

"You know I bet there's a bit more diversity in some more professional fields," Hugo said, taking a sip of his water.

"I bet so. That brings me to what I wanted to talk to you about."

"Oh?" Hugo's face brightened.

"Yeah. Um, I don't really know how to say this, but I have no interest really in staying with Java City. I've been with them for twelve years, and it has been good, but it's just time to move on."

"I could see that. What do you want to move on to?"

"Business."

"What type of business?"

"Kind of like an MBA."

"That is wonderful. That is wonderful!" Hugo cried.

"Yes, I have been looking into it. My friend knows someone who did a program with Rainy City University."

"Now what is that? That's no university I've ever heard of."

The man from the counter brought over their gyros.

"It's a specialized certificate program for professional advancement," Adrian announced.

"Of course," Hugo responded.

"Anyway, they get you ready for a career in business in just eight months. I think I want to do it."

Hugo looked at his gyro but did not take a bite. "Like I said, son, I think it is wonderful for you to pursue professional advancement. I fully support you."

"Can you help me pay for it?" Adrian asked, turning slightly red.

"What?"

"I was wondering if you could help me pay for the program. It isn't much, just a couple thousand a month."

Hugo took a big bite out of his gyro, as though chewing on such a delicious meal promised him escape from this conversation. Finally, he responded, saying, "I'm afraid I can't do that, son." He used the word "son" as though there was a level of intimacy between Adrian and him.

"I understand," replied Adrian as he ran a hand through his hair. "Can I ask why?"

"Why? You want to know why? When you look at me, you are seeing someone who created himself. Was there anyone to help me pay for college? No. Was there anyone to hold my hand through accounting school? No. The simple answer is that I worked hard and made my own path when there wasn't one, and I want the same for you. What I want is for you to create yourself, because you will be better off for it. Does that make sense?"

Adrian nodded slowly.

"Now, remind me," Hugo began, "what was your undergraduate major in?"

"Photography."

"Ah, will they let you into the program if you don't have a background in business?"

"Yes, they welcome almost every undergraduate degree."

"What degree do they not welcome?"

"Um. I don't know. But I called a representative and talked to them about my situation. They said it was totally all right that I had my background, and they even offered to pre-accept me for the program."

"What did you have to do to be 'pre-accepted'?"

"I just called them and told them about my college education."

"Well, I do hope that you are post-accepted posthaste," Hugo said, smirking. "So when does the program start?"

"About a month."

"All right."

"I'm really looking forward to it. I've already thought about leaving my notice at Java City."

"I bet you have."

"The café has been good to me. It has offered me twelve years of a stable career, a way to keep busy, a means to afford my rent, but I think it's time I got serious about my career. I want to move up in the world, not stay where I'm at."

Hugo was nodding slowly as his son was speaking. "It all makes perfect sense to me. What you are saying is you want to grow up a bit."

Adrian found this wording a tad bit harsh, but he was forced to agree. "This could really be my chance, you know?"

"I do know."

They finished eating their gyros quickly. After all, Adrian's lunch break was not a long one. Only for a little while could he be away from the espresso machines, those devices that were capable of bringing such joy to so many people, or rather, of preventing much misery. Adrian was well trained in the art of the thirty-minute meal, but Hugo was not able to finish his meal. He left the last third of it on his plate, and the two of them shuffled out of the restaurant quickly.

He had not realized it, but they had, in fact, walked downhill from the café to the gyro shop, and so now they were presented with a climb to make. He was huffing as they walked up the slope, but Adrian was unfazed by the walk. They reached the café and Hugo extended a hand to shake. They promised to keep in touch, and Hugo mentioned he looked forward to hearing more about the program once it started.

3.

He woke up in the middle of the night.

He flipped over his digital clock, his eyes burned by the neon red. 4:18 am. He rolled over to face the other side of the bed. He began to cry. He gripped the pillow in his hands tightly, nearly shaking it, sobbing. All alone, he thought to himself. I am all alone.

He sat up on the bed and looked at the other side of it, at the empty space. He placed a hand on that side of the bed. Then he wiped the tears from his eyes with an old tissue. Up he got from the bed, heading into the bathroom, in a daze. Unsure of what he was doing in the bathroom, he went back to his bed. It was cold. He pulled the blanket up close and tight. Why me? He continued to sob. He picked up the pillow and threw it across the room. Breathing heavily, he picked up the other pillow and positioned his head under it.

For the rest of the night, he was not able to fall back asleep.

4.

The sun was shining down on the city gloriously. Hugo raised a hand to wipe a drop of sweat from his cheek as he stared at the front door of his house. He opened it and entered. After he put away the groceries, he walked up the creaky steps to the closet. He reached far into it, looking for the vacuum cleaner, and once he had it, he pulled with all his strength. It didn't seem to want to budge. He pulled harder and out it came, practically flinging him backward. Over to the nearest outlet he went, where he plugged in the cord and proceeded to vacuum the carpet. As was always the case, he was meticulous, not missing a spot. If a scrap of paper at first did not want to come up, he simply ran the cleaner over it again and again until it changed its mind. He proceeded in this way for a while. Having done accounting for a vacuum cleaner company, he felt indebted to the device for providing him with years of labor.

After he put away the vacuum, he opened the nearest door and walked into his bedroom. The sheets were a mess. He had been in such agony the night before, such suffering, that he had not even bothered to put the sheets back the way they were meant to be. So he went over to the bed and pulled up the sheets. He repositioned the pillows and made sure everything looked perfect. Gazing at the nightstand, he saw the tissue, still slightly moist, and he picked it up and threw it away. Then he saw the photograph.

Sitting on the nightstand was a framed picture, taken long ago. He looked at it only for a second and then he couldn't bring himself to continue. He picked up the photograph, walked over to the closet, and placed it in a drawer. Looking back upon the bedroom, now cleansed of the picture, he was pleased.

As he walked down the stairs he held onto the railing with his hand, leaning on it occasionally. The living room, as seemed to be the trend, was a mess. Having retrieved the vacuum cleaner, he took another go at it, getting annoyed when the vacuum seemed to be stuck under the coffee table. The magazines sitting on the coffee table were in a random pile. He remedied this by throwing away half of them and keeping the others. Some of them, after all, were from more than two months ago. When he opened the trashcan to throw out the magazines, he was greeted by a massive pile of waste. He tied up the bag of trash and took it to the container outside near the curb.

The rituals of spring-cleaning were sacred to him. Every year, it was his pride, his joy, to sweep through his house, looking for refuse, putting things in their place, getting rid of waste. Yet this year felt different. It was as though he was navigating through a minefield, never really sure when he was going to encounter something. What, exactly, he was going to encounter was a mystery, but it existed nonetheless. So he went about his business.

All morning he was busy cleaning, but he hardly made a dent in things. On and on he continued, moving from one room to the next, on high alert for anything that might set him off.

Now he was in the study, a room he rarely ever used in his entire life. The floor of the room was covered in papers. He picked these up and looked at them, one-by-one. There were copies of tax documents, sketches and doodles, and financial statements, to name just a few things. But he looked at these papers and was intrigued by the stories they told. He peered over one of the financial statements and determined that it was most likely important to hold on to, so he placed it in a pile to keep on the desk. Finally, beneath some papers, he saw the annuity statement. He picked it up, clutching it tightly, and then placed it in a pile to be shredded. He had no interest in reading about what this document had to say. Walking out of the room, he bumped into the piano leaning against the wall. It had not been played in months.

Then he saw it.

Sitting on the floor, a few feet from where he was standing, was the bracelet. It had diamonds on it. What was it doing in here? He put it on the desk and left the room.

5.

The phone was ringing.

He muted the television, sighed, and picked up the receiver.

"Hello?"

"Hey, big brother!"

"Hi, Martin."

"How's it been going?"

"Oh, fine."

"Good to hear, good to hear."

Hugo looked around, as though there would be something in the room to distract him from the phone conversation.

"Retirement treating you well?" Martin asked.

"Well enough."

"Yeah, well I've still got a little while before I can reach that point. At least another year. A few more kids to teach."

"Well it is your passion, isn't it?"

"Yes, yes of course. I love teaching high school. In science, we get to do the coolest things, and I love seeing the progress in students from the beginning of the year until the end. It's incredible."

"Good to hear." Hugo was watching the television ad for a product that would cure baldness. He wasn't bald, but he was mesmerized.

Martin lived on the other side of Lake Washington, in the sleepy suburb of Kirkland. He had lived there for years, raising a family, working as a teacher, and he always made an effort to reach out to Hugo, to keep in touch. Such gestures, unfortunately, were not always received with the same zeal. Martin was an enthusiastic person, with bright red hair and a positive attitude. He could take any situation and figure out how to look at it positively. The two brothers were six years apart in age, and there had been no other children in the family. Martin lived with his wife, Patricia, and they had a son, James, who had a young daughter named Cassandra. It was not uncommon for Martin to invite Hugo over to the suburbs to spend time with his family, time that Hugo found to be pleasant if a little draining. The brothers were reasonably close, despite the age difference, for they kept in touch regularly. In Hugo's eyes, Martin felt it his duty to look out for his older, aging brother, who would soon need to be locked away somewhere in a nursing home. But Hugo had no plan to go, at least so long as he had a say about the matter.

"You must be busy this time of year," Hugo said without interest.

"Yes I am, yes I am. The end of the quarter is coming up soon, and there will be many tests to grade."

"Always fun."

"Always fun. Say, what are you doing later on next week? What are you doing next Thursday?"

"Let me check." Hugo walked into the kitchen to take a look at his calendar, hoping that he had something planned. But he didn't. The calendar was blank.

"I am available. Why?"

"Well, I was wanting to have James, Cassandra, and Barbara over for dinner, and was hoping you could make it."

There was a pause. "Yes, I think I can make it. Can you pick me up?"

"Of course."

"Great."

"So what have you been up to?"

He hated being asked this question. He despised being in the role of someone who had a need to report what they had been doing to others, as though it really mattered. He always did the same things, and he was pleased with such a routine. Was his routine really anyone else's business?

"A little of this, a little of that."

"Nice and specific answer," Martin teased. "I have been so busy with work. I just haven't been able to see up or down. Things will quiet down soon enough, though."

"I bet they will."

"It'll be great."

"I just remembered. I do have something planned for tonight." He was standing in between the kitchen and the living room, staring at the television screen.

"And what is that?"

"Taking Paul to the jazz show."

"Well, that should be an awesome time. That's the guy you play chess with?"

"Yep."

"Yeah, well good for you, getting out there, doing stuff."

"Well, I better get going," Hugo said with a tone that indicated finality.

"Yes, you should. Have fun tonight. Say hi to Paul for me."

"I will."

"Bye!"

"Goodbye."

Hugo rolled down a sleeve to look at his watch. 5:00 pm. If they were going to eat dinner and make it to the show, they would need to get going soon. He walked into the kitchen and poured himself a glass of water. Staring at the refrigerator, at magnets of tropical locations, he got lost in his own thoughts.

It was enough of a disappointment that Adrian worked as a barista for the last twelve years, building nothing in the way of a career. But what was even worse was the lack of a wife or kids. Here Hugo was, retired, and there was no sign of a grandchild appearing any time soon. It would have been pleasing to him to have a little grandson to read stories to, to teach math to. Hugo built a lot in his career, an empire perhaps, and he needed to feel like it was being passed on, into the right hands. The step into the business program certainly was a good start on Adrian's part, but time was ticking if the Java City barista had any plan for finding a wife. Meanwhile, Martin was wildly successful as a teacher, garnering awards and the adoration of countless students. Martin had a son and a granddaughter, and a peaceful existence in the suburbs. Hugo knew it was not helpful to compare himself to him, but he did it anyway. He held their lives up, side-by-side, wondering where he had gone wrong to cause things to play out the way they had.

Having finished his water, he walked out the door of his house, locking up, and went over to Paul's door.

"I've been really looking forward to this," Paul said, as they were walking towards the bus stop.

"Me too. Tonight it's Lewis Beck playing with his band. It should be good." Hugo realized at once that he was sounding like his brother.

They stood at the stop not far from their houses. Fifteen minutes passed, and the massive bus stopped in front of them. Hugo swiped his bus card, but the reader indicated that he was out of funds. He looked up at the driver, who folded his arms.

"I have a five," Hugo said.

"No change," the burly driver replied.

"Wonderful..." Hugo said as he found a seat.

The city passed them by through the window. While they were in North Seattle the view was green and lush. There were many people out, walking about. The bus was ready to break down at any moment. The road was rough and bumpy. Always wary about riding the bus, Hugo looked out the window and tried not to think about how nervous he felt. Paul wore a serene expression, evidently excited about going to the show. With a turn, the bus careened onto the highway. Traffic, as was always the case this time of day, was horrifyingly dense.

"Great," Hugo muttered.

Their progress was slow, gradual, and the feelings of exhaustion among the riders was palpable. Hugo looked around him, viewing bored youngsters and people of a different class occupying the hard seats. The driver was forceful. Upon making a stop, when he realized that several onboarding riders did not carry correct fare, he yelled at them, reminding them of the policy of the bus towards those who could not pay the fare. As far as Hugo figured, the extra amount he paid to board the bus should mean that he got a deluxe seat, removed from everyone else. That, or the extra money should enable one of these poor souls to board the bus despite being short on cash. Out the window, in the distance, was downtown, their destination. Hugo looked at the buildings, tall and proud, reflecting in a bright gleam the shimmering water below. He saw the rolling hills which were dotted with small houses that had withstood years of wild rains. Hugo thought about how nice it might have been to own one of those houses up on Queen Anne. He had spent only a little of his own time walking through there, up and down the hill, breathing heavily. The impression left on him by Queen Anne was a distinct one: evidently, it was a lovely place to live. There was a certain park on that hill that afforded a glorious view of downtown, the space needle resting practically in the palm of the hand of the beholder. Hugo wondered desperately as to what the name of that park was. He asked Paul, who said he didn't know. Oh well. Perhaps some mysteries were best kept concealed. At least the mystique of the hill would be preserved.

Such slow movement on behalf of the bus was hardly bearable. Hugo worried that they were going to miss the show, though they had two and a half hours to go until it started. The Purple Door was the premier jazz club in the city. All of the acts who mattered, at least in Hugo's mind, came through when they were playing. Tonight's show would be wonderful indeed. In fact, Hugo had been looking forward to it for the last couple of weeks. He remembered how he saw it, etched into his calendar, every time he bothered to look at his schedule he was again delighted by the impending show. Music, jazz was special for him. It was a way of escape, of transcendence, and he believed that he needed tonight's show more than he knew. Indeed, they would eat at the Purple Door and then enjoy an evening of world-class music. In the meantime, all he had to do was make it through this traffic.

They got off the bus in the heart of downtown. Never one to spend time here, Hugo was disoriented as regarded which direction to go. Paul, on the other hand, led him confidently west, towards the water. It was a warm, early spring evening. The sun came out, and the streets were filled with busy cars carrying busy people. Hugo walked close to the buildings as they made their way, anxious about the passing cars.

"It isn't much farther," Paul reasoned.

"It better not be."

Paul was an avid fan of jazz as well. The two friends had been going to shows, on and off, for years. They loved the thrill of watching a performance and then discussing it, analyzing the musicality of the performers, sharing and bonding in the experience.

They crossed a street and Hugo was afraid that a large truck was not even going to stop for them. Paul was calm and at ease.

"Want a coffee before we get to the venue?" Paul asked.

"You know I don't drink that dirt."

"Oh, how could I have forgotten? Well, I would certainly like some."

"Then let's step inside," Hugo sighed.

They opened the door of a café, the second one Hugo had been in that month. The air was rife with the scents of coffee. The two friends walked towards the long line and waited somewhat patiently until they made it to the front. Paul ordered an iced coffee and they walked over to the counter to grab it.

"Want a sip?" Paul offered.

"Nope."

They exited the café.

"Are we close?" Hugo asked.

Paul enjoyed his beverage for a brief moment, and then answered, "We are. Just a few more blocks."

They crossed the street and continued onward, past a group of tourists taking a photo in front of a fountain. The city was truly alive. To the left of where they were walking, only a few blocks away, was Pike Place Market, the sprawling complex of shops and eateries where, in Hugo's thinking, one could be robbed in exchange for trifles of luxury. They continued on their way. The road sloped upward, and Hugo at once felt irritated that such a strain was being put on his legs. His ankle, which was healed considerably, was not giving him too much trouble. At the top of the hill, there was a door that was purple. The two friends looked at each other and smiled.

Paul opened the door and held it for Hugo. Inside, they were greeted by a waiter who had a waxed mustache.

"Reservation?" he asked.

"Under Fenway," Paul replied.

They were seated not far from the stage.

"Pretty good seats," Paul said.

"Yes, but they could be better."

They were brought glasses of water and menus, told to take their time before ordering.

"Well, we only have...." Hugo looked at his watch. "We only have an hour and a half before Beck takes the stage."

"It'll go by fast," said Paul.

"These guys really are something. They have been touring up and down the coast, and I am glad we are finally seeing them. It's about time. Their drummer plays with the most intricate technique, diving into all kinds of rhythms. The trumpet can fill the room, and the piano sounds nice and warm."

"You should be a music critic," Paul remarked, "you have a way with words when it comes to describing it."

"I just like it a lot. Let's leave it at that."

"Okay."

"I have always liked jazz. It has been there for me. I grew up listening to it."

"Kind of like with chess."

"What?"

"You grew up listening to jazz and you grew up playing chess," Paul explained. "You are a fellow who enjoys his passions."

"I do."

"It is an excellent thing. I like jazz a lot, too. I like other types of music as well."

"Like what?"

"Rock and roll. Folk. I even like some of the electronic stuff that is coming out these days."

"Electronic?"

"Oh yes." Paul seemed excited. "There's this folk singer I like a lot. He uses pitch-altering technology on his voice, to change the sound, and the result is really special. It has a very emotive quality to it."

"That sounds like a bunch of garbage to me." Hugo was incensed.

"Why?"

Hugo paused to think, and then said, "Technology and music have a delicate relationship. In the '60's and '70's, they made a lot of progress in recording technology. That is all well and good. But these days you can't even separate the technology from the music."

"So?"

"The other day I saw an ad for a band: Neon Gorilla. I looked at the picture and saw that all three of the band members were standing in front of keyboards hooked up to computers. It's terrible."

"Why is it terrible?"

"Because," Hugo said, "music is about the expression of a person's soul through performing with instruments and with the voice. It is supposed to be organic. It is supposed to happen in a live setting, and it should require technical ability to perform. These buffoons with the laptops, all they do is push a button and then music starts to play. Or they sing into a magical microphone, it alters their singing pitch, and we are supposed to be in awe of their singing ability. It makes me sick just to think about. Here's my question. What I am wondering is this: where did the talent go? Those bands, jazz as well as rock, from the '60's, what happened to them? Today all we are left with is the technology. The humanity is gone."

"That's a lot to think about," Paul answered. After they ordered their food Paul said, "As far as I am concerned, music is all about self-expression. It's about taking what is in the soul and disseminating it through sound. I don't think music needs to be live. There is still a type of talent that is involved in making music even if it is prepared before a performance and then played back. I don't see any need to place a requirement on music as demanding strict technical ability. After all, it's not like some of those rock and roll bands were playing the most sophisticated stuff."

"Yes, but that's exactly it: they were playing it."

"And I don't think the human touch is gone from music. I just think we have found a new way to express it, namely through technology. The marriage of human sounds with technology is a powerful thing. I know that band you were talking about, Neon Gorilla. I listened to some of their tunes, and I must say I quite liked it."

"Really?"

"Yes. They use computers to make sounds that no one else can. They have created their own sonic footprint. Every saxophone sounds similar, but every computer has the potential to sound entirely different."

"Oh, every saxophone does not sound similar!"

"Anyway," Paul had a sip of water and then continued, "I don't think the increased use of technology in music is anything to worry about. There are bigger things to worry about. There will always be a human touch to music, because guess what? Music is always made by humans. That means there is always room to connect with it, to feel it deeply. At least that is what I think."

"Well, what I can say is I am glad we are going to a jazz show, where the music is intricate, and performed by musicians who are in the room, playing."

They were brought their food. Eating relatively silently, Hugo was annoyed by the loud music that was playing through the speakers. By his estimations, computers played a substantial role in the creation of the music, and he didn't like it one bit.

It was not much longer before the lights in the room dimmed, a man standing on the stage before a microphone.

"Good evening, ladies and gentlemen. Are you ready to hear some of the Lewis Beck Quintet?"

A cheer sounded through the room. The loudness caused Hugo to start to feel excited.

"Well, here at the Purple Door we are proud to bring you high-quality jazz music. But first, before we bring them out to play, we want to talk to you all about our new Purple Door member rewards program. You see…"

"I hate this kind of stuff," Hugo whispered, "just yet another scam to try and get our money."

Not much longer after that, the man thanked the crowd and left. The spotlight focused on the center of the stage, where three men and two women entered. They came out with their instruments with the exception of the drummer, whose set was already prepared. The audience's cheering was joyful and ecstatic. Hugo was clapping his hands, hollering loudly.

A man with horn-rimmed glasses grabbed the microphone and looked at the audience. "Good evening, Seattle. Are you ready to hear some tunes?"

"Yes!"

"My name is Lewis Beck. This is my band, and we are going to be taking care of y'all tonight. You see, tonight we are going on a journey, a musical journey, and you are all invited. We are going to see sights, and hear things, and it's going to be...well, it's going to be something. I'm not great with words. I'm better at the whole music thing." He picked up his trumpet, turned to his band, counted them off, and they proceeded to play.

Hugo was whisked away by the music. As the trumpet soared, so too did he. He became lost in the sounds. He felt the drums deep in his bones. One instrument played a solo and then another. For the first time in two months, he felt free. It was as though he had been shackled, and now the shackles were no more. It felt as though he was flying over the Seattle night sky, passing through the buildings, surveying all that was below. He was smiling at Paul, who likewise was enjoying the show. For that time, there was nothing but the music. In the dimness of the Purple Door, light reflected off the chandelier onto the instruments, creating a resplendent glow. Hugo watched Lewis principally, who played his trumpet powerfully, facing his band, then the audience, pointing his instrument towards the ceiling, blowing into it with full force. The piano was like a gentle rain that cascaded down the side of the window. He listened to the trumpet solo, following each and every note, hanging on to the notes, as though they were a form of salvation, as though they were the only thing available to grip in the word. The band was playing, and then soon enough they were finished. The evening had run its course.

The audience applauded for minutes. Hugo thought about standing up to clap, and decided to do so. He was in awe of this band, of their abilities, of the trip they had taken him on. He wanted to cry, but there were no tears. Lewis thanked the audience, and then they were gone.

Paul reached for his jacket. "Well, that was special."

"Yes, it was." Hugo was still smiling from the performance.

"Should we be going?"

"Yes, let us go."

They stood up and began to move out of the venue. It was crowded, so it took a while for them to be able to leave.

"Could you believe that piano player?" Paul asked.

"How about the trumpet?"

"They were all spectacular."

All of a sudden any discussion about technology and music, about human connection, seemed insignificant, for the two friends had experienced, directly, the human connection of music that night. There was little in the way that words could do to capture the magic that swept over them.

They made their way outside. It was getting cold now. Not nearly as many cars were in the street, nor were there so many people beyond those who were trying to leave the venue in a crowd.

"Which way to the bus?" Hugo asked.

"I will show you."

They crossed a street, past a neon sign indicating the presence of a bar. Hugo was following after his friend, trying to keep up, trusting that he knew what direction they needed to go. They passed a beggar who smiled at them.

"Not today," Hugo said.

They continued, crossing several more streets. Hugo couldn't help but notice how unpleasant it was to be downtown at this hour of the night.

"Here's where the bus comes," Paul said.

"All right."

They stood together, in silence.

"When does the bus come?" Hugo asked.

"Let me check." Paul began toying with his phone.

Hugo was nearly shivering in the cold. He thought of how nice it would be to be at home, in his warm bed, maybe drinking a cup of tea. He might well have been reading a good book, as he so often did late at night. He looked over at Paul impatiently.

"How long?"

"Not sure."

"Can't you check with that thing?"

"I can, but it's taking a while to load."

"So you can't."

"What?"

"So you're saying you can't check when the bus comes."

"Right now? No."

Hugo sighed. "Wonderful. I am stranded downtown."

"At least you're not alone."

This made Hugo smile. "No, I'm not."

Across the street was a small crowd of people gathered. "I wonder what all the fuss is about," Hugo spoke, pointing.

"Don't know." Paul was still looking at his phone.

Then Hugo's face brightened. "Is that...I think it is!"

"What?"

"Over there. It's Lewis Beck." The horn-rimmed glasses were unmistakable, even in this city.

"Should we go say hi to him?" Paul wondered.

"What if we miss our bus?"

"It's across the street. We won't miss it."

"All right then."

They shuffled across the street. The crowd was difficult to move through, but they managed to push their way to the front, where they beheld Lewis.

"What do you want?" he asked Paul.

"You're Lewis Beck."

"Yes, I am."

"You put on a great show tonight," Hugo raved.

"Yes, we did."

"Will you sign an autograph for me?" Paul asked, who was clearly star-struck.

Lewis was wearing a green sweater and had shoulder-length hair. It appeared as though he was chewing gum. He had an apathetic air to him. "No, I don't do that kind of thing," he said.

"Really?"

"Nope."

"Oh, okay, thanks."

Lewis said, "Yup."

The two friends got out of the way of the crowd, crossed the street, and stood where the bus, allegedly, was supposed to arrive.

"He was certainly a ball of sunshine," Hugo said.

They laughed together.

"I can't believe he wouldn't sign an autograph," Paul said.

"These musicians, they get it in their minds that they are famous, and that they have a right to treat everyone else like garbage."

"Now, now," Paul replied. "You can't generalize. Just because one jazz artist was unkind does not mean that they are all like that. Musicians and artists are just like any type of people. You have those who are nice and humble and those who are less so."

"Sure," Hugo assented, "but all I'm saying is that we are really big fans of this musician. We came out to see him, and I had an amazing time at his show. Then when we finally got the chance to meet him, he was a jerk. How can a jerk make such beautiful music? What's the deal with that? And where is this damned bus?"

"Be patient, it will be here any minute."

Just at that moment, a bus came around the corner. It stopped before them and opened its doors, its presence a relief to the now-shivering Hugo. They climbed aboard and paid their fare, Paul loaning Hugo the necessary funds. It was thirty more minutes before they got off the bus in their neighborhood, where they proceeded to walk. Hugo said goodbye to Paul as they approached their houses. Inside, Hugo did not dive into a good book or make tea. Rather, he climbed straight into bed, astonished by how late it was, and proceeded to lie there, thinking.

6.

He held the annuity check from WiseLife Insurance in his hand as he walked towards the bank door. He opened it and held it for a lady who was walking behind him. At the front of the bank there stood a teller who was smiling with a beaming expression.

"Hello, Hugo!"

"Hello, Richard."

"What do you have for me today?"

"Just another check."

"Ah." The teller held the check in his hands, as though it somehow was capable of communicating profound, hidden truths to whoever was prepared to listen to it.

"You do know you can set up to have this directly deposited, don't you?"

"Yes, I know."

Hugo kept looking around him, evidently uncomfortable to be in the bank.

"I'll just go ahead and take care of this," Richard spoke, who disappeared momentarily.

Hugo looked around the room. The ceiling was high and the windows were spacious. Cars were passing outside the window, under an overcast sky. Hanging on the walls were special promotions for events and offers that the bank was making. Not far away, the same lady who Hugo had held the door for was seated with a banker. This lady, who appeared to be about Hugo's age, looked at him momentarily, the two exchanging eye contact briefly. It seemed as though she was looking through Hugo, at whatever was on the other side of him. It made him feel even more uncomfortable.

"And we're back," Richard said, reappearing.

"Fantastic."

"Everything is processed and you are good to go. Would you like a copy of your statement for the account?"

"No, that's quite all right."

"All righty, Hugo. Anything else I can do for you today?"

"No."

"All righty, Hugo. Thank you so much for coming in today. You have a great day now!"

"You too," Hugo mumbled.

He walked back down the hill. There was a palpable heaviness to the clouds hovering overhead. Hugo wondered when, if ever, spring would arrive. But he also knew it would be here before he knew it. What he was left with was the promise of spring, a promise that would soon be made good on. Today he was feeling a bit of a pain in his left leg and he couldn't deny it. Often he felt pains everywhere in his body, but the prospect of being hindered in his ability to walk was deeply alarming to him.

Despite the iciness of Lewis Beck in person, nothing was done to diminish how much Hugo had enjoyed the show. He looked back on it fondly and was already thinking about future shows to get tickets to.

As he opened the door to his house he thought of something. He walked upstairs to his bedroom and opened the closet. He opened the drawer and took out the picture he had placed there.

He looked at the picture for a long time, and then he put it back in the drawer.

April

I.

There was a knock at the door.

Hugo slowly walked over and, preparing himself for the onslaught of positivity, opened it.

"Hey, big brother!"

"Hey."

Martin wrapped his arms around Hugo in an embrace. The hug lasted a long time, Hugo smelling Martin's rich after-shave. Martin looked at Hugo as though he was looking for something in his face. Hugo hated this.

Martin had red hair, green eyes, and was much taller than his brother. The two of them looked funny standing together, Hugo in his tie, with his disappearing hair, and Martin towering over him in a cardigan.

Growing up, Hugo had been older by a substantial margin, six years, yet he never lorded it over his brother, preferring a peaceful co-existence with him. Rarely did they fight. But the two brothers were certainly different people. As Martin always chose to be positive, to view the good in life and in others, Hugo chose pessimism, or "realism" as he touted it. When it came to political beliefs, the brothers growing up disagreed sharply, with Hugo rejecting the establishment and Martin embracing it. Then, it seemed that, just as soon as Martin was old enough to have a more mature relationship with his brother, Hugo was already preparing to leave Edmonds for college. While Hugo was interested in books and school, Martin was more involved with athletics, playing baseball from tee-ball to the high school varsity team. The two brothers made an effort to stay connected, particularly after their mother died. She passed away a decade before.

"You look great," Martin said.

"I feel okay."

"Shall we?"

"Yes, let's."

They stepped out into the pleasant evening. Spring was in full bloom. Hugo's garden was coming along very nicely. He had azaleas, daffodils, and a cherry tree to tend to. As was characteristic in Seattle during this time of year, it was raining more. But the shift in mood, overall, was certainly a good one. The days were steadily becoming longer.

They entered Martin's car, which was nice and luxurious, and Hugo bit a nail as he waited for his brother to get situated.

"You ready?" Martin asked.

"I am."

The car pulled out of the driveway, turned around, and sped along the road.

"Can you slow down a bit?"

"Sure thing, big brother."

The decrease in speed was so drastic that it felt as though the car was no longer moving.

"You need to be sure to yield here," Hugo said as they approached an empty residential intersection.

"Gotcha."

The car came to a sharp halt. Martin moved his head rapidly left and then right. The car accelerated back to its slow speed. They approached the neighborhood bar and took a left turn. Before long, they were on the freeway.

Hugo looked at his watch, for it was thankfully still light out. It was 5:00 pm. By his estimation, crossing Lake Washington and making it to Kirkland was going to be a horrendous ordeal.

"Traffic is going to be lousy," he grumbled.

"That's all right. How was the jazz show you went to?'

Hugo's expression lightened. "It was great," he said, "but the performer himself was a real jerk."

"Really? That's interesting."

"Yeah, oh well."

They were making steady progress along the freeway, but now all of a sudden there was utter gridlock. Coming to a complete stop, the brothers looked at each other.

"This could be better," Martin remarked.

From where they were seated they could see the entire expanse of the lake. Water flowed freely for miles, resting beneath the rickety bridge that carried the dragging cars. The sky was clear and the sun was sitting above the buildings of downtown to the west. In the distance the end of the bridge was visible: the East Side suburbs, that mysterious kingdom where shopping malls and franchises reigned supreme, where people carried groceries in plastic bags, and where a car was necessary to get anywhere. Hugo despised it. He had grown up in a small town, but he never realized how awful a place it was until he made it to the city. Looking back, he felt embarrassed regarding where he grew up. Martin, on the other hand, was content with where he lived, even pleased by it. This was unfathomable to Hugo. No matter how hard he tried to understand it, he was unable to comprehend how anyone could enjoy living in the suburbs. No longer did he think about it much. Simply put, there were city people, and then there were others.

"Well I hope you're hungry," Martin said, "Patricia is making burgers. Lamb burgers."

"I have little doubt that I will be hungry by the time we reach your home."

Martin patted him on the back. "Big brother. Always with the funny lines. You crack me up."

"So how is school going?" Hugo asked without interest.

Martin was merging lanes. "Like I said, it's been busy. Been real busy. Right now we are wrapping up our big unit on the law of thermodynamics. The kiddos usually understand for the most part, but there can sometimes be some confusion about the content."

"Well, that's what you're there for!"

"Correct, big brother. I do my best to make sure that every kid is prepared for success, and as you know, I have been teaching this stuff for a while now, so I understand pretty well the places where kids get stuck, and I know how to help them out, generally speaking."

"That is good. To be excellent at one's profession is one of the highest pleasures in life."

"It is, it is. But you know what?"

"What?"

"I'm getting tired. I've been teaching for...thirty-four years now, most of those at the same school. You know what I've found to be the case? While the kids stay the same age, I keep getting older! It's hard for me to deal with. Sometimes it feels like I can work my absolute hardest until my body is tired, but there is still so much teaching, so much learning left that needs to happen. It's enough to make me feel like I'm not even making a difference."

"You are making a difference, Martin. What you need to do is to focus on your own sphere of influence, on what you can do every day to make learning happen. If you control what you can and work hard, the world will benefit." Hugo was struck by how positive he was becoming. He decided he needed to get out of this car.

"Thanks for that, big brother. But I kinda dread retirement, you know. It scares me."

"Scares you? Why?"

"Just...all that time free, with nothing to keep me occupied. I don't know what I would do with it. I suppose it would be all right."

"Martin, retirement is the best thing that ever happened to me."

"Really?"

"Yes, I get my days open and I am free to live as I like. I can swim, work in my garden, spend time with Paul, or just be by myself. It is a wonderful thing." Hugo was lying, for what he wanted in life was the fulfillment a career brought.

The traffic was opening up slowly.

"So you spend a lot of your time with hobbies and that sort of thing. I suppose that must be pretty great. But I don't know if that is for me. I was created to teach!"

"Yes, and I was created to do accounting. But times change. We get older, we slow down. Life slows down. It's all natural. It's part of the process."

"That doesn't sound like a process I want to be a part of," Martin proclaimed.

"Sorry to say it, Martin, but it's something we all have to deal with. We all slow down!"

Martin turned to look at his brother. His expression was skeptical. "You're happy, being retired?"

Hugo nodded. Still, a part of him, a small voice, was nagging out, wanting to declare that he was in fact lying and that he was not happy at all. Hugo tried his best to suppress this voice, but it was still there, inside him. Horrified, Hugo paid no attention to the fact that his palms were sweating, and instead, he focused on the grotesque traffic in front of him.

It was another forty-five minutes before they crossed the lake, traveled north, and found the exit to take off the freeway. Hugo looked out the window, at the dense coverage of trees, the minivans traveling along the road. Martin turned the wheel one way and then the other, clearly fully aware of where he was headed. Up a hill they traveled and then turned into a neighborhood, past a sign reading, "Lavender Heights".

A seemingly endless stream of houses passed by Hugo's window. Higher and higher they traveled until Hugo felt that there was no way they could go any farther up. At last, they pulled into a cul-de-sac. Martin turned to his brother and exclaimed, "Home, sweet home!"

They got out of the car. Night was quickly approaching, the sun descending beneath the trees. Hugo followed his brother up the staircase that led to the front door.

On the outside, the house was large, ornate, painted light blue, with windows that climbed high up to a sturdy roof. Inside, the home was spacious and precious. Immediately visible were some old family photos that depicted Martin, Patricia, Barbara, James, and Cassandra, along with some other relatives all looking slightly to the right of the camera. There was a giant table in the kitchen that was already set. Rows of shoes lined the floor near the door. The smell of lamb was immediately apparent to Hugo. Clearly, this was a home and not just a house.

"There they are!" a voice cried.

"Hi, honey!"

A slim woman with silver hair stepped into view and hugged Martin. Patricia radiated the same warmth and positivity as her husband. She turned towards Hugo and hugged him. Hugo decided he had reached his hug quota for the year.

"How have you been, Hugo?'

"I am fine. And you?"

"Doing great!"

Patricia worked in real estate. According to Hugo's arithmetic, she was largely responsible for such a nice house, the high-quality school for the child, and everything else the family needed.

"Is Dad back?" a voice called.

In stepped James, who was fit-looking and had light red hair. He was tall, like his father. "How's it going, uncle Hugo?"

"Oh, fine." Hugo extended a hand to shake, irritated that he was forced to answer this question multiple times.

"Don't run in the house, sweetie."

Cassandra came trotting through the kitchen, followed by Barbara, her mother.

"Great-uncle Hugo!" Cassandra cried.

Hugo gave her a hug and then turned to look at the front door, briefly.

"So," Patricia said, "we are all here now. The burgers should be ready soon."

"That's great!" Martin said.

"It is," Patricia assented.

Eventually, they took their seats at the table. Every conceivable topping and condiment for lamb burgers were available at Hugo's disposal.

"All righty," Martin said, "I'll pray. Dear Father God, we just thank you so much for this day. We thank you for this home, for the sun, for family, and we pray that you would bless this food. In Jesus' name, we pray. Amen."

Hugo felt no need to pray at his meals, but he contented himself with this ritual of his brother's.

He did not pay much attention to the conversation that was unfolding around him at first. What he was more interested in was eating. All that time spent in the car had caused him to feel famished. Occasionally, when a question was asked of him, he would answer tersely.

"How is the retired life?" Patricia asked.

"It is good," he grunted.

"Still swimming?" James asked.

"I am."

"How are things in Wedgwood?" Barbara asked.

"Nice and quiet."

This was often how Hugo functioned in social situations. It wasn't that he disliked interacting with others socially, rather that he preferred to operate more on the periphery. That being said, if a choice topic arose, if something of interest was brought to his attention, he had no trouble at all chatting away about it: accounting, soccer, and gardening were just a few such topics. However, it proved to be infrequent that dinner conversations involved gardening.

"It's going to be great in July," Martin beamed.

"Why is that?" Hugo wondered.

"Didn't you know?" James blurted out.

"It's going to be wonderful," Barbara said.

"What is going to be wonderful?"

"In July we are going on our vacation to Lake Chelan. We are going to be at our condo for a full week," Martin smiled. "While we are there we will enjoy walking around, mini-golf, cycling, swimming, stopping into town for a while, maybe jogging, and more."

"It's going to be fantastic!" Patricia cried. "You will be able to come over, won't you Hugo?"

All of the pressure in the room was now resting on him. "I, er, I don't know. I mean, I just don't drive on roads like that anymore."

"That's all right," Martin reassured, "we'll pick you up. It would mean a lot to us if you could be there, big brother. Of course, we understand if you have other things going on."

One of Hugo's greatest, most vital goals in his affairs with others was to be polite, to maintain harmony. For this reason, he had no problem stating, "You know, I will think about it."

"It'd be great if you could go," James said, "I bet Cassandra hopes great-uncle Hugo can come."

"I do!" she proclaimed.

"When is it in July?"

"The 14th through the 20th."

"Ah. Let me think...I don't think I am busy then, but I will have to see."

This had been more than enough attention for Hugo to handle for the evening. The prospect of going on a trip with anyone, and particularly with these people, filled him with dread. Sure, it would most likely be an enjoyable time, with reading good books and taking plenty of naps. After all, he was the reigning senior in the family, and so he was afforded a certain level of freedom and respect when it came to how often he decided to take a nap. But to be around so much positivity for such a long time, in such a high concentration, was more than he could handle. Truthfully, he would think about going, considering it carefully. Sure enough, Martin would ask him again concerning whether or not he would go. Hugo was beginning to think about joining, envisioning what it would be like when he decided to tune himself back into the conversation.

"It has been pretty slow, to be honest," James said before taking another bite of his burger. He was the proud owner of the local bookstore, a frequent point of interest to Hugo.

"Why do you think that is?" Patricia inquired.

"I'll tell you why it is," Hugo said. "Kids don't read like they used to."

James said, "You don't think?"

"No. Not with all the screens and video games they have now."

"I think there is some truth to that," Martin added, "but don't you get a lot of kids who have ebook devices that they use for reading? Don't kids read books on their tablets?"

"They do," James said, "but it's hard for us to compete with that. It would be nice if we sold ebooks at Bookworm."

"That would probably help your business," Hugo asserted. "I myself have never been one for the electronic books. They just aren't the same as holding one in your hands."

Martin looked at Cassandra. "What do you think?"

"I like to read on my tablet," she spoke.

"Well, there you have it, ladies and gentlemen. James, son, it sounds like you need to start selling ebooks."

"But do you really think that's what kids are using them for?" Hugo challenged. "Cassandra, sweetheart, I am sure that you do plenty of reading on your tablet. But aren't most kids playing video games and what have you on their devices instead of reading? It's not like you have any kids who are reading *War and Peace* on that little screen.

"Well," Patricia said, "I'm sure you don't have many kids reading *War and Peace* at all."

James said, "What I can say is that I know sales for that book are very high."

Hugo was astonished. "Are they really?"

"Yes, but there is an edition of the ebook that is totally free. The copyright for it is expired, so it is available for free."

"That can't be good for sales."

"No, Hugo it is not." James started to laugh.

"I have lived on the same street for thirty years..." Hugo began.

Martin was smiling pleasantly at him.

"What?" Hugo demanded.

"Nothing. Please go on."

"Well, yes, anyway, I have lived on the same street for thirty years, and I tell you, it is amazing how many fewer kids I see playing outside. They must all be inside, playing video games, or whatever it is that they do now."

Martin said, "Or maybe they are reading on their tablets."

Hugo looked around the table, realizing that he could not defeat their optimism for the future of humanity. "I suppose so," he finally said.

Later on, everyone hugged and said their goodbyes. Martin led Hugo down the stairs to the car. Already tired, Hugo was looking forward to a short, swift drive back home, to where he would be reunited with his bed. They got in the car.

"Well, that was a tasty meal," Martin rhapsodized, "don't you think?"

"Yes, it was," Hugo agreed.

"Yessir, Patricia has still got it. She's still got it."

The car pulled out of the driveway and soared down into the heart of Lavender Heights.

"Well we really hope you can make it to Chelan," Martin said. "It would be great to have you."

"I'd like to go."

"What's stopping you?"

"Um, I'm not sure. You know I have a calendar at home, I'll just need to check it to make sure that I can be away from home for so long."

"That's fair, big brother. It is a long time to be away from home."

They continued on in silence for a while. A few turns later and they were back on the bridge. The moon was hovering above, its light reflected on the waves of the lake in streaks of yellow. Dark, the suburbs were quickly vanishing from view. In such blackness, it appeared as though the car was suspended in motion, simply floating over the water indefinitely, rather than heading for a destination on the other side. As they passed over the lake Hugo became aware of the spaciousness, of just how vast it was. It was enough to incite a sense of awe in him.

"So, big brother," Martin said, "how many months has it been?"

"What do you mean?"

"You know...since—"

"Oh, I don't want to talk about that."

"But—"

"Did you hear me? I said I don't want to talk about that. Let's change the subject."

A pause followed, Martin gripping the steering wheel loosely, occasionally looking behind him before making a lane change.

"I know it must be hard to talk about," Martin said calmly.

"Not really. I just don't have any interest in talking about it."

"But I think it's important that you talk about it. Isn't that what the healing process is about? I think so. I think you need to have people in your life who you can talk to about this stuff, and I'd like to be one of those people."

"To be honest with you," Hugo said, "I'm just not in the mood to talk about it. Here we had a nice and pleasant evening, with a great meal and company, and then you want to make things all heavy. Why?"

"I just want to support you, big brother."

Another pause came. "I know," Hugo said.

"You do know how much we love you, don't you?"

Hugo smiled. "I know," he said, "and if you want to show that you love me, then I think the best thing we can do is just move forward and focus on all the good things in life. Why get caught up in the past? I already told you in the car ride earlier that I am as happy as can be. I have never felt better. I feel comfortable in my own skin. So why make things heavy?"

Now the car was pulling off the bridge, entering the freeway.

"Well for what it's worth," Martin continued, "our parish holds a widower support network, and I think it would be really valuable for you to at least come and check it out."

"There is nothing to talk about!" Hugo yelled, slamming his hand on the dashboard. "I already told you I'm happy, and all I need is for us to move forward. I don't need to get caught up in the past. I am living my life doing the things I love with the people I love. What could be better than that?"

"Don't you—"

"The last thing I need is to sit in a basement of some church, in a circle, talking about my feelings with a bunch of strangers, especially when there is nothing to talk about."

A few minutes of silence later and the car rolled up Hugo's street. Climbing out of the car, Hugo heard Martin say, "Like I said, big brother. You do know that we love you a whole lot, don't you? We just want what's best for you."

Not wanting any more conflict, Hugo replied, "I know, Martin."

"It was great seeing you today. Please let me know if you're in for Chelan. Hope you can make it!"

"I will."

"All right, big brother. Love you!"

"Love you, too."

The car sped away and Hugo made his way up to his room. He prepared for bed, turned off the lights, and pulled up the covers. The very idea of a widower support network was an affront to him. Why, he wondered, had Martin mentioned such a thing? Of course what had happened to Hugo a little more than two months earlier had been painful; the agony had been beyond any words. Hugo knew he was lying when he said that there was nothing to talk about, but he didn't see what the use was in talking about it. As far as he was concerned, every time someone attempted to bring it up, it was like he was being stabbed anew with tiny blades. It saddened him to think that the people in his life would set out to hurt him in such a way. As he had mentioned to Martin, what he was interested in was pursuing the good in life, focusing on family and friends, on his hobbies, on all the life that still rested before him.

But occasionally, despite his best efforts, a memory or a thought would surface in his mind, and he would feel himself begin to panic, his palms sweaty, his heart beating rapidly. This would happen, and then he would pour himself a glass of water, go swimming, or do something else to help him escape whatever was hounding him.

I am happy, Hugo reassured himself as he lay in bed. I am happy.

In a darkness, stronger than the depths of Lake Washington, Hugo slept a troubled sleep.

2.

The small lights of the Wedgwood recreational pool reflected gently in the water. He was making strokes, breathing on every third one, traversing up and down his own solitary lane. Beneath the water there was a pattern of red and blue tiles that guided him forward. It felt like he was moving in slow motion as he reached with one arm and then the other, as though he was in actuality making no real progress.

Having reached the end of the pool, he took a deep breath, his heart beating rapidly and firmly, and proceeded to perform a flip turn. With the best kick he could muster he pushed off the wall of the pool deck, hoping to gain some momentum. 175 yards, he told himself. 25 to go. He was not getting enough air, as hard as he tried to breathe deeply. His feet were kicking with plenty of vigor, but he was feeling fatigued. Reaching up his head to take another breath, a small amount of water entered his mouth. Through the filtered world of his goggles, everything was dark blue. Now he was steadily approaching the end of the pool. Every stroke felt agonizing. Air became precious. Finally, reaching out an arm, slicing through the water in a haphazard stroke, he was overjoyed to feel the tips of his fingers reach the end of the pool deck.

He pulled his face out of the water and looked at the clock. Evidently, it was not his day for swimming. He was more than twenty seconds late for his next 200. He struck the water, making several splashes, and proceeded to lean over the end of the deck and simply breathe.

For a minute, he floated there and breathed, mindful of the swimmers in the other lanes who continued to go, who were much faster than him. All at once he was aware of his own body, of its weight. His arms felt heavy. His feet felt heavy. Clearly, he was not in the same shape he had been in when he was younger. Age was something that was steadily catching up with him, and there was nowhere to hide. When he was younger, there was no issue for him with swimming lap after lap, miles at a time, for hours. In high school, he was a member of the school swim team, where he swam long distance races. What he loved about long distance swimming was its meditative quality. While swimming for long periods of time, there was nothing to focus on but the sensation of the body passing through the water, of the rhythm of breathing, or the feeling of kicking off the wall. Swimming for him was calming, a source of comfort. He remembered, too, the way in which he slept as an adolescent on the swim team. Like a rock, he slumbered for the few hours afforded him before he had to wake up and get ready for school. During the swim season, swimming and school met in a beautiful harmony. At the swim meets he felt the sense of fiery passion, the ecstasy of being alive that was invoked when he was busy swimming, heart beating wildly, arms slicing the water. The world was his and nothing would ever take it away, as though things would always be this way.

But here he was, huffing out air desperately, his body tired, wondering how things could possibly have changed so much. No longer was the water his friend. Tonight, the pool was a cruel foe who laughed in his face. He wondered how much longer he would be able to swim. The reason he continued with this particular sport was because of how low-resistance it was, how easy it supposedly was on the body. But tonight it felt like swimming was very rough on the body, as though the pool chewed on him and spat him out. It was his routine to go swimming in the evening on Monday and Friday. Such had been his custom for decades. Never did he swim with others, and never did he interact with other swimmers beyond basic etiquette. He always strove for the same thing: 3,000 yards. He swam fifteen 200's. Yet tonight was different. He had only completed 12 of his 200's, and he was so tired and dizzy he felt like he was going to fall over. So he decided that he would complete one more 200. For the first time in years, he would not attain his goal.

After another two minutes of recovering, he dove back into the water, resolved to make his swimming count. But his arms sluggishly slapped against the water. He was hardly able to move his feet. Already he was wondering how much farther there was left to go, something he normally never did. Looking up, he estimated that he was about half-way across the pool. The pain he was feeling was unbearable. He felt like he was suffocating. Every subsequent stroke was more painful than the one that came before it. Having reached the end of the pool, he declined to make a flip turn, and instead attempted to climb out of the pool.

His first attempt to get out proved to be unsuccessful, with him falling back into the water in a massive splash. He tried again, feeling the aching sensation in his arms, and managed to exit the pool. He walked into the locker room, took a shower, changed his clothes, put his wedding ring on his left ring finger, walked to the car, and drove home, utterly defeated.

3.

"You know, I think this is going to be great," Paul said.

"Me too. It's a shame we are stuck in traffic yet again."

Paul was alternating the placement of his foot between the gas pedal and the brake pedal. They moved slowly, the other cars around them going faster than them. Nevertheless, it was a lovely spring afternoon. The sun was shining above, and there was a crisp breeze in the air. Flowers were in full bloom. This was precisely what the two friends were after: to see a beautiful, blooming display at the annual tulip festival in Mount Vernon.

"Good thing we left when we did," Paul asserted.

"Well, hopefully there are some flowers left by the time we get there."

"The flowers aren't going anywhere."

Hugo looked at Paul, at his black hair, his wiry frame, reminding himself that Paul was, at his heart, a realist. For this was the founding point of their friendship. Paul's realism complemented Hugo's incessant cynicism rather nicely. The two shared a view of the world that was cautious, at times nervous, and usually critical. Paul, however, was more at peace with things than Hugo. He was better at knowing how to let go. Hugo would not say that he had a terribly large amount of friends, but he prided himself on what he possessed in Paul, which was a deep, rich friendship.

"I feel like wherever I go," Hugo began, "I run into traffic. In the last twenty years, traffic has only gotten worse and worse. "

"You just need to be a little more patient. It isn't that bad."

"'Isn't that bad?' It's terrible! It's awful. I can't bear it."

"Well, you don't have much of a choice in the matter."

"Hmmph."

"Sometimes you have to be patient. You have to accept things as they are. So you get caught in traffic every now and then? It happens. You have got to take what life offers you and deal with it. Take a look outside. What do you see?"

"I see a fast food restaurant."

"Uh-huh."

"And other cars."

"Yup."

"And that's it."

"That's all you see?"

"What do you see, Mr. Poet?"

Paul breathed in deeply. "I see a blue sky, and a bright sun, and horizon that is vast."

"Beautiful," Hugo said, "but we aren't paying good money to see the pretty sky. We could have done that at home. We are paying money to see the tulip festival, an event that only happens once a year. We go every year. I can't stand the thought of missing it this time."

"You won't miss it. You don't need to hurry. You've also got to remember to take time to stop and smell the roses. Er, tulips."

They both laughed at this. As upset as Hugo might be sometimes, he could count on Paul to cheer him up.

"I don't have time to stop and smell anything. I'm going to be dead soon. If I wait around and accept things as they are, I'm going to miss seeing the things I want to see."

Paul looked amused. "That's a rather morbid appraisal of things. I still stand behind what I said."

So they sat in traffic. It was another forty-five minutes before they passed Everett, and they still had another thirty miles to go. Traffic, thankfully, lightened up after that point, and Hugo rolled down his window so he could feel the breeze on his cheeks. They were moving along steadily when all of a sudden traffic once more was bad. Out of instinct, Paul slammed on the breaks and they came to a stop, narrowly avoiding the car in front of them.

"What are you doing?" Hugo roared. "Are you trying to kill us?"

"I'm—"

"You can't be driving like that."

"I'm sorry," Paul choked. "I didn't expect traffic to get bad again."

"No one ever expects it," Hugo replied.

They were quiet for the last forty-five minutes it took to reach Mount Vernon. Hugo was breathing loudly. When he was younger, Hugo and his mother were involved in a car accident. He was twelve at the time. They were driving through their neighborhood when Hugo's mother forgot to look both ways at a yield sign. The result was that they tee-boned another car. To this day Hugo remembered the loudness, the sound of glass cracking and metal colliding. The sensation of being rocked back in his seat left a deep impression on him. In addition to the loudness and the rocking, there was the horror, the sheer terror of realizing that the world was full of danger. Neither Hugo nor his mother were seriously injured in the accident. The other driver was fine as well. However, their cars took some serious damage.

For weeks Hugo was afraid to climb into a car. The horror of being rocked in his seat, the feelings of helplessness and lack of control were with him when he thought about going for a drive. Eventually, he was able to overcome his own fears. But every now and then, every decade or so, he would have an episode in which residual fear surfaced and he would be terrified of driving. He might be sitting in traffic when panic would all at once seize him and he would be paralyzed. It was his joy to give up driving and his car when he retired. After all, everything he needed was located in his neighborhood. He also had Paul and Martin to depend on when it came to other driving needs.

When they reached Mount Vernon, it was his relief to climb out of the car, having finally arrived at his destination.

"So where are the tulips, anyway?" he asked as they walked through the massive parking lot.

"We should be seeing some very soon."

They passed under a hedge archway. Before them were crowds of people walking in one direction and another. People, young, old, of every description, were present. Tulips had the power to bring together people from around the world.

"I remember where to go now," Hugo said. "Follow me."

"No, it's this direction." Paul was pointing towards the left.

"Follow me," Hugo repeated.

They went with his plan and walked along a narrow pathway that led to the bathrooms and a trash can.

Paul shrugged.

Walking back along the pathway, the two friends were quiet for a while.

"Been to mass lately?" Paul asked, breaking the silence.

Striking Hugo as a strange question to be asking given all circumstances, he replied, "No, I haven't been."

"When did you last go?"

"What are you getting on my case about?"

"Just curious. Just making conversation."

"Okay."

"So when did you last go?"

"Hmm," Hugo put a finger to his chin, "you know, it's been a number of months."

"I see."

"I just haven't really felt a need to go."

"No?"

"Life has been, well it's been good. I guess what I am saying is that I have felt spiritually quenched, for the time being, anyway."

Paul was effectively a secular person. However, being re-alistic, he recognized that there were certain benefits that arose from a cultivation of the spiritual life, regardless of which tradition one chose to pursue. Knowing that Hugo was raised Catholic, Paul understood it was beneficial for Hugo to be involved at least at some level. A sense of com-munity, social engagement, and an awareness of a reality beyond one's own life were all things to be gleaned from liv-ing spiritually.

Hugo was raised in a devoutly Catholic family. He had vivid memories of his mother upstairs, praying the rosary, or of his father with a Bible open. These images were some-thing that he carried with him. As a child, he spent hours sitting in mass, feeling incapable to wrestle with the over-whelming boredom, the droning tones of the priest echoing off the stained-glass windows. He and his brother were en-rolled in a special class as children, where they showed up weekly to have Bible stories read to them and play games. Some of his good friends growing up came from this group.

Growing up, the values of discipline, compassion, and for-giveness were stressed on Hugo. He was taught to take his faith and integrate it into his life. Throughout high school, he went to mass regularly. Once in college, he drifted away from it. When he got married, she told him that the Catholic faith was important to her, and he agreed to participate. They were married in the precise church he grew up attend-ing. So life went on with them going to mass. They had Adrian, and they raised him to follow in the faith just as they had. Yet when Hugo compared Adrian's spiritual upbring-ing to his own, it was safe to say that it was much less severe in tone and intensity. To be honest, Hugo was clueless re-garding how to apply the message of the Christian story to the profession of accounting. Working with numbers, bring-ing a sense of balance and order to the world, it seemed that there was no room for grace or mercy. Still, there was beauty in the order that Hugo's work produced, and it inspired him to look to the spiritual realm.

But these days thoughts of Christ or God were far from Hugo's mind. He was much more interested in the smaller facets of his own life, of his garden, his soccer team, his swimming stroke (though as of late he was not interested in that either). He went to mass a few times, but he found it to be boring and uninspiring. The message of the priest in his homily was far removed from the reality Hugo was living. So he was content to stop going. Hugo had a peace of mind in this. After all, Adrian was minimally practicing, so it was not as though Hugo had an image to maintain for the sake of his own family. Hugo couldn't care less what his son did as far as religion was concerned, because he thought it was none of his business.

Martin, on the other hand, was a different case altogether. Brimming with faithful energy, he and Patricia gave themselves to the church, reading from the altar, serving at the food bank. Genuinely and passionately Martin believed in his relationship with God, and he raised James to be the same way. In turn, James raised Cassandra in the faith, thus continuing the family legacy of faith for several more generations.

For some reason, Martin felt it his need to occasionally have a spiritual dialogue with Hugo, a matter which irked him more than almost anything else. Hugo recalled the sentimental heaviness, the way in which Martin would earnestly ask his brother about faith, nodding with sincerity, asking probing questions, as though it was his divine duty to monitor Hugo's faith. Such conversations were the bane of Hugo's existence. The brothers had not talked about the subject since Hugo consistently stopped going to church, so he knew that he had another one of these interactions to suffer through coming up very soon.

Paul, not being religious, was only curious about Hugo's practices in a more general way. Therefore, it did not bother Hugo much when his friend said, "It is good to hear you are feeling spiritually quenched. What do you think is the cause for you feeling this way?"

"I don't know."

"Is it swimming?"

"It certainly isn't swimming," Hugo mumbled.

"Are you exploring other faiths?"

"No, I am not. The truth is I'm not all that interested in religion. I don't feel like I need it. I just like to live my life, and that's how it is. Isn't that how it is with you?"

"That's fair," Paul conceded, "and yes, that is how it is for me. I am content to live my life as it is. I don't look beyond the chores I need to do, the game of chess I am playing, and that is enough for me. That doesn't mean I don't occasionally feel like there might be something more to all of this, though."

"What do you mean?"

By now the two friends had taken the path back to the main area, continued on a separate path, and were standing before a sprawling field of tulips. There they were: long streams of flowers colored orange, yellow, red, purple, and pink. The sight was enough to bring a big smile to both of their faces. Other people were standing about, taking photos, pointing at the flowers. Children could be heard laughing. The sun was shining down from above as though it approved of all that was taking place.

"Take this for instance," Paul said. "It's really amazing, this view of tulips. Now I don't know about you, but at times I can't help but wonder if there is a God out there, some sort of cosmic order that causes something as beautiful as this to exist."

"Well, I don't think there needs to be a God for this to exist."

"You don't?"

"Of course not! Humans exist. Tulips exist. We find tulips to be pretty. Perhaps it is as simple as that."

They continued to survey the flowers when Hugo sneezed. He continued speaking, clutching his flower-decorated tie in one hand, saying, "Besides, you are talking about two different things."

"Am I?"

"Yes. On the one hand, you are talking about God and spirituality, but then you are asking me about my attendance at mass, which is just organized religion. What do the two have to do with each other?"

Paul was caught off guard by this question and laughed nervously. "Well, I don't know. Maybe the two have less to do with each other than we might sometimes think."

"Let's say I go to mass. A chorus sings a song, a priest speaks, there are pretty stained-glass windows and the church has a high ceiling. All of those things are manmade or are man himself."

"Or herself."

"Whatever. The point I'm trying to make," Hugo argued, "is that I don't know if we can separate 'God' from what comes from humans. So what's the point of pursuing God if all I ever arrive at is human?"

"Hmmm."

"What's the point of talking about spirituality and all that if it's so far removed from me? What's the point if the closest I get to 'God' is a piece of round bread that I would have every week at communion?"

They walked away from the field of tulips, unaware of what higher being, if any, to attribute the beauty.

Along a narrow path they walked. The day was turning out to be rather warm. There was a steady, oceanic breeze coming in. Mount Vernon was located not far from the water, a small settlement situated on the edge of the estuary. Hugo felt himself practically sweating. He was energized by the conversation he was having with his friend. He was, at last, being given an opportunity to give voice to thoughts and feelings that he had been holding onto for quite a while. They reached a second field of tulips, and he had no trouble continuing where he left off, saying, "Tell me, Paul, do you have tulips in your garden?"

"I do."

"So do I. This is my point: the giant field of flowers is all well and good. It is very pretty. But isn't it nice to have some flowers in your own little yard? Isn't it nice to be able to have something smaller, more manageable to work with? That's how I feel about my life. You and I can spend an afternoon here, looking at flowers, but when we go home we spend ninety-nine percent of our time with our own little gardens, and you don't see me complaining. I love my garden. In the same way, I could spend a bunch of my time preoccupied with God or whatever, but I'm much more content to focus on my own life, including my garden!"

"Ah!"

"Like I said before, it's very tricky to separate 'God' from human creation."

"Yes," Paul admitted, "but isn't the whole point of it that the human creations, the church building, the priest, it's all coated in the divine, and God is supernaturally at work through it?"

Hugo was slightly astonished to be having this conversation with Paul, who did not practice any religion. But Hugo knew Paul well enough to know that there was no conversation they couldn't end up having.

"If the Roman Catholic Church is coated in the divine, then I have been made a very big fool of. Looking at the world and at history, at the atrocities committed in the name of the church, I think it is safe to say that it is fully human and not at all divine."

"Sure, but what about all the good of the church? What about the food banks, the schools, the hospitals, the answered prayers?"

"What about them?" Hugo replied. "Humans are capable of doing mighty good things. No need to label it as coming from up above. It could just be the goodness of people."

"That's not the Hugo I know! Hugo would never say such positive, nice things about humanity!"

"You caught me!" Hugo was grinning.

The two friends spent the rest of the afternoon looking at tulips, trekking from one field to another, continuing to talk about the spiritual, laughing, arguing, and enjoying one another's company wholly and thoroughly. When it was time to leave, Hugo even sensed a pang of sadness.

4.

Ambling through the aisles of the supermarket, Hugo felt a sense of malaise. He looked down at his list, at the things he needed to purchase, and then up at the cart he was pushing, which contained apples, onions, cucumbers, red peppers, and a head of lettuce along with four shopping bags. The list was not long. He couldn't wait until he would be able to leave the store.

Turning the cart he walked down another aisle, putting things in it without looking at the price tags. Usually a meticulous shopper for deals, today he wanted to be on his way quickly, and so he picked out items indiscriminately. All of a sudden he stopped his cart. A rather large man and his cart were blocking the entire middle of the aisle. Waiting impatiently, Hugo stood and looked at the processed, synthesized food sitting on the shelves. In the background, there was the sound of schmaltzy, sentimental guitar-music playing.

"Excuse me," Hugo intoned.

The fat man didn't budge. Apparently engrossed in comparing coupons, this individual seemed to be stuck in place.

"Excuse me!" Hugo exclaimed.

The man and his cart moved to the side, creating a path through.

Hugo pushed his cart rapidly, making it through before the man returned to looking at his coupons.

Irritated even further, he continued on his way through several more aisles. After a while, he looked down at his cart and realized that it wasn't filling up at all. He continued on his way.

Now he was in the sweets section.

Looking about him, he saw the despicable, abominable sugary goods that he knew would kill him if he got close enough. He walked past a rack of donuts, careful to not even look at what was contained within. Sugar, he knew, was one of his great enemies in his life. Everywhere he looked, he was bombarded with it: donuts, cake, cookies, brownies, juice, soda, the list went on and on.

By no means even remotely big, Hugo was as small and slim as someone his age could aspire to be. If all things worked out according to his careful planning, he would live to be at least a hundred. This, of course, was without him taking into account medical advancement. Hugo was typically sure to exercise, eat right, and to sleep plenty when he was able to. However, lately, he was struggling in these areas. Feeling more lazy, he was content to eat whatever was lying around the house. Idle eating was undoing all the progress he was envisioning for himself. Then there was exercise. In the weeks that passed since his failed swimming experience, he continued to go to the pool, being disappointed more and more. Some place in his mind was infected with a toxic form of thinking, and now his own brain was getting in the way of his ability to spread his arms and move through the water.

Regarding sleep, Hugo was not getting much of it.

Still moving the cart, practically closing his eyes in order to avoid the evils surrounding him, he finally looked up and realized he had escaped the wasteland that was the sweets section. He gazed at his list again. In fact, the only thing left to purchase was lunchmeat.

Several other people were standing near the deli counter. Hugo took his place behind a young couple. Easily his least favorite part of shopping was procuring lunchmeat. He stood there, nearly leaning on his cart, waiting as the attendant helped one customer and then another. The young couple in front of him seemed to not know what they wanted. They spoke together, as though picking meat to purchase was a discussion they had to publicly conduct. Hugo was gripping the handle of his cart tightly. Finally, after what had felt like an hour, the man grabbed a bag of turkey and was on his way.

"Can I help you, sir?" a young lady asked.

"Yes, I would like the deli counter turkey."

"How much?"

"A pound."

The attendant proceeded to slice the meat using a large metal apparatus. This process was slow, gradual, and Hugo felt ready to burst with impatience. The attendant placed the bag of meat on the scale: .945.

"Is that all right, sir?"

"No, I said I would like a pound."

Back to using the apparatus, Hugo was left to wait. Then the attendant placed the bag on the scale: 1.125.

"Is that all right?"

Wanting it to be just right, Hugo asked if the attendant could remove some of the meat. The meat was taken out of the bag, and it read .970.

"Is that—"

"Yes, that's fine," Hugo huffed. He took the bag and thanked the attendant, overjoyed that the ordeal was ended and he had acquired what he set out for.

He pushed his cart towards the front of the store, wondering how bad the lines would be.

He was not prepared for what he saw.

Across the store, each and every checkout lane was filled to the brim with other customers who had carts filled to the brim with items to be scanned, bagged, and paid for.

Sighing, he took his place in the line that appeared to be the shortest.

An older-looking man was scanning the food. He had a tattoo of an eagle that went along his neck. Hugo began to think about how idiotic tattoos were. They were like a public display of stupidity, he thought. This grocery store employee was chatting amicably with the brown-haired woman who was preparing to pay for her groceries.

"Can we do a little less talking and a little more working?" Hugo asked.

The employee looked at Hugo. "Sir, I will be with you shortly."

"What do you mean?" Hugo gestured at the ocean of food that separated him from the employee. "Do you think you're going to get through all of this 'shortly'?"

"Sir, please calm down."

"I am calm. I am—"

"Please excuse him, sir," another voice from behind Hugo said, "he won't be causing any more trouble."

Hugo looked behind him and saw a woman with long blonde hair and a pearl necklace. Certain that she was familiar, he could not place his finger on where he had seen her from.

"How's it going?" she asked. "Having a tough time?"

"I'm not having a tough time. I'm just trying to purchase my food and be on my way."

"I know. It's okay. The line is long, but they get through it fast. You just wait and see."

"Who are you? You look familiar."

"Me? I'm Lily. Remember? The owner of the Blue Hen. I brought you a glass of water."

All at once aware of who she was, he smiled, relieved that he was in the company of someone he knew.

"How have you been?" she asked. "Haven't seen you at the bar in a while."

"I haven't been going."

"I know. How come?"

"Just haven't been as interested in my team."

"But I thought you loved your team. You told me those stories about how you grew up watching them play."

"Yes, I guess I haven't wanted to wake up so early to catch the games."

"That's fair. They're on pretty early."

A customer had already made it through the line. Progress was taking place as Lily and Hugo took a step forward.

"Well I have been there early most days," she continued, "making sure everything is going right. It's all part of being the manager, you know. They're a good bunch, my servers and staff."

"That's good to hear."

"It'd be nice to see you again sometime. You should bring your wife. I'll give you both a Guinness on the house. Like I said before, I like to reward my regulars."

"That's a kind offer."

He looked into her cart and saw that she, like him, had not picked out much. This made waiting in line all the more unbearable, the fact that one was trying to purchase very little, and yet a wait in the line was still necessary. They both took another couple of steps forward, the sea of groceries before them steadily shrinking.

"Your groceries look very healthy," she said. "Lots of greens and fruits and the like."

"Yes, well I try to be conscious of what I eat."

"That is good."

"Sebastian used to make the best salads. He put in nuts and fruit and whatever he could find. They were delicious!"

"Who is Sebastian?" Hugo asked.

"Oh," she turned red. "I'm sorry. There I go talking about my late husband again. I didn't mean to. It's just a force of habit. He was such a big part of my life, you know."

"I do know. How long has he been gone?"

"Oh, on August 6th it will be seven years."

"Uh-huh."

"We don't need to talk about that. Here I go, at the super-market, talking about loss! I'm sorry."

Moved, Hugo said, "It's no problem. Don't concern your-self over it."

Now it was Hugo's turn to check out his groceries.

"How are you doing today, sir?"

"Fine, fine."

"Excellent. Will you be—"

"I have my own bags."

By the time all of the groceries were scanned and placed in the bags, Hugo realized that only two of the four bags had even been necessary. This seemed odd to him. He was eager to leave the store, and so he said goodbye to Lily.

"Like I said," she began, "come on back to the Blue Hen. A free round waits for you!"

"I got it, thanks."

It was raining outside. The coverage of clouds was dense and dark. The water was coming down in a light sprinkle, nothing that was too bothersome.

Hugo felt no need to tell Lily that he would not be able to bring his wife to the Blue Hen. It was a personal matter, and he possessed no need to talk about it. But he was struck by the way in which she so openly discussed her own dead hus-band. Who was this woman, and why did he keep running into her? On one level, he had much more in common with her than could seem possible. There had surely been an opportunity for them to connect over a shared experience, but it was a personal matter.

He walked through the rainy Wedgwood afternoon along Mason Street, glad that the winds from earlier had come to a stop. He took a turn and went towards his own street. It was not a long walk. He gripped the handle of one bag in each of his hands.

Already standing on the front steps of his home, he waved at Paul who was tending to his garden. Hugo opened the door and entered, the receipt nearly falling out of a bag. He proceeded to put away groceries, which didn't take long.

Was it possible that it was worth talking about it with other people? Martin had mentioned a support group. Martin said that one needed to have people in life who you could talk to about this sort of thing. Lily was unable to help herself from talking about it. No, Hugo reminded himself. It was a private, personal matter. Talking about it didn't help; it only led to unnecessary suffering and pain. Why focus on the past? All he wanted to do was move on towards the future.

Hugo looked in the refrigerator and realized how sparsely stocked it was. Feeling a tear form in his eye, he ran into the bathroom and ripped off a piece of toilet paper to wipe his eye. Then he blew his nose. He looked in the mirror, at his yellow argyle tie, at his mustache, beholding his own loneliness. I'm happy, he told himself as he wiped his eye again.

May

I.

Opening his eyes, he was awake. He picked at a scab on his left arm until it bled. He removed his blanket, took his morning medication, and climbed out of the bed. Stumbling into the bathroom, he banged his elbow on the side of the doorframe. He brushed his teeth forcefully and splashed cold water on his face. Then he walked down the stairs, to the kitchen where he poured himself a large glass of water. He turned on the news but was appalled by what he heard: another terrorist attack in some distant city. He turned off the television, sat on the sofa, and drank some water, festering in his own thoughts.

The telephone rang. Knowing that he now had to interact with someone, he felt bothered. He looked and saw that it was Adrian calling.

"Hello?"

"Hey, Dad."

"Hi, son."

"How are you?"

"Fine. You?"

"Doing good. I was wondering if I could come by for a little while, just to have a drink and chat."

Hugo gazed out the window of the living room, looking at his lawn. "Yes, that will be fine."

"Okay, I'll see you soon!"

"See you soon."

Realizing that he needed to get out of his pajamas, he went upstairs and changed. On his way up the stairs, he tripped and fell upward, stumbling all the while. Prepared to kick the stairs out of annoyance, he refrained and continued on his way.

Now he was walking into the study, the room where his bookshelf was. He scanned the spines of books and picked out an old mystery he had read before. Though he had previously read it, he had no recollection of what it was about, let alone who perpetrated the crime.

On the sofa he sat, reading, sipping his water, waiting for his son to arrive. After an hour of waiting, his temper had mellowed somewhat. Behind him, he heard the sound of a car engine coming to a halt. Adrian was here, he knew. Hugo stood up and walked towards the front door. He opened it and greeted his son who was walking past the azaleas.

"Hi, son."

"Hi, Dad."

Despite their relationship as a father and a son, there was still a tone of formality to any visits that took place. Since it had been nearly three months from Adrian's last visit, there was a sense of a gap in how much time they spent together at Hugo's house, so he was always sure to hold the door open for his son when he arrived, to offer him a drink, and to let him speak first. In his manner, Hugo was a formal person.

Hugo brought a glass of water over to Adrian.

"Want anything to eat?" he asked somewhat begrudgingly.

"No, thanks. I already ate."

"Good."

Then Hugo waited for his son to speak first. Obviously, there was some sort of business that needed to be attended to. There always was when a visitor came by.

"I have been doing pretty well in the program," Adrian said.

"Good to hear!"

"I am learning a lot," Adrian continued. "They really like to 'fill your head with knowledge', as the teacher puts it. The classes are only two months long, so they cram a lot of material into it. You try to keep up, but it's hard to not feel like you are drowning."

"Did you have an okay time paying for it?" Hugo felt no guilt.

"I had to take out a loan-a small one. But that's fine. I am paying for it fine."

"Good, good. So what are you learning about in this program?"

Adrian had a sip of water and crossed his leg. "Right now I am taking two separate classes: human resources and participating in a global economy."

"Sounds valuable."

"It's pretty neat."

"Are you enjoying it?"

"It's a good way to get ready for my new career, you know?"

"Yes, I do know. But that's not what I asked you. Are you enjoying it?"

Adrian paused before answering. Finally, he said, "It's all right. It's pretty stressful, but I think it could be useful for my career."

"Okay."

It was surprising to Hugo that his son was interested in business school. As a young child, Adrian was always been drawn towards the creative passions: painting, writing stories, and taking photographs. Hugo attempted to guide his son towards being more interested in math, science, and literature. Reading and literature had been where they met. However, for the most part, Adrian was set in his own ways. Particularly he was interested in taking photographs. Hugo could remember, fondly, them walking to the local park, where Adrian would take photographs with his tiny disposable camera, documenting butterflies, the sky, trees, and the playground among other things. They would go home, and a week later, when the camera's storage was full, they would develop the pictures. Hugo would take the photographs and show Adrian how to place them into a special book, where the memories would be preserved for years. In Hugo's study, next to the bookshelf, there was a small pile of these picture books. Inscribed onto the back of each photo was the name of the people in the picture, along with when and where it had been taken. It was Hugo's intention to give these books back to his son, but Adrian claimed he had no storage for them.

When Adrian announced that he wanted to major in Photography, Hugo was skeptical. Still working at the time as an accountant, Hugo did not consider taking pictures to be a valid profession by any means. It was true that he enjoyed those trips to the park, as well as the time spent filling out the books, but he thought it best to leave it at that. Hugo thought there was no need to try and make a career out of it. Still, Adrian was resolute in pursuing photography as his principal field of study. Class after class was devoted to techniques, how to take photos, how to decide what to photograph, and how to present what was photographed. Adrian enjoyed his studies and was successful at it. After college, in addition to working for Java City, he spent the summers taking pictures of weddings, at first for friends, then for friend-of-a-friends, and soon he had his own operation going.

But with time Adrian grew tired of photographing weddings. His aspirations, it seemed, were bigger than this creative outlet was, for he felt constrained. It always seemed to be the same, the picture of the groom waiting at the altar, the picture of the kiss, the picture of toasts, the picture of the getaway car, the sentimentality of each wedding more or less being the same. Hugo advised his son to consider going back to school, maybe becoming a teacher of photography or looking at a new degree altogether. But Adrian chose to put his time back into Java City, and that was how the next twelve years went: more or less smoothly, with little in the way of change or development. That was until now.

"Do you think that maybe there is a way you could combine photography with business?" Hugo asked.

"I'm not interested in photography, Dad."

"Okay."

"Right now I want to really apply myself to business, and see what I'm made of. I am interested in learning how to be a part of a team, generate innovative ideas, and use classic practices and principles of business to lead to success. I was thinking of finding a company that I believe in and then applying once the program is over."

"What kind of company?"

"I don't know, but I was thinking of something in finance. There is a lot of growth in that particular sector, especially in Seattle."

"Well that all sounds great to me," Hugo replied, "but the little Adrian I remember in my mind, Adrian the child, was passionate about drawing pictures and taking pictures of butterflies. Don't you still have interest in that? It was what you studied."

"Not really," Adrian answered before taking another sip of water.

Again Hugo was feeling anger well up inside of him. How could his son go and act like he had completely transformed what he was interested in? It felt like Adrian was trying to create distance between himself and his past, and since Hugo was a big part of that past, it felt like distance was being created between them. Still, he was fully in support of his son working towards a professional career; it relieved him. He spent far too many years hearing dull updates about Java City, with nothing in the way of real progress taking place. So Hugo was supportive and oppositional towards the idea of Adrian abandoning photography for business. This internal divide, this dissonance that was produced in him, only made him angrier.

"You know," he began, "I never imagined you for the business type. What draws you towards it?"

Adrian, who felt like he was defending himself, said, "I want to make the world a better place. I want to create connections between myself, others, and the world. I want to help make products and services reach people in a way that makes a difference. What could be better than that?

"That does sound nice." It sounded empty to him.

"Plus I think my mind is built for it. I feel like I have always been a real people-person, that I have the outgoing attitude and the energy that is necessary to be really successful in finance, or in whatever sector I end up working for."

This was not the Adrian that Hugo knew. It hurt him to think that his son might indeed be changing, as though the memories of the past were being eroded away. While Hugo had no desire to live in the past, he did hold a high reverence for the pleasures of memory. Hugo did not believe what his son was saying, anyway, so it made no difference. It was not a matter of Hugo thinking that his son was lying so much as that Adrian was mistaken in his own assessment of himself. How could those books of pictures of butterflies and trees come to mean nothing? This was not Adrian. Hugo was annoyed, taking a sip of water and then leaning back on the couch.

"Where do your classes meet?" he asked.

"Over in Fremont. We meet in this really nice business tower that was just built in the last five years."

"Sounds lovely."

The two of them chatted for a while longer. Adrian claimed that his classes were demanding all of his free time. It was a bit of an adjustment going from Java City to this program, and transitions always took time. Hugo agreed, and spent a while reminiscing about when he had transitioned from accounting school to his first actual job in the field.

"When does the program end?"

"October. There are four rounds of two-month classes."

"A great time to be looking for a job."

"Yes, it will be. How is Martin and the rest of the Larsons?"

"They are doing well, as always. I am going on a trip with them to Lake Chelan in July."

"That should be fun!"

Adrian was not close with this family, but he still felt a desire to check in on them, to hear about how they were doing, for he knew that they were a powerful force in the effort to make sure that Hugo was not too lonely. Meanwhile, Hugo said he was looking forward to the summer getaway a great deal. The father and son took a while longer, talking about the program and about life in general, and then around 4:00 pm Adrian mentioned that he needed to get home and study. Hugo was understanding, and as he watched his son leave the front door and walk towards his car, he thought of how great the moment would have looked as a photograph.

2.

The lilacs in Hugo's garden were now clearly coming into full bloom.

He crouched down low so he could feel the stem of the flower between his fingertips. It was May, and he thought his garden was looking spectacular. The late-spring sun was shining down warm, radiant rays on the back of his neck. There was no breeze. The air was decidedly dry. In the other corner of the garden, the tulips, purple and pink, were looking marvelous, like glowing lavender.

He took a step back to admire it all, the culmination of many hours of hard work. But he could not look at it for long, for there was one issue still needing to be addressed, mainly weeds.

Throughout Hugo's garden, festering, growing rapidly, expanding, were weeds that threatened to suffocate the beautiful plants he cultivated with such intentionality. Just the mere thought of the weeds taking over the garden filled him with dread. So, getting his gloves and a bucket, he proceeded to grab them by their grassy edges and toss them away.

It was difficult work. He would pull a weed only to find that the roots still remained, which were a promise of more weeds tomorrow. He would dig in the soil, searching for every last bit of root, and then toss it into the bucket. His search for roots would lead him across corners of the garden, under other flowers and near bushes. Eventually, he had to make peace with the fact that some of the roots were not going anywhere. It really felt like there were more and more weeds with each passing moment. He nearly stepped on one of his azaleas while he was going about his business. All the while he was lost in his own thoughts.

Spring, to his thinking, was the best season. It was the time of rebirth, renewal, change, and of course the return of flowers. After the long and dreary winter, full of dark nights and cloudy skies, spring presented itself as an opportunity for all that to be done away with and for life to return to the world. But Hugo himself felt too old, too tired for change, for renewal. His body was old and his soul was even older. Spring was a young man's game. With its sense of energy and vitality, spring was a time ripe with opportunity, but Hugo didn't think it was his to seize. He felt old, and he was angry at the fact that he felt old. It was as though the world, which seemed to cycle through seasons with little thought, was passing him by, leaving him in limbo while all the young people rejoiced. He had his garden, it was true, but each year it took more and more effort to maintain it. An increasing amount of energy was being demanded of him, and he was anxious to meet it. Already, after little more than twenty minutes, his wrists were aching with a sharp pain. His legs hurt from sitting on them. His back was bothering him from all of the hunching over. Meanwhile, his garden, his prize, his gem, was being blocked out by these little monsters. He was angry at the weeds, and he was angry at the loss of beauty implied by their conquering the seeds he had planted. In bitterness, disillusionment, and fury, he persevered to uproot the weeds.

The world, he knew, was full of weeds: terrorism, violence, unchecked greed, environmental decay, calamities, injustice for many groups, and hegemonies of many descriptions. But the biggest weed of all, at least as far as he was concerned, was the body of lies that existed in the world. People lied each and every day, in little ways and big ones. The biggest lie of all persisted: that life went on forever. Hugo was seething as he pulled a root from the ground, thinking about the fact that, despite all efforts undertaken, his own days were numbered. As Paul would say, it was true that there was good in the world: the hospitals, schools, food banks, everyday acts of compassion and love between people that were both small and big. But in the same way that it was hard for Hugo to not feel like the beauty of his garden was being undermined by the weeds growing all around, it was difficult to not think of the world as a flower, maybe a tulip, being choked by a weed wrapped around it tightly.

Hugo pulled up weed after weed, grunting and sweating. He felt the dirt with his hands. He turned his head to look around the garden.

He was not the only one who had loved the garden.

The flowers looked beautiful. The sun above was astonishingly peaceful and serene. There was a quietness to the street, a spirit of tranquility that hovered over each and every house on the block. At that particular moment, Hugo was trying, unsuccessfully, to drag a root out of the ground and toss it into the bucket. In one surge of strength, he pulled with all of his might, only to find that the root stayed firmly in place. He brushed some of the dirt off his hands, looked around again, and stood up. He picked up the bucket of weeds and dumped it into the green waste bin. Then he turned to Paul, who was watering his plants, and waved a friendly wave.

3.

Hugo closed the door behind him, locking up, and headed towards Martin's car. It was a cloudy day, the street covered in an ominous darkness. Yet there was the warmth of May present. The flowers in the garden, in fact, did look lovely, particularly thanks to some significant weed eradication efforts that had been undertaken.

Opening the door of the fancy car, Hugo had a seat and looked at his smiling brother.

"How you been, big brother."

"Not bad. You?"

"Been good. Been good. Is it all right if we head to Rosarita's?"

"That works for me."

Martin looked in the mirror of the car at Cassandra, who sat in the back.

"How's Mexican sound, sweetheart?

"Sounds great!"

"Great!"

The car sped along, Hugo reminding his brother of the usual yield areas, feeling uncomfortable all the while.

"So what have you been up to?" Martin opened up the conversation.

"Not much."

"Been swimming?"

"A little."

"Watch any soccer matches?"

"No."

"Oh, that's too bad. Garden looks great."

"Thanks. I've been working on it a lot. Those damned weeds have given me some trouble."

Martin laughed. "They will do that, big brother. So do you think you can join us for Chelan?"

Hugo was dreading this question. He knew, immediately after they had last talked, that his brother would bring it up, and he had even gone through the trouble to prepare an answer. But no amount of preparation could allow him to be ready for one of Martin's emotionally heavy pep talks.

"Yes, I would like to go," Hugo sighed.

"Great! Fantastic! Wonderful!"

Hugo at once partially regretted his decision to come along on the trip, but still he thought that it would be, all things considered, a beneficial one for him to take. The small bubble Hugo inhabited in Wedgwood was comfortable. He was at peace to roam the same places and do the same things indefinitely, but he also recognized the real benefit in occasionally breaking out of the bubble. After all, it was only in doing so that he was capable of acquiring an expanded perspective, in turn appreciating Wedgwood even more. Plus, the scenery afforded by the Lake Chelan area was undeniable in its compelling beauty. It would be a hectic seven days, overflowing with activities, people, and positivity, but Hugo suspected that it would offer him some valuable time of solitude away from home, and that, more than anything, was why he accepted the offer to go on the trip.

"I'm so glad you can come. Isn't that great news, Cassie?"

"It sure is!"

"Looks like we're approaching the restaurant."

Martin took a sharp turn and parked the car in the back lot of a worn-down looking building. They got out, under the cloudy sky, and stepped towards the entrance of the restaurant.

Inside, they were greeted by a waiter named Federico, who led them through the dim space of the restaurant to a back corner, where the only incoming light was from a window several yards away. In the background, there was the sound of Mexican music playing. They were brought water and proceeded to chat.

"Work has been even busier," Martin mentioned. "End of the year is coming up fast, and I'm trying to get everything ready for the last test and for final grades."

"Sounds like a lot of work," Hugo said, taking a sip of water.

"It is, it is. But I've done some thinking, and I think next year will be my last."

"That's great to hear! You'll be welcomed into the magical kingdom of retirement."

"It wasn't a decision I made lightly, but that's where I'm at in life. There are more important things than teaching, right little one?"

"Right," Cassandra answered.

"Anyway, that's what's going on with me, big brother. Oh! We were just talking on the phone to one of the guys we share the condo with, and he was saying that they have been doing some remodeling. It sounds like the place is going to be extra nice!"

"That's nice to hear," Hugo stated, and then turned to Cassandra. "How's school going for you?" he asked.

Cassandra was in third grade. Precocious, she learned to read before most of her peers learned the alphabet. It was Larson family practice to read and imbue an appreciation for reading into everyone. Hugo himself always loved reading, reading anything, really. Now Cassandra was carrying forth the Larson spirit of academic achievement. Her teachers mentioned that she was extremely smart. Her music and physical education teachers praised her aptitudes. It was James and Barbara's philosophy, in addition to cultivating positivity, to rarely shield their daughter from the world of adults. For this reason, Hugo and Martin felt perfectly comfortable carrying forth a grown-up conversation in her presence. In short, she was a peer of sorts.

"School is going good," she said. "I'm reading *Treasure Island*."

"*Treasure Island*. Now, I haven't read that one in a while. I don't remember how that one goes."

"It's really great," she continued. "I like the descriptions."

Then they were brought their food. They spent a while eating quietly. They were practically the only ones in the restaurant. The light only appeared to be growing dimmer. The walls were decorated with colorful tiles, but they were hardly visible.

"So," Martin effused, "any tips for someone who is getting ready for retirement?"

"Yes. Enjoy it."

"Anything else?"

"Nope."

Hugo had been retired for three years. The truth was that he, like his brother, had been apprehensive about making the transition. For accounting had been more or less his life for decades. But the time came and felt right, so he decided to enter into a new phase of life. He remembered the initial boredom and the lack of feeling fulfilled. But these feelings quickly passed as he settled in.

Now they were reminiscing over a story from the past, trying to fill in the cracks of information as to what precisely had happened.

"What happened next?" Hugo asked.

"Well, you were all up in those trees across the street from our house. You had made your little wooden platform."

"Tree fort," he corrected.

"No, big brother. It was a couple of planks of wood nailed between the branches of the two trees. You and Mark were sitting on them when I came to find you."

"What had you wanted?"

"I'm not sure. I think I was supposed to tell you that dinner was ready or something like that. But I came to the bottom of the trees and started calling at you."

"Ah, yes, and we told you we wanted to stay right where we were."

"Right, and I got mad. I got so mad, I started to climb up the trees, even though I was scared. They were tall trees!"

"You climbed up, and then what?"

"I think you two climbed higher up to get away from me," Martin suggested.

"Mmhmm."

"I didn't go up very high. I looked around me and decided to start climbing back down. I got near the base of the tree, but there was a big gap between where I was and the ground. I wasn't even sure how I had made it up in the first place!"

"How did you make it up?"

"I don't know. But anyway, it was like a ten-foot jump down to the ground."

"No, it wasn't. Or you wouldn't have been able to climb up in the first place," Hugo reasoned.

"There must have been some branch I used to climb up that I missed coming down," Martin said. "Anyway, I was stuck. I called out your names, but you were as silent as the trees. It was scary!"

"Poor thing!"

"I thought you had climbed up so high that there was no way you were going to be able to come back down."

Hugo asked, "You thought we weren't going to be able to make it down?"

Martin nodded. "I thought I was going to have to fall out of the tree, limp back home and get Mom to call the fire department to come and rescue you."

"That's silly!"

"Is not!"

"So how did you get down, from the three-foot gap?"

"I think I jumped. I rolled and tumbled a bit, but I was fine. I was fine. Then I ran inside and cried, 'Mom, I think they're stuck in the trees'. And you know what she said?"

"What?"

"'Oh, those boys will be fine.'"

"Have we talked about this story before?"

"We must have," Martin said.

"It's a great story," Cassandra proclaimed. "I like hearing these things."

"Mom said you would be fine," Martin continued, "and so she paid no attention to you. I thought she was crazy for not caring. But then when I walked back outside, guess what?"

"What?"

"You had come down from the trees and were standing there, in the cul-de-sac. I think you were smiling. Or maybe you looked more concerned, like you didn't want me to tell Mom."

"Which you did."

"Which I did."

"How about the story about the magical snow elves?" Hugo asked. "You want to hear that one, Cassie?"

She nodded.

Martin was already laughing. "You think of the worst stories to tell, big brother."

"Or the best stories!"

"Right. So it was winter. I think I was six. It had been snowing all winter. A very white Christmas. We were inside, reading or playing or something. All of a sudden, you turn to me and say, 'You know what Marty? I was outside a minute ago, and I think I saw a couple of magical snow elves.' 'Really' I asked. You were nodding through and through, then you said, 'But you gotta hurry outside real quickly if you want to see them. They appear only for a minute, and then they vanish.' I was wearing my pajamas- it must have been in the morning- and I ran out the back door of the house into the snow. I stepped on that snow, and boy was it cold! It was cold. I could see my own breath. 'Run out farther, they're slipping past the trees!' you called to me. So I

102

kept running, on that cold snow, across the backyard, towards the pocket of trees. I reached the trees and looked around, but there was nothing. I was devastated because I thought I had missed my chance to see some snow elves. Feeling disappointed, I walked back towards the house. What I didn't realize at first was the fact that you had locked the door. You locked it, big brother!"

Cassandra and Hugo were both laughing.

"Anyway," continued Martin, "I thought I would run around to the other side of the house. So I cut through the garden. I reached the stairs and went up. I slipped and fell on one of the steps and banged up my hand pretty badly. By the time I reached the front door, you had locked it too! 'Climb in through the window!' you called. 'On the roof?' I asked. 'Yep,' you answered. So I leaned over towards the edge of the front deck and grabbed the side of the roof. I wasn't strong enough to pull myself up, so I just stood there, on the front deck, gripping the roof. Then, finally, the door opened and you let me in. There, are you happy?"

"We are," said Hugo, "thank you for sharing that wonderful anecdote." It made Hugo pleased to hear stories from the past, for, through stories, the world Hugo and Martin had shared as children was given new life. Everything in the past seemed to have a shiny, pearly glint to it. Hearing of the past was a welcomed relief from the anger and frustration Hugo was feeling lately.

They finished their meals, paid, and left the restaurant. They continued telling stories as they were in the car, tales that showed how the two brothers had goofed off together, growing closer in the process. These were their stories, stories that they shared together as they went through life, and there was a comfort in that.

"See you soon, big brother!" Martin called as Hugo walked up towards his front door.

4.

He was walking down the street and not thinking of much in particular. The weather was strange. There was a covering of clouds, but the sun kept periodically breaking through. The air was warm. The sun would set soon. The days were getting to be longer and longer.

He passed a house that was designed in the modern way. The roof had grass growing on it. Each window was a massive square that perfectly refracted the sunlight. Narrow and angular were the stairs. Colored brown, with cream stripes, the house was hideous to Hugo. He turned his attention to the other side of the street.

There was a small, green house. An open fence led towards the front door, which was wide open. This house had a small garage and sturdy-looking roof. The windows were small but open.

Hugo started to reflect on the way in which houses tell more about a person than one might think. Hugo's house was only three houses up the street. It was painted a light blue, had average windows, a red door, a nice small front lawn, and a second story that was as big as the first. There was also a garden to consider.

Hugo only had another street block to go. His ankle, which had been injured months before, was as good as new. For months he had had full movement capability, something that he hoped to never lose. Looking both ways, he crossed the street, moving to the side of a roundabout. Only a few houses left.

There was a great variety in the houses that lined the street. True enough, each house told a particular story, a piece from the city's history. Some of the houses were old, as though they had held many owners, surviving numerous eras. Other houses, like the modern one he had walked by, seemed to evoke a different era. Houses like these ones were more of a statement, delivering some sort of message about the world or about the ambitions of people. Either way, it seemed to Hugo that Seattle had been settled, founded, and developed in a rather random way. Some houses had small lawns and hardly took up any space. Others were massive, inefficient, having no regard for space. It seemed that the pastiche of houses that lined this Wedgwood Street was unlike any other street in the country. But Hugo knew better. He knew that streets looked like this in cities all across America and also across the world.

Between two small houses, in the middle of a small lawn, there grew an enormous tree of gala apples. The owner of the tree, a Kim Schaefer, had eagerly given permission to all the residents in the neighborhood to enjoy the apples that grew from this tree. The sun was clearing the clouds as Hugo stepped towards the tree. Several apples, some more ripe-looking than others, sat on the ground beside the tree. He reached up and inspected a few apples. One was too premature while another was past its prime. At last, he beheld one, predominately red, one that fit snugly in his hand. He looked around and then took a bite. For once, he thought, it was nice knowing the people who lived in the neighborhood. He stepped back towards the sidewalk. The taste of the apple was tart and juicy. He turned and moved back to his home.

It was not a long walk, he knew, but it was an excellent way to clear his head, to center himself, so he was pleased to travel the route frequently, especially when the weather was cooperative.

As he was fond of reminding people, it was a fact that he had lived in this home in this neighborhood for over thirty years. He remembered when he moved from his previous apartment to this house. He tried to remember what the neighborhood had looked like then, but it was quite hazy. What he knew was that there were many more trees back during that time. There had been a lot fewer houses, and a lot fewer people. The neighborhood was much quieter. The truth was that the neighborhood was still quiet, but there was something special about the Wedgwood of Hugo's youth, when it was a dormant kingdom, a sleepy place where families were being raised. It was a more than suitable place for Adrian to grow up, and the commute to work was relatively painless for Hugo.

Hugo crossed a street, remembering teaching Adrian to ride a bike across this very intersection. Always coordinated, it had not taken much to teach Adrian how to ride. Now that he had been a barista for twelve years, that coordination had only been further refined.

No longer did Hugo recognize the neighborhood. Too many little things had changed: the paint color of a house, a tree cut down, new people living in a house, newer and newer cars speeding across the street. Hugo took a bite of the apple and then looked at his left hand, at the lines that comprised it. He wondered, had the neighborhood changed, or rather had he changed? Surely he was not the young professional pushing his son around on a bike he once had been. Was he old? Compared to plenty of people living in the neighborhood he was not old by any means. But what did that mean? Death is death, he told himself.

Having reached his front door, he took a final bite from the apple. Inside, he disposed of the core, had a seat on the sofa, and read the morning paper, which he had neglected all day.

5.

Many people would have found an Introduction to Statistics course lecture to be dull, but not Hugo. He sat in the second row, taking meticulous notes, looking up at the professor every now and then. Currently, they were learning about standard deviations, and he felt the sheer pleasure of learning as the professor droned on and on. He was utterly in his element.

The lecture hall was massively cavernous, though only one-third of the seats were occupied. Dimly lit, it was an old building. The professor, who had a beard, glasses, and wore a beret, was referencing a slide that demonstrated what he was discussing. No one was sitting next to Hugo, for it was a common courtesy, when possible, to sit a seat apart. But he was so engrossed in the content he was learning that he didn't notice how many students must have been skipping class. Despite the bleakness of the lecture hall, the fact remained that it was a clear, sunny day outside, the end of spring term signaling vivacity and change.

It was Hugo's second semester at the University of Washington. He already knew he wanted to get into business school and then study accounting. Another year of taking introductory, survey courses would afford him the opportunity to at last apply to business school. He had taken classes on religion, literature, history, popular music, and math, among other things. A lover of learning, he had enjoyed all of the classes, and though he felt called towards accounting he could appreciate the value of other areas of study as well. Wanting to be part of a globalized, urban school, UW had proven to be a logical choice. He had worn purple and rooted for the Huskies with a mighty fervor. In short, he loved his school.

On this particular day, he had special plans, to see his girlfriend, Sandra. Before he knew it, the lecture was finished and it was time to leave the lecture hall. The other students shuffled out of the area quickly. Hugo grabbed his backpack and headed for the door.

Outside, the air was warm and pleasant. He was standing in Red Square, the central meeting place on campus. Lined with bricks, an obelisk statue sitting not far off, Hugo could see the other buildings, cathedral in style and scope, that lined the perimeter of Red Square. To his left, there was Suzzallo library, a building that had colored glass windows and stood tall. He stepped towards the center of Red Square, wondering where he should head next, and then he remembered that he needed his bike. The plan had been for him to meet Sandra in her neighborhood, southern Capitol Hill. So he walked across the brick expanse, past the tables with students organizing a revolutionary movement against the establishment and then the church kids giving out free hot chocolate. He walked by Suzzallo, moved up some steps, and entered the quad.

In full bloom, the quad had grassy stretches, with kids sitting under cherry trees reading. Others were fully engaged in tossing back and forth a Frisbee. In the distance there stood the building that housed the business school. He looked at this building longingly. Forward he continued to walk, on the brick path that sliced through the center of the quad. He turned to the left, and then to the right, and saw elegant, old buildings, gothic in style, that housed the music school as well as the visual arts. Up another set of stairs he moved, nearly at his destination.

Walking long distances was a standard currency as a student at UW. It was expected, on any given day, to spend up to an hour and a half if not longer walking to and from classes. Fortunately, Hugo derived great pleasure from walking and running about. The rolling, sprawling nature of the campus was part of its charm for him.

Beneath blue skies, he approached the dorm bike rack. He reached into his pocket and pulled out the key for the lock to the bike. Having unlocked it, he climbed onto his blue bike, kicked off the ground, and rode down the gentle slope away from the dorm. He heard a voice call his name from above.

Stopping the bike, he turned around and looked up. "What?" he asked.

"Hey, Hugo," it was Thomas, his roommate.

"Hey, man. How's it going?"

"Going well. Where you off to?"

Hugo fidgeted with the gear shifter. "Going to go and see Sandra," he replied.

"Right on, man. Well, are you free later for a late-night ice cream run?"

"Of course!"

"Cool. Have fun with Sandra!" Thomas said.

"Later!"

Just as he was soaring down the hill off of campus, so too his spirit was soaring at the prospect of getting to see Sandra. They had been together for a little over a year and their relationship was special. When he was with her, he felt comfortable, at ease. They could talk about anything. He had someone he could share life with. They enjoyed playing sports together, reading, and traveling around the city. It was Hugo's hope and belief that they were going to spend the rest of their lives together. But what he needed to keep reminding himself of was to slow down and take things as they came. Inside him was a passionate love that needed escape, but it seemed that life was telling him to take things one step at a time.

Sandra attended Seattle University, a smaller, Jesuit school located only a few miles from UW. They had not wanted to attend separate schools, but Sandra had not had the grades for UW, and he had not been interested in attending SU's business school. The two of them were at peace with the fact that they did not live far from each other. They saw each other every weekend, and occasionally during the week when life wasn't too hectic. Sandra was studying journalism and was hoping to find work with one of the local papers soon.

Still, at times when he was alone in his dorm room, staring out his window, it had felt as though she might as well have been on the other side of the world. They talked on the phone frequently but at times he wanted nothing more than to be with her, to hold her. Thomas was someone who Hugo had confided in about his struggles, and in him, he had found an understanding friend. Thomas and his girlfriend would occasionally go on dates with Hugo and Sandra.

Hugo looked forward to the day when they would be separated no more.

Now he was cruising, riding down the hill near the medical center and approaching the Montlake Bridge. Next, he rode up 23rd Street, turned at Aloha, and got on to 12th avenue. Along this road, he went for a while longer and then soon he was approaching SU's smaller, but humble campus. He parked his bike near the quad and proceeded to walk towards the café they were to meet at.

In the streets, there were still more college students walking around, laughing, swearing, eating, reading, and throwing Frisbees. He crossed the street and entered the Perfect Grounds café.

At once he saw her sitting in a corner, reading. Feeling his heart beat powerfully, as though this was his first date, he approached her. In her hands, she held *A Portrait of the Artist as a Young Man*.

"That's a good book," he said, "I like the part where-"

"No, don't!" she cried. "I'm almost done. I can't put it down."

He sat down across from her and smiled. "Hi."

"Hey. How are you?"

"Doing pretty well," he said. "How about you?"

"Not bad."

"How's your week been?"

She sighed. "It's been busy. I've been working on this paper. For my Intro to Social Justice class, I have to write a paper on what I think is the most pressing social issue in our society."

"Well, that's easy."

"Are you gonna get any coffee?"

"Yes, I think I will."

When he returned he had a seat and said, "Your paper is an easy one to write about. Just write about the war."

"That's too obvious, and I don't think it has the right scope."

"Scope? What do you mean?"

"Well, all the fighting going on in Vietnam is terrible. It's awful and we shouldn't be there, obviously. But think about the number of people who are being directly affected by it."

"Do you want me to give you some figures on how many of our peers have been killed, injured, or imprisoned?"

"That's okay," she laughed, always eager for a lively discussion. "What I mean is that there are other, more pressing social issues, ones that are affecting millions of people."

"Like what?"

"Like poverty. The unequal distribution of wealth in our society."

"Ah."

"I think this is a more pressing issue that needs to be solved."

"It definitely is. "

"I mean, think about us. We are so lucky that we get to come here and get college educations. We are privileged. We were born into privileged families, and a lot of opportunities were sent our way. That is not the case for a lot of people, especially people who live here in this part of town. Don't even get me started on how broken our schools are!"

"No need," he said. "I'm well acquainted. Not personally, though."

"No, you and I are not personally acquainted with broken schools in the slightest. Hillcrest High School was a wonderland. It produces college students. It may be hard to imagine, but not all high schools are like that."

"Nope."

"Anyway, if I am going to write about poverty in America, I need to figure out how to approach it."

"An interesting question," Hugo added after taking a sip of his coffee. "Why not start with an exposition on the current state of poverty in our country: unemployment, homelessness, underemployment substance abuse, etc. then move on to the solution to the problem. Do you need to have a solution?"

"A proposed solution, yes."

"Okay then. What do you got?"

She put a finger on her chin. Her black hair was lovely.

"Wanna hear what I think?" Hugo teased.

She laughed. "I know you're eager to give me the one solution to the problem, but I think it's better that I reason through the problem on my own and arrive at something that is mine and original, don't you think?"

"Fair enough."

"I think," she said, "we need to focus more on social programs. Invest more money directly into education. Make our colleges better as well as our K-12 schools. By expanding the public sector we can create more jobs. Increasing the taxes on the wealthier classes would provide more resources for everyone else. Also, investing in affordable housing would be a good thing."

"I don't know, Ms. Lee..."

"Stop it," she said, smiling. "These are just my thoughts. I don't need you to approve of them."

"Just kidding. I think you have some great ideas. I agree wholeheartedly. It sounds like you solved the problem!"

"I guess so. But that's only the beginning of my week. We had a soccer game on Tuesday, which we lost. Playoffs are coming up pretty soon, and I don't know how good our prospects are. Then I got asked to prepare a brief message for my Theology class."

"Is that the Catholic class?"

She nodded.

"How's that going?"

"Pretty good. I want to say something that comes out of the book of John, but I don't know. I try to write something down, and then I get stuck."

"I get that. Being creative can be difficult."

"How about you? How's your week been?"

"It's been good! I was getting ready for another midterm yesterday."

"What class?"

"Introduction to Environmental Studies."

She nodded at this.

"I've been playing a lot of chess, too."

"Sounds like life is going pretty well for you. You're always up to the same things."

"Well, you know. I have my things that I like to do, and that's how it is."

She put a hand in his. "I've missed you," she said.

"I've missed you, too. I'm glad we can be together now!"

"I look forward to when we're together always."

"The day is coming," he prophesized. "But for the time being, we get to enjoy things as they are. It's not so bad living a few neighborhoods apart. Some people date from different states, or different countries."

"Yes, and it's terrible!"

"I suppose so. Well, like I said, we're only going to be living closer to each other as time wears on."

"It's true," she said, smiling.

"Listen," he said, "you want to go on a walk?"

"Sure," she was still smiling.

He chugged the remains of his coffee and stood up. She grabbed her book and followed him out of the café. The air outside had grown cooler since they had been in it. They held hands and walked down the street, south towards Cherry Street. It was here that he had all that he needed, he was in the company of the girl who he loved, in the city that he loved. How could he begin to describe that feeling of completeness, the comfort, the sensation of being at home with another person? His life had problems, of course. School, while enriching and enjoyable, was an ever-present source of stress. Recently he gathered that his parents hadn't been getting along. He heard stories from Martin about nasty arguments that took place between them. But despite any stressors or anguish, in this moment he was happy, for this was a perfect moment, crystallized in time.

"Where are we headed?" he asked.

"I know a place."

"Sounds good."

At Cherry Street, they turned left and kept walking. Off the main thoroughfare of SU, they were moving towards more houses. These houses were as old and vibrant as the neighborhood itself, which was brimming with life and energy.

"Darling..." he said.

"What is it?" She looked at him and he noticed how elegant her hair looked when it was tied back.

"I've been nervous about something lately."

"What's that?"

"My parents, they have been fighting a lot, I guess."

"Arguing and stuff?"

He nodded. "Can we talk about it?"

"Of course."

"Well, I don't really know where to begin. I guess I'm just afraid they might split up."

"Don't get too caught up in that. Do you know why they have been fighting?"

"Martin says that he's not sure. You know my dad drinks right?"

"I do."

"My guess is that his drinking habits have gotten out of control again."

"Again?"

"Well, he likes to drink. He has never been violent or anything, but he becomes careless when he drinks. My mom has found him passed out around the house. He also drives recklessly sometimes."

"Okay."

"And every few years, growing up, it seemed like his drinking would flare up and get worse, almost like there was a cycle to it."

"Interesting. I mean, that's horrible, but it's also interesting. What you are saying is your dad has a steady pattern of drinking that includes spikes in consumption."

"But he has always been sober at important things. He was sober at my high school graduation, and the same goes for my swim meets."

They stopped walking for a moment. Before them was a green space that spanned the block. There was a grassy hill and several benches to sit on. They had a seat on one of the benches.

"So you think your dad's drinking has got something to do with your parents fighting," Sandra assessed.

"Yes, that's about it. I wish he would get treatment, you know?"

"That would be nice. But it takes a lot of courage and fortitude to embark on the journey of sobriety."

"That sounded very profound, the way you worded it."

She blushed. "Thanks."

"My mom doesn't always make things much better. She has a temper. She gets really angry and lashes out at him when he has been drinking."

"Well, how would you react?"

"I don't know, but it just seems destructive."

There was a pause as they sat there. One of Hugo's favorite things about being with Sandra was precisely this, the fact that he could be silent around her and it was all right. They often talked about things that went beyond what words could say: hopes, fears, everything and nothing, the future, the past, and anything else they could think about. But they both knew that there were things that words could not capture, and so they were content to simply sit together, to be together, in the process taking a stand against a big and cold world.

"Man," Hugo said, "the world is controlled by adults. And what do they do? They fuck things up."

"You sound like an author I've read. You shouldn't be so harsh on people or the world," she said. "The world is a beautiful, if broken place, and it's up to us to go out and make it better."

"If I sound like an author, then you sound like your social justice textbook."

She started laughing. "I was reading through it earlier today, in fact. I know that it's scary with your parents, but no matter what happens, it will be all right." She squeezed his hand. "We have each other."

"Yes, we do."

"Won't we always be together?" she asked aware of her sentimentality.

"Yes," he replied.

They sat on that park bench and chatted for several more hours. Eventually, they got up, kissed, and walked back towards her dorm. Strangely enough, the walk back seemed to take less than a minute. Standing in front of the door to her dorm, they hugged for a long time, basking in the feeling of holding and being held.

"Love you, Sandra."

"Love you too. When will I see you again?"

He started walking towards the stairs. "I'll call you tomorrow and we can discuss our next jaunt."

"Okay!"

"Okay. Bye."

"See you!"

Leaving her was always the most difficult part. It was a ritual at this point, the walking down the stairs from her room at the end of a date, feeling emptiness, a loneliness creeping into his heart. It was his desperate dream to end the day with her, and he looked forward to that day with every beat of his heart. At the bottom of the stairs, he walked towards where he had locked his bike, undid it, hopped on, and rode off.

It was getting dark. The breeze was cold against his body as he rode. The ride before him was like traversing a valley, with him going down several hills before going up some more. He was still thinking about his parents as he rode. What if they split up? When he got home he would need to give Martin a call, he decided. It was odd to think that the fighting between their parents had brought the two brothers more closely together. In Hugo's mind, he tried to block out the image of his dad, drunk, spewing out nonsense, then passed out in the doorway. Likewise, Hugo imagined his mother finding his father, screaming at him in her shrill voice, the two of them fighting again. These images haunted Hugo, at times keeping him up deep into the night.

He was cruising along Montlake Bridge when he nearly witnessed an accident. A car stopped just inches before the one in front of it. A pang of panic surged throughout his body. His heart was beating wildly. His breathing was deep. Just keep riding, he told himself. He was able to disregard the scene and continue on his way.

Taking a turn at the medical center he ascended the gradual slope towards home. He started to worry about something else. What if he didn't make it into business school? That's all right, a reassuring voice in his head said. There's always something else to study, maybe English or history. The truth was Hugo loved to read and to have stimulating conversations with other people. This was principally true when it came to his relationship with Sandra. The two of them were active readers, constantly consuming the pages of one classic and then another. In turn, they loved to have deep conversations about what they were reading or thinking about. They were frequently talking about what they were learning in their classes, and doing so allowed them to become connected in a more intimate way, for it felt like they had taken on the course load of one another.

Parking his bike in front of his dorm, Hugo walked up the stairs only to be grabbed by Thomas who was heading down.

"Where-" Hugo exclaimed.

"Ice cream time, hermano."

Thomas and Hugo walked through the chilly evening air to the student-run ice cream parlor located just a few blocks away. In order to reach the ice cream, one had to enter one of the other dorms and then walk into the basement of the building. The place was happening, full of hungry or bored students. There was talking and laughter in the background of Mick's Café, as the establishment was affectionately referred to.

"Ever since dinner I've been thinking about this," Thomas said.

"Come to think of it, I'm actually pretty hungry."

"Well, nothing will nourish you like a big old cone of vanilla."

"That's right!"

They made it to the front and ordered. Hugo went with vanilla, his favorite, and Thomas had chocolate. The two friends sat at one of the tables and enjoyed their treats.

Someone poked his head out from around the corner. "Hey, guys." It was Lester, another student who lived in their dorm.

"What's going on?" Thomas greeted him.

"Oh, not much."

"Did you have ice cream?" Hugo asked.

"Yeah, I already did."

"Well, have a seat. Don't be shy!" Thomas cried.

Lester sat with them and they chatted for a while.

"So, Hugo," Thomas began, "are things heating up with Sandra?"

"I guess you could say that. What we have is something special."

"Something special? Good grief! You sound like a regular romantic."

Hugo shrugged, not knowing how to react.

"Are you gonna get married?" Lester asked.

"I think so."

"Really? I can't even imagine getting married. It just seems so, I don't know, adult of you," Thomas replied after licking his ice cream.

"Yes, well, that's part of life. You grow up and you do more adult things. You become an adult."

"Way to be a downer."

"There's nothing wrong with being an adult. A guy can't spend his whole life goofing off and eating ice cream."

Lester said, "And why not?"

"Well, I mean I guess you could. But what would be the benefit in that?"

Lester and Thomas looked at each other. "There is a lot of benefit in that!" Thomas exclaimed. "But listen, man. I really am happy for you. You are in love, and that is an awesome thing. You have all of my love and support. Just promise you'll always have time to get a cone every once in a while. Sound good?"

Hugo smiled. "Only every once in a while."

Lester and Thomas led the way out of the parlor. Lester invited them over to hang out, and Thomas agreed to go, but Hugo declined. Preoccupied with thoughts of his parents and his future, Hugo had other things on his mind.

June

I.

Gentle and magnificent, Green Lake was a sight to behold. It was a warm day, the sun occasionally peeking through clouds and shining down below. There was a strong breeze, particularly next to the water. Under the cover of trees, the trail ran around the lake infinitely, traversing it, revealing new sights every lap. The water rolled against the shore calmly. In the air there was a feeling of tranquility. Birds flew from one branch and then another. Skaters, bike-riders, runners, and people walking moved around the lake endlessly. One only had to travel around it one time to realize that there was no end to its hidden wonders, the new experiences awaiting an adventurer. People walked, sipping iced coffee beverages gotten from local cafes. Others wore shorts and walked their dogs. It was on this day, when the lake was the center of so many peoples' day that Paul and Hugo were walking together.

"When is the last time you saw her?" Hugo was referring to Paul's daughter, Janet.

"It's been a while."

"Does she have any plans of visiting?"

"Yes, in September."

Paul had long been divorced. For reasons unknown to Hugo, his friend's wife and he split twenty years before. From what Hugo knew, it was relatively amicable. Together they raised one daughter, Janet, who bemoaned the loss of her parent's union but was old enough to cope and understand. Janet went to college at UW, and when she graduated she signed up to teach English in Argentina as part of a special service program. While the program only lasted a year, she enjoyed it so much that she had chosen to stay year after year, eventually becoming a citizen and then a certified teacher of English in the country. Eventually Janet married a local man, who worked in business, and the two had a life together just outside of Buenos Aires. They had no kids of their own, but they were happy. Once a year she managed to fly up for a couple of weeks, and Paul enjoyed this time with his daughter. Time and distance made them less close, so Paul looked forward to having a chance to learn more about what kind of woman she was growing up to be.

As Janet lived in Argentina, Paul lived by himself. At times he was lonely, but for the most part Paul was quite happy with his life. He deeply valued his friendship with Hugo. In a sense, the two were a bit of a family of their own. Together the two friends raised their kids, watching the neighborhood grow and change. They celebrated holidays together and played many games of chess. But the fact remained that, as close as they were, there existed a distance between the two friends, a disconnect that needed to be addressed. Paul knew that they both felt this, so he decided to try bringing it up again:

"How have you been?"

"Fine," Hugo answered. "Are you making small talk with me?"

"I mean, how has life been, you know, without her?"

Hugo swallowed. Initially, his reaction was to say that he didn't want to talk about it, but this was changing. Rather than feel a need to evade the topic, Hugo had a desire to engage with it more directly. Hurting, he wanted to talk about the topic, to practically attack it, in hope that doing so would alleviate the suffering he endured.

"I have been struggling," he said softly.

"Tell me more."

"I don't see why it had to happen, why it had to unfold the way it did. There was so much suffering and pain. It seemed so needless. It's not fair. She and I weren't perfect; there were flaws in our marriage, but what we had was special, and it was taken away from me. No one asked me if it was all right for her to be taken from me. She had a lot of life left to live. I have been robbed, and it makes me bitter."

"I see. Do you feel like the universe is cold or uncaring?"

"I do. Life is such a fragile thing. Some people live to be old and ancient, and others die young. Why? It's all so unfair. I hate it. I despise the fact that we have no control over our lives, and I despise living without her."

Paul turned his head to look into Hugo's eyes. What he saw was pure hurt, like an animal that had lost a leg.

With another curve in the road, they were passing the Green Lake boat rental facility, which was unsurprisingly packed with people hoping to go out on the water. A man nearby was selling ice cream. There were tall trees all around.

"I understand that you are hurting. You know that I care a lot about you. It means a lot to me that you are sharing these things with me. I can't imagine how much you must be suffering. But you are strong. You are so strong, and I know that she would be proud of you. Think about it. She would want you to continue to live life, even without her. There are other things that make life worth living."

"Are there?"

Concerned that they were diving too deeply into pointless philosophizing, Paul shifted gears in his approach, saying, "What my wife and I had was not something special. True, there were special times, but overall it was a rocky and dark time in life for both of us. One of the greatest sources of light in our family was Janet. Now she is gone from me, and in a sense, I feel like she was taken from me. We talk on the phone every now and then, and occasionally when she has time off she comes to visit, but it's not enough. I miss her so much. Anyway, the point I'm trying to make is that you lived in a special marriage, where you loved each other wholly and selflessly. A lot of people in life never experience that. So you should feel very happy that you got to. Even if she left too soon, you still had a lot of time together, and I know that doesn't ease—"

"You expect me to just smile and be thankful for what we had, rather than focus on the reality of things? She is gone, Paul, and she is never coming back. I don't even know if I'll ever see her again, and that really scares me."

"Sure. Like I was going to say, it doesn't ease the pain or anything, but—"

"No, it doesn't. I don't even know why I talk about this stuff because it just makes me feel so upset.

"You need to talk about it."

"What is there to say? That I can hardly sleep at night? That every little thing I run into in my house reminds me of her? I'm supposed to talk about it, but there is nothing to talk about."

"I know you are feeling a lot of things. But please don't shut yourself down from it."

"Don't you have days where you wish you could just be with Janet?"

"Yes, I do."

"What do you do?"

"Sometimes I feel so sad that I miss her. But I let myself feel that sadness, because it's a feeling, and it has meaning to it. Your feelings have meaning to them."

"What meaning? I feel terrified, sad, angry, bitter, you name it, and there is no point to any of it. In this life, we are just all wandering around, in the dark, in one direction and another, and there is no point to any of it."

"Why is there no point to it?"

"Because," Hugo said, breathing deeply. "We can't bring back the ones we love, and ultimately they are always taken away from us. That, or we are taken away from them. Everyone dies."

They walked on in silence for a while. Snippets of conversations were audible around them from the other people who were moving about the lake. Hugo wondered what these other conversations, the ones of the younger people were like. Were these people talking about lighter things, like weddings, jobs, and plans to have fun? What about the other old people like himself? Were they acquainted with loss? It didn't matter, because Hugo knew that no one understood how he felt. No one else had lost someone who was as precious as he had. He was completely alone, and he knew there was no benefit in talking to anyone about his pain, because he couldn't make anyone else feel it like he did.

Now they were reaching the seating stands on the other side of the lake. There were people out on the water, paddle boarding and kayaking. Another curve in the road led them past a small golf course.

At last, Paul spoke, "I know you don't believe this, but it will get easier with time."

"Get easier? It sure as hell won't. I don't want to live life without her. I don't want to forget her and go on with my life. My life ended when hers did. I couldn't do that to her."

"Do what to her?"

"Betray her."

"Listen, Hugo. In this life, we are all passing through. Now I don't have the answers to the big questions, about God or the universe or the afterlife, but what I do know, and you know this too, is that life is short. It goes by fast. You don't have to forget about her in order to go on with your life. But you can't sit around, pretending things are all right when they obviously aren't."

"I haven't pretended to do or be anything."

"The last few months I wanted to talk to you about her. I wanted to hear you tell stories about her. You know I knew her well, and I thought if we could remember her together it might bring about some healing for you. But you weren't willing to talk about it. You would change the subject. You avoided it. Now you are finally beginning to open up, and I think that is a really good thing."

"Well, I'm glad my misery is a 'good thing'."

"It is, because you need to allow yourself to fully feel all the feelings that are there."

"There is no point! Why suffer so much? She is dead. She was here, she was alive and with me. One day we were together, watching television, and then a few months later, one day, she was gone, lost, away from me forever. She was the light of my life. She brought so much joy and peace and comfort and warmth into my life, and with her death, all of those things have vanished, and I will never find them again. I am old. Pretty soon I will be dead, too. It's basically over for me. There's no chance to make a fresh start. There is no reason to make a fresh start."

They were walking down a gradual slope, in between trees. A bicyclist passed by them, startling them. Hugo turned and looked out at the water, at the gentle waves. He thought about how she and he used to come and walk around this very lake, stepping on this very path, together.

Paul pointed towards the horizon. "There's the parking lot."

They had walked a lap around the lake together.

As they got into the car, while buckling his seatbelt, Hugo said plainly, "She was here, and now she is gone."

2.

Hugo was early at Paul's house.

Paul opened the door and let him in. He led him back, through the living room, to the backyard, where a circle of chairs was already in place. In Hugo's hands, he held a fruit salad. He asked where he could put it, and Paul took it off of his hands. The sun was shining down in full rays. The day was going to last for hours and hours. Paul's backyard was a verdant place, with flowers in bloom and trees to provide shade coverage in the corner.

"Others will be arriving soon, I think," Paul said.

It was his custom each and every year, right in the middle of June, to host a get together for the neighborhood, to allow people to come and be together and enjoy food. It was a way of welcoming in the summer of sorts. Paul had been a happy host, enjoying having the opportunity to bring people together. Hugo, who was mild in social situations, came each and every year, this being one of the few times of the year that he even saw some of the other people who came. As neighbors moved in and out, the guest list changed with time. Hugo felt like he was a constant, as though he always came to this party, year in and year out, no matter what, and that made him feel strange. Did he have anything better to do than to be at this party? A big part of why he went was to spend time with Paul, but Paul was frequently preoccupied with entertaining guests, and besides, Hugo knew he could come and see him nearly any time. So why did he keep going? Well, he thought to himself, perhaps he might figure out the answer to this question this year. It seemed like a great opportunity for such a revelation to take place.

Hugo sat in one of the chairs, feeling the sun beat down on the back of his neck. He had forgotten to apply sunscreen, which was a compulsion for him this time of year. Getting severely burned was a strong source of anxiety for him. Typically, he was sure to put on sunscreen before he went outside for long stretches of time, particularly when he was gardening. Alas, he told himself, it was best to leave the matter be.

"How have you been?" Paul asked Hugo, taking a seat next to him.

"Fine."

"How's the garden?"

"Good. I have some chrysanthemums coming in right now. They are great."

"Excellent! Been working on the weeds?"

"A little. It doesn't feel like I can ever really get rid of all of them."

"I hear you. Well, hopefully it keeps on raining."

Recently, June Gloom had proven to be an apt description for the weather in Seattle. Over the last few weeks, rain was the norm.

"I worry about the rain we are going to get this summer," Hugo said.

"What do you mean?"

"I just hope we get enough of it. You know how dry and barren it gets in the summer."

"I do."

"So here's hoping for rain."

"It gets dry and barren in the summer, but you know that it's the same every year. We always get through it."

"Yes, but you know that the seasons are changing," Hugo said, referring to the phenomenon of climate change.

"Yes, summer is coming soon."

"No, that's not what I mean. Climate change. The winters are getting colder, and the summers are getting hotter. It is all based on extremes. There is a bulk of scientific data supporting the fact that our global climate is being rewired."

"I see."

"So let's just hope that our gardens stay all right. In a couple of months, around the country, it will be a heat dome or something like that. It will be hot and humid. It will be unbearable. It gets like that every year, but it gets worse and worse if you look at the trends over the last few years. Thank goodness we live where we do."

The Pacific Northwest was insulated from the rest of the country. As half the country was covered in snow during the winter, and then scorching hot during the summer, the northwest remained mild, cloudy, protected on every side by mountains, shielded by bodies of water. Layers upon layers of waters separated Seattle from everything beyond it. To the west, there was the sound, the peninsula, and then the ocean, fathomless in its depth. To the east, there sat the Cascade Range. So, really, the Seattle area was like a sliver of precious, sacred land sitting in an unknown corner of the world, distant from so many people, talked of as though it was a sort of mystical location that could be visited in the imagination only, or not talked of at all. But for people like Hugo and Paul, this was home, where they lived their lives.

"Don't you think," Paul began, "that it's indeed possible that the changes in climate are the result of larger, natural climatic phenomenon that takes place over the course of thousands of years?"

"That is a common argument. But then the question remains this: why are the changes in climate taking place over such a short interval of time? In the last one hundred years, the carbon dioxide content in the atmosphere has gone up exponentially, and temperatures have soared. Scientists are in agreement about what the causing forces are. It's the public that has more reservations about it."

"You think?"

"There is a lot of money, money from powerful industries, that is going into keeping people misinformed and ignorant about the whole thing. "

Hugo put a hand on the warm back of his neck. "Yep," he said, "we're all doomed."

Paul turned his head and noticed someone walking towards them. "Oh," he said, "we have another guest here. How are you doing, Nathan?"

"Doing well. Hi Paul."

Paul turned to Hugo. "You've met, haven't you?"

"I don't think so," Hugo said, crossing his arms.

Nathan reached out to shake hands. Hugo shook with the vigorous grip that had always been his practice.

Paul was, in a sense, born to bring people together. In his career, he had worked in sales, and he had been happy to connect with all sorts of people, to form relationships, and so it seemed only natural that he was hosting this party. He had made an effort, much more so than Hugo, to get to know the people who lived in the neighborhood. Consequently, he knew virtually everyone living on the street. He wanted to connect Hugo to these people, but he didn't make it easy for him.

"Well, it really is a nice day," Nathan said. "Especially after the last few days we've been having, this is nice."

"Yes, it is," Hugo answered like a robot.

Nathan looked at Paul. "Well, I brought over some chicken thighs to grill. Is it all right if I use your grill?"

"Sure thing. Let me get it set up for you."

The two neighbors walked a few steps away from the circle of chairs. In the distance, Hugo heard the sound of more voices. More guests were arriving.

A woman, a man, and a young adult boy entered.

"Oh," Paul said. "Carol, Dave, Rex, how are you?"

"We're great," Dave, the father, answered. "How are you?"

"Good, good."

127

Paul introduced them to Hugo, who stayed seated in the circle of chairs by himself. Carol and Rex, who were carrying food, walked up the stairs into the house, leaving Dave to have a seat next to Hugo.

"So," Dave began.

"So," Hugo echoed.

"I've seen you out tending to your garden. It looks really great."

"I work hard to take care of it. Which house do you live in?"

"Oh," Dave replied, "I'm in the brown house just across the street from you. I see you sometimes when I go for my afternoon jogs."

Hugo remembered that this brown house was the modern house that he had despised seeing. Now, here he was, talking to the owner of that house, chatting with him. Hugo started to regret that he had even come to the party. Already it was shaping up to be a deeply unpleasant experience. He hated having small talk, particularly with these people who he didn't honestly care about. Being here seemed like a sort of service to Paul. A lot had been on Hugo's mind lately, and he had been struggling with feelings of anger and bitterness. Here he was, at Paul's dinner party, talking to Dave, the doctor living in the modern house.

But Hugo, being aware, knew that he couldn't simply leave the party, and he also couldn't simply refuse to interact with anyone. He would need to do his best to be social, to be personable. It was while thinking about this that Hugo asked Dave, "How's work?"

"Oh, you know how it is. A patient comes to you with something wrong. You tell him your professional opinion, and then he argues with you. It's all very nice."

Hugo smirked at this. "I know I've done that with my doctor," he said.

"I'm sure you're not as headstrong in your opinions as some of my patients," Dave chimed.

"Perhaps."

"A mom brings in her son, who is fifty pounds overweight. I finish the physical, and then I mention to the mother that her son needs to lose weight. They don't usually take this very well. Pretty soon I'm sitting in my office, wondering what I'm doing. What I want to do is—"

"Take care of people."

"Right. I want people to be healthy and live the fullest lives they can. But sometimes I feel like people don't want those things."

"Maybe people inherently want to be ill?" Hugo suggested.

"No, that doesn't seem right. But people seem to be drawn to unhealthy lifestyles: being sedentary, eating processed foods, not doing intellectually fulfilling things. You know, stuff like that."

"I do know," Hugo answered, "I for one take excellent care of myself. I haven't been to the doctor in over a year."

"What do you do to take care of yourself, Hugo, if I may ask."

"I go swimming. I read a lot. I buy fresh food and cook it. It's as simple as that. Plus a game of chess here and there helps keep me sharp."

"I bet it does. How old are you?"

"Sixty-six. You?"

"Forty-five. And you are retired, right?"

"I am."

"What did you do for a career?"

"Accounting for Smartest-Tools."

"Is that the company that sells vacuum cleaners?"

"Right."

"How did you like that work?"

"It was great." Hugo was in a rhythm of speaking now since he was able to talk about himself. "I came in every day, looked at the numbers, managed accounts, that sort of thing. It was work that made sense to me."

"I bet. How do you like retirement?"

Carol and Rex came walking out. "How are you doing?" Carol asked them.

"Doing great!" Dave called.

Hugo noticed that Rex appeared rather sad and gloomy. He was looking at the ground frequently, hands in his pockets, his feet shuffling anxiously. Rex had light brown hair, blue eyes, and wore a logo-less sweatshirt.

"Oh, look!" Carol cried. "There's Stephen. Let's go and say hello."

She and Dave disappeared at once, leaving Hugo with the young man who was looking at the ground.

"Well, how old are you, young man?"

"Nineteen."

"Sounds about right. Are you in college?"

"Yeah, I go to Western"

He was referring to Western Washington University, a school located up near the Canadian border, known for the bohemian, countercultural ideals and practices of its students. In a sense, it was no different than any other college, but it seemed as though it embodied this hipster, "granola" essence to a particularly high degree. Located in Bellingham, Hugo had spent some time in the town, but not much on the school campus.

"Do you like going there?"

"It's all right, I guess."

"What are you studying?"

"Haven't gotten into a major yet. Still taking general electives."

Hugo wondered if this fellow was capable of speaking in sentences that were longer than they had to be.

"What is your favorite class you took?"

Rex looked at Hugo. It felt like he was looking straight through him, at one of the trees behind him.

"I took several piano performance classes, and I liked those a lot," he said.

"Ah, you play?"

"Yes."

"What are your favorite composers?"

"Debussy, Erik Satie, Charles Ives."

"Excellent choices," said Hugo with genuine earnestness.

Hugo had listened to his wife play the piano. In fact, he still had a small piano in his study. When she had been with him, he would listen to her play for hours at a time, the sound of her voice a comforting force for him.

"What do you like about playing?" Hugo asked.

"When I play the piano, it makes me feel free."

"I understand that. It is a beautiful thing."

There was a pause, a lull in the conversation, and then Hugo spoke:

"So you think you might major in music performance?"

Rex shrugged. "Maybe."

"What else do you like to do?"

"Not much. Go for walks."

"Me too."

"I've seen your garden. It looks very nice."

Hugo said, "Thank you. I work hard to keep it maintained. Pretty soon I'm going to need to mow the lawn. That won't be much fun."

"No."

"Maybe you could come and mow the lawn for him sometime," Carol suggested, who had returned with Dave.

"Maybe," Rex answered.

"That would be splendid," Hugo said. "So, Rex, you are here for the summer?"

"Yes, I am."

"Well, I hope to see you around soon. It has been nice talking to you."

"Yes, the same goes for you, Hugo."

Hugo took a few steps away from the circle of chairs. What was it with this kid? He hardly spoke, and it seemed like he was possessed by a ghost. Had Hugo been like that at that age? No, he reasoned. He had been filled with energy, energy and optimism about all things. He had gone out, eager to partake in his passions, of which there had been many. No, Hugo thought, there simply was no connecting with the youth for him. What did young people believe in? Hugo decided that he had no interest in spending any more time with Rex, that it was a waste of time. Hugo felt angry that his generation had worked as hard as they had to create a beautiful world only to watch subsequent generations take it for granted and spoil it.

"There you are," Paul spoke. "It's time to eat."

Hugo walked upstairs and helped himself to some fruit salad, chicken thighs, potatoes, and regular salad. He then brought his food out to the table that sat not far from the circle of chairs. Naturally, Hugo sat next to Paul, and to his right was a woman, also older in age, who he couldn't name.

"Hugo, that's quite a full plate you've got there," she said.

"Yes, well, one does need to eat."

"I suppose that's true."

"Remind me of your name."

"Kim Schaefer," she said. "The lady with the apple tree."

Hugo's eyes brightened slightly. "I have enjoyed your apples a fair bit. I have made it a habit to walk over and pluck an apple from your tree every few days."

"Yes, there are more apples that come from it than I know what to do with."

Aware that the conversation had run its course, Hugo turned to Paul, practically begging him to save him.

"Hugo," Paul said, "there's someone I'd like to introduce you to. This is Sophia, sitting across from us. Sophia has spent, how many years was it?"

"Fourteen," she said.

"Yes. Sophia has spent fourteen years living in Bosnia, in Sarajevo. Isn't that neat?"

"What were you doing there?" Hugo asked.

"I was practicing law," she said. She had short blond hair and kind eyes.

"Law? Seems like a strange place to practice it."

"There is a lot going on there. There is a great need for justice, for someone who will fight to protect the people."

"I suppose so."

The truth was that Hugo had left North America only a few times in his life, for short intervals. It wasn't a matter of him being ignorant of the rest of the world; he had read far too many books to be ignorant. More to the point was the fact that Hugo didn't really feel any need to go anywhere terribly far from his own home in the Seattle area. Consciously, Hugo viewed the Northwest as being his native country. He didn't identify with the politics or ideology of the rest of the country. When he had traveled, he had felt a strong bit of alienation, as though he was terribly different from other people. He remembered when his work had required him to take several trips to the Midwest and Texas. Well, he didn't think he could have felt more out of place than he had when he had gone on those trips to those places. Consequently, Hugo was happy where he lived. Viewing life on the most micro level, he was pleased to live in Wedgwood. For all intents and purposes, Wedgwood was his country. Sure the occasional trip to the coast or to a place like Chelan was enough to satiate any feelings of cabin fever or over-familiarity, but for the most part, he liked where he was. For this reason, when he did talk to people who came from other parts of the country and of the world, he had felt slightly ill at ease in interacting with them, not knowing what to talk about, what questions to ask. Even when it was a person from somewhere as close as California, he felt unsure of how to proceed in talking to them. If he met someone who came from somewhere else, then his own faith in the Northwest as being all-sufficient for his needs became threatened, because here was a person with a different mindset or culture, who seemed to also live a happy life. Hugo was forced to proceed as though the Northwest was the only place where a happy life was possible, because it was the only place he was ever going to be. Hugo didn't want to be bothered by people who came from other places. Simply put, what he desired above all things in his life was to not be bothered.

After dinner, the sun was beginning to set quickly. Paul walked over towards the fire pit and lit it. Crackling, bright, and smoke-filled, the fire became a source of warmth that summoned the neighbors to sit around it. Hugo sat in a chair next to a fat man who wore a ponytail.

"So, what do you do?" Hugo asked, trying his best to be social.

"I'm a software designer."

"What does that entail?"

"I write and edit code that goes into programs for computers."

Hugo was already lost.

"It sure is nice to be here at this party," the man said. "It's great that Paul puts this event on each and every year."

"What's your name?"

"Marcus. Yours?"

"Hugo."

"Pleasure to meet you, Hugo."

"Same."

"What do you do for a living?" Marcus asked.

"Nothing."

"You're retired?"

"Mmhmm."

"Oh, that must be nice."

"I don't mind it."

"For me, it feels like retirement is so many years away. I feel like I'm going to be spending years writing code!"

"You are."

"Oh, well. A man has got to work, hasn't he?"

"Unless he's retired."

"There you go."

Bored with the trajectory of this conversation. Hugo started to think about this man, who had a hideous ponytail and was clearly too fat to be healthy. What would Dave the doctor have said? Probably the same thing he tells so many of his patients. Was Hugo being harsh regarding the size of another person? Perhaps. Hugo felt no pity for the man who was eager to be through his career and in retirement. Life is not a race, Hugo told himself. Death is waiting at the end, so what's the point in being caught up with the next step, the next upcoming change in phase? If a man is not pleased with his career, if he dreads the upcoming years of labor that await him, then he is responsible for having chosen to go into an unsatisfactory field. It was as simple as that. Hugo had not always liked his job. He had spent year after year working at it, through ups and downs. He had always persevered, working towards the next goal while still enjoying the present day of labor.

"So where did you work?" Marcus inquired, trying to keep the conversation alive.

"Smartest-Tools."

"Is that the—"

"Yes, it is the vacuum cleaner company."

Hugo had known that, on a certain level, the capacity for Smartest-Tools to improve the state of the world was relatively minimal. Yet he had been devoted to his company, believing in his work because it was honest. Practicing accounting, performing the job in all of its requirements, had been a source of fulfillment precisely because it had been a job that needed doing. Ascribing meaning to one's work was one of the most important tasks in the life of an adult, so long it was a professional career and not a job as a barista.

"Did you like working for them?" Marcus continued.

The conversation went on and on, endlessly. So the group of neighbors sat around the fire, talking for quite some time. In total, Hugo had talked to Dave the doctor, Rex the moody pianist, Kim the apple tree lady, Sophia the Bosnian lawyer, and Marcus the software engineer with a ponytail. It was more socializing than Hugo was accustomed to. What this evening really did for him was it led him towards realizing precisely how little he knew the people living on his street, in his neighborhood. He did not know these people well. The interactions he had had with these people were superficial and vapid in content. Feeling empty, Hugo was also angry that he was forced to fend for himself throughout the evening. In years past when he had come to this party he had brought his wife, a person who was there for him, a pair of eyes for him to look at immediately after talking to a weird person, a hand to hold, a person to share food with. Now all of those things were gone. He was representing himself at the party. Had he done a good job representing himself? Socially, he had been competent enough. It didn't, however, prove to matter much, because he really didn't care what these other people thought of him. The only person whose opinion mattered to him was now gone forever, and instead, he was left with a parade of idiots.

3.

Hugo woke up from dreams he couldn't remember. He tossed and turned, trying to fall back asleep. His breathing was short and shallow.

He looked at the clock and saw that it was 2:17 am. For a few seconds he wiped his eyes, and then he stared at the ceiling, though he couldn't see anything. Realizing he was the only living thing in his large, dark bedroom, he began to feel unsettled. Turning his head both ways he looked around at all the blackness that was surrounding him. His heart rate beginning to spike, panic coming arriving, he reached for the lamp and turned it on. At once a blast of precious, life-giving light poured generously into the room. There was a comfort that couldn't be put into words at being able to see one's surroundings. He could see the shadows of the cabinets spread outward. It was quiet. Nothing in the room was moving.

In an attempt to remember the dream he had just been having, he found that he couldn't recall what it had been about. Strange, for only seconds ago he had been having that dream, and already it was gone, slipped away into the shadows. To his left on the dresser, there was a glass of water, which he picked up and proceeded to drink from. Having finished the glass, he was still thirsty, and so he decided to walk downstairs and pour himself some more. Did he dare venture out into the savage night? He decided it was worth it.

Slowly, he climbed out of his bed and walked towards the front door, it feels as though the shadows all around him were following him. Through the hallway he walked. He held on to the banister rail as he navigated the stairs. Taking his time to move down, he breathed deeply, hoping that his heart rate wouldn't spike again.

His doctor had told him that he had high blood pressure and that he needed to take care of his heart. For this reason, he had been particularly conscious of what he ate. The feel-

136

ings of panic, the attacks of anxiety, were a recent phenomenon, one that had started in the last couple of weeks. He would be doing something mundane when he would be seized by the feelings and sensations, and he would not know what to do. The panic was like a lion waiting in the corner, ready to pounce on him at any moment, and he knew that if it did, he would be overwhelmed. Therefore, he was rather on edge as he stepped onto the ground floor of his home.

Into the kitchen he walked, taking steps slowly. In each room and hallway that he entered he turned on the light, gradually flooding the entire house in a luminous glow.

Opening the fridge door, he reached for the water pitcher and poured some into the empty glass he was holding. He noticed that his hand was trembling as he held the glass, shaking restlessly. He took a seat at the kitchen table, had a sip of water, and admired the fortress of light that he had constructed in his house. Surely the light that he had brought into his house would keep the dark feelings away. Surely, he was safe.

For fifteen minutes he sat and enjoyed his water. Then he got up, opened, the fridge, and looked inside for something to eat. There was nothing that was appetizing to him, and he felt no need to eat for the sake of eating, so he resumed his seat at the kitchen table.

Hugo had been the primary one to cook in the household. As Adrian had grown up, it was the routine for Hugo to come home from work and proceed to prepare a meal: pasta, cooked meat, salads of many styles. There was no particular reason for him being the head chef, but he did enjoy it.

With a look around the room, he realized that he was sitting in the precise seat he sat in for so many meals, for so many years. Across from him was an empty seat.

All at once, he felt his body give way to the raw feelings. Quickly, he rose from the table, walked upstairs, and jumped back into his bed. He gripped a pillow in his hands and squeezed it as hard as he could. He was breathing deeply. His palms were sweating. His head was aching.

So he sat, waiting for it to pass. But it wasn't going anywhere at all. He started to punch his pillow. Striking harder and harder, he hit the pillow with all the force that he could, groaning with anguish. A minute passed in this way, though it had felt more like an hour. Wiping the sweat from his forehead, he sat on the corner of his bed, wondering what he had done.

4.

He was sitting on the floor of the study, looking at books. The shelf was half-full. Below Hugo, at his feet, there was an enormous pile of them. There were mysteries, westerns, science-fiction books, and, of course, classics. Reading the classics, the literary opuses that pushed boundaries and enriched the mind particularly well, was always their favorite way to spend time. So many books to get rid of, he thought to himself.

A book caught his eye. He picked up *To the Lighthouse* and looked at the cover. He read the back of the book and was reminded once more why this story had appealed to him. As he opened the first page he observed her name written inside. He looked at the handwriting, the curves in the letters, the faded quality of the writing. The name was resting there on the page, and he looked at it practically meditatively. Then he put the book on the shelf.

She read it a long time back. Had it been during high school? Either way, it was long enough ago that it was all hazy to him. She read it, and then she loaned it to him. So he too read it. He enjoyed it, but he struggled more with Woolf's experimentation. His wife seemed to have no problem with reading experimental literature. Her mind was always wired that way, free-flowing, abstract, drawn to feelings. This particular book was one of her very favorites. She spent half of college talking about it, or so it seemed.

He continued to look at books for some time, occasionally smiling, occasionally sighing.

5.

The car was speeding along the freeway, across the lake, towards the suburban wasteland to come. Hugo was looking out the window at the sunlit scenery. In the distance there stood the Cascades, the rigid range of mountains threatening to rip the sky apart. Lines of trees hugged along the rim of the lake.

"I'm glad you were able to come, big brother. It means a lot to Cassie that you can come, right?"

"It does," she answered.

"Of course. I am happy to come."

The truth was that Hugo was eager to be out of his house. Lately, things had become strange there; perhaps it was a matter of having spent too much time in it. Regardless, what he knew was that those things were unsettling, uncomfortable there. It felt like his world became too small, as though the walls were closing in on him. After that night a few weeks ago, when he was kept up wide awake, something seemed to change in him. No longer was he at peace staying in his home for too long at a time. To occupy himself, he spent more time in his garden, mowing the lawn, and tending to his flowers. In particular, his pink roses were looking very nice. His flowers gave him a sense of hope, a promise of relief from the darkness that was all around him.

"You know," Martin began, "I was looking at the twenty-five-day forecast, and it looks like it should be very nice in Chelan. Very nice."

"Yes, but the weather can change a lot in twenty-five days."

"That is true. But if you think about it, weather prediction technology has really come a long way in the last couple of years. It's amazing to think about!"

"I suppose that is true. But it's not even July yet, is it?"

"It's actually the third week of June."

"Oh, well all right."

Having crossed the bridge, the car was speeding towards Kirkland, but not to Lavender Heights. Instead, Martin drove along the main drag of Kirkland, towards the Elementary school. Tonight was the annual end-of-year music concert. Cassandra would be playing her recorder with her classmates. Hugo was happy enough to be coming along and being a part of his brother's granddaughter's concert.

"I'm sure you're gonna dazzle us with some fantastic music tonight, sweetie," Martin beamed.

James and Barbara were busy running errands, so Martin picked his granddaughter up from school. They spent the afternoon together and then traveled across the lake to pick up Hugo. James and Barbara were intentional about living close to James' parents because they wanted Cassandra to grow up close to her grandparents. What they wanted was to have a full family experience for her upbringing. Martin, though he was busy with teaching, was beyond happy to be there for his granddaughter.

They pulled into the parking lot of the school and got out. While walking towards the entrance, Cassandra saw several of her friends from school, and so Martin let her go with them to find their music teacher. The two brothers wandered around until they found the gymnasium, which was packed with parents sitting. In fact, there were so many parents present, that the backspace of the gym was reduced to standing room only. Martin, after all, had never been known for his punctuality, at least not like Hugo.

Finding their way to the back left corner of the room, the two brothers stood and chatted. Hugo occasionally looked down at his tie, which was full of musical notes and staffs.

"The schools sure ran late this year," Martin remarked.

"Yep."

"That's all right, though. It just means that we have a longer period of time to spend anticipating things like this concert." Martin pulled out his phone. "I have full bars here. Great!"

Hugo was never bothered to purchase a smartphone. What he owned was a primitive, large phone that functioned for communication purposes primarily. Hugo always carried his phone, but it was rare that he used it. He had a computer, but he hardly knew the first thing about how to operate it. This explained his inability to connect with Marcus, the software engineer with the ponytail at Paul's dinner party. Hugo held a disdain for technology. In his mind, the advent of smartphone technology, tablets, and computers, had become a force that was shrinking the attention spans of its users, in other words, the young. He didn't like seeing people always with their phones out, looking down at them or else raising them up to take a picture. It was technology that was causing people to become less present in life, he thought. He himself would settle with a good book over the pleasures afforded by a video game any day of the week, for what he was more interested in was enrichment, in stuff with substance.

"It looks like they're starting!" Martin exclaimed.

An older-looking lady was standing at the front of the gymnasium with several rows of children standing behind her. Cassandra, who wasn't terribly tall, stood in the front row.

"Good evening, ladies and gentlemen, and welcome to our end of the year concert..."

Hugo found himself spacing out during the teacher's speech. Before he knew it, the kids were holding their recorders, playing a rendition of "Ode to Joy". The song was over in a flash, and then the parents were applauding. Many adults were taking video and photos with their phones. Then the kids continued to play another song, and another, and another. Cassandra, who held her recorder confidently, played well. The concert, which didn't last more than thirty minutes, was over very quickly.

With one final round of applause, parents began to go and find their kids. Hugo and Martin met up with James and Barbara, who were standing with Cassandra.

"You sounded so wonderful," Barbara said.

"You sounded splendid," James offered.

"I agree!" Martin squeaked.

"Thanks, everyone."

Throughout his life, Hugo attended a number of functions for Adrian. He went to countless soccer games, cross-country meets, marching band competitions, and also attended photography exhibitions. It had brought him pleasure to be there for the people who he cared about, and though he was happy to do this for Cassandra, it would have been nice, he thought, to do so for his own grandchild. He could imagine going to a music concert for an Adrian Hugo Larson, and hearing him play "Ode to Joy" and many other songs.

Very soon the gymnasium was empty except for a few kids and adults standing around, including the Larson family.

"So, Cassie, sweetie," Martin said, "I'll see you real soon, okay?"

"Okay."

"Great job today. I'm really proud of you. You are one awesome kid!"

Hugo waved. "Bye, Cassandra."

"Bye, Hugo! See you in Chelan."

Those final words echoed through his consciousness. At once it became clear to him that he was really going to be spending an entire week in a scenic location with this positive, upbeat family. Dread threatened to take over, but he was resilient, reasoning to himself that, surely, the trip would be an enjoyable one.

"Shall we head out, big brother?"

"Yes, let's go. It's past my bedtime," he joked.

"Why, it's only 7:30!"

"I know. Let's go."

The sun was still far from setting as they stepped out into the parking lot. Hugo got in the car, and they drove back along the main street of Kirkland. Generic, cookie-cutter houses lined both sides of the road.

"That was a neat concert," Martin said. "I always enjoy getting to hear Cassandra play."

"Yes, it was really something."

There was a pause as Martin drove. Hugo was feeling the same bit of tension that he had experienced the last time Martin drove him home several months earlier. He felt like a volcano that was about to burst at any moment. It was hardly bearable. Should he say something? Well, this time was about as good as any.

"I think I'm ready," Hugo began.

"Ready for what, big brother?"

"To talk about things...about what happened in January."

Martin didn't speak immediately, instead keeping his concentration on the road. They were floating over the dark lake once more. It was as though they were becoming dissolved within the folds of water, disappearing fully.

There was more silence before Martin spoke. At last, he breathed in deeply and then said, "That is very good to hear. I know what happened in January is not easy to talk about, so it doesn't surprise me that you didn't want to for a while. But it is a sign of progress that you are opening up. How are you feeling about it? I mean, obviously, you are not feeling great, but what's going on?"

"I feel hurt, angry, bitter."

"I get that. Tell me more."

"She was the love of my life, the source of light, comfort, and peace, and she was taken from me so cruelly. It hurts me to my very core. A part of me died on January 12th, and that part of me is gone. I don't know if I can reclaim it."

"I know it's hard for you to hear this, but you know time will make things get better. You remember how much it hurt us when Mom passed, but things have healed a bit in the years since then."

"Yes, but this isn't the same thing," Hugo countered. "We had so many more years ahead of us, she and I."

"Perhaps it is not the same thing, but pain is still pain. Hurt is hurt, and what I am saying is that time will heal the pain, even if it doesn't ever go away completely. You say you have been feeling angry?"

"Yes, I woke up the other night and started punching my pillow like a wild animal. I feel like I have been losing control over myself. I have been having experiences, little episodes where my body freaks out."

"What do you mean?"

"I get these weird feelings, where I start to panic, and my body goes into this sort of survival mode. It is very frightening."

"I bet that is a natural response of the body to loss," Martin reassured. "Did you feel better after you punched the pillow?"

"The answer to that question is not important. The fact of the matter is that I punched my pillow like some sort of madman. What is wrong with me?"

"I don't think anything is wrong with you. You are bereaved, and you are slowly dealing with it."

"I don't feel like myself. Ever since that day in January I have felt different, like a shadow of myself. What am I supposed to do?"

"Move forward."

"Move forward?!"

"Yes. You need—"

"Easy for you to say. The man with the lovely wife, the kid and the grandkid tells the bereaved, angry old psycho to simply let go and move on. Look at all that you have, Martin. You have so much. You have your career, your family, and a peaceful life in the suburbs. Do you have any idea how darling Cassandra is? I was thinking about it when I saw her playing her recorder tonight. Anyway, who are you to tell me that I just need to move on? Do you think it's easy to? Maybe if you were in my position then you would understand why it's so hard. But that's just it. You don't understand. I am alone."

"You aren't alone."

Hugo continued, "I told you last time we were driving on this road together that I was happy. That was a lie. I am not hiding behind lies anymore. So I'm being honest with you when I say that it's too late for me to move on. There is no new life out there waiting to be found. I had my life. It was long and full of good memories, but so much of what made it great was that she was in it. The honest truth is that I am a wreck. I am falling apart, and my friends and family are watching it happen right before their eyes. But you know what? Don't worry about it. You have your sunny disposition to keep you going. Being positive is something that always guides you through everything. It's easy for you to be positive, because nothing has happened to you. Don't mind me. I'm just waking up in the middle of the night, punching my pillow, crying myself to sleep, unable to enjoy anything or think about anything except for the fact that she's gone."

"Big brother..."

"Did I appreciate her as much as she deserved? Well, you know I did the very best I could. But still, a voice nags at me, telling me that I didn't cherish her enough, that I didn't live fully enough into every moment that I got to spend with her. While we're on the topic of feeling bitter, I never said this before, but I feel bitter that you have so much and I have so little. It pisses me off because I tell myself that if I had what you had I wouldn't take it for granted. If she was with me still, I would treat every second with her like it was the most precious flower in the entire world. So that's it. I'm done talking. I don't have anything else to say. I don't think I want to hear whatever you have to say to me either. I can't say that I'm looking forward to our trip to Chelan, but I will be going. I will be there. You know why? Because I am desperate, and I need to be around people. I don't even know what I feel anymore. One minute I am panicked, the next I am angry, the next I am all right. I have lost the person who was more important to me than anyone else, but I'm not ready to give up on the other people who are still with me, at least not yet. I need help. There, that's it. I'm finished."

They had reached the city and were approaching Wedgwood.

"Would you be willing to see a therapist?"

"Yes."

"I know someone who does great work. He is a close friend of mine who specializes in post-traumatic stress disorder. He also does work with grief therapy. His name is Christopher Stevenson. I can put you into contact with him."

"Do you think that could be helpful for me? I have never seen a shrink."

"I think so, big brother. It's all about taking small steps in the right direction. Can I ask you another question, big brother?"

"Yes, what is it?"

"Since January, have you been to the grave?"

Hugo sighed. "No, I have not."

"I know it must be a very challenging thing to do. But I think it could be a good step in the right direction for you. Just something to think about."

"Okay. But that has nothing to do with any of this.

Now they had pulled up at Hugo's house.

"Well, here we are," Martin said.

"Here we are."

Hugo opened the car door and heard his brother say, "I'm glad you shared all of this with me. I really am. Thank you."

Hugo laughed and said, "You're welcome."

"One more thing."

"What's that?"

"I'm looking forward to this trip to Chelan. I think it's gonna be good. It's gonna be good. And I'm glad you're coming with us. You being there will only make the trip better."

Hugo started to cry a little bit. "I'm glad to be coming, too."

"Maybe sometime when we get back, we can get you in touch with Christopher. I think that would be good for you too. Also, when you're ready, I'd like to take you some time to visit the grave. How does that sound?"

"I don't think I'm going to be ready anytime soon."

"That's okay. Take your time."

"All right. Love you."

"Love you, big brother."

6.

In his bedroom, he opened the closet and then the drawer. Pulling out the photograph, he looked at it. The photograph depicted him and her standing at the observation deck of the Space Needle. In the photograph, he was not looking at the camera directly, but she had insisted that it was a good picture, that it had a charm to it. Standing alone in his bedroom, he looked at the photograph and smiled.

July

I.

The sun was up a couple of hours when he awoke. He got out of bed suddenly, looking around, and then proceeded to do his morning stretches. Not wanting to wake anyone he tiptoed outside through the sliding glass door. Already it was getting to be warm out. If today was to be anything like the previous three days, then it would be a very hot day indeed, the temperature soaring well into the 90's. The sunlight rained down.

Standing outside, he took a few steps, feeling the cool grass on his feet, and he approached the lawn chair. He sat down in it and looked up. Immediately in front of him, in its gigantic splendor, was lake Chelan, a crystalline pool of water that swallowed the horizon. Reflective as glass, the water was bright blue. In the sky a few clouds, light and feathery, hung in the air, lazily drifting across the lake. Behind the clouds, there were the dark red hills that surrounded the lake. There was a powerful feeling of sweeping openness to the view. Running along the mouth of the lake were houses, well built and nice looking. These houses were colorful, many of them with docks leading out into the lake.

The condo property was located on its own peninsula. Each condo unit was homogenous in appearance but possessed its own particular charm. A small stretch of grass was afforded to the owners before there came the dock and the water. Hugo continued to look at the view, feeling as though he was on a different planet. His world, Wedgwood with its trees and clouds and gentle slopes, was completely alien to this expansive, dynamic landscape.

How had he gotten here? He was picked up by Martin a few days ago. They drove to his home in Kirkland, where they packed into James' minivan and the seven of them, including Cassandra's friend Daisy, embarked on a trek across the Cascades. Their drive led them up higher and higher in elevation, through wooded stretches and rocky hills, along winding, narrow roads, until they reached the summit of the pass. Hugo, who did not enjoy driving in general, was on edge for the entirety of this ride. Then, after reaching the summit, they made the descent back down. They ended up in a clearing, the land of Central Washington sprawling outwards mysteriously. The fields they passed were starkly, richly yellow. It was only another hour or so of driving before the lake was visible.

The car conversation was chipper and sporadic. Hugo kept to himself, attempting at several points to fall asleep but failing to do so. Instead, he was forced to look out the window, thinking about the little world he was leaving behind, wondering if he might be leaving some of the pain and misery behind as well. So many of the associations he had emotionally with her were intertwined with the house in Wedgwood and the surrounding neighborhood. All at once, while driving, Hugo felt a sense of how big the world was, of how small he and his life were in the scheme of it. Strangely enough, he found this to be a comforting thing.

They reached the condo and spent the first day getting settled. The next two days were filled with reading, napping, walking around the condo property, and swimming. They had not yet stopped in the actual town of Chelan, so perhaps today would be the day for such a venture. The days so far were full but went by fast. In Hugo's imagination, the rest of the trip, like most things, would fly by as well. But he was not interested in thinking about the end of his time in Chelan because he had a feeling, a sense that there was something he was meant to learn, to experience from his time here. Therefore, he was living his life with eyes wide open, attentive to his surroundings and to the people around him.

The rest of the family were not getting on his nerves too much, thankfully. After all, he was free to go off and sleep if he needed to escape a particularly positive moment. He was, it was true, a gifted sleeper, so this was no problem. The meals together tested his tolerance for positivity a bit. The other night at dinner, there was a conversation about how wonderful and beneficial a particular nonprofit organization was. Hugo mostly tuned the conversation out, because if he didn't it made him a little angry. But for the most part, the larger Larson clan was good to him, and he was thankful for them. He was thankful to not be alone.

All was quiet and still as he sat in the lawn chair. His eyes were wide open; he was fully awake. Looking at his watch he noticed that it was just after 6:00 am. Should he do it? He decided it was a good time to go for a swim.

Back inside the condo, he tiptoed about until he found his trunks and goggles from his suitcase. He went back outside again and gathered that the sun was making steady progress, though it was still hidden behind the dark red hills. He walked along the grass down towards the dock and dove into the water at once. Something he had learned from all his years of swimming was that it was never beneficial to test the water temperature or seek to gradually become accustomed to it. Instead, he thought it was always better to go ahead and dive in immediately. The water might be cold, but with time it would quickly warm up as the body adjusted. Plus, the shock to the system of diving into cold water was healthy and a nice reminder of being alive.

He was swimming with clean, smooth strokes towards a buoy resting in the water fifty yards or so from the dock. Since the poor performance months earlier, Hugo took time off from swimming, but the trip to Chelan, he considered, was an opportune time to get back into the habit of exercising. For a while, he was totally uninterested in swimming, angry and bitter at the fact that he struggled so much that one night. But a change in surroundings might prove to be just the catalyst necessary to get him swimming again. As he swam, he glided through the water, kicking powerfully, breathing on both sides. The water was chillingly cold, but he didn't mind. Every time he raised his head up to breathe, he looked at the world outside of the water, and it appeared as though he wasn't even moving at all, the lake remaining unfathomably massive, swallowing up all that was inside of it.

What he wanted to do was reconnect with why he loved swimming in the first place. To his thinking, this shouldn't have been too difficult of a thing to do. But during the few swims he had gone on since that particular episode, he similarly struggled, unable to swim all of his 200's. Today, there was no way to measure 200's precisely, so he decided he would swim to the buoy and back to the dock 50 times as a workout. It was not long before he completed 15 trips, and he was feeling good. It felt great to be awake before the rest of the world, to be basking in his own private space, removed from everything and everyone else.

He was thinking about her again as he swam. He was thinking about how injured he felt without her, how wronged he had been. Where this thought came from he had no idea, but he knew that it was very real and had substance to it. With one stroke and then another, he was pulverizing the water, destroying the angry thoughts and feelings as they arose. What he found to be the case was that he was able to swim more quickly and smoothly than he had in quite some time. Had he finally found a constructive outlet for his anger?

Amazingly, he was practically flying through the water. Every time he reached the dock or the buoy, he had to quickly turn his entire body, shifting momentum, and then proceed to swim in the opposite direction, which was highly demanding of his energies. But he accomplished this feat again and again. He had boundless energy. In the water, there was only him and his thoughts, and he was slicing through his thoughts with every stroke. Now he had completed 40 trips. He was positively on a roll, with no sign of stopping anytime soon.

Having completed 50 trips, he stopped for a moment by the dock. Floating gently in the water, he started to realize just how cold it was. He looked up at the dock, the grassy hill, the sleepy condo, and then decided to make 10 more trips. Once more, these trips went by smoothly. It wasn't that Hugo suddenly figured out how to become invulnerable as a swimmer, but rather that he unlocked the secret to channeling his own inner state of being into an effective approach to athleticism.

So he completed 60 trips, and all at once he was starting to feel tired, for it caught up to him. He reached the dock and climbed out. His arms were so tired that this was a challenging task. Now that the morning had worn on a bit, the sun was just over the edge of the hills, and he could feel its rays on his body. It was a pleasing sensation, to be wet, and then to gradually dry off in the sunlight. He let his feet dangle in the water below the dock. He turned around and looked at the condo, wondering if anyone else was woken up yet. Martin was known for sleeping in when he possessed the opportunity, not that his job allowed him to sleep much.

So Hugo was left to enjoy the peace of solitude. This was strange, for when he was in the water, the feelings of loneliness were deeply unpleasant, but now that he was by himself and drying off on the dock, not far away from others, he felt a solitude that was enjoyable. Looking out at the water, it was as though he had left all of his feelings, his hurt, in it. The lake had accepted his offering. He felt cleansed, purified, vital. He looked out at the water for some time. An occasional boat would speed by, creating small waves. He could see people stirring in some of the other houses, and he could hear the sound of cars passing through the condo property. How had the Larsons ended up with this condo to begin with? Not needing an answer, he eventually stood up and walked towards the sliding glass door on the backside of the unit.

Inside, he encountered the rest of the Larson family sitting at the table, apparently waiting for him.

"Good morning, big brother. Have a good swim?"

"Yes, I did in fact. It was great."

"Great!"

"How is everybody doing?"

"Wonderful," Patricia cried.

"Fantastic," James answered.

"Marvelous," Barbara cheered.

"Good!" Cassandra and Daisy spoke in unison.

"Oh," Hugo replied. "That is good to hear.

They ate breakfast together. With joy, they recounted how they spent the previous three days, and they discussed their plans for the upcoming one.

"What is planned for today?" asked Hugo.

"Well," Martin answered with verve, "we were thinking of going on a little hike in a couple of hours. Then, we could head to the other side of the peninsula for some mini golf. Finally, we were thinking of going into town for dinner."

"Sounds like a full day."

"It is, big brother. It is. But it's nothing we can't handle, right, girls?"

"Right!"

"Outstanding. Now you girls go ahead and finish your breakfast so we can head out on the hike."

"Yes, Mr. Larson," Daisy answered.

"Please, call me Martin."

It was not long before it was time to depart for the hike. The location of the venture was a little more than thirty minutes away, situated high in the hills facing away from the lake. The group piled into the car and James pushed his foot on the gas pedal. They sped away, out of the condo property, and towards the road that ran around the lake. It was another warm, sunny day, the sky a clear, pure blue and now devoid of any clouds. The sun seemed to float above in a fixed, still position, not moving at all as the car drove higher and higher into the hills. Through the right window of the car, there was visible the deep, rugged earth that comprised the hills, colored a rusted red. To the left, there was the expansive view, which included the lake down below, the town on the northern edge of the lake, and the many winding roads that ran up and down the hills. Trees dotted the hills, appearing rugged and worn under the mighty weight of the simmering sun.

Before long, the car pulled into a lot and James turned around smiling, and said, "We're here!"

They got out of the car and stood around for a minute while Martin tied his hiking boots. Next, he unfolded a massive map and proceeded to survey it carefully.

"Let's see...if we go this way...but if we go there..."

"Martin?" Hugo tapped him on the shoulder.

"Yes, big brother?"

"Are we ready to go?"

"Yes, we are. Yes, we are."

In front of them was a steady climb up a sloping hill, which initially looked rather intimidating. But the truth was that every member of the Larson family, including Daisy, was in better than good enough physical condition for the venture. Hugo, with all the swimming and walking he did, would have no problem making the climb.

"Who wants to race to the top?" James asked, pretending to start running.

"I do!" Cassandra yelled and sprinted up the first twenty feet of the trail.

"Well," Patricia said, "looks like we have our work cut out for us."

So they set about their way. James and the girls were in the lead, then came Barbara and Patricia, and then came Hugo and Martin in the rear.

"I kinda still can't believe we really made it here," Martin noted.

"Why?" Hugo challenged. "You come here multiple times a year for your condo."

"Yes, but there's something about this place, about all the beauty and the escape of it that makes it feel magical."

Believing that few things were truly magical, Hugo replied, "I suppose so."

"I just look at the girls, thinking about how much fun they are having, and it brings joy to my heart."

"That's good."

"Do you remember the magic of being a child?"

"I do," Hugo said, "but I left it where I found it: in my childhood."

Martin was in many respects a more sentimental person than Hugo. Sensitive, caring, and outgoing, he seemed to be the opposite of Hugo. Growing up, their mother, Heidi, doted over Martin, he being the baby in the family. She lavished gifts and privileges on him, and in turn, he developed into an emotionally literate young man. This had proven to be useful when raising James, who went through a fairly rebellious adolescence. Martin was devoted to being there for his son, unlike many of the other fathers of his generation. Adrian, on the other hand, was relatively straightforward to raise, causing little in the way of trouble or mischief. Things were easy for Hugo. He had not really known what he had been doing as a father, but all things worked out well. So the two brothers raised their children. Year after year of life passed by, and now here they were, hiking up a hill just outside of Lake Chelan.

"How is Adrian?" Martin asked.

"He is doing well. As I told you before, he is working on getting a business degree of sorts."

"You didn't mention that to me."

"Oh, well he is working very hard on earning this credential. It is an intensive course load. I was talking to him on the phone just last week, and he said he was drowning in homework: textbook readings to do, quizzes to take, projects to work on. It all sounds like a lot of hard work to me."

"It sounds like a lot of hard work to me too, big brother. Is he not interested in photography anymore?"

"I don't think so. For the time being, this is what he is really interested in pursuing, and I fully support him in the venture."

"That is excellent to hear. I wish him the very best."

"I haven't seen much of him since he started the program. He hasn't always answered my calls, either."

"But that is understandable, isn't it? He is hard at work, making his dreams come true, so surely it makes sense that he isn't so available. I know that at times when I get bogged down in teaching I don't always have the headspace for some of the people in my life. That's why I'm so happy to be here, on vacation!"

"Vacations are a great thing," Hugo conceded, "but I often found that, in my own career, I spent the majority of my vacations wishing I was back at work."

"Ah, it is not always so easy to simply be and enjoy time off. For us teachers, it is particularly a challenge, because we are given summers off. That's a large amount of time!"

"I don't know how you can handle having so much time off at once. In my practice, we had two weeks around Christmas and a week in the summer. That was it. And that was more than enough."

"I suppose every field has its own benefits and costs," Martin conceded. "Like I told you before, I am thinking this is going to be my last year of teaching before I retire."

"Forget what I said before about enjoying retirement. Enjoy the work while you have it. It's all you got."

"Tell me, big brother. Do you ever miss working? Be honest!"

Hugo was breathing deeply as a result of walking upwards at a sharp incline. "To be honest, I do miss working. I like to present myself as being happily retired, but the truth is I get restless. Sometimes I wish I could pore over some numbers again, or call an old associate, if just for fun. I wonder how that vacuum cleaner company is doing, who is managing their accounts now. Ever since I retired, I have been pretty out of the loop as regards the company."

"I see, I see."

In that moment, Hugo was feeling angry that he was retired. He was annoyed that aging had caused society to relegate him to a status of inactivity. Sure, he worked hard to stay busy with all of the things he liked to do, but it wasn't the same. Gardening and swimming were hardly a substitute for honest, salaried labor. What he craved was that deep sense of fulfillment that comes from work as an accountant, providing real and tangible services to others. Hugo's portfolio of work was impressive. He managed his accounts well and built up a vast network of contacts throughout the industry. But what did any of that amount to now? It seemed that all his work and toil had come to nothing, and that was heartbreaking for him to accept. If anyone asked, he loved retirement, but the truth was he could hardly stand it.

"Yes," Hugo said, "being busy is a part of life, and you won't find it in retirement, so you might as well enjoy teaching for what it is, while you can."

"That is an excellent attitude to adopt, big brother. Now tell me, do you think we were always so busy as we were these last few years?"

"Of course we were. I remember when I was working as an intern for a big bank and attending classes at UW at the same time."

"Right, and I had my teaching practicums and then student teaching. Those were very busy times."

"Yes, precisely because you and I were at the beginning of our careers and still figuring things out. With time, you learned to become a more efficient teacher, to plan, grade, and instruct with increasing speed and efficacy. I learned how to practice accounting more efficiently as well. What happened next? Our jobs had responsibilities added to them as we improved. I took on a larger workload. You became the head of your school's science department, yes?"

"Correct. I became the department head, which meant I played a major role in the selection of curriculum and the delivery of instruction. My responsibilities certainly increased, big brother!"

"As you gained responsibilities, you only continued to improve. Pretty soon, after a few years, you were at the top of your game. You and I were the best at doing what we were doing, right?"

"Right! Oh, this is making me excited."

"So, really," Hugo concluded, "you are currently at the best place that you can be. You are on the top of the teacher food chain. Your knowledge and skills are at their peak levels. Of course, this will change after another year of teaching. You should spend as much time as you can being a teacher, because, despite the suffering or hardships you may experience day in and day out, this is the best place you can be. There is nothing waiting for you on the other side of retirement. Nothing at all."

"You really think so?"

"I know so because I have made the transition myself. So enjoy yourself, and know that I wish I could be in your position."

"But, big brother, don't you think it's possible to stay occupied, to continue to grow well into the retired years?"

Hugo sighed. "I don't know. I have done my best to continue to live in a fulfilling way. But at times, it feels like I am just biding my time before I die."

"What a dark way to look at things!"

"I mean, I don't know what I am growing at other than petty little hobbies. My mind and body are only getting older every year. I am slowing down."

"You may be slowing down, but that doesn't mean you can't do so with grace, that you can't continue to grow even as you slow down."

Hugo looked at him skeptically. "I don't think what you are describing is possible. Are we at the top now?"

All at once, the ground had become flat. Hugo, who was looking at his feet and focusing on the conversation he was having, turned his head up and had his breath taken away. The view before them offered a panoramic take of what seemed to be the entire world. For miles in every direction, they were able to look, seeing the lake below like a blue orb, the red hills sprawling endlessly outward. The houses and buildings of the town were little more than tiny boxes below. The air possessed a thin quality and the breeze was softly gentle. In all, Hugo thought the hike was quickly justified by this view.

They spent a while standing at the summit, taking photos together, eating the lunches they packed, enjoying themselves immensely. Hugo's thoughts wandered as he started to think about how his conversation with his brother directly paralleled the hike, for what was growing in one's career but climbing a mountain? Like a long hike, navigating the professional world was rigorous, tough, and difficult, but what did it offer at the end but a view that surveyed everything around and a deep sense of reward? Hugo experienced awe in that moment, an awareness of the grandness of things in the world.

A few minutes after they ate, they decided it was time to head back down and get ready for mini golf. As is always the case with hiking up to high elevations, the trek down is much smoother, faster, and easier. It only took a little more than an hour for them to return to the car. The sun was making steady progress across the sky. It was getting warmer by the minute. They drove back along the same winding roads. After a hike and swimming, Hugo was feeling tired, so he closed his eyes and dozed for a little while. It was a sudden awakening when the car pulled into its spot in front of the condo.

They went inside so people could change and get rid of some of the gear they had brought. Then, once they were all gathered together, Martin said, "All right, ladies and gentlemen, it's time for some mini golf!"

"Hooray!" Cassandra exclaimed.

"Are we driving there?" Hugo wondered.

"No, silly. It's just on the other side of the property. We'll walk!"

"Great," Hugo muttered, who was exhausted.

Locking up the condo, they stepped out into the hot day. They walked together in pairs, Hugo walking next to James, but not speaking to him.

"Hey, Martin!" Hugo called.

"What is it, big brother?"

"I'm feeling a little tired. I think I will go back to the condo and rest for a while."

"Okay. Perfectly all right. Will you come to meet up with us later?"

"Sure thing. Where is the mini golf course?"

"It's just over that way," Martin said, pointing.

"Okay, well I will see you soon then."

"Okay!" Martin handed him the key.

Turning around, Hugo marched towards the condo, along the pebbled trail that traced the side of the lake. His head was relatively empty as a result of all the exercise he had gotten. Since he woke up so early, what he wanted desperately was a chance to get some rest.

He approached the door to the condo and unlocked it. Inside, he found his bed and practically collapsed onto it. He was asleep within minutes.

After he woke up, he was not able to recall them with any specificity, but Hugo had experienced troubling dreams.

It was the sort of nap that he woke up from feeling foggy, and it took him twenty minutes and a glass of water in order to feel like himself. The remnants of the dreams hung over him, a dark shroud. Sitting in the chair in the main room of the condo, he experienced the joy of a bit of solitude after having spent so much time in the company of other people. Should he go and join the others at all, or rather simply wait for them to come back? Deciding it was best to be a team player, he put on his shoes, stepped out the back door, locked up, and was on his way.

Yet again he walked across the pebbled trail. In the distance, there were trees, a swing set, and a small beach area where families were swimming. Hugo shuffled along, past the beach area, and on to the grassy field that led to the other side of the peninsula. The sun was shining down directly on him now. Good thing he remembered to apply sunscreen, he thought. He walked through the grass, past several young people playing fetch with a dog, past a boy playing catch with a friend, under the cover of trees when they were available, towards the mini-golf course.

To the right of the paddle board rental facility, not far off, was the course. It was small and not fancy in appearance, but a number of the holes possessed deceptively simple obstacles, as Hugo remembered. He was able to obtain a golf club with no difficulty, for it was a free service of the condo property. He picked out a red ball, which matched the red tie he was wearing. Red was his favorite color. Looking across the course, he saw his family standing around the ninth hole.

"Well, look who made it after all!" Martin bellowed.

"Glad you made it," Barbara said.

"Happy to be here," Hugo replied, clutching his golf club proudly.

"Why don't you go ahead and have a turn?" Martin asked.

"Sure," Hugo said.

He stood over the ball, looking for the hole intently.

"Where is it?"

"Where's what?" Martin asked.

"The hole I am aiming for."

"Oh, you have to hit it through that tunnel over there. It will drop you out on the other side, which is where it is."

"Okay, got it."

He held the club steadily in his hands, looking at the ball. With a swing, he watched the ball bounce off one wall and then another, missing the tunnel completely.

"That's all right," Martin reassured him. "Give it another go."

Frustrated already, he quickly made a stroke with the club and saw the ball bounce off the edge of the mouth of the tunnel, traveling towards where it had started from.

The par for this hole was four. Hugo made it to the hole in seven strokes, and then it took another three strokes for him to knock the ball into the hole. Fortunately, they were not keeping track of scoring. They moved on to the next hole, which was a straight shot past a large windmill.

"I'll go first," Cassandra said, who stood before the ball and made a stroke. The ball moved up past the windmill and into the hole in a single shot. Everyone cheered and applauded.

Daisy, Barbara, and Patricia took turns next, then James and then Martin. Everyone was able to dodge the rotating blades of the windmill. Now it was Hugo's turn. Rattled from his poor performance on the previous hole, he summoned all of the strength and courage he had in him and stood over his ball. Hitting the ball, he watched it move right into the windmill blade, bouncing off it and returning back to where it had begun. Fuming with rage on the inside, he nearly muttered a curse word, but restrained himself, knowing that children were present. He aimed his club again and struck the ball at the windmill, which deflected the ball back at him. Finally, on the third try, the ball moved past the windmill and towards the hole.

He moved the club back and forth gently, calibrating his shot before he took it. Then he executed a stroke and watched the ball pass over the hole. He slammed the ground with his golf club. All he wanted was to finish playing. It was another two strokes before he was able to finish the hole. Everyone else was supportive of his efforts, displaying unimaginable patience.

Because she went first and he went last, Hugo had an opportunity to visit with Cassandra, to learn more about what was going on in her life.

"Are you enjoying your summer?" he asked, hoping to forget about mini golf for a while.

"Yes, I am enjoying it very much."

"What's your favorite thing you have done this summer?"

She thought about it for a moment and then said, "This trip!"

"Good to hear."

"What about you, great-uncle Hugo?"

"I would probably have to say this trip as well. It has been a lot of fun, hasn't it?"

"Yes, it has."

"Are you looking forward to going back to school soon?"

"Yes, I am. I love school!"

"Good girl. Fourth grade...that's a pretty big deal, don't you think?"

"Yes, and then in fifth grade I will be the biggest kid in the school."

"Well, that will be pretty cool."

It was Hugo's turn to hit his ball. He took a break from talking with Cassandra to do so, no longer angry that the ball was not remotely going where he had wanted it to. Then it was Cassandra's turn. After she had gone, they continued to chat.

"What are you looking forward to about fourth grade?" Hugo asked.

She thought about it and said, "Music!"

"Your concert was great."

"Thanks, great-uncle Hugo. Next year we get to play band instruments."

"Really? What instrument do you want to play?"

"Trumpet."

"Really? Why?"

"Because Miles Davis is really cool. I want to play the trumpet and be like him. "

Hugo, the avid fan of jazz, replied, "That certainly is a good reason. He has made some terrific music."

"Will you come to my band concert next year?"

"Yes, of course."

"Great!"

"What else are you looking forward to about fourth grade?"

"I want to do a lot of reading."

"Excellent. Anything in particular?"

"I want to read mystery novels."

"Those sure are fun to read!"

They continued to talk in this way throughout the round of mini golf. It was Hugo's aim to be supportive, caring, and enthusiastic when he talked to Cassandra. In effect, she was his own granddaughter. Martin was successful in making Hugo feel like he was a part of his family, and for this, he had to be grateful, especially considering how mean Hugo had been to Martin when they were kids. Despite any bitterness or jealousy, Hugo still felt a sense of ownership over Cassandra. He was invested in her success, and he often offered, unsolicited, advice to James and Barbara concerning how best to raise her. But perhaps Hugo's favorite reason for talking to Cassandra was because it reminded him of what it was like to be a child, enabling him once more to live in that magical world. One day, if Adrian had a child, Hugo would strive to be the very best grandfather in the world. For the time being, he was somewhat content to pour his love over Cassandra.

At last, after many trials and struggles, Hugo had survived and completed the mini-golf course. Still tired, he had a sudden desire to have a glass of wine, to drift off a little bit. This was curious, for he did not often crave alcohol.

"Well, that was a lot of fun, wasn't it?" Martin suggested.

"It was, Martin," Daisy assented.

"Wonderful to hear! So here's the plan now, everyone. I am thinking we head back to the condo, rest up for a minute, and then head into town for a little bit. Sound good?"

"Sounds great!" everyone but Hugo chimed.

It was shaping up to be a rather full day, Hugo thought. But this was part of the way Martin ran his vacations: each day was packed to the brim with adventures because spending time doing anything else was a waste. They walked back to the condo. Hugo went into his room and sat on the bed. It felt like only a few minutes had passed before Martin was calling everyone to get ready to go.

Stepping outside, Hugo climbed once more into the front seat of the van. Martin hopped into the driver's seat and looked at him, smiling.

"We're off!" he called.

The car navigated through the condo property and headed out on the main road, driving along the edge of the lake towards town. It was the hottest time of day now. Light from the sun reflected off the lake in a shimmering, glistening display. The car sped along, Martin eager to drive quickly, and soon the town was coming into view. Martin parked the car next to a fountain and they all climbed out. Some clouds were visible in the sky above, but the sun reigned supreme.

Nearby was a large bridge that crossed a river. The river fed into the lake itself. They walked towards the bridge and stopped to take photos on the bridge, for the view it afforded of the entire lake was sweepingly stunning.

"If you look just over there," Martin said, pointing, "you can see our condo."

"I don't see it," Cassandra said.

"It's there!"

"Right over there, sweetie," James spoke, also pointing.

But Hugo, again, was thinking of other things. At that moment, he was preoccupied with the very idea of bridges, how they linked two things together, serving as a transition. He knew he went through many transitions in his life: child to teen, teen to young adult, young adult to husband, husband to parent, and parent to retiree. But where did that leave him now? He was experiencing the sensation that, as he stood on the bridge, he was in the midst of a transition himself. He knew where he had come from, but he had no idea where he was headed. What waited for him on the other side? What was it about vacations that caused him to feel so reflective all of a sudden?

After they walked across the bridge, they continued on a main drag of the town. Chelan was small. There was a little bustle of cars heading one direction and another. Other people, many of them no doubt tourists, were out walking about, taking photos, all seemingly drawn towards the views of the lake. Hugo and the others were walking past a café, and several restaurants, towards a park, an open green space.

Walking next to James, Hugo started to talk to him, asking, "So how's the bookstore?"

"It's all right. This time of year can be pretty good. Lots of kids doing their summer reading. By the time late August comes around, we get a rush of kids who are picking up books for their school classes, so that helps. But like I think we talked about before, it is difficult to compete with electronic markets."

"That is good to hear. I always worry that kids aren't reading like they used to."

"Oh, reading is very much alive and well. We certainly sell a lot of young adult books."

"Young adult books? What are those?"

"It's a genre of books intended for teens. They contain a lot of themes of teen life such as rebellion, growing up, and being true to yourself. I can't think of any titles to name off the top of my head, but they sell really well. I've read a number of them myself, and I gotta say I actually enjoyed them a fair bit."

"They sound horrible."

"Why do you say that?"

"What kids and teens need is to be enriched," Hugo preached. "They should be reading the classics. Why are

166

they wasting time with this artificial trash when the really good stuff is already out there, waiting to be discovered?"

"It's not trash, uncle Hugo, it —"

"It sounds to me like someone decided to make a quick buck off of young people by making up a genre for them to read, and it is preventing them from reading the stuff that is actually good for them."

"But don't you think that young adults need to be cared for and nurtured in a special way? Don't' you think what they need is books that speak to their own experience?"

"No, I don't think so. What I think is that they should read the same things that kids have read for generations, and that is the classics. When we were kids that is what we read."

"Don't you think the world is changing? That what kids need from their books is changing?"

"I agree that the world is changing, more so than I would like, but I don't think this is something that needs to change. What seems obvious to me is that certain companies and authors are making money off exploiting vulnerable teens, and that is despicable!"

"Making money is part of the business. It's not the teens who are losing money, it's the parents, and it's not exploitation, it's a special form of nourishment."

"Call it what you want," Hugo said while straightening his posture, "I stand behind my assessment of things. You won't see me reading any of those books."

"Well, they aren't really intended for you. Different groups of people have different kinds of books for them."

"Really? You believe that? Because it is my conviction that quality is quality, simply stated, and that all books are for all people."

"Sure, but I'm not going to see you reading a romance novel, am I?"

"Probably not."

"And nor will I see you reading a young adult book. So, therefore, there is such a thing as taste and preference, and that's okay."

"I still believe quality is quality, wherever it is found."

"So do I."

167

It may have seemed as though the banter and the back-and-forth between Hugo and James were tense, but in actuality, it was merely a part of the Larson family culture of discourse and discussion. The members of the family were happy to have debates, to talk about a subject of conversation from multiple angles. It was not uncommon for participants to change views in the middle of an argument. James, in particular, was drawn towards such conversations. Growing up, he was a rather rebellious adolescent, one who had debated endlessly with Patricia and Martin, about bedtimes, chores, and allowances. Many in the family thought that he would go on to attend law school. However, his love of reading, together with a savvy sense of business drew him towards opening his own bookstore. Despite the struggles and difficulties he highlighted when talking to family, he was truly a successful businessman.

James and Hugo were watching the girls run about the green space, playing catch with a Frisbee.

"The world sure is changing quickly," Hugo said, brooding.

"You think so?"

"I can't imagine the world these girls are growing up in. I don't recognize it."

"Why not?'

"All the technology. The phones, computers, and tablets, it is changing things. Plus, the world is much more violent than it has been in years."

"I think you've been watching too much of the news," James challenged. "If you think about history, The Cold War was a source of immense violence and suffering. Sure, we have our own unique challenges for today, like terrorism, but I don't feel like the world is any less safe than it has ever been."

"You're right. The world has consistently been unsafe," Hugo smiled.

"Besides, the solutions to the violence exist."

"It's true. Good diplomacy and tactical, minimal military action when necessary would solve most of the problems."

"But at the same time," James added, "there is a certain timelessness to all the wars. It's in the Bible. There will always be war. In the 20th century, we have seen our fair share of wars, but it's no different than any other century, really."

"Except that we now have the technology available to annihilate every living thing on the planet."

"Well, there is that."

"Just because a book written two thousand years ago says there will always be war does not mean that it has to be that way. One shouldn't believe in some sort of divine inevitability."

"Maybe so, but the track record of history is in pretty good harmony with what the Bible says."

"Perhaps so, but we need to hope for a better world," Hugo answered, now feeling empowered. "Even if we are in fact doomed, it is human nature to aspire to something better, a better life for our children and grandchildren."

"That is surprisingly idealistic and optimistic of you, uncle Hugo."

"It's just me being as realistic as I can be. I know I can be a bit of a cynic, but I need something to believe in."

A little while later and the girls had had enough of throwing the Frisbee, and the group continued on walking. The houses and buildings of downtown Chelan were old and worn-looking. Hugo was feeling particularly irritated at James, at how gifted he was in debating issues. Normally, the discussion and the people having the discussion were kept separate from one another, but today Hugo felt resentment towards his nephew, and in turn, he felt resentment towards the world itself. He hated how chaotic and messy the world was, how unsafe it was. All of it seemed so unnecessary to him: humans slaughtering one another for no apparent reason beyond ideological orientation, which to him was a petty reason for fighting in the first place. Disregarding these feelings, he was hungry. Maybe a glass of wine would take the edge off, he pondered.

They approached a restaurant: Mike's Diner. It seemed benign enough, he decided. Entering the restaurant, they had a seat outside. By now, it was truly hot out, Hugo sweating a fair amount.

They ordered their food and enjoyed one another's company. Hugo had his long sought after glass of pinot gris. As he sipped it, he felt himself slip away a little bit. Throughout his life, he enjoyed drinking responsibly and casually. In college, he did not have a drop to drink until he was old enough, instead settling for coffee. It was his philosophy that alcohol was a nice treat and that it was nothing more than that. Abusing alcohol, he thought, was easy enough to do, and so a healthy sense of caution was always justified when approaching the substance. Hugo's own father abused booze to the point of becoming utterly dysfunctional, and so Hugo always took it very seriously. It was his intent, as a way to honor his father, who was long dead, to always drink in a responsible, restrained manner, to only have one drink per day. When Hugo was raising Adrian, he was conscientious of his drinking habits. Hoping to set a positive model for his son, he rarely enjoyed a glass of wine at the dinner table, and often enough he didn't drink at all. Adrian, Hugo was proud to know, hardly touched the stuff.

For a long time, they sat at the outdoor table of Mike's Diner, the sun now beginning to make its descent. Hugo thought about how far away he was from so many things. He watched the people who walked along the streets, who were from all over the country and even the world, and he imagined for a moment that he was somewhere like Mediterranean Europe. There was a warm touch to the breeze that threatened to knock their napkins off the table. For the first time in quite a while, Hugo felt at peace. He looked out at the view of the street, the lake hovering in the background, the red hills even farther back. He was, he knew, surrounded by people who he loved, and who loved him.

Eventually, Martin announced that it was time to head back to the condo. They paid the bill and walked back into the warm air. Hugo adjusted his sunglasses and walked beside Patricia. A magic was hanging in the air as the town prepared for the falling night. Orange light reflected off the sides of the buildings. The stores were emptying of people as the bars and restaurants began to fill up for the evening. They reached the car and pulled back once more onto the narrow road, which at this point was as familiar to Hugo as any road he ever knew.

The sunset was beginning to unfold as the car pulled up in front of the condo. Behind the red hills, the sun was making its disappearance. The family along with Daisy headed out to the back of the condo, where there were a table and chairs.

Watching the sunset, Hugo thought about the idea that he himself was inhabiting a nighttime of his own. Night, with its darkness and unknowable features, was a state of being that complemented Hugo well. The sensation of wandering through the blackness, reaching out and feeling for things, captured how Hugo was feeling. There he went again, he told himself, being so reflective. What for?

Seated next to Patricia, he asked her, "How has the summer been for you?"

"Busy," she replied, "lot's of work."

"I understand that."

"Then there is also what happened in June."

"You mean Matilda's passing?"

She nodded.

"I'm so sorry," Hugo said. "That must have been really hard on the family."

"Yes, but it is how life goes, as they say."

"True enough."

"But you're right. It was really hard. As you know, she had cancer. Horrible disease."

"It really is. Did she suffer much?"

"Very much. They had her on steroids, doing sessions of chemo, and working closely with a specialist doctor. She suffered for months and months."

"I'm so sorry," Hugo said.

"I'm just glad that Cassandra got to know her a bit before she passed."

"Yes, that is a good thing."

Feeling under the full spell of Chelan, the caring support of his family, he was ready to share. He decided it was worth talking about, though he resolved to keep his emotions in check.

"You know I have been struggling myself," he said.

"I know," she said, running a hand through her hair. "It was January, right?"

"Right."

"How have you been doing?"

"Not great. I have found myself feeling very angry and bitter at times. I don't know how to deal with it."

"Martin mentioned he had had some conversations with you about it. "

"Yes, and I was not always the most kind during those."

"It is understandable. Death is a lot to deal with for anyone."

"That is an understatement."

Patricia smiled. "I don't always know how to have these conversations. I try to say what's on my mind, but sometimes I say silly things, like just right now."

"It's all right."

"Martin mentioned getting you in touch with Christopher. Would you be open to that?"

"Yes, I would be open to it."

"That is good. He does very good work. At least that's what I am told."

"I don't doubt that he does excellent work. He is a trained professional. What I am more nervous about is the idea of sitting on a couch and sharing all my anguish with another human for an hour at a time. That doesn't really appeal to me."

"Therapy is not always easy. It is hard work. But it is good, and it leads to real progress."

"Sure it does. But I don't really have things sorted out."

"What do you mean?"

"How I am doing, what I am feeling, what I am experiencing, none of it has been hardened into a concrete form yet. I don't feel ready for therapy."

"You can wait before you start," she said, "but don't feel like you have to have it all together before you begin. Remember, that's why you are doing therapy, to sort through things with another person who can help you figure things out."

"I suppose that is true."

"I think it will be very good for you. You know we all just want to be here to support you in any way we can as you are going through this tough time."

And Hugo began to softly cry.

"It's all right," she said.

"I know," Hugo said, his voice shaking. "Everything is all right. That's what everyone keeps telling me, but I feel like I am living in hell. She is in heaven, and I am in hell. One minute, I am angry, the next I am happy and content. It feels like I am betraying her when I feel happy, like it is wrong."

"Why do you think it is wrong? Don't you think she would have wanted you to be happy, even if she wasn't there to experience it with you?"

Hugo looked up at the hills and then said, "I was never a very happy person in life. So much of what did make me happy was her, and she was stripped from me, just like that."

"I understand that," she said. "What do you remember about her?"

Around them, the others were talking, laughing, carrying on conversations about one thing and another. Here was Hugo, crying, wiping the snot from his nose, completely bare and open. But didn't it feel good to be vulnerable? Taken back by what she had asked, he thought carefully about his answer to her question.

"What I remember about her is her smell, which seems like a weird thing to remember. It was a sweet scent, like cinnamon, that attached itself to everything she wore. I remember the colorful clothes she wore. I remember her calm, serene manner. What I remember more than anything else is her laugh. It was high-pitched and filled with passion. When she laughed, the world stopped for a moment."

"Mmhmm."

"But the truth is that, even in the last six months, I am forgetting more and more about her every day. It gets harder and harder for me to picture her face. Those green eyes, the black hair, it's starting to blur a little bit. Forgetting what her

173

face looks like makes me feel like a traitor, so I look at photographs of her, which can make me cry or smile."

"You're not a traitor. You're a human being. Part of living is coming to terms with death. I'm not trying to tell you what to do or how to live your life, but what I am telling you is that your life is far from over. She was a big part of your life, and that will always be true, but it is possible for you to still live a life that honors her even in her absence."

"You really think so?"

"I do."

"I just don't see it that way," he said. "When she died, my life froze in place. How am I supposed to progress without her?"

"You don't have to 'progress'. You just have to go on living. There will inevitably be highs and lows, joys and sorrows. The last month has been a lot for Martin and me, what with my mother's passing. I can't act like I haven't felt the precise same way you do now at times, but you need to figure out how to move forward while still looking backward in remembrance."

"That sounds like a tall order."

"Yes, but it is doable. People around the world, throughout history, have dealt with loss. Have you spent any time thinking about that? In all the earth, among all the people who have lived, people have had to wrestle with loss. Does that comfort you at all?"

He had a sip of wine. "Not really," he said. "Because no one had what I had."

"But don't you think that, maybe, some people have had something that was similar to what you had?"

"No," he answered. "No one has been close to having what I had."

"Well, I'm sorry you feel that way."

They returned to the condo. Long ago the sun had disappeared behind the hills, the final rays of light glowing in a gentle, delicate flash. Darkness was creeping over the surface of the lake, which looked cold and metallic, and was reaching towards Hugo and his family. The mosquitoes were vanishing and it was getting colder by the minute. The sounds of other condo tenants talking and laughing could be heard. Hugo started to think about his situation. They still had another three days to be at the condo. What else was in store for him during his time here?

Martin walked over and stood by Hugo. "I have a challenge for you, big brother."

"And what is that?"

"The girls —Daisy and Cassandra — want to see who is the fastest swimmer between you and me."

"Martin, it's late and cold. I'm exhausted."

"No need to hide cowardice, big brother," Martin said, smiling.

"What are the terms of the race?"

Martin pointed towards the lake. "See that buoy? Whoever can swim to it first and then return back will be declared the champion swimmer. Sound good?'

Figuring that he had nothing to lose and everything to gain by defeating his brother, aware of the absurdity of the activity he was about to participate in, he went inside and changed into his trunks.

The buoy was faintly visible in the hushed night. The two brothers stood behind a stick that was declared the starting line by Cassandra. On the count of three, they proceeded to trot towards the water. Hugo dove into the water with a clean, streamlined form and proceeded to take strokes. Exhausted, he realized that he was moving a lot more slowly than he had been earlier that day. He couldn't sense where Martin was, but he was taking no chances. He swam with full force. The water was unfathomably cold, chilling him deeply. At last, he reached out a hand and touched the buoy. Turning around and summoning his strength, he continued on his way. Nearly colliding with Martin, he maneuvered to the left to avoid him. Pleased that he was in the lead, he kept swimming, feeling that his arms had become as heavy as lead.

He reached the shore, ran up the grassy hill, and passed over the wooden stick in triumph. Not far behind there came Martin. There was much cheering and applauding for both participants.

"It's all part of any complete vacation," Hugo heard Martin declare.

Later that night, after everyone else went to bed, Hugo was outside, wearing a sweater and his pajama pants, soaking in the night. He sat in the coldness, thinking about how his day started and ended with swimming. Certainly, all of the conversations he had had throughout the day had given him plenty to think about, particularly his conversation with Patricia.

Beyond the occasional lit lamp, all was dark. It was quiet and still in a way that was unattainable in Seattle.

Alone, Hugo gazed into the deep night, wondering if, after all, there was a way for him to move forward in his life without her.

August

Two things were clear: it was hot out, and the lawn needed mowing.

Summer was in full effect throughout Washington. The daily temperature was hovering in the 80's, getting close to the 90's for days at a time. The air was dry. Weeks passed without precipitation, with only an occasional day getting any substantial cloud coverage at all. Indeed, every day the sun was shining down on the city, contributing its scorching heat. All Hugo wanted to do was stay inside.

The day had started off simply enough, with him being focused on doing laundry. As he pulled his clothes out of the washing machine, he sniffed them and thought about the scents. Then he went up into his bedroom, where he folded his clothes and put them away. Where, he wondered, had he accumulated so many clothes? Deciding that it would most likely be best to do so, he made an extra pile of clothes he would take to the local thrift store one of these days.

Then he did something he did not often do. Feeling lethargic, tired, and weak for no reason in particular, he climbed into his bed, shut the blinds, and decided to take a nap. But no sleep came to him. Rather, he drifted between levels of consciousness without ever decidedly falling asleep. The experiences and sensations were unpleasant. He rolled from one side to the other, clutching the blanket tightly. In the semi-dark room, he tossed and turned. This went on for about an hour. It was so hot he could hardly stand it. In fact, he had considered temporarily relocating his bedroom to a room on the first floor of the house, but this sounded like an awful lot of work.

Eventually, he realized and accepted that no sleep was going to come to him. He felt disoriented. Here it was, the middle of the day, and he was in bed. What was most common in Hugo's lifestyle was to wake up early, stay active and awake all throughout the day, and then to finally go to bed late at night. Today that natural sleep-wake cycle was disrupted. No sleep was going to come; it simply wasn't in the cards.

There was the sound of a knock at the front door, which he could hear even up the stairs and through a door. He knew who it was, and that he really ought to go and answer it, but he also knew that he didn't have to. It was by no means an emergency. He was expecting this visitor, for they had scheduled this time to meet, and looking at the clock he could see that it was 3:00 pm. He did, however, feel guilty at the thought of not answering the door.

He motioned to get out of the bed, but he was not able to. For some reason, due to forces beyond his understanding, he was stuck in place. There was no physical barrier to his getting up, so it must have been in his mind, he thought. His brain was telling him to stay put, to close his eyes, and shut out the hot, encroaching world outside. So he remained there, his eyes closed, digging deeper beneath the covers. Yet it was far too hot to be under covers, and he was beginning to sweat. This is comfortable, he reasoned to himself, isn't it?

Once more there was the sound of a knock at the door: three quick, courteous knocks. The sense of urgency felt real to him, but so did the call of the bed. It was agonizing for him, for it felt as though he was being pulled in two opposite directions at the same time. What had gotten into him? After all, such behavior on his part was so very out of the norm. Typically, Hugo was an active man who strove to be occupied and busy, pleased to live in such a way.

He was sweating through the covers, tossing and turning, his eyes closed. It seemed like the walls of the room were closing in on him. It was so hot that he could hardly think.

A few more minutes passed with him lying in this way. There was no more knocking at the door, and just as its sound vanished, so too did his dread about answering. Now he was free to be in bed for as long as he liked.

Surprisingly, he did fall asleep. He woke up and looked to see that it was now half past three. At once, he rose from the bed, casting the covers aside with force. He walked downstairs and poured himself a glass of water. As he imagined it, he was likely dehydrated from all the sweating he had done, and it was now the warmest time of day. Thankfully, it was much cooler downstairs. The last few days had been so hot he had not been able to do much for his garden.

Again someone was knocking on the door.

Hugo walked through the kitchen, into the living room, and then up to the front door. He looked through the little hole in the door to see who it was, and it was precisely the person he had been expecting earlier: Rex, the son of Dave the doctor.

He opened the door quickly. "Hello," he greeted.

"Hi," said Rex, who was already radiating an aura of moodiness. "I came by earlier, but you didn't answer. My mom told me to come back."

"And I'm glad you did," Hugo said, trying to smile but failing. "If you'll follow me, I'll take you to the mower."

Hugo's backyard was not large, but it had an enchanting charm to it. The roses were looking lovely, and there was a big tree in the center of the yard, old and worn-looking. Lining the perimeter was a white fence with chipping paint. Along the back, above the fence, there was the cover of trees, preventing one from seeing any of the other lawns.

A small shed stood in the back right corner of the yard. It was painted a blue that matched the house. Hugo led Rex towards it. Inside, there were musty, earthy smells. Along the walls, there were gardening supplies hanging: a rake, shears, gloves, a hat, and a hoe among other things. There were plenty of pots sitting in the corner of the shed. Nearby, there was a push mower, which looked broken but wasn't.

"Here it is," Hugo said, picking it up.

"Thanks, Mr. Larson."

Hugo could have corrected Rex and told him to refer to him by his first name, but he didn't. He found such a spirit of formality to be nice and enjoyable, for it reminded him of his working days.

"Now, if you'll follow me with it..." They stepped out of the shed and into the backyard. The sun was pouring down fiery rays. Even the air itself was warm, carrying with it a sense of lightness. The old man and the boy stood in the shade of the tree.

"You can start by covering over this backyard," Hugo said. "This thing may look like it's about to fall to pieces, but if you give it a good push you will see results. Any questions?"

"No."

"Then begin."

Rex proceeded to push the mower around the perimeter of the lawn. Hugo went up onto the back deck, and into the house to pour himself a glass of water. In the kitchen, he stood by the window and sipped his beverage. For reasons he couldn't explain, he had an urge to have a glass of wine, just one. He went and poured himself a glass of chardonnay to go along with his water. Then he had a seat at the kitchen table. Sipping on his drinks, he was reminded of Chelan.

For a while he sat, taking sips from his drinks, able just barely to see Rex laboring in the sun. It made Hugo feel good to know that he was able to facilitate honest labor for another person, even if that meant less work for himself. Sovereignty, the ability to say that he could do all that he needed to by himself without help, was something that he held in high regard, but he hated mowing the lawn. Rex's mother had seemed resolute about him coming over, so Hugo had obliged her. As he sipped on the wine he sensed a faint buzz come over him. Things seemed to melt away just a little bit.

A little while passed and his glass of water was half empty. He rose from the table, grabbed a pitcher, and filled it. Opening the freezer door, he poured some cubes into the pitcher for added effect. Then he refilled his own glass and poured water into another glass. Feeling charitable, he stepped outside with the extra glass and walked towards Rex, who had nearly completed his circuit.

"Here's something to cool off with," he said, handing a glass to the boy. "It's so blasted hot out."

"Thanks, Mr. Larson."

Hugo turned his head one way and then the other. "It looks good out here, like it's coming along."

"That's all I can hope for."

"Will you be ready for the front yard soon?" Hugo entreated, smiling.

Rex took in a deep breath. "Yes, I will be," he said.

Several minutes later and Rex was done with the backyard. Hugo stood and watched him finish the job. He gestured with his hand for the boy to follow him, and they walked through the side yard and towards the front.

The sunlight was practically reflecting on the pavement. Each house was a shelter, an abode tucked away from the brutal heat. No children were out playing today. Cars passed only occasionally. For a second, Hugo surveyed his garden in the front yard, feeling a fondness for each of the many colorful plants and flowers that thrived under his care. It made him proud to claim this plot of land as his own.

Turning to face the boy, who was covered in sweat, he instructed him to continue mowing. Being bossy reminded Hugo once more of his working days. It was Hugo's hope that the direct sunlight would purge Rex of his moody aura, and so it seemed to. Rex spoke more expressively, using more words, and making a wider variety of facial expressions than he had at the dinner party so many weeks before.

Hugo walked about the garden, inspecting a flower here, touching a plant there. Behind him, he heard the sound of Rex pushing the mower and breathing deeply. Hugo took the two empty glasses and placed them at the base near the front door. Next, he went inside and back into the kitchen. He had a seat at the table, agitated, and had another sip of wine. His daily glass of wine was nearly gone, but that was all right. He had a faint desire to have more to drink, but he knew that acting on this urge only led to trouble, and his will was strong. Rising from the table, he stepped back outside.

He walked towards his orange roses that were in full bloom. Placing the stem of one rose in his hand, he was careful not to touch any of the thorns. He lowered his head and sniffed the flower, delighted by the fresh scents. Strangely enough, the smell of the rose reminded him of just-washed laundry.

Looking up from the rose, he saw Paul tending to his own garden. Hugo waved a hand and greeted him.

Rex was finished mowing. Hugo went up and placed a hand on his shoulder. "Well done," he said. "It was hot out here, but you did a good job."

Rex, who didn't seem to like having a hand on his shoulder, forced a smile.

Hugo said, "Please, come in for a few minutes. Have another glass of water."

They made their way back into the house. It seemed to Hugo like he was entering and exiting the house far too many times, but this was how it always was on days when he did anything that involved the yard or garden.

They sat at the table. Hugo stood up and poured another glass of water from the pitcher. "It's important to stay hydrated on days like this, you know."

"I know."

Hugo sat down again. "You're not old enough to drink wine, are you?"

"No, I am not."

"That is a shame, for a glass of wine on a day like this is quite nice. But, if you'll believe it, a glass of water is even nicer."

"I do believe that."

They sipped their water. Hugo wondered if the boy was going to get up and leave suddenly. But he didn't. Rex stayed put, making slow progress on his own water.

"I have a request," Rex broke the silence.

"What is it?"

"If you don't mind, I would like to play your piano."

There was a glow in Hugo's eyes. "Why, yes, that would be marvelous. Let me show you where the piano is."

They rose from the table, walked back into the living room, and into the study. The piano was small and unimpressive. The wood was worn from years of passing from one owner to another, but the instrument still functioned as well as any. Hugo stepped to the side and stood by the bookshelf.

"Please, play as much as you like. Do you mind if I watch?"

"No, I do not mind."

Rex had a seat, cracked his knuckles, and began to play, offering a rendition of Debussy's "Arabesque 1", which sounded lovely. Hugo swooned as he heard the playing. This was the first time in months that anyone had played the piano. It was as though the piano was dead, and now life was being injected back into it—pure, flooding, explosive life. Hugo was grinning as he listened. In particular, he appreciated the incredible sense of gentleness, the delicate way in which Rex played, treating each note as though it was of illustrious importance. Hugo hung onto the notes, deriving comfort and peace from them.

"Well done, well done," Hugo cried, as he had a seat on the bench next to him. "I am impressed that you know that song by heart."

"Why shouldn't I? It occupies a place close to my heart."

"Makes sense to me. If I look here..." Hugo reached into a bin that contained books of sheet music. "I should be able to find it...yes, here it is." He placed a book of Debussy on the piano. "You know, I have always loved Debussy's music myself, but it has been so long since I heard it played in this house."

Rex picked up some sheet music and began to play "Arabesque 2", the companion piece. His playing was a bit rough; he missed several notes and had to slow the tempo down considerably, but it was still recognizable. After all, the piece Rex was playing was much more technically demanding than the one he had earlier played, though no more or less lovely. Eventually, after about a minute of playing, Rex stopped.

"I can't," he said.

"No," Hugo corrected, "that sounded great. Please keep playing. I am impressed that you can play such a difficult piece."

"All right."

Rex stared at the music with an intent focus and then continued to play, still fumbling over the notes, but getting through it. By the time he finished the piece, he felt exhausted, but he also was overjoyed, because he had once again encountered why he loved playing the piano so much.

"That sounded great," Hugo praised. "What else do you know?"

They spent the bulk of the afternoon seated on the bench, Rex playing songs, sharing what he knew and what he only partially knew. Rex clearly had a larger understanding of classical music. As he played, they bonded in the magic of the music. Hugo learned that Rex's dad Dave was actually his stepfather, and Hugo shared that his own parents had nearly separated at a time in his life, but that their marriage endured. Rex shared also that he had struggled with depression, and that music was an antidote, that it had kept him away from negative influences when he was in high school. They chatted, learning more about each other, and eventually, it was time for Rex to be off.

Hugo opened the door for him and noticed that it was cooling off. The sun was setting behind the cover of a particularly tall tree. Hugo waved to Rex as he walked away. They had agreed that in the next week or two Rex would come back over and that he would mow the lawn again. Additionally, they agreed that he would play more of the piano. Hugo closed the door and walked back into his house. He went into the study and looked through several of the books of music he owned. For a while he sat there, on the floor, leafing through the books, allowing the memories to all return to him, thinking about how often the piano used to be played.

2.

Hugo asked, "Should we go and watch the penguins play?"

"Sounds good to me," Adrian answered.

Hugo took the zoo map in his hands and looked at it carefully. By his estimation, they were on the north end, near the entrance, and to reach the penguins they would have to head south and east, past the lion savannah.

It was yet another scorching August day. The heat made it almost unbearable to be out and about, but it didn't prevent people from enjoying seeing all the animals.

"Follow me," Hugo said.

The father and son walked past a group of small children who were being wrangled together by several chaperones. They headed past a small food court area and Hugo made inevitable comments about the dangers of sugar. They passed a cage that contained several monkeys, and so they stopped to watch.

One of the monkeys, a lemur, was hopping from branch to branch, taunting one of its peers. Hugo watched, wondering what life must have been like for the creature in its natural habitat. Continually the lemur jumped across branches, moving quickly, and it was a source of endless entertainment for the small crowd that was watching. Eventually, Hugo became bored and nudged his son to continue walking.

The left side of the path had shade provided to it by trees, so that was where they walked. There was a turn in the path, and they were headed towards the lion's field. Excited, Hugo sped up his walking.

"This should be pretty neat," he said.

"I bet!" Adrian agreed.

Open, sprawling, the simulated savannah was impressive. Nearby there was a binocular device, and Hugo poked his head inside of it, eager to see some lions. Scanning left and right he looked, but he was unable to see any.

"Maybe they're in the shade, sleeping," Adrian suggested.

But Hugo was skeptical. "We'll see one soon enough," he said.

Still, he was looking through the binoculars when all of a sudden he saw a lion. On a long, smooth rock, lying quietly and still, was a lion, beautiful in all of its glorious splendor.

"There it is!" Hugo exclaimed.

"Let me see."

Hugo shared the binocular device.

Understandably, Hugo's enjoyment of the outdoors led him to tap into his own inner child whenever he was at the zoo. There were feelings of passion, eager expectation, and joy that accompanied him every time he visited this place, the aquarium, or the botanical garden. It was not something he could really explain, something that he could put into words, but he knew the feelings were real. Most of the time, Hugo felt old, but it was on choice occasions such as this that he felt young, possessing a sprightly energy. He was happy to spend all day long at the zoo, going from one exhibit to another, and it brought him an additional, special joy to be able to share all of this with his own son. Growing up, Adrian had been taught to admire the outdoors and to care for animals, in the same way his father so genuinely did.

So the father and son took turns looking through the binoculars. Adrian took out his phone and attempted to snap a photo of the lion.

"Take one of us together."

"Sure thing."

Adrian held the phone up, changing the setting so he could see his reflection in the camera, and snapped several photos of his father and him, the lion sleeping lazily in the background

"This is so neat," Hugo said. "That thing is the absolute king of the wild. To be able to see one up close is an amazing experience."

"It sure is."

They kept walking, now getting close to where the penguins were.

"I'm glad you were able to come here with me," Hugo said, "to take some time out from your busy schedule of studying."

"Mmhmm."

"How is that going?"

"You mean the program?"

"Yes."

There was a palpable pause. Adrian seemed to be thinking carefully about the words he was going to use next. Hugo looked at him, examining his thoughtful expression, becoming slightly alarmed.

"You are still doing well in the program, aren't you?"

"Dad..."

"What happened?"

Adrian looked at the ground as they were walking and said, "I quit the program."

"What?"

"I said I quit."

"But why?"

Adrian said, "As you know, the class moved along at a very, um, rapid rate."

"Yes, I did know that."

"The truth is, I was able to keep up with it for a while, but it got to be too much. There came a day when I was sitting there in the lecture, having no idea what they were talking about. I was scoring low on quizzes. I was going home at night with a bunch of homework and I had no idea how to do it. I talked it over with my instructor. He told me he couldn't advise me on what course to take, but he was understanding and accepting of me taking time to think things over."

"'Think things over'?"

"Yes, I spent a week going to class and reflecting on it. I realized that business just isn't for me."

"But...son...you were talking not long ago about how passionate you were about business. You said you wanted to go into finance."

"Yes, and I guess I'm sorry to say that I was wrong."

187

As far as Hugo was concerned, life presented people with challenges, and the whole point of existing was to struggle against these challenges, to buckle down, to work hard, to conquer. This at least was the story of Hugo's own career. So it seemed wrong, un-Larson even, of his son to go and give up.

"Well, that's all fine, but what are you going to do now?"

"Good question."

"What's the answer?"

"I don't know."

"You don't know?"

It was one thing for his son to quit the business program, but another one altogether for him to not have a plan for what he was going to do next. It worried Hugo to think that his son didn't have a career.

"There is always Java City, isn't there?" Hugo wondered.

"Not really."

"Why not?"

"I worked there for so long. I just couldn't bear to go back there. Too many bad emotions associated with that place."

"But, son, you have to work."

"I know, and I am going to figure something out, but right now I could really just use you being understanding of where I am at."

"I am understanding, and what I understand is that you haven't thought things through. You're thirty-three years old. You've spent a third of your life as a barista, and you have no plan for what you want to do with your life. Can't you see how hard I've worked to give you the very best? I made sure there was always a meal on the table. I supported you as you made your way through college, and that degree didn't amount to anything, because here you are, lost."

Adrian, voice shaking, said, "My degree didn't amount to nothing, Dad."

"Well, it certainly seems like it. You've spent your life serving coffee, and you have nothing else to show for yourself. I try to be patient and understanding. That sums things up: I try to be patient and understanding, but you give me so little to work with, Adrian. The truth is that I am disappointed in you. I still love you. I am here for you, to support you in the ways that I can, but I need a bit more from you. You're thirty-three years old. I don't know if you need to work harder, or just work better, but I need more from you. Does that make sense?"

"It does. You know, it hasn't been easy for me. Not knowing what you want to do with your life is not a pleasant feeling. I understand that you were able to figure out that you wanted to do accounting pretty early on, and it's great that you were so successful at it. The truth is I just didn't know what I wanted to do. You know I liked art. I enjoyed taking pictures and shooting weddings, so I studied that, but I really didn't know what I wanted to do. I guess I did this business program for the wrong reasons, because I thought it would make you proud of me, because you would have thought that I was walking in your footsteps."

"I didn't know that that was why you did the program."

"I think it was a big part of why. That, and because society told me that I needed to find a traditional, professional career path, that I needed to start making money. But those are not good reasons to go into something."

"No, they are not."

"But you were lucky. You found what you were passionate about, and it did happen to be a traditional, professional career path."

"It wasn't really a conscious decision," Hugo said. "Going into accounting felt inevitable, like it was destiny that I would start practicing it. The truth is I didn't think about it a lot. By the time I got to UW, I knew that I wanted to get into the business school, and so pretty much one thing followed after another from there. What you say is true, though. It's not about the money. It's about the passion. I know it sounds like a cliché to the point of risking meaning, but in this life, we have to find what we are passionate about. That's all I wanted for you."

"What?"

"I wanted you to find what you were good at, that brought you fulfillment, and for you to pursue that with your whole heart."

"It does sound cliché, doesn't it?"

"But so anyway, you don't think photography is your passion?"

Adrian shook his head. "I don't think so. I just don't see how it could to turn into a job."

"Fair. And you certainly don't think any form of business is your passion."

"Definitely not."

"Then it seems like you have some soul-searching to do, my son."

They left the lion field and were still heading towards the penguins. Everyone they passed, children, parents, young people, all seemed to have one thing in common: they looked happy. Meanwhile, Adrian was trying to wipe tears from his eyes using the sleeve of his shirt. There was a tension between father and son, but they tried instead to focus on what had brought them to the zoo to begin with, which was the animals.

The penguin area comprised a large structure painted like an iceberg with a small pool of water below. Hugo and Adrian stood, watching them, black and white creatures of whimsical fun. As they swam in the water and came up for air. the penguins bumbled around, bumping into each other. They were staring at the sky as though expecting a meal. A few minutes passed and then a man with a net full of fish appeared to feed the penguins. Ravenously hungry, the penguins ate the fish and continued to swim about.

"That's what we're like," Hugo said. "All of us, we are like penguins. We swim a little, trot around a little, and occasionally, when we are lucky, we get a big helping of fish. Really, it's all we can aspire to. You can be a businessman, or a doctor, or a lawyer, or a chef, or something else, but the outcome is the same. If you work hard, you get a big helping of fish at the end of the day."

3.

The morning was wearing on and he was going to be late for his game, a rare occurrence. Having donned his jersey, he went into the kitchen and thought, Sure, why not? He went and poured himself a glass of chardonnay. Sipping the beverage slowly, he thought about how nice it was that the heat had temporarily abated. Now, if it would only rain. The garden was yearning for precipitation.

The wine had a sweet taste to it. It brought him pleasure to drink it, feeling his nerves settling a little with each sip. It seemed that, lately, he was drinking with increased frequency. This, however, did not concern him, for he held himself to just having one drink per day. So long as he met this standard, he didn't think that he was in any sort of danger of overdoing it. Today he met his limit rather early. It was only noon. Still, it didn't seem to matter terribly much to him. Drinking a glass of wine was drinking a glass of wine.

He looked at his watch. It really was time to be getting going, he thought. Rising from the kitchen table, he headed towards the living room. He closed the blinds, opened the front door, checked that all the lights were off, and left his house.

Walking to the bar, he sighed multiple times. There was a dull aching sensation in his chest. It created a sensation of heaviness, as if a weight was pressing down on him. Perhaps because he hadn't eaten, the wine had a particularly strong effect on him. It even caused him to be a little bit dizzy, which was rare for him. It was strange to him that he didn't feel anything today. Anger, sorrow, shock, and nostalgia were all emotions that he became well acquainted with in the past six months. Yet today, for the first time, none of those feelings were present. What he was left with was a belly sloshing with chardonnay.

As he reached the bar he bent down to tie his shoes, and then he entered. Secretly, he was hoping that she wouldn't be here today, the owner of the bar. Uninterested in having any polite conversations with her, he seated himself and looked up at the screen. Already the game was twenty minutes in. His team had the ball and was up 2-0.

"What will it be today?" a man with a scruffy beard asked.

"Just a glass of water, please."

"Sure. Anything to eat."

"No, thank you."

"Sir, I need to ask that you order something off the menu. Do you need time to think?"

Hugo grabbed the menu and leafed through it in seconds. "Onion rings, please."

"Coming right up."

Left to watch his game, he was relieved his team was winning. There was peace in being allowed to enjoy the game without fear of being disturbed. He hadn't seen Lily, the owner, so it seemed unlikely that she was going to come and bother him. Really, what Hugo was interested in was being able to enjoy the game. It had been a while since he had come to the bar. Since he didn't have cable on his television and he wasn't interested in fiddling around with computers, there was no way for him to watch his team play except by coming to this establishment. In fact, it seemed as though it had been months since he had been to this bar, which seemed peculiar.

"Your onion rings, sir."

"Oh, thank you."

Hugo had no interest in eating onion rings.

"Anything to drink?"

Remembering his quota, he replied, "No, thank you."

"Very good."

Looking up at the scoreboard, he was concerned to notice that it was now 2-1, with the other team carrying the ball.

He started thinking about Adrian. It was a little over a week since they went to the zoo together. They had not talked since then. Had he been cruel to him? In his mind, all he did was be honest. Valuing honesty above all virtues, Hugo was true to himself in how he had interacted with his son. Recently, the distance between them changed somewhat, with them communicating more and more. But with Hugo hearing the news that his son had quit the program, he felt such raw emotion, being so upset by the news, that he had had no option but to speak his mind. After all, that was what his son deserved, he thought, to hear an honest assessment of the situation. Who else in Adrian's life was going to be honest with him? As far as Hugo knew, his son didn't have anyone else in his life who served as an older, mature source of wisdom, a guide. But, their time at the zoo was potently tainted by the conversation they had had. An awkward tension still lingered in the air as they said good-bye to each other that day.

Hugo was left to worry. What would his son do? For most of Hugo's life, he had not worried about his son. All throughout his life Hugo believed that things would work out in his son's favor. Yet now that conviction was being shaken to its very core. Adrian was not getting any younger. Was it too late for him to make a new start? What was Hugo's role in being a parent to his son? Would things be figured out? His head was racked with questions as he heard a voice from behind him.

"Enjoying the game?"

It was Lily.

"I um, yes, I am enjoying the game quite a lot."

"You just got here, didn't you?"

"Correct."

"Because the game started a while ago. I must say I'm surprised that you wouldn't be here for the start."

"Yes, well, I had some matters to attend to. How did you know when I got here?"

She laughed. "I see all."

"Right. It is an excellent game, if my team can just hold onto the ball."

"Yes, that certainly is important. Where is your wife? I told you to bring her."

Hugo gulped. "She is deceased."

"Oh, I'm so sorry. I didn't mean to...I'm sorry."

"That's very all right," he said. "Now, if you don't mind, I think I will get back to my game."

"Of course."

She was gone, and he was left to enjoy soccer. A few minutes passed, and then she returned with a glass of red wine.

"You strike me as a wine drinker," she said. "Enjoy, it's on the house. In honor of me insensitively bringing up painful memories."

"I told you that was quite all right. It's part of the past."

"Listen," she said, "I'm about to start my lunch break. Do you mind if I eat with you? I'm not hitting on you, just a widow being friendly towards a widower. I understand if you want to be left alone."

He thought about it. What he had set out to do was enjoy a game of soccer by himself, to get lost in it, and most importantly to be alone. But here he was, being offered the company of someone who might be able to understand his experience, being offered friendship.

"Sure thing. You can eat with me."

She disappeared and then came back with a salad. "I only have thirty minutes or so," she said. "If I disappear long enough, this place starts to fall apart. You know how it goes."

"Sure."

"Do you have any kids?" she asked.

"Yes, a son."

"Very cool. What does he do?"

"He is on a journey of self-discovery."

"Ah, best wishes with that. I have two daughters myself. One is an engineer and the other is a writer."

"Good to hear."

"They are very precious to me. When I lost Sebastian, I thought it was all over for me, but they were very supportive and helped me through a lot of the struggle."

Hugo was wondering why she was being so forward, how she could talk so openly about her dead husband with a man who she hardly knew.

"When did you lose him?"

"About seven years ago."

"Is it still hard?"

She sighed as she had another bite of her salad. "Yes, yes it is."

Then she asked, "When did you lose her?"

"January."

"Oh! So recently. I am so sorry. Now I feel even worse."

"Don't."

"That must be an inconceivable loss to deal with. How have you been faring?"

"Not great," he said while tapping his finger on the table rapidly.

"What is going through your mind? How do you feel?"

She was really getting to the tough questions, he thought.

"I don't feel much. It has only been very recently that I have started speaking about it openly."

"That makes sense. For a while, the pain is so great we don't know what to do with it, so we hold onto it. We let it build up. Then, eventually, it comes out. One way or another, it eventually comes out."

"True." He looked down at the glass of red wine, which he hadn't touched.

"Well, she began, "it is brave of you to talk about it openly. It is a sign of courage. So you should feel good about that, not that there's a lot to feel good about."

"No, there is not."

He was giving short answers. He was having a tough time carrying on this conversation. He was left with nothing to say.

"Are you gonna touch that wine?" she asked.

Breaking his vow for the first time, Hugo had a sip. It tasted bitter.

"Yes," she began, "I lost Sebastian about five years ago. Pancreatic cancer. It was a long fight. He spent two years battling it. We gave him every support we had. It took all of our money. But it seemed like we just couldn't stop the life from being sucked out of him. It was unbearable to watch my husband slowly disappear from me. You surely understand that pain. If I may ask, how did she go?"

"I don't really want to go into it, to be honest."

"That's okay," she said, "the details of it don't matter. What matters is the loss, the lingering absence in our lives of someone we love."

He started to sip the wine more frequently. When he arrived at the bar, his body had nearly processed the chardonnay he had consumed at home. But this red wine brought him back that buzzed effect, that lessened ability to think too long or hard about anything.

"How have you been able to live your life without Sebastian?" he asked.

"Oh, I only have fifteen more minutes. Time flies! I have not always done the best job of living without him. The truth is it has been hard, really hard. How old are you?"

"Sixty-six."

"Right, well I am fifty-nine, and I was fifty-two when he died. I was not really ready for what happened. But that's how it goes. Life doesn't really ask us if we are ready for what it has planned, does it? We take on what life gives us and endure. So, anyway, you are a bit older than I was when I lost Sebastian. There were a lot of things that helped me get through it: meditation, hiking, painting, my daughters, time, those sort of things. But I think time made the biggest difference. I don't really believe that time heals all. Time doesn't do that. What it does do is pass, and as it passes, some things can be easier to deal with. The wound is still real and there, but we become stronger, more aware, and we adjust to living in that absence. Time changes us."

"I suppose it's true what you say about time. But I don't feel like I am patient enough. Hardly any time has passed since I lost her. It has only been seven months. There has not been enough distance created for me to see things with any clarity."

"Mmhmm."

"For a while," Hugo began, "I didn't want to move on. In fact, only very recently, like in the last month or so, have I begun to conceive of living a life without her. But I don't know how to create such a life for myself."

"It's not something we come up with overnight."

What struck Hugo about Lily was the way she spoke, using the word "we" and "us". It came across as very special to him, because it made him realize that she and he were entrenched in the same struggle, the struggle to live amidst death.

"For a while," Hugo continued, "I was angry. I was bitter that she was taken from me. I still am angry and bitter sometimes, if I am being honest, but it's not as bad as it was."

"What do you feel now?"

"A little bit drunk."

They both laughed at this. "What I'm feeling," he continued, "is not much at all. I feel heavy. I feel like life is so difficult and pointless. What's the point of going on if we are going to die?"

"Do you not want to live?"

"No, that's not the case. I want to live. I want more of life. I want life to not end! But it does."

"Yes, but even as short as life is, with all its pain and struggles, there is still purpose to it, isn't there?"

"You don't sound convinced."

She laughed. Her salad was now gone. "I guess I want to hear your thoughts. I believe life is full of purpose, but it sounds to me like you aren't so sure."

"I'm not so sure. I spent my life hard at work, building up to something I thought I could hand off to my son, to pass on to the next generation. That and my relationship with my wife were the source of meaning for me, but both things have been taken from me. My son is nowhere close to having kids or even a career, and she is gone."

"Hugo..."

"Normally, I would cry at this point," he said, "but I haven't cried in a while. It's like I don't' feel anything at all. I am numb. I miss being able to cry when I think of her. Am I forgetting her?"

"I don't think so. Your mind, heart, and body are just processing the loss."

"That sounds like sentimental nonsense."

"It may sound sentimental, but it's a fact. Grief is an emotionally complex process, with all of the feelings being involved."

"Sure it is. I'm sure happiness is involved in grief as well."

"Well, maybe not happiness, but certainly a fondness for remembering things about the lost one."

"That's true. I feel that way sometimes when I look at old photographs."

"See? You're navigating a process, and it takes time. Just don't give up hope on the idea that there is a purpose to all of this, to the human experience, because there is."

"I'm still skeptical about that."

She looked at her phone. "I got maybe two minutes. Let me ask you a question. The answer may seem obvious, but I think it's worth asking: do you feel hopeful?"

"No."

"I understand feeling that way. For years, I felt like there was no hope, that things weren't going to get better. But you know what? They did."

"You felt this way for years? I don't think I can handle that!"

"I'm not saying you are going to feel any way for any amount of time. Every grief journey is a very personal, individual thing. Who knows what your journey has in store? I need to go, but I have another question: what are your sources of support?"

"I'm not sure," he replied, "and you need to get back to work."

"That's true," she said, "but I have really enjoyed having this conversation with you. I feel like we were meant to meet. Anyway, I need to go, but I hope that we can talk soon."

They exchanged phone numbers, though he knew already where he could find her. After saying goodbye, she walked away from him, but then she turned around, her blonde hair shaking.

"One more thing!" she cried.

"What is that?"

"I know I have been giving you a lot to think about, but that question I asked you about the supports, it is important. You need to know where you can find comfort, peace, and strength in your life, whether it is activities, or people, or places. I would encourage you to think carefully about your answer to that question, and to pursue those things."

He finished his glass of wine, watching the game until it was finished. His team lost 3-2.

4.

It was only the early evening, but he was tired. He went into the kitchen and poured himself a glass of wine. It was his second for the day, but he felt no guilt at having adjusted his quota. Many people had more than three or four glasses in a single day, so what was wrong with two?

The chardonnay caused him to be sleepy. He went upstairs, changed his clothes, and got into bed. He was asleep before eight.

Morning came and he resisted getting up out of bed. He stayed where he was, festering in his own thoughts. He looked at the clock and realized that it was an hour past when he said he would meet with Paul. I need to be going, he thought. He summoned the strength that he had and got out of bed.

Having taken his medication and gotten ready for the day, he walked outside, turned left, and went towards Paul's house. He knocked on the door quickly.

Paul opened the door and said, "Morning, sleepyhead."

"I'm sorry. I know I'm late."

"It's all right. I came by earlier and you didn't answer, but it's not a problem. Are you ready to go now?"

"Yes, I am."

Paul seemed to be surveying Hugo. "How are you doing?" he asked.

"Been better."

Hugo had a mild headache, probably a result of lying in bed for such a long time, he had decided. They walked over and got into Paul's car. The car pulled out of the driveway, and sped towards the heart of Wedgwood.

"That's surprising about the loss," Paul remarked. "They had been looking good all season."

"Yes, but that's not even the most surprising thing that happened to me when I was watching the game."

"What was?"

"You see, I have sort of become friends with the owner of the Blue Hen. Her name is Lily."

"Friends?"

"Yes, but just friends."

"Oh, well, that's great." Paul pointed at himself. "Friends are great."

"Yes, they are. She's a widow."

"Oh."

"She seems to have a lot of wisdom about things. She was asking me all these questions and trying to support me. It was really weird."

"How did you become friends with Lily?"

"She started talking to me when I was at the bar. Then I ran into her at the store. I don't know. It's weird."

"That is weird, but kinda nice too, isn't it?"

"What do you mean?"

"Well, you have someone who, while not having the exact same experience as you, has experienced a loss very similar to you, who can help guide you along in ways that I, frankly, can't."

"What do you mean you can't?"

"Well, I haven't lost my wife. We divorced, which is like losing her, but very different. I also sort of lost Janet when she moved to Argentina. I mean, I still get to see her, but so much of our lives are separate. Those two things are the extent of my experience with loss. I don't have quite the same experience as you, at least not like Lily does. It can be hard for me to know how to support you, because I don't always know what you are thinking or feeling."

"Often, I don't feel like I know what I am thinking or feeling, either."

They laughed. They left Wedgwood and were headed north on the freeway, towards Northgate Mall.

"I have started to drink more. Not a lot. Just a little bit more," Hugo said gripping his cat tie.

"How much more?" Paul inquired.

"Two glasses of wine per day instead of one."

"Oh, well that seems pretty harmless."

"I think so, too."

Paul said, "Tell me something interesting."

"About what?"

"Anything."

"You know I'm no good at being a conversationalist."

"Well, tell me about these fancy shoes we're going to pick up."

"If we find the right shoes," Hugo began, "they are blue, with in-sole padding, and have yellow laces. That's all I know about them."

"What's the brand?"

"Don't know."

"What store sells them at the mall?"

"I think Shoez does."

"Shoez?"

"Indeed."

"Isn't that a store for women?"

"No, it is not. It is intended for both genders."

"Sure it is."

"It is!"

"We're just two men, off to buy shoes," Paul sang.

"That is precisely what we are doing."

It wasn't long before they pulled off the freeway, the vast, sweeping mall looming not far off in the distance. The parking lot itself seemed to be bigger in size than all of Wedgwood. They parked in the back, far from the mall, and walked towards it.

Nearly menacing, mammoth in size, the mall was the premier shopping center in Northeast Seattle. Unsurprisingly, Hugo hated coming here. He despised going shopping. But there came times in his life when such an activity was unavoidable, particularly when he needed shoes. His feet were sensitive, and so most shoes made for an uncomfortable fit. Consequently, when he needed new shoes, he bought a particular brand that he couldn't remember the name of.

Effectively, the layout of the mall was one large, long corridor. Streams of people walked up and down this corridor, browsing in shops, making purchases, drinking coffee sold by the stand. Since it wasn't December, the crowds were not as bad as Hugo was anticipating. Still, the signs of mall fatigue were beginning to wear on him, and he had only just entered the mall. I'm getting to be too old for this, he thought.

"So where is Shoez?" Paul asked.

"I don't know. Let's find a map."

"Where is a map?"

They turned their heads one way and then the other, looking for one of the large maps that oriented shoppers, but they didn't see one.

"Let's look over here," Paul pointed.

"No, I think Shoez is this way."

"Are you sure?"

"Yes. You would think they could just put a map in front of the entrance where shoppers are coming through, don't you?"

"You would think so, but you would be wrong."

"Anyway, let's go this way. I think the map is nearby."

"All right," Paul said.

They walked north along the corridor, moving quickly. Smells and scents emanated from each of the stores they passed, evoking different products. But there was no map anywhere in sight.

"Should we turn around?" Paul asked.

"No, I think we are close to the map. Let's keep going. We can't keep walking back and forth or we'll never find anything in this mall."

"Fair enough."

So they kept walking. Pretty soon, the smells of food were in the air. They had reached the northernmost end of the mall: the food court. An abominable combination of lipids, sodium, and processed chemicals, the food court was the stuff of Hugo's worst nightmare. Immediately he experienced an urge to turn around and leave, but he saw a map near the front entrance of the mall.

"There it is," Hugo called.

They shuffled towards the map and examined it carefully. Hugo traced over the map with his finger, looking desperately for Shoez.

"Where is it?" Hugo asked.

"There it is," Paul said.

"Where?"

"At the bottom of the map."

"And where are we?"

Paul laughed.

"Where are we?" Hugo repeated.

"At the top of the map."

"So we need to turn around and make our way back the way we came," Hugo concluded.

"Looks like it."

"All right, well let's get going."

Feeling a sense of urgency, they walked back through the sweeping corridor towards the south end of the mall. They passed by where they had entered and continued onward. Then, across from a skate shop, they observed Shoez in all its glory. Inside they were bombarded by walls of shoes.

"Do we need to find someone who works here?" Paul asked. "After all, you don't know the name of the shoe brand."

"No, we can find it on our own."

From one row of shoes to another they looked, scanning each and every shoe, looking for a pair that matched what Hugo described. But while there were plenty of shoes, including skater shoes, basketball shoes, and hipster shoes, there was no pair of shoes that matched what they were looking for.

Paul said, "I'll just ask someone who works here for help."

Tapping a man on the shoulder, Paul said, "Excuse me, we are looking for a particular type of shoe."

"Sure thing. What kind of shoe are you looking for?"

Paul described the shoes.

"Oh," the attendant said, "the Algot 2016 is what you are looking for."

"Yes, do you have it?"

"No, I believe we sold out just the other day. They are in pretty high demand."

"Wonderful," Hugo mumbled.

"Do you know anywhere where we could find a pair?" Paul asked.

"Hmmm. You could try The Shoe House."

"Where is it?" Hugo asked in desperation.

"Other side of the mall, by the food court."

"Thank you so much," Paul said.

"One more thing," the attendant said. "If you leave me your phone number, I can call you as soon as we get a shipment of those shoes."

"That would be great. Thank you."

The two friends walked out of Shoez and went towards the food court. They passed clothing store after clothing store until they reached The Shoe House. Inside, they found a massive space, more like a warehouse, filled to the brim with shoes. Every couple of aisles had an attendant walking through, answering questions.

"Let's take a look," Hugo said as he walked down a row of shoes.

"Shouldn't we ask someone for help?"

Clearly, the two friends possessed different approaches to shopping. Hugo wanted to not be bothered, and he didn't want to bother others, so he declined to ask for help when he was able to, and instead sought to find whatever he was looking for by searching independently. Paul, on the other hand, wanted to be as efficient as possible, so he always wanted to be helped by someone who worked at the store. Who had a more complete knowledge of where to find a product than someone working at the store? Here, then, the two different philosophies concerning shopping clashed.

Hugo traced one row of shoes and then another, fruitlessly. Meanwhile, Paul found an attendant, who informed him that the store just recently had sold out of the Algot 2016 and that it was unknown where a pair of them could be located. Paul followed after Hugo, who was looking at two boxes of shoes, and delivered the sorry news to him.

"Oh well," Hugo sighed. "What's the point? They're just shoes. Not worth all the trouble. In another year, I'll have worn through them and need yet another pair. It's all so very meaningless."

"Whatever you say, my friend."

Walking back towards where they had entered, Paul's phone began to go off. He answered it. It was the attendant from Shoez, with news that, after looking in the back of the store, he was mistaken, and that there was one last pair of the Algot 2016 available for purchase in Hugo's size. Overjoyed, Paul led Hugo towards Shoez. Hugo tried on the shoe and found that it fit. Paul was so excited that they finally found what they were looking for that he wanted to hug Hugo. But Hugo, on the other hand, was in a gloomy mood.

"They're just shoes," he said while riding in the car back home. "Nothing to get too excited about. We went through a big hassle to find them, and now we have them. Big deal. I spent half my day looking for shoes when I could have been doing something else with that time."

Then again, it was not as though Hugo would have spent that time doing anything else more meaningful. As far as he was concerned these days, doing any one particular thing held no more meaning than another. Riding home in Paul's car, holding the shoebox on his lap, Hugo stared out the window.

September

I.

Walking through Sunnyside Park on a crisp evening, Hugo became aware of just how special a night it was. Paul's daughter, Janet, was spending the week visiting from a small town outside of Buenos Aires. She and her husband, Alejandro, had flown up to Seattle, and were staying with Paul. Already, Hugo had seen plenty of them both. He had never been to Argentina, but over the years, with all the visits, he felt he had gotten to know the Marquez family well. In the last four days, he saw and talked to them several times while outside gardening.

On this particular evening, Hugo was invited over to have a lavish meal of pasta. They had enjoyed one another's company, good wine, and great conversation. They talked about what life was like in the Southern Hemisphere. Janet worked as an English teacher at an impoverished school, and the experiences she recounted were rich indeed. Alejandro worked for a bank.

Having decided that it was far too pleasant an evening to stay indoors, the four of them went outside and walked towards the park, which was not far away.

Sunnyside Park was one of the most vital green spaces in all of Wedgwood. It was not large, but it contained trails that wound through patches of trees in an enchanting fashion. The small forest in the park was just big enough to get lost in for a little while. There was even a little playground for children to play on.

"It really is quite lovely here," Janet said.

"Yes, fall is a nice time to be here, though I suppose technically it isn't fall yet."

"Where we live, it is just turning into spring. The whole world is coming alive after a long winter, not that it got to be as cold there as it is here in the winter."

"The climate is a lot warmer in Buenos Aires, isn't it?"

"Yes, for the most part. There are fluctuations in the weather—polar air that sweeps in—but it doesn't really get to be all that cold. It is the rainiest season of the year, but it's nothing compared to here."

"Interesting."

"Yes, I remember I was in for quite an adjustment when I first moved there!"

"I bet."

"I was just a young college kid, you know. I wasn't ready for the world that awaited me in such a big city as Buenos Aires. It really is a world-class city. Did you know that it has more bookstores per capita than any other city in the world?"

"I did not know that."

"Yes, and writers like Borges proved to be invaluable in the development of today's literature."

"I have read Borges," Hugo remarked. "I must say I quite liked what he wrote. My wife was even more interested in him."

"Mmhmm."

"Now tell me something: honestly, do you ever bemoan moving down there? Do you ever wonder what life would have been like for you if you had stayed here, settled down, and gotten a regular job like everyone else?"

The group passed under an arch formed by tree branches and headed deeper into the forest. Soon the sun would be setting. The lingering light from the sun reflected off of the trees marvelously. The tips of the tree branches, like human fingers, all were pointing to the sky. Alejandro turned around and said something to Janet in Spanish.

"What did he say?" Hugo asked.

"He was remarking on how beautiful it is here. He was quoting a famous poem in Argentina that describes a sunset."

"Ah."

Though Alejandro spoke English fluently, it seemed that he was more comfortable speaking in Spanish, and that language proved to be a bridge of intimacy between him and Janet.

"Do you have an answer to my question?" Hugo pressed.

"Yes, I do. The truth is I have thought in my life about the many different paths I could have gone down. What if I had been sent to serve in Korea instead? Germany? What if I stayed here and got a regular job as you describe it? It is like the seemingly infinite library from Borges' famous story. There is an unfathomably massive chain of possible paths down which one can wander. But in the end, one can only take one path, and one must accept that that particular path, the path taken, possesses meaning in it. I may have wondered what life could have been like outside of Buenos Aires, but my heart never left it."

"I understand what you are saying."

"After all," she continued, "what's the use in becoming too preoccupied with such questions, if not solely for the sake of whimsical fancy?"

The air was cool, and Hugo was clutching at the sides of his Jacket. He zipped it up, but not without taking a second to look at his tie, which had sheep dancing on it. It was one of Hugo's sillier ties, but he enjoyed it nonetheless. There was certainly a crispness in the air, a cold atmosphere. The days were getting to be shorter, and the seasons were changing. The days had been warm, but the nights were getting to be cooler and cooler.

"You know, I had an opportunity to move, when I was younger," Hugo began.

"Really?"

"Yes, I remember it well. A few years after I had gotten on with my company, they had an offer for me. It was for a position in Los Angeles. It would not have been moving up at all; it was doing the same work at a different branch of the company. However, I was enticed by the offer. Here I was, just a couple of years out of college, young, rife with energy, and I was being offered the path to a new city."

"So I assume you didn't take the position. Why?"

"Well, I spent a long time thinking it over. The truth is I wanted to stay close to my family, which was in Edmonds. I wanted to be near my friends, and also I had a wife to think about. She was developing as a journalist, working for a local newspaper, and I didn't want to uproot her from that."

"I see."

"But now, all of that is a part of the past," Hugo lamented.

"It's true that it's a part of the past, but that doesn't mean it doesn't matter. Every decision we make leads us farther along on the path that we are traveling along. Each decision, each junction we reach, leads us somewhere new. It all matters, even if it's part of the past."

"You're right. Lately, I have felt like so much of who I am, my life, is a part of the past. It feels like it is gone, and all I am left with is a box of photographs in my study. Where did everything go? Do you think I am still passing junctions at my age?" Hugo thought that Janet sounded a lot like Lily in how she was speaking.

"Of course you are!"

"It doesn't feel like it. It feels like I am stuck in one place like I am not moving."

"Well, believe it or not, you are still making decisions and navigating life. Life is far from over for us!"

"Hah. Speak for yourself. How old are you?"

"Thirty."

"I am much older than that. I have seen and experienced much. I reckon I have lived a full life. It's hard to not live life looking backward, thinking about what could have been and what wasn't."

"I believe it is possible to look backward appreciatively and forward expectantly."

"I like that."

"It's how I try to live."

210

"You know," Hugo began, "you and I are like a case study. We are an examination of what happens when life somewhere far off calls. Of course, Los Angeles is a far cry from Buenos Aires in terms of distance, but I think the point remains. We both had an opportunity to take a job somewhere else, to have novel experiences. Whereas you went for it, embracing it fully, I stayed put. I tried to work on building connections with my family, being a husband, and growing in my career from here in Seattle. I felt at peace with staying put, but a little bit of curiosity remained as I wondered what it was I was missing in California."

"That seems pretty reasonable to me. It would make sense that you would wonder about what could have been as you made a major life decision."

"It's funny," Hugo said, "because this all happened forty years ago. Yet right now it feels so fresh in my mind. I feel like I am making the decision all over again."

"I think the central challenge of it all is to arrive at a place where you can be accepting of the path you are on."

"Of course I accept the path I'm on. I just wish that the path hadn't gone by so fast. I wish I could walk down the path again."

"I don't think you are the first person to ever feel that way."

"But you say you have no regrets, right?"

"Right. I'll let you in on a little secret. Since we're talking about paths, what I've found to be the case is that it really doesn't matter what path we take. Of all the paths, the entire library of Borges, the fact remains that each and every path, whether you go to Los Angeles, Buenos Aires, Seoul, Madrid, or stay in Seattle, what I have come to believe is this: whatever path you end up going down, there are wonderful and marvelous things to observe no matter what. All you have to do is be paying attention."

"I understand."

"Just as you can go to Buenos Aires and be dissatisfied, you can stay in Seattle and derive great joy and fulfillment from what you do. You, Hugo, spent time developing your family and planting roots, and I have little doubt that you found that to be a satisfying thing."

"It was a satisfying thing."

"See? There is a comfort in knowing that, no matter what, you are on the right path."

"I suppose you're right."

"Now, that's enough talk about paths!"

They walked through the forest and were now looping back through the park, towards the entrance. They passed through a field. Leaves had only just begun to fall. For the most part, they were still hanging from the trees. It was now dark out. They reached the entrance, took a turn, and were at once heading back on residential streets towards Paul's house. The houses looked peaceful in the gentle night, though it was achingly cold out. Alejandro had an arm around his wife.

Having reached the house, they went inside and warmed up.

Paul began pouring the wine. "Want a glass, Hugo?"

He obliged his friend and had a third glass. The misty, swirly contentment that wine brought him was substantial. Hugo sat on one of Paul's couches, staring at the others, not saying anything, simply absorbing the conversation.

With each passing day he was diving deeper into the world of his own thoughts, lost.

2.

He was holding the roses carefully in his hand, fearful that he might be pricked by the thorns. It felt like an illustration of what he was doing: he was delicately handling something, afraid that he might be cut by it. But if he was cut, at least then he would know whether or not he felt something.

It was a cool, sunny day, the sky clear and the breeze chilling. He was walking along a road not far from his house. In his hands, he carried a bouquet of roses. The sense of dread and unease that he felt was nearly overwhelming. His

212

heart was beating rapidly and he was sweating. Again and again, he strove to clear his mind of all the thinking. It was not much farther before he would have reached his destination.

On his left, there was the Blue Hen. Did he dare go in? Not feeling capable of dealing with what he was going through sober, he entered the bar and ordered a glass of pinot gris. Lily was nowhere to be seen. Must be her day off, he thought. Sitting, sipping away, he looked at the flowers which rested on the table before him. The roses were orange, cut from his own garden. He thought about all the time, care, and effort that had gone into producing these roses. It brought him a sense of pride to think that he was responsible for their creation. The thorns of the roses rested against the smooth surface of the bar table. Hugo spent twenty minutes there until he had finished his drink, and then he continued on his way.

His nerves settled a bit, he walked down Mason Street, only minutes from where he was headed. He passed by one house and then another. Imagining the happy families that lived in these houses, he considered the people to be unacquainted with carrying out a duty as solemn as the one he was tasked with. A few houses later and he made another turn, onto a more residential street. The sun was out and the day was so pretty, yet he still felt on edge. Fortunately, the alcohol numbed the pain just enough so that it was bearable so that he wouldn't turn around and head home.

For months he thought about doing this, anticipating it, deliberating it over in his mind. There had been several days when he heavily considered going, but he refrained. The horror of it was too much for him. Today marked the first time he decided to go for it.

Walking through a lonely field, he felt empty.

What was this emptiness? Why had it become so common? Hugo felt slow, as though he couldn't walk or think as fast as he usually could. In the last few months he was all over the map emotionally, and yet now there was nothing. Was this the new normal? Was this how things were going to be from now on? Desperately he wanted to feel something, anything, but he feared the pain that might accompany feeling. Well, at least fear was present as an emotion for him.

A part of why he was drinking more was because it afforded him a feeling, a sensation to grab onto. Being buzzed, or even a little drunk, was something, rather than the overwhelming nothingness that seized his heart at nearly every moment. Lately, he was drinking more. The other day, he had had three and a half glasses of wine, a new high. He was sleeping and drinking more, and he didn't seem to mind.

The reason why he slept so much was precisely the opposite of why he drank, he thought: it was an attempt to escape feeling, to be away from reality, to settle into the emptiness and dwell in it for a while. When the sun rose and Hugo's alarm went off, he would roll around onto his other side and go back to sleep, rejecting reality.

The field was coming to an end and on the side, there were the hedges. Hugo knew this place well from all his walks through the neighborhood, but it never felt more troubling to him than now. A little way past the hedges and he saw the open gate.

He looked through the gate and saw the tombstones.

Panic seized him, his heart beating wildly in his head. He dropped the flowers, turned around, and walked back the way he came. Then, realizing that he didn't have the flowers, he returned for them. Picking up the roses, he noticed that one of his fingers was bleeding: a prick after all.

So many feelings, images, and memories were flashing through Hugo's consciousness that for a moment he didn't know if he would be able to get home. He stood still, paralyzed, unable to enter the cemetery and unable to leave.

He stood still for several minutes. Then he took a step back towards his home, and he was on his way.

He walked quickly through the field, ashamed that he had been unable to go to her grave. They had said that it was a great sign of healing and progress to be able to lay flowers at the grave and to simply stand there, fully embodying grief.

But the simple truth was that he wasn't ready, and he didn't know when he would be ready, if ever.

In the middle of the field, having changed his mind, he intentionally dropped the flowers on the ground, deciding that maybe someone else would find them who wasn't a coward.

3.

Taking another sip of water, Hugo said, "It was very nice to have Janet here. She was only here for such a short time, though."

"It's true," Paul replied. "It was nice but short."

Hugo looked out the window of his living room, at the leaves which had just begun to fall from the trees. "She and I had an interesting conversation about how I almost moved to California in my youth."

"I remember you telling me that story."

"Yes, it is hard for me not to look back on that story without a sense of loss to it. There was such a wonderful opportunity presented to me, and I passed on it. Who knows what I missed out on by not making the move?"

"Well, we would have never met, so there is that."

Hugo laughed. "It's true. I guess there is loss no matter what one does."

"You can choose to look at it that way, or you can say that there is gain no matter what one does."

"Ah! There is light in every darkness. How mystical!" Hugo snapped.

"It is mystical, if you think about it."

"I suppose so. But I tend to only see the loss in life, not the gain."

"That is just one way of looking at it. You should expand your mind a bit and open it to the rest of reality. However, if I am being honest with you, I'm not really as optimistic as I may seem to be. You see, something happens to me every time Janet visits. In being with her, I become reminded of just how much time I spend without her around, and there is a very real sense of loss to that. I have spent years of my life apart from my daughter. You have always been very close to your son. That is a fortunate thing, my friend."

"Yes, it is a fortunate thing, except when there are challenges involved with being a parent. Maybe sometimes distance is nice. For example, I am quite frustrated with Adrian's career situation. Did I tell you about that?"

"Yes, you did."

"I just don't know what to do. I don't know what to say. Yesterday we talked on the phone, and there were many pauses in the conversation. It felt so difficult to carry it on. I feel a very real sense of loss with my son's career. There used to be something there, Java City, which I, of course, was never wild about, but at least there was something. Now he is unemployed, and his money is starting to run out. What will become of him?"

"I don't know, but he'll figure something out. A Larson always figures things out," Paul said.

"True enough. Would you like a glass of wine?"

"No, thank you."

"I'll be right back."

Hugo walked into the kitchen and poured himself a glass of chardonnay. It was early in the day, but he had the urge to drink, and so he acted on it. He was still making an effort to track how much he drank each day, so he wasn't all that concerned. Taking a sip of the beverage and looking out at the backyard, he admired it.

Back in the living room, Hugo had a seat and made himself comfortable. He was sipping his drink quickly. He asked, "How do you live with Janet's absence?"

"I live with it the same way people always live with awful things: I just do. Like you, I go through my life, doing the things I enjoy, one day at a time, and often I sadly am not even aware of her. She is so far away! I have thought about going down to visit her, but I just feel too old to make a big trip like that."

"I don't blame you for feeling that way. I wouldn't want to travel that far."

"That doesn't surprise me."

"Indeed not!" Hugo had another sip of wine.

"Then there is the way that Janet makes me think of her mother, which makes me feel more loss. The way she speaks with such a keen intellect, her eccentric little qualities, it all reminds me of her, which causes me to think back on the twelve years we spent together. You know, I had not wanted to be separated from her, but in the end, there was no option. There is loss on top of loss!"

"There is," Hugo answered. "It is all very terrible. Why not have a glass of wine and forget about your troubles for a little while?"

"Hugo, you know wine is no solution to your troubles. I don't mind you drinking, but I must ask: why it is that you have started to drink more lately?"

"I haven't had that much more to drink lately, really," Hugo defended. "Maybe a little bit more, but not much. It isn't anything to worry about. I am perfectly in control of my lifestyle, thank you very much."

"Sure thing."

There was a pause, as Hugo finished his beverage, and then Paul said, "You know what? We should go on a trip."

"A trip?! Where?"

"To the coast. We could go to Grayland for a weekend. Wouldn't that be fun?"

"I don't know, Paul."

"Come on! Why not? The two of us are preoccupied with loss. I think it could be good for us to find a reason to celebrate some gain in our lives by going somewhere. It doesn't have to be a big trip. We could just go for a couple of days."

"I guess I could consider it."

"That's all I ask. Think about it. Consider it. I can do all the planning, and I would drive of course."

"When would you want to go?"

"Hmmm. How about sometime in November, before Thanksgiving?"

"Okay. I will let you know if I want to go."

4.

The tide was still low. They were walking across rocky sand, past logs, over swaths of seaweed, towards the horizon. In the air, there was a misty quality. Overhead was a thick ceiling of clouds, bright and impenetrable. Though it was cold, they were still having a nice enough time being outside, walking.

"It really is a good day to be at Golden Gardens. It really is," Martin said with excitement.

"Sure is," Hugo agreed, mild as the weather.

"I love when we have the opportunity to come and spend time in Seattle with you."

"Yes, it is nice."

"I also love this time of year. The leaves are changing colors and falling off the trees. The days are getting to be shorter. It's colder. Oh, it is a wonderful time indeed."

Hugo liked fall well enough. There was no season that he was smitten by, but he knew that he despised summer and winter. He disliked summer because of the heat, and the winter he hated because he feared that snow would fall. Hugo hated snow. It was true that there remained something profound to be admired about fall. During fall, there was a whiff of change in the air, a space for reflection as the world transitioned into darkness.

Hugo was walking with his brother, and Patricia was walking with Barbara. James had stayed at home to work on a project, and Cassandra was not feeling well. So, the three of them had decided to pick up Hugo and head to Golden Gardens, a beach in western Seattle.

"How is the school year going?"

"Oh, it is a busy time, big brother."

"Tell me more."

"The school year has only just begun, but already there are tests to grade, lessons to plan, and students to manage. I am so very happy to admit that this is, in fact, my last year of teaching, though I really do enjoy it."

"If you enjoy teaching so much, why not keep doing it?" Hugo already knew the answer to this question.

"I just don't feel like I have it in me to keep going. I'm getting old, big brother! I had thought that the previous year was going to be my last year, so it is a big deal that I decided to teach for yet another year."

"Fair enough. All I know is that it was a sad day the day I left my job."

"That is reasonable. That is reasonable."

They stepped over a particularly large log, Hugo holding his starfish tie as he made the big step over to the other side. In the distance, he could hear the gentle sound of waves kissing the sandy surface, the breathing of the earth.

"I have a question for you, Martin."

"Yes, big brother?"

"This was a long time ago—many years. Do you remember when I was working for my company, and I was given the option to move to Los Angeles to work the same job?"

"You know what? I do remember that. That was a big decision that you made."

"Well, honestly, do you think I made the right choice?"

'You mean to stay in Seattle?"

"Yes."

"Well of course you did. Your family was here and so was your wife's family. You love living in Seattle. It's your home. By staying here you were able to come and see me, and so our relationship continued to grow. It was a great thing that you stayed here."

"But don't you think maybe, just maybe, there are some things I missed out on by not going?"

"Why are you thinking about this, big brother? It was so many years ago!"

"True. I guess I have just been thinking a lot lately about things...reflecting."

"The truth is there might have been things you missed out on, but there are also things you would have missed out on if you had left here. Besides, things fell together the way they did."

Seasons changed, the weather changed, but the path worn by Hugo through his life, the trail of footprints in the sand, remained utterly immutable. For some people, this was a comforting thought, but for Hugo it was terrifying. He was afraid that he had made mistakes. Regret loomed in his mind, a curiosity that nagged at him as he wondered if, perhaps, some of the choices he made in his life had not been the best ones. Sure, he made the best of his choices, but this was different from making the best choice. If Hugo was preoccupied with a scenario that took place more than thirty years ago in the past, what else was there for him to feel regret for?

"I tend to think more about what is lost than gained," Hugo said, brooding.

"I know, big brother. And you know I tend to think more about what is gained."

"I just feel like there is so much loss. Loss is all that I see."

"I understand." Martin put a hand on Hugo's shoulder. "How have you been doing?"

"I feel like there is loss in Adrian's life, around his career and his lack of family. There is loss in my life as I think about her. There is even loss in my garden as some plants die. I have tried my very best to live life to the fullest, but it feels like everything around me is unraveling."

Martin smiled. "Not everything is unraveling."

"I was talking to Paul the other day about his daughter, Janet. You know about her, right?"

"Yes."

"Anyway, he and I were talking about how his daughter lives so far away, and we became preoccupied with all of the loss in our lives. What a heavy load it is to carry!"

"Yes, it is a heavy load, but you don't have to carry it alone."

"That isn't always true."

"What do you mean?" Martin asked.

"Well, you can't help me carry the load of having lost my wife. I have to do that all on my own. No one can help me but myself."

"Big brother, that simply isn't true. You know that we are all here to support you, and there is professional help. I really should get you into touch with Christotpher—"

"I don't want to go see some shrink! There's no point in doing anything like that. I have a load that I have to carry, and it is heavy, and I am all alone. You know what? There is no point to me even carrying this load. There simply is no point. I keep saying the same things over and over again."

"Don't you believe that we can help you carry the load? Don't you think that we were able to be there with you when we were over in Chelan?"

"You were there to support me, but I still had to work through things on my own. I am still working on things, but I am making no progress. I am going nowhere. The other day, I tried to go to the grave."

"And what happened?"

"I couldn't make it inside of the gate."

"I understand."

Hugo was tired of hearing his brother say that he understood because it really felt to him as though he did not understand. Martin still had his lovely wife alive, along with a career and the rest of his family. What did he know about loss?

"I couldn't do it," Hugo continued, "I just couldn't."

"What was going on at the moment? What were you feeling?"

"Now it really feels like I am talking to a shrink. Thanks for that."

"Big brother, I am only trying to help. I am trying to be here for you. Do you think the last eight months have been easy for us? Look, I know you have experienced a loss that can't be put into words, but it hurts all of us when you try to create distance from us. I can't help you if you just discredit me as being a would-be therapist. We love you and want to be there for you in any way that we can. We want to help you move forward with your life. You yourself talked to me about the idea of moving forward not that long ago. What happened to that thinking?"

"I don't know," Hugo answered with hesitation, "but I think I gave up on that notion."

"Look," Martin said, "I need to be honest with you. You've been slower in your movements and your speech. You answer the phone maybe half the time I call. You even had a glass of wine at brunch today. Now, I know it's just a glass, but you never do that! Not ever. The big brother I know is energized, active, and sober-minded. So what happened? Because I don't recognize this gloomy, overly reflective guy in front of me. All you seem to want to talk about is how things are pointless and have no meaning. Well, let me ask, what does have meaning for you?"

"I don't know. Nothing."

"Do I hold meaning for you? Do I mean something to you?"

"Yes, of course."

"Then something does have meaning!"

"You tricked me!"

"I didn't trick you, big brother. What I did is I put things into perspective a little bit for you. There are other things in your life that hold meaning to you, too. What else?"

"I did listen to that neighborhood boy Rex play the piano. That was nice."

"Okay."

"My garden, Paul, Adrian, my home, my tie collection, I don't know."

"That's not a bad list to start."

"But that's just the thing," Hugo bemoaned. "Those things I listed, including you...while they may contain meaning for me in an intellectual sense, I don't feel that they hold meaning for me in my heart."

"Mmhmm."

"We are like the sand of this beach. We stick together, and we are pounded continually by waves. Eventually, every last speck of sand is sucked up and dissolved in the sea."

"I suppose that's true."

"Everyone dies. Everything is lost eventually."

Hugo was aware that he was becoming melancholic again. But he didn't know what to do, for all he was doing was reflecting how he truly felt. He was being true to his own experience.

"Not everything is lost," Martin answered, "I didn't want to go there, but I will. We have promises from God of being made new. We have the promise of eternal life. This life, it is fleeting, fragile, and delicate, but the life that is to come is vast."

"Yes, but I don't feel it. I don't feel the truth of God's promises. I don't see the eternal life. All I see is what I don't see, which is my wife of forty-three years! Now you may find it easy enough to believe in a loving, all-powerful God, but I'm not really interested in that. What I am interested in is what I can see, what I can feel and touch. The truth is that there is no way to know if there is a God, and even if there is one, it makes no difference if you believe or not. There is no point in believing because the afterlife is absurd."

"What's absurd about the afterlife?"

"Eternity is absurd. The idea that people would be eternally punished or benefited for a finite life is absurd and makes no sense."

"Yes, but God is mysterious and we were meant—"

"Sure thing. God is mysterious. Here I thought you had all the answers, but you have to appeal to mystery to explain the unexplainable. I don't want to hear it. All I want to do is to try and enjoy the rest of this walk. Is that all right?"

"Yes, big brother. That is all right."

They walked on in silence, their footsteps, the gentle hush of the ocean waves, and the breeze the only sounds that could be heard.

5.

He had consumed more glasses of wine than he could count.

His head was riotous, a raging swirl of aching pain, filled with spite.

He lay down in bed. It was only half past eight, but he was ready to sleep. Closing his eyes, he found he couldn't keep them shut. Tossing and turning, he pulled the blanket over himself. Then he climbed out of the bed, nearly falling over. He stumbled into the closet and ran his hands through the drawers. Having found the photograph, he looked at it and began to feel an anger that consumed him. He took the photograph, ripped it up, and tossed it into the trash bin.

Downstairs, he looked for more wine but could find none. He thumped his knee on the kitchen table as he walked by. He cursed, and then made his way to the couch. He couldn't think. He couldn't sleep. Looking for the phone, he wanted to call his son, to tell him that he was a disappointment and a disgrace to the Larson family, but he couldn't find it.

Hearing the sound of the wind rustling the trees outside, feeling afraid, he began to cry.

6.

Wearing a light green sweater, Sandra was smiling a big grin. Her black hair was shoulder-length, and her eyes shone like bright emeralds. Hugo had on a tie with a picture of mountains on it. He ran a hand through his light brown hair. She was the one pushing the stroller. They were making their way towards the bus stop. Sitting in the stroller, Adrian was placid, as was so often the case.

"I've never been up it before," Sandra said. "This is exciting!"

"The view is just stunning up there," Hugo answered. "It really is amazing."

They passed one house and then another, moving slowly, enjoying a chilly, cloudy day. After all, they were in no hurry. It was an early Saturday afternoon. Sandra, who was working hard on a report on a city financial scandal, found the time off from work to be with her family, and Hugo never worked on the weekend.

They reached the bus stop and stood still.

"So," Hugo began, "we will take the 48, and then transfer to the 9. That should get us to Seattle Center. Then we can eat or picnic. We don't want to be spending money at the top of the Space Needle; it will be astronomical."

"Sounds good to me. Glad you made a plan."

"Happy to do it."

The bus arrived and they got on board. Hugo used all of his strength to lift the stroller onto the floor of the bus. After they paid their fare they sat down near the front of the bus, and off the vehicle sped.

They were zooming through the neighborhood, the houses passing by in flashes, the trees green blurs. Hugo looked towards the back of the bus and saw the rough, disheveled people who were also riding. Next, he turned down to look at Adrian, who was smiling and reaching forward with his hands.

"Car," Adrian said.

"Yes, sweetie, we are riding on a very big car," Sandra smiled.

"We are off," Hugo said, "heading towards adventure."

The last few weeks at work were quite stressful for Hugo. He was working under sharp deadlines, and was struggling to meet them. Though he was known to be a ferocious worker, the load that was set before him was a heavy one, demanding every last ounce of his time and energy. He spent several nights late at the office, hard at work. It was true that he liked his job, but as he sat at his desk, looking at the photograph of his wife and baby son, he couldn't help but miss them dearly. All that work had taken a toll on him. There were small bags under his eyes. For this reason, Hugo was so very glad to be spending time with his two favorite people in the world, to be able to escape his job, if for only a little while.

A few years earlier, Hugo was offered a job working in Los Angeles for the same company, but he turned it down. Now, sitting on the bus with his family, in the city that he loved, he felt not even an ounce of regret over the choice he had made. There would be no looking back, he resolved, not now and not ever.

The course of the bus was rickety as it made its way closer to the heart of the city. They would catch their second bus downtown. Hugo and Sandra owned a car, but parking around Seattle Center was such a hassle that they decided it was better to use public transportation. Besides, it made everything feel like a little bit more of an adventure to use the bus.

It wasn't long before the skyscrapers of downtown came into clear view overhead, the bus approaching the tunnel station. Again Hugo lifted the stroller, and they walked towards the stairs leading up to street level. Outside, the air was crisp. In fact, it was cold.

"Let's go, sweethearts," Hugo called.

Leading the way, Hugo took a turn pushing the stroller. The streets were bustling with people walking about, off to work, shopping. As the crosswalk light changed colors, Hugo was cautious to look both ways multiple times before leading his family along. He moved forward, fully certain of where he needed to go.

"Come on!" he shouted to his wife, who walked a few steps behind him.

"Coming."

They passed a tiny espresso stand, took another turn, and headed towards the financial district. In fact, they were not far from Hugo's office. Here the buildings were massively tall. In the distance, to the left, there was the large, neon red Public Market sign, undoubtedly filled to the brim with tourists. Eventually, Hugo stopped walking, having reached the sign for the bus stop.

"Here we are," he said.

"How are we doing on time?"

Hugo looked at his watch, then at the bus sign, saying, "Four minutes."

They stood as the throngs of people passed them on both sides. Cars navigated the traffic chaotically but without accident. In the distance there were the sounds of drilling and hammering, indicating construction. The city was building upward.

"He's being awfully good today," Sandra added, pointing at the stroller.

Adrian began to cry.

It was a loud, wailing sound, accompanied by sniffling and the shaking of arms.

"I'll take him," Sandra said. She took him out of the stroller and held him gently, hushing him, rocking him in a back and forth motion. Still, he continued to cry. She turned around patted his head gently. He was slightly calmer.

"It's all right, little guy."

"Do you want me to take him?" Hugo asked.

"No, that's all right."

The second bus was approaching them, and Adrian was tranquil once more. They placed him back in the stroller and climbed onto the bus. This bus was significantly older than the first one they had ridden. The bus was packed with other riders of all sorts of descriptions. There were old men who appeared raggedy and possibly living on the street, young women and men wearing business attire, the elderly, and young college kids who snickered to themselves, among others.

Having sat down, the bus sped off towards Seattle Center. Hugo held the stroller with both hands and looked at his son. He smiled a smile of fond love, thinking about how happy he was that Adrian existed and belonged wholly to him. What Hugo saw in Adrian was a promise, a hope for a new future, a new generation of prosperity. What, Hugo wondered, would Adrian do for a career? Maybe he would be a fireman, or a doctor, or go into business, or any other number of things. Would Adrian get married? Would he have children of his own? Hugo thought about his own parents, how only a few years earlier it nearly appeared as though they would divorce. They had argued bitterly, and Hugo's father, Matthew, was drinking heavily, but the couple endured in their marriage. Yet, despite all the marital progress, to this day, Matthew's drinking was significant, a cause for concern. Hugo didn't live with his father anymore, obviously, so he was left to wonder what Matthew's drinking habits were really like. Whatever happened to Matthew, Hugo hoped that his own son would never personally know what alcoholism was, the toll that it took on the drinking individual and all those around that person. Hugo had been intentional to minimize and control his drinking, having no more than a single drink on any given day, and he was true to this resolution. Matthew's father, and his father before him were drinkers. A generation of savage alcoholism had followed another for as many generations as Hugo could trace. But finally, with Hugo, that cycle was broken, and with Adrian, there was the possibility of a new familial pattern, one marked by the responsible enjoyment of alcohol. Indeed, Hugo looked upon his son and imagined the schools he would attend, the friends he would make, and the places he would go. All that Hugo saw in his son was possibility.

As the bus navigated the dense city streets, the buildings shrank in size rather quickly. Downtown Seattle was not sprawling in its size, but it did contain some tall buildings. With a look out the window, Hugo saw it, the Space Needle, standing upright and proudly, piercing the sky. Viewing it always instilled in him a sense of awe, as he thought about what man was capable of engineering. For him, the Needle was a symbol of the future, of hope, of promise.

The air was even cooler as they got out of the second bus, stepping onto a smooth sidewalk. Nearby there was a grassy field. The Space Needle was so close it seemed to be touchable, but it was at least a few hundred yards off. Hugo continued to push the stroller, looking at his wife and smiling. They walked along a narrow path, past several experimental pieces of art that were installed on the side. One of these pieces of art was a red, cubic sculpture, one that captured Hugo's imagination. Nearby, there was a statue of a flamingo, colored a dark, jade green. Birds gathered in the grassy field, flying off as Hugo's family walked by. Tourists from all over the world passed by Hugo, taking photos, speaking languages other than English.

Hugo stopped pushing the stroller.

"How about here?" he asked.

"Works for me."

Sandra reached into the back compartment of the stroller and pulled out a blanket. She put it on the ground, removed Adrian and placed him down, and removed a basket that contained their lunch.

"I've been looking forward to this," Hugo beamed.

"It will be good. Thank you for making the sandwiches."

"Happy to do it."

They sat down and enjoyed their sandwiches. Hugo loaded them with plenty of turkey and cheddar cheese. Between them, they shared a bottle of water, and then they proceeded to eat baby carrots. For Adrian, they brought some small crackers. It was strange, thought Hugo, to remember that here it was September, and that Adrian would be turning two years old in January. Hugo's birthday was December 4th, and Adrian's was January 8th. It seemed like only the other day that Adrian was born, and already he was crawling and walking, saying words and phrases. It was strange and it was scary to think about this, for the time seemed to move by so fast.

Hugo and Sandra took their time in having a child, deciding to wait and enjoy being together. Both of them made substantial developments in their careers, as Hugo was established at his company and Sandra was making progress as an investigative journalist for The Seattle Times. Her specialty included political topics, with her contributing a column two mornings a week about current events. Sandra was passionate about justice and truth, and so it made sense that she had her job.

They spent a while eating. Hugo didn't manage to finish his sandwich, so he put it away, saving it for later.

Adrian stood up, and pointed at the Space Needle, saying "Big!"

"Yes it is, sweetheart," Sandra affirmed, picking him up. He started to laugh, and so she laughed along with him.

Hugo lay down on the blanket, staring at the cloudy sky. He was wondering when they would go up the Needle. There was no rush to go about it; they had all day.

"Should we go up?" Sandra wondered.

"Sure, why not?"

They put Adrian back in his stroller and walked towards the main area of Seattle Center. Walking along the path, they saw South American musical performers, a glass neck-lace salesman, and a man who was jamming on a saxo-phone. The crowds were exceptionally large.

Approaching the Needle, the sounds of big band jazz were playing in the background. There was a line of people that wrapped back and forth for dozens of yards.

"This might take a while," Hugo sighed.

"Not a problem," Sandra chirped.

They stood in line. Hugo looked at Sandra and held her hand. He thought about their relationship, all the time they had spent together. Remembering their time as college students, he pondered how difficult that time had been, when they were attending different schools. During that era, it seemed as though they never would be united together. It had appeared it was their destiny to be apart from each other. But this was no longer the case. They were together, and as far as Hugo was concerned, they would always be together. He imagined them growing old together, all the adventures they would go on, the countries they would visit, the smiles they would share. It warmed his heart to think that she was his.

Surprisingly, the line moved quickly. It was not long before they stood at the kiosk where tickets were purchased.

"Hello," the attendant greeted.

"Hi," Hugo said, holding the stroller tightly. "Three tickets, please."

"Your child is free."

"Oh, wonderful!"

Hugo paid for two tickets, and they waited for the elevator to come down. The jazz music continued to drone on, partially drowned out by the sounds of people talking. In the distance, the cityscape was visible, the buildings of downtown forming a jagged ridge. There was a beeping sound, and then the elevator opened. Several people walked out, and then the elevator was clear. Hugo pushed the stroller in and instinctively reached to press a button, realizing suddenly that there was only one destination.

"Here we go!" Sandra cried.

Up the elevator went, rising higher and higher into the sky. Since the front wall of the elevator was made of glass, Hugo could watch as they rose. The people and buildings below began to shrink in size, the buildings of downtown coming more closely into view. The world around them, the horizon, was growing in size even as everything below was shrinking. Hugo thought that surely they had reached the top, but they only continued to go higher. The Cascade Mountains were visible in the east, and the Olympics in the west, looming, extensive, and grand. Just before the Olympics, there was the water of Puget Sound, which was still, a clear blue.

Another beeping sound signaled they were at the top. The door opened and they stepped out. Before them was the entrance to a restaurant, which they were not interested in, and to the right, there was a path towards an observation deck. They walked along it, and within moments they saw the full view.

Hugo's breath was taken away. It had been years since he went up here. The shape of the city was principally the same, but the nuances and details had changed tremendously. Hugo picked up little Adrian and held him.

"Look!" Hugo whispered.

"Pretty...blue," Adrian marveled.

It was true that the view was quite blue. The sky, which had cleared up considerably, revealed the sun breaking through with rays of lovely sunlight. Patches of the sky were blue, the water in the Sound was blue, looking in the other direction Green lake, despite its name, was blue. In all, there was a great deal of blue to behold.

Hugo turned to Sandra and smiled. "It's great, isn't it?"

"Sure is."

For a while they walked around the observation deck, Hugo carrying his son and pointing out features of the view to him, Sandra following close behind with the stroller. There was a strong breeze at this altitude that could be heard even from inside. Once more Hugo became aware of just how high up in the air they were. Finally, he turned to Sandra and asked, "Want to head down?"

"Sure."

They made their way towards the elevator, but without Hugo taking one final opportunity to bask in the experience of having made it to the top of the Needle. One last time, Hugo looked at his family, then out at the view, and thought about how deeply connected the two were.

"Wait," he said.

"What?" Sandra asked.

Hugo took out his camera. "Let me get someone to take a picture of us."

A kind passerby was happy to take a photograph of them.

The elevator had arrived, and so they walked in. The ride down was uneventful, but it was a relief to know that the ground level was getting closer. With a beeping sound, the elevator signaled that it was time to get out. They walked outside, into the cool air, and stood together for a moment.

"That was great!" Sandra proclaimed.

"Yes, it was."

"Should we head back home?"

"Maybe not just yet."

"Where should we go?"

"Walk?" Adrian asked.

"Let's walk around a little," Hugo assented.

Seattle Center was a vibrant place, full of people ambling about. They followed the path before them, heading past a roller coaster, a carousel, and then a cotton candy stand, towards a clearing. Before them was a pit, at the bottom of which there was a fountain, spewing out water in synchronization to upbeat music.

"Should we enjoy the fountain?" Hugo asked.

"We still have to get home, honey."

"You're right."

They walked past the fountain, up to where there was an ice cream stand. Now that the sun was out, such a treat was much more appealing. Painted a bright green, the stand was old-looking. A youngster was serving ice cream to people, and he looked bored.

"What can I get for you?" he asked Hugo.

"Vanilla, please."

232

"I'll take strawberry, please," Sandra chimed in.

Enjoying their ice cream at a nearby table, Hugo allowed Adrian more than a few licks of the vanilla. Inevitably, Adrian ended up getting ice cream all over his face and cheeks.

"Let me wipe that off for you, sweetie," Sandra said, rubbing his face with a napkin.

Then Hugo and Sandra looked at each other, aware that something smelled foul.

"Is there a bathroom nearby?" Hugo wondered.

"I see one over there."

"I'll take care of it," Hugo answered, pushing the stroller with Adrian.

Sure, changing diapers was not the most pleasant thing in the world, but there was something satisfying about cleaning up a mess, a pleasure in seeing the face of a young child after he has been changed, looking so very innocent. Hugo gazed upon Adrian, proud that he was his. The two of them returned to where Sandra was sitting, still licking her strawberry ice cream.

"Thank you for taking care of that, sweetheart," she said.

"Not a problem. Happy to take care of it," he said, meaning it sincerely.

For a while they remained at Seattle Center, the sun poking through the clouds for a while, only to then become obscured by them again in a sort of rhythmic dance. Rays of sunshine would come down, blessing their day, and then be replaced by that crisp September gloom. After they finished their ice cream, they took Adrian over to a grassy patch and allowed him to walk around. It was amazing to think about how quickly he was learning to speak. Here he was, piecing together little words and phrases, pointing at things. Hugo picked Adrian up, placing him on his shoulders, and walked around, making the noises of an airplane. Then he placed his son on the grassy floor and gently patted his head.

Soon, it felt like the day was beginning to come to an end. They made their way along the winding path back through Seattle Center, just under the reach of the Space Needle, towards where their first bus would pick them up. Fortunately, they only had to wait a couple minutes for it to arrive. They rode the bus back into downtown, which on a Saturday evening was becoming relatively desolate, and then continued onto the second bus towards Wedgwood. As they left and stepped towards their home, the sun was setting.

Outside and gardening was Paul, who waved at the Larsons. "Have a fun day?"

"Yes, we did!" Hugo grinned. "Want to come over?"

"Sure."

Paul walked over and entered the house with them. Inside, Hugo offered him a glass of wine. Hugo himself settled with water, and Sandra was poured a glass of wine. Sandra had a sip of her drink, and then walked upstairs, where she placed Adrian in his bed, and proceeded to read him a story.

Paul and Hugo talked about the day. While Hugo visited the Space Needle, Paul was busy mowing the lawn and tending to his roses. Hugo asked where Paul's wife was, and he explained that she had to work.

"It was a lot of fun," Hugo said. "It's actually a shame to see the day come to an end."

"Yes, but you can rest assured that another enjoyable day will come very soon. Boy, Adrian is really growing fast, isn't he?"

"Yes, he is. In fact, his birthday is coming up very soon."

"December and January are good months to have birthdays in."

"Are you still trying to have kids?" Hugo asked.

"Yes, we are. Thinking and hoping that it will happen soon, but you know how it goes."

"I'm sure it will be soon."

"You're right."

"Just be sure," began Hugo, "that you stop to be appreciative for all the moments that come, all the little things that happen, because they happen fast, and you can't go back."

"Good advice."

"I'll be right back." Hugo rose up and walked upstairs to Adrian's room. He kissed Sandra on the cheek and then looked down at his son, who was asleep. He lowered his head down and kissed Adrian on the forehead. Then he motioned towards leaving the room, but not without looking at his son one final time.

October

I.

"Want to play chess?" Paul asked, standing in Hugo's doorway.

"No thanks, I'm not really feeling up for it."

"You okay?"

"Yes, I will play with you later." Hugo closed the door and went upstairs.

The phone rang, and it said it was Adrian, but he chose not to answer it, despite the fact that it possibly involved information regarding the fate of his son's career. Looking up at the ceiling, Hugo knew that he needed to bathe, but he was struggling to muster the energy. He wandered downstairs to watch television. He made sure that he had a steady flow of wine going in his system.

Later on, lying in bed, he longed for that sense of escape, the dissolution that was sleep. But it didn't come to him. He closed his eyes and felt the room bounce a little, but he was wide awake. He was wired. A splitting headache was forming, but he didn't mind it much. He didn't mind anything much. Tossing and turning, he moaned to himself.

The gray light from outside was penetrating through the window, leaving him in a silver glow. Thinking about the fact that he had originally scheduled an appointment to see a counselor, he was practically laughing on the inside, for that appointment was at five, and he had no intention of going. For Martin's sake, he said that he would see the counselor, but he was not really interested in going because there obviously was no point. What did some shrink know about what he had been through? Nothing, he told himself, absolutely nothing.

Spontaneously, he threw the blanket off the bed. He got up out of it and walked to the window of the bedroom. Outside it was raining a steady mist. Turning around, he went through the bedroom door and downstairs. He turned on the television and went to the news. There was nothing going on beyond the most recent governmental scandal. He lay down on the sofa for a moment, once more closing his eyes, once more feeling that aching pain in the back of his skull. He told himself that he needed something to drink, that he needed to make those feelings and thoughts go away. Up he rose from the sofa. He moved into the kitchen and reached for the bottle of Riesling he had been working on. To his devastation, he realized that it was completely empty. As he remembered it, there was a third of the bottle left, so where had it gone?

Scrambling through the kitchen, he was looking for something to drink, but there was nothing. The kitchen was empty. Settling at last for a glass of water, he had a seat at the kitchen table and sipped it, lamenting that no relief was coming from drinking it. Then he knew what he needed to do, namely, that he needed to go to the liquor store, which was closer to where he lived than the grocery store. He was resolved to go, at least in his mind, but his body was not following. He walked into the living room and fell down onto the sofa.

He stared at the ceiling and thought about nothing. But doing this only made his heart beat rapidly.

Still, the television was blaring the news in the background. It was a noise that clashed with his headspace. Irritated, he reached for the remote to turn it off, but it sat on the coffee table beyond his reach. He got up off the sofa, walked up to the television, and at last turned it off. The silence that filled the entire house was potent.

Unable to bear the silence, and at last fully prepared to leave, he stepped outside his house, locked the door, and walked down the street. Terrified that he would run into

Paul and have to face him, he continued on his way. Fortunately, it now being October, the weather was steadily in decline, and so people were spending less time outside working on their gardens. Hugo kept walking, stopping at a busy intersection, and then turned around in surprise when he heard his name called.

"Hugo Larson," she continued. It was Kim Schaeffer, the owner of the apple tree.

"Um, hello."

"How are you?"

"Fine, I am fine. How are you?"

"Oh, still alive. You know how it is." By Hugo's estimation, she must have been in her nineties, so such jokes about mortality were nothing to be unexpected.

"Well, I will see you—"

"You know," she began, "you should come by for tea sometime. It would be nice to have a visitor."

"I don't know, I'm quite busy, you see."

"Too busy to visit a dear old lady?"

Feeling trapped, he obliged her, saying, "On second thought, I suppose I could make time."

"Bring that friend of yours, Paul. We can have ourselves a merry little tea party!"

"I will be sure to do that," Hugo answered. "Now, I really must be on my way."

"Where are you off to?"

"Church. I am late for mass."

She pulled out a watch and examined it slowly. "You certainly are late," she said. "It's four forty-seven. When did your mass start?"

"Well, it is not a mass. It is a prayer service. It is the sort of event that you can come and go to. I really must be off."

"All right, well I will not stand in the way of a man and his Lord."

"Thank you."

Continuing on his way, Hugo walked along the street, taking a right. In the distance, he could see the liquor store in a parking lot. He walked up to it and entered. Inside, he was greeted by beer, spirits, wine, and all sorts of alcohol that would reach the same effect through different means. Feeling excited, he walked through the white wine aisle and decided instead to look at their selection of reds. He found a bottle that came from Chelan and considered the connection to be a fitting one. It looked to be cheap stuff, not having an actual cork but being screwed on and off. He also reached for a brown bag to purchase. Walking back towards the front of the store, under bright lights, he paid for the wine, walked out into the parking lot, opened the bottle, and had a big swig of it.

He made his way over to a bench not far from the liquor store and had a seat. He continued to drink out of the bottle, shielding it with the brown bag to avert suspicion. Things were starting to feel a bit hazy.

Sitting on the bench in the parking lot, Hugo began to think about death.

He did not fear death. For much of his life he, like most people, was preoccupied with living and the concerns of life: work, play, spending time with loved ones, the simple things. Death was unknowable, an abstraction, a distant reality that bore no relevance to life because it was its precise opposite. People lived and people died, this being an intellectual understanding that Hugo reached. For most of Hugo's life, he was too busy with work and raising his family to even begin to think about such a thing as death. Yet, when Hugo's mother, Heidi, passed away it was difficult. A source of continuity that Hugo had, a timeline that he could trace all throughout his own life had been disrupted. Hugo was not interested in talking about the fact that she had died, but Martin was. Martin was eager to read from the Bible, pray, and talk about Heidi's passing as though it would somehow make the loss less painful. Hugo chose to view life and death as a transaction. People are given life, which is like a loan, and they eventually must pay back that loan. No matter the person and no matter the life, death is always the natural consequence. So Hugo had been preoccupied with earthly matters, particularly his family, and he had not bothered to look up and see the dark specter of death hovering in the air, not far away. In young Adrian, Hugo saw so much life, such shimmering, lovely life, how could he even conceive of something like death? All that rested before him was a future of hope, promise, and life. But with each passing year, he watched as Adrian too started to age, with no child of his own on the horizon. The brightness of Adrian's life began to dim and dull. Then there came what happened to her, to Sandra. It happened suddenly. It happened irrevocably. She fell ill. It was so sudden. The doctor said that she had two months left to live. The next nine weeks were unfathomable, full of terror, tender love, nostalgia, and desperation. She being bedridden, Hugo had not left her side during that time. For hours, he held her hand, looking into her eyes, wanting to see what was there. He placed his head close to her head, wanting to feel her warmth, wanting to embrace the life that was in her. Even when he was this close to death, he denied its existence. Then, one day, a day like any other, she did not wake up. He woke up, but she did not. He was not able to comprehend what happened. Panicked, he called Paul, who called the ambulance. They took her to the hospital, but it was too late. Hugo remembered holding her hand even then, noting that it was not warm. Always her hands had been warm, but now they were not. Her fingers were still, and her eyes were closed, meaning he couldn't see into them. There were so many things he wanted to tell her, but all he wanted to tell her more than anything was that he loved her one last time. But he couldn't tell her that he loved her again. She was gone and he was left, abandoned to live with her absence. For her the transaction was complete.

Sipping steadily from the wine, Hugo thought about walking back home. He stepped towards the sidewalk, but just as he was about to continue, a bus came speeding up by him, halting right where he stood. Feeling bold and drawn to the unpredictable, he stowed the wine in the bag and boarded the bus. He had a seat in the back and proceeded to sip his beverage in a clandestine manner.

The city bus sped along, taking a turn and moving out of Wedgwood. The tree coverage quickly vanished as the bus approached the freeway. Feeling dizzy, he spent a few minutes not drinking. The bus passed over the freeway, just to the left of Green Lake, and moved towards the water. Neighborhood passed by the window after neighborhood, an endless stream of houses. People boarded the bus and got off. Hugo continued to enjoy his drink. The bottle was half gone.

Having come to a halt, Hugo was surprised to learn that this was the final stop the bus made. The driver, a skinny man, kindly asked Hugo to exit the bus. He did so, stumbling his way towards the exit. He nearly fell to the ground when he got off the bus. He looked around, wondering where he was. All around him were small houses. Walking, he sipped the wine and laughed to himself. He genuinely felt rather jolly. He turned a corner and found that he was standing in a busy intersection, cars passing by at rapid speeds. Again he sipped from the bottle, burped, and nearly crossed when he wasn't supposed to. Other people were watching him, but he was not aware of it. Realizing that he was passing a grocery store and that he was running low on alcohol, he set down his bottle, straightened himself up, and walked inside. He was able to pass off the appearance of being sober and purchased another bottle of red wine.

Standing outside the grocery store, he finished the first bottle and decided to save the second one for a little later. He kept walking, wondering what he would find next. He turned off the busy street and moved through several blocks of houses that sat under the cover of verdant trees. In the distance, he heard the sound of a dog barking. Frightened, he ran, tripped, and fell onto a grassy lawn, dropping the bottle in the process. He reached for the unopened bottle, climbed up to his feet, and continued on his way. Then, taking a step past yet another block of houses, he was astonished by what he saw next.

There was the sea. Hugo could make out the gentle, foamy surface of the water as it met the sand. Where, exactly, was he? Carefully, he stepped down the sandy hill and walked towards the shore. No one was out. As he reached a log not far from the water, it began to rain. Water fell from the heavens on Hugo, who simply kept walking, having no destination in mind.

His paper bag was getting wet, so he removed the first bottle and threw it on the shore, near the water. He then opened the second bottle and began to sip from it. The air was misty; he could not see very far ahead of where he was moving. His thoughts wandered as he walked.

Who, he wondered, was he? He knew he was Hugo Larson. Named after his great-grandfather, who immigrated to the United States from Spain, he had a family name of sorts. He was a man who had worked hard to provide for his family. But now he was effectively without a family to provide for, so what then was his role? Here he was, spending all of his time on activities that were meaningful to he himself, but what did he do for others? Since she died, what had Hugo done for another human being? He, too, found his sense of identity in being an accountant, but now that was gone as well. He knew that he was Hugo Larson, and he knew as well that he existed, but he didn't know who or what he existed for. What was the purpose of it all? If death had the final say, which it certainly appeared to, then it seemed that there was nothing more to life than to treasure it for what it's worth, while it lasts. But here Hugo had run out of reasons to enjoy life. All he was left with were his petty activities, which had left him feeling hollow lately. Some people suggested that love, pure love was the meaning of life. Well, Hugo had run out of sources of love. What was love? Love, thought Hugo, meant being willing to sacrifice one's self for others, to even die for others. Who in Hugo's life could he say he would be willing to die for? Of course, he would die for his son, but this seemed only natural, and hardly capable of counting. Would he die for Paul? He knew that he liked Paul, that he enjoyed spending time with him, but would he really, truly sacrifice himself for his friend? He didn't know the answer for sure. Then there was Martin. Hugo didn't really want to think about Martin and love, for the resentment he was feeling towards him was overwhelming. Martin's own understanding of love inevitably involved theology and the love of God, which Hugo was not interested in. Hugo had another sip of his wine. Now he was really starting to feel dizzy. Things around him, like a log and the water, were spinning a little bit to him. He picked up a large rock and tossed it feebly into the water. It made a small splash. This, then, was an illustration of the totality of Hugo's existence. All he was, his life, was a rock making a splash in the ocean, there one second, gone the next. As hard as he tried, there was no way that he could do or create anything that was of lasting consequence. Sure, he had amassed a considerable body of wealth through his career, but that money would end up with his son and then disappear. Besides, what did it matter if he made a lot of money for his family and himself? Wasn't it selfish to only be preoccupied with his own family? No, he argued, it was noble and right to work hard to provide for one's family. It was part of being alive. When she was alive, he had felt a sense of meaning, a trajectory in which his life was moving. In short, it was then that he felt loved. The notion of the rock splashing in the water was not the best one available to describe his life, he decided. What Hugo and his life represented was a small piece of wood, floating out towards the center of the sea, floating carelessly about, struck by storms, crashed by the tides, at the mercy of whatever force happened to be present. Previously, he was a piece of wood floating with his wife, and they were together. What Hugo realized in that moment was the fact that the life he was living was not really a life at all, but was a form of walking, wakeful death. He was abandoned to live in an uncaring world. He did feel the love of the people close to him: Paul, Adrian, and Martin to name a few, but this love was blotted out by the overwhelming void of love that existed, the empty space in his bedroom, the photographs, the books, the clothes, all of the little things that were imbued with traces of her spirit. This void was threatening to obliterate him. He could feel himself existing in a delicate balance with it. Succumbing to the void was not a matter of dying; Hugo knew grief wouldn't kill him, but the consequences of it went deeper than death, to a form of spiritual annihilation. It was entirely possible that Hugo would go about living his life, doing the little things he liked to do with the people he liked to do them with, and that all the while he would be living in silent desperation. Halfway through with the second bottle,

Hugo could drink no more. He threw the bottle into the sea and tumbled, crashing over onto the sand, where he fell asleep. The rain pelted him as he slept.

When he awoke, it was no longer raining, but it was still cloudy. It was getting to be dark. He rose from where he slept, covered in sand, his head feeling as though it was split in two. Where, he wondered, had the wine gone? He looked for it until he realized that he had gotten rid of it. Filled with remorse for throwing it away, he walked along the shore, thinking that he needed to get home.

Leaving behind the misty, foamy sea, he stumbled up the sandy hill, moved through the cover of several trees, and arrived back on the residential street. The world was unchanged, as though nothing had ever happened to it. Now it was really getting to be dark. It was also quite cold. Hugo put his hands in his pockets as he walked to keep them warm. A bus passed and then another, but they were not the route number that would get him home. He was, he realized, in Ballard, walking along the edge of western Seattle, moving with the sea.

All Hugo was interested in doing these days was drinking and sleeping. Did he need to make changes? This was a question that demanded a great deal of thought, but he decided that, no, he did not need to change. The way in which he was living his life was perfectly suited for him. Thoughts of losing people close to him invaded his mind. What if Paul died? What if Adrian died? How would he proceed to live without these people in his life? Better not think about such things, he told himself.

After an hour of walking, he finally found a bus stop that would lead him home. He stood at it, touching his head with his hand, and waited patiently for the bus. Finally, it arrived and he rode it home. Having arrived home, he went upstairs, had a shower, and went to bed. He fell asleep immediately and slept soundly all throughout the night.

2.

Looking down at his feet carefully, he navigated the terrain. They were walking up a sharp incline, and he could feel it, he breathing in and out deeply. Above, there were trees that protected them from the faint misting that was coming down. Adrian, who was not in the greatest shape but had the advantage of thirty or so years, was leading them forward. Mindful of rolling his ankle, Hugo walked cautiously, stepping around one rock and then another. Occasionally he looked up, and when he did, he beheld the beauty surrounding them. There were walls of trees, green, full, and vital. Beyond the trees, there was the view of down below. Layer of trees descended upon layer of trees, and above, in the distance, there were the other grassy hills that rose high up into the sky. These hills rose around the contours of the freeway, which edged along.

"How much farther do we have to go?" Hugo asked, complaining.

"Not that much more to go."

"Good, I'm feeling tired." He couldn't remember the last time he had gone hiking other than in Chelan. In fact, he could hardly remember the last time he had done anything physically demanding. Poor weather meant that he had been less inclined to go swimming.

They had been walking upwards for at least two hours. Hugo's stomach was growling with hunger. He was the type of person who was capable of enjoying working out and complaining at the same time. Still, he resolved to buckle down, keep walking, and be strong. He didn't want to appear aging or weak before his son, so he had that to motivate him.

"How's life back at Java City?" Hugo asked.

"It's not too bad."

"Have things changed much since you left there?"

"There are some new faces working there, but for the most part things are the same."

"I see."

"It doesn't feel too great to be back, to be honest."

"Why not?"

Adrian paused, and then said, "It feels like walking back to a place you wanted to leave, your tail hanging between your legs. It feels like letting go of all your remaining pride. It just feels, I don't know, undignified."

"Yes, but this was the choice you made, wasn't it? You decided that the business program hadn't been for you, and so you chose to return to the job that you chose to return to. It's honest labor, isn't it?"

"It is honest labor, but it's not fulfilling labor."

"I understand that. But what other option do you have at this point? In a complex situation like this, you need to take care of a multitude of needs. You have your short-term needs and your long-term needs. Long-term, you need to find work that is meaningful and fulfilling, but equally importantly, you need to find work that can meet your short-term needs. Like it or not, Java City meets those short-term needs."

"It's true, it's just a bitter pill to swallow."

"Well, you don't have to stay there long. You just need to figure out what you want to do. You're young. You have plenty of time and opportunity to make a new start." Hugo thought he was starting to sound more like Martin than himself.

With another curve in the road, they passed by a wall of rocks. They kept walking, the only ones present on the trail. As of late, the weather had taken a turn for the worse. Virtually every day in the last week had been predominately cloudy, with plenty of rain, wind, and cold. Being a native of the northwest, Hugo didn't mind. What he did mind, though, was the threat of power outages as a result of an oncoming storm scheduled for the next couple of days. This storm, apparently, would be severe, powerful, and lasting.

It had been a few days since Hugo rode the bus to the beach in a drunken stupor. The previous couple of days saw him drinking only once or twice a day, substantially less than he was having before. Feeling antipathy towards the notion of drinking less, he simply proceeded in living his life the way he did. Life seemed rather passive to him. One day passed after another. He had not seen Paul or Martin in a while, though they kept calling. He wanted to make seeing Adrian a priority because he wanted to connect with him about what was going on in his life. As he was walking, Hugo found that he had no urge to drink, which was refreshing. For all intents and purposes, nature was presenting itself as his alcohol, his source of calm, ease, and relaxation.

There was no dramatic moment between Adrian and Hugo, in which Hugo articulated the resentment that he felt towards his son's situation. Instead, a week or so earlier Adrian sent Hugo a letter, which explained that he regained his job at Java City and that he was itching to hike Rattlesnake Ridge sometime. In turn, Hugo called his son, speaking to him gently and kindly, saying that he would be pleased to go on a hike with him. So here he was, suffering, trying to enjoy time with his son, though the discussion was not quite comfortable. The conversation flowed easily enough between them, but it was not comfortable, for it was as though they were not on the same page.

Hugo was not sure how he felt about his son's working at his old café. He supposed it was fine for the time being. But he was left wondering, in eager anticipation, to know what was planned next. What Hugo wanted to do was to be a role model figure for his son, to guide him on the path that he would take. But what did Hugo know about paths?

One final stretch of steep climbing rested before them. Hugo was already panting, out of breath from the gain in elevation. Adrian was walking just a bit ahead of him, and so he mustered his available strength to meet his son. They walked past a large rock, and all of a sudden, the view was afforded to them. In a three-sixty panorama, there was an expansive view of forests, rife with lush, green trees, just below the hills, all of it under the hovering clouds. In fact, from where Hugo and Adrian stood, they were above several layers of clouds. They could see outward for miles, and all at once Hugo became aware of just how small he and Adrian were. In the scheme of things, the cosmos, creation, the earth, across all time, Hugo and Adrian were just two people, creatures prone to fear.

Hugo and Adrian had a seat and ate their lunch.

"I was going to wait to tell you about this," Adrian began, taking a bite of an apple, "but I suppose now is as good a time as any."

"Tell me what?"

Adrian reached into his backpack and pulled out a piece of paper. "I saved it for you!"

Hugo took the paper in his hand and inspected it. "The Seattle Academy for Excellence in Photography."

"What is it?" Hugo asked.

"It's a program in photography. It trains you to become a master photographer, offering courses, intensive internships, one-on-one mentoring, and help finding a job or setting up a private practice."

Overwhelmingly sensing déjà vu, Hugo asked, "Now, son, do you think this is the right thing for you to be doing?"

"I do. I looked into it. I grabbed coffee with an alumni of the program and asked him all about it. The program lasts two years, so it's a much slower pace than the business program was. They start classes all the time. Plus, unlike, the business program, this is actually a field that I'm passionate about. I care about photography!"

"I know you do. But I thought you said there were no jobs in photography, and that there was no point in pursuing it."

"I thought so, too. But I've been doing a lot of thinking in the last month. The truth is you gotta follow what you are passionate about in life. That's what you did, right?"

"That is what I did."

"Now I feel like I am ready to do the same."

"You do?"

"Yes. The classes are part-time, so I can still work at Java City even while I am taking them."

"Well, you know that I can't help you pay for the program. Like I said before, I believe that we need to work hard in this life to make our own way. That's what I did for myself, and that's what I want you to do, too."

"I understand, Dad."

"It sounds like you have done your research, and you have found a program that works for you. I offer you my full support."

"Thanks, Dad!"

Hugo patted him on the side of the arm. "Should we head down?"

"Sure, let's go."

Walking, Hugo was nervous, thinking about the news he had just heard. But surely this situation is different than the last one, he thought. Also, there was the fact that Adrian was following his passion to take into account. What was passion? What was that driving force that led people in such different directions? Unconsciously, Hugo's passion was accounting. Adrian, on the other hand, seemed to be very aware of his passion, and it looked like he was prepared to follow it with all of his heart. Hugo felt happy for his son, but also a bit nervous, afraid that for some reason this program wouldn't work out, either. Not knowing that he could handle another devastating loss in his life, Hugo was anxious to hold onto things as they were. At least when Adrian had been exclusively working as a barista there had been no devastating failures to reckon with. Then again, as Hugo believed very strongly, working a mediocre job and never bothering to even aspire to be more was the greatest failure of all. Not trying something new was its own form of loss.

The truth was that for the last few years Adrian and Hugo were estranged from each other, but that had changed in the last year. In fact, they had grown to be rather close. So when Adrian decided to do something, to try something, it implicated Hugo. Perhaps that was the consequence of living in relationship with another person, namely, that you felt like you were a part of them and that they were a part of you. When one of you was hurt, so too was the other. Hugo would be sure to watch Adrian closely in the following months, to check in with him, to monitor his progress in a loving, fatherly way.

They hiked all the way back down Rattlesnake Ridge until they reached Adrian's old, beat-up car. They drove home, speaking more about the new program, the sense of excitement, of gain, palpable.

3.

The bright, fluorescent lights of the drug store were oppressive as they shined down on Hugo. He was walking through the cereal aisle, towards the back area where the pharmacy was housed. Of course, there was a line of people waiting to pick up their drugs. Annoyed, Hugo waited in line, watching one person walk away from the front desk and then another. Finally, it was his turn.

"Hello," an older looking lady said in a white coat.

"Hi."

"What can I do for you today?"

"Here to pick up."

"Your name?"

"Hugo Larson."

"Date of birth?"

He gave her the necessary information she asked for, and then watched as she scurried off to retrieve his pills. Holding the bag in his left hand, he paid his co-pay and then left.

"Have a nice day. Stay safe out there," the pharmacist called.

"Hmmph."

The city was placed on high wind alert and was expected to remain in such a state for the next three days. Rumors of a massive storm were circulating in Hugo's circles. The people he knew talked about wind and rain, about power going out, about danger. Just the other day Martin called and asked if Hugo wanted to spend the next couple of days living with them in Kirkland, just to be safe. He declined, citing how thoughtful Martin had been, but said that he was perfectly safe on his own in Wedgwood, thank you very much. Truly, Hugo had lived through enough storms in Seattle to know that, really, they just weren't that big of a deal. He had plenty of supplies that he might need at home and he was resilient, so there was no need for concern. Additionally, he had two bottles of wine at home.

Stepping out of the drug store, Hugo was met by a blustery, fierce breeze. He looked up and saw that trees were swaying from side to side, that a heavy rain was falling. Great, he thought to himself, wonderful. The rain, which fell at a slanted angle, cascaded in direct opposition to the direction in which Hugo was headed. Each step was demanding all of his energy to take. Within minutes, he was utterly soaked. His hands were cold, so he placed them in the pocket of his coat. In an ironic gesture, he wore a tie with the sun on it, but it seemed that his magical charm was powerless in the face of such brutal weather. The few people who were out walking about were all wearing hoods and looking down towards the ground. Hugo had no hood to wear, for he did not own a rain jacket. As he approached a crosswalk, he stepped right into the center of a massive puddle, the water rising up to his calves, and he cursed to himself.

It seemed as though the walk home was never going to end. But as endless as it had appeared, before Hugo knew it, he was taking the turn off Mason Street, towards his street. He continued walking, as briskly as he was capable, heading down the gentle slope that led towards his home. The sky was dark, rainfall obscuring the trees in the background. The houses looked like small, delicate shelters from the storm that were being attacked by wind and rain. Now he was passing by the apple tree that was owned by Kim Schaefer. He wondered if she was staying safe in this weather. People seemed to worry about Hugo staying safe, so how was a woman who was fifty percent older than him to get by? However, he was not left to ponder her well being for long, for he was faced with more immediate concerns. He looked at his garden, which looked pitiful in the barrage of falling water. Then he thought of the lawn, which was getting to be overgrown once more.

Still walking quickly, Hugo turned and headed up the path to his door. Inside, the relief he experienced was joyous. Casting off his sweater, he watched as droplets of rain fell all over his carpet. He took off his shoes and then walked into his bedroom. After changing his clothes, he went back downstairs and sat on the sofa for a moment.

Bothered by his thoughts, struggling at first to get up, he eventually made his way into the kitchen, where he opened a bottle of chardonnay. He had a big swig of it and looked through the glass sliding door. Next, he went over to the table.

He sat down. The storm around him was growing. The sound of rain pelting the roof increased in volume until it seemed as though a hole was going to form. Thunder could be heard in the distance. Hugo sat, sipping his beverage, and soon the glass was empty. Filling the glass with more wine, he continued to drink steadily from it.

It was not long before he finished the first bottle. His head was a mess, and he felt dizzy. Deciding that he would go and lie down for a bit, he rose from the table, stumbled up the stairs, and fell onto the bed. He closed his eyes and drifted off to sleep.

In his sleep, he dreamed that he was standing on the edge of a dock, overlooking a massive crater. He stood alone, the feeling of loneliness penetrating to his deepest recesses. Standing there, he began to cry, and his tears fell into the crater. He cried and he cried. He cried for Adrian, for Paul, for Martin, for Lily, but mostly he cried for her. His tears filled the crater, and after a few minutes of crying, he saw that the crater was now full of water, that it was a lake. Turning around, he was going to leave the dock, but he tripped and fell backward, into the water. Unable to swim, he waved his arms wildly in the water, and eventually, he sank into the water, into his own tears.

Hugo woke up quickly. He was horrified by his own dream. How had his mind fashioned such frightening, strange content to pass off as a dream? First and foremost, Hugo was not a crier. He was never known to be one to break down into tears. Actually, this was not true. In the past few months, he had done plenty of crying. He simply liked to present himself as being someone who was too strong to cry. Secondly, Hugo was more than competent as a swimmer. There simply was no way that he was going to drown in a lake of tears. The issues with the reality of the dream not-withstanding, he was deeply disturbed by the dream. He still felt the effects of the wine.

There was the sound of someone knocking at the door. All he wanted to do was escape from his own life, to disappear. Certainly, he didn't want to be in the company of others, whoever it was. Most likely it was Paul knocking, wanting to check in on him during the storm. Declining to answer, he sat on the bed, running a hand through his hair. He rolled around in the bed, wanting to go back to sleep. For the next thirty minutes, he rolled around in bed, restless.

Finally, he got out of bed, walking into the bathroom. He ran cold water against his face, enjoying the chilling effect it had. He looked at the mirror and thought about how big it seemed to be. Then he walked downstairs, taking a look out the window. Still, the rain was falling with a ferocious intensity, the wind blowing just as powerfully.

The phone rang. Hugo considered answering it, seeing that it was Martin, but he didn't want to get into a conversation with him at the present moment. He listened as the phone rang, its tone gratingly repetitive. A minute later and all was quiet again. Once more, if for only a moment, Hugo felt a peace at being in solitude. But lurking in the shadows of the room, around him, there were demons of loneliness that were settling. Hugo went into the study and picked out a book. He sat down on the sofa, behind the light of the big windows, and read.

He read, but his thoughts were all over the place. Hardly could he concentrate. Again and again, he found that he was reading the same sentence, that the lines of text seemed to blur together on the page. Frustrated, he put the book down, and lay down on the bed. It was too cold to try and sleep. He got up from the sofa and walked over to the kitchen, to where his second bottle of wine sat. By his estimation, it was time to start drinking again.

Realizing that it was dark in the room, he reached for the light switch, but when he flipped it, nothing in the room changed. He turned the switch on and off over again, but the room remained shrouded in darkness. He had lost power.

Of course, it was getting darker, the sun behind the clouds was setting. He would drink, he decided, but first, he should get some things ready. He walked over to the closet, which was next to the study and across the hall from the bathroom, and looked inside until he found a flashlight. He turned it on, went into the kitchen and made sure he had food to eat that would not necessitate actual cooking, and then sat down in front of the bottle.

Someone was knocking at the door yet again. He sighed and waited, but when he heard the knocking sound one more time, he realized that he could not ignore it any longer. He walked across the living room and answered the door. Standing, shaking with cold, dripping rainwater all over the ground, was Paul.

"Hey there," Paul said.

"Hi."

"Can I come in?"

"I'm actually a bit busy with—"

"I don't have power or any flashlights. I am sadly unprepared."

"Sure. Come on in."

Paul stepped inside and hung up his jacket. Clearly, he was soaked in only the few seconds he spent walking outside. Since it was getting darker they lit some candles. Paul had a seat on the sofa and looked at Hugo.

"So," Paul said.

"So?"

"No power here, either?"

"Nope."

"That's okay." Paul turned and looked out the window. "Quite the storm, isn't it?"

"It's pretty severe."

"They made it sound on the news like it was going to be the end of the world. It's not that bad, though."

"No," Hugo agreed, "it's not that bad."

"How have you been?" Paul asked.

"Fine, and you?"

"Not too bad."

There was an awkward pause between them. "Can I offer you a drink?" Hugo offered.

"No, thank you."

"Why not?"

"I'm just not interested. I appreciate the offer, though."

Hugo poured himself another glass and sat back down in his armchair, facing his friend.

"Have you thought about the trip?"" Paul inquired.

"Yes," Hugo replied, "I don't think it is a great idea."

"Really? Can I ask why?"

"It's just not a great time of the year. The weather is going to be like this," he said, pointing out the window. Then he said, "I want to be close to my home, to my family, and I don't want to burden you with having to drive."

Paul sat up straight on the sofa. His green eyes had a sparkle to them. "Well, I don't think the weather is going to be much of a problem. It's not going to be like this in Grayland. The storm is just a temporary thing. As I recall, your family had been irritating you. Wouldn't it be nice to have a little space from Martin and them? I'm not trying to pull you away from your family or anything; it's just that some space apart could be nice. We would only be gone two nights. It's not like a week or anything. Lastly, it's no burden to me to have to drive. You know I actually enjoy a good drive, and this trip is full of beautiful scenery to admire."

"Okay."

"So, I guess I'm not trying to invalidate how you feel, but I want to make the case that going to Grayland could be really good for both of us. We spent a while talking about loss, and those conversations weighed pretty heavily on me. I don't doubt that those conversations didn't weigh on you as well. I have spent my whole life going on little trips to Grayland. It is a place that is pretty dear to me, and it would be my joy to share it with you. Wouldn't it be nice to escape for a little while?"

"Yes, I suppose it would be."

"Then let's go! Think of the adventure!"

"I don't know..."

"Hugo," Paul said, "I came over here twice today in the rain because I wanted to talk to you about this trip. There is no one I would rather go to Grayland with than you. I am really excited by just the prospect of going. Please?"

Hugo could tell that Paul really wanted to go on this trip. In Paul's eyes, there was a desperate hope that Hugo would agree to come along. He started to think about what he had at stake in going on the trip. At this point, he couldn't care less about being apart from Martin and his family for a couple of days. He was just making excuses as to why he didn't want to go, and what he was finding was that his excuses were collapsing. He needed to go on this trip. He, too, was acquainted with loss, and there was much to be gained from a trip to the coast, however small such a venture might appear to be.

"All right," Hugo said, "I'll go."

"You will? Fantastic!" Paul practically rose from the sofa in celebration, but Hugo stayed put.

"How about a glass of wine to celebrate?" Hugo asked.

"No, thanks."

Paul's declination caused Hugo to become aware of his own habits. Was he drinking too much? He didn't know, but it made him uncomfortable to think that he was working through his second bottle of wine for the day while his friend was completely sober.

"You should have something to drink," Hugo asserted, "It will be good for you."

"Really, I'm fine."

There was a pause as Hugo sipped his beverage. He was starting to feel dizzy.

"Hugo..." Paul began.

"What?"

"Don't you think, maybe, you've had enough to drink?"

"Why do you ask?"

"It just seems like you are drinking awfully quickly. How much have you had today?"

"A couple of glasses."

Then Paul saw the first, empty bottle sitting on the kitchen table in plain sight.

"Hugo," Paul spoke, his tone rising, "You need to stop."

"No, I don't."

Paul got up from the sofa and walked into the kitchen, towards the second bottle.

"What are you doing?" Hugo asked, who had also risen and was walking into the kitchen.

"I'm cutting you off." Paul grabbed the second bottle and started to pour what remained down the sink.

"What are you doing?!"

"No more. You've had enough."

Hugo slapped Paul across the face. The bottle fell to the ground, shattering into pieces of glass shards. Paul shrank back a little, but he stayed on his feet.

"Hugo, this isn't you."

"What do you mean? I have only ever been the same person I always am."

"This is wrong, Hugo. You need help." Paul said. A red mark was already beginning to form on his face.

"I don't need anyone. I don't need you. So stop trying to help me! I'm fine!"

"Okay," Paul said.

"Okay, what?"

Paul turned, left the kitchen, walked to the front door, and let himself out. Hugo stood in the kitchen. What he was most angry about was the fact that he no longer had any wine to drink.

4.

"I just can't find a reason, to be honest."

"A reason...to live?"

Hugo sat uneasily on a large, leather couch, looking into the eyes of his new counselor. Highly uncomfortable, he didn't see any point in answering the questions that were asked of him.

"Yes, I don't see the point in living when my reason for living was taken from me."

"I see. There was a reason, but it is now gone, and there is nothing that can take its place."

"Well, nothing can take her place. So no."

"I understand. Do you think there is any other way to find a reason to live?"

"Another reason?"

"Yes, something that gives you a feeling of fulfillment, that makes you happy. Do you think you could live a life that pays tribute to the person that Sandra was?"

"She deserves the best."

"Mmhmm."

"So if I were to find a reason to live that honored her, it would need to be the best reason of all. "

"And why should it not be?"

"But I can't find anything."

"Which brings us back to where we started."

Hugo felt annoyed. "Yes, it does."

It was only their third session, and in Hugo's professional opinion it was not going well. They were trying to get to know each other, but this was difficult to do when Hugo didn't believe in the process. The only reason he was here was because of his brother. Further, in his mind, there was no sense in going to therapy, because there was no way things were going to get better.

"Does anything bring you fulfillment? Any fulfillment at all?"

"Yes."

"Like what?"

"I feel invested in my son."

"Tell me more."

"I have been watching him develop his career, and it brings me a lot of joy to see him as he learns and grows. She and I raised him together, and so part of me feels like," Hugo looked around the office and then said, "part of me feels like if I can raise Adrian well, then I can make her happy."

"That's beautiful."

"Yes, it is beautiful. But like I said. There's no point, because she is gone. She is not even aware that I am raising Adrian the way that I am, because she is dead."

"You're bumming me out!" Christopher cried.

"Sorry, but it's the truth. When we die, we are gone. Worms eat our flesh. We decompose over the course of months and years, and eventually, every last physical trace of us is gone. There is nothing left. The only hope is for us to have children who have children."

"Having children is an important part of the human experience, yes."

"Do you have children?" asked Hugo defensively.

"Two sons."

"Do they bring you fulfillment?"

"Yes, they do. Now, will you answer one of my questions?" Hugo sighed. "Okay."

"You say that Sandra is gone. Do you really believe that? Is there not a part of you that believes that she has a presence in your heart? Is there not a part of you that believes that somehow, somewhere, she is looking down, watching you and smiling?"

"That sounds like New Age nonsense." Hugo was reminded of Lily.

"Your call. What else brings you fulfillment? Even just a little bit of it."

Aware that Martin had asked a similar question months earlier, Hugo replied, "Oh, well I care about my brother. I care about my friend Paul, or at least I did."

"What happened? Why don't you care about Paul?"

"You ask a lot of questions."

"You answer a lot of questions," Christopher answered, smiling.

"I don't really want to go into it."

"Okay."

"He came over and he poured out all of my wine. How could he do that?"

"Pour out your wine?"

"Yes."

"Well easily. He probably just went up to the sink and—"

"So I like to enjoy wine. Big deal."

"Big deal."

"It's not like I'm telling him how to live his life."

"How much do you like to drink?"

"It varies."

"Ballpark?" Christopher was occasionally making notes on a notepad, but more so he was locked into the conversation.

"Well, to be fair, I had a lot that day."

"What day?"

"The first day of that big storm last week."

"Gotcha."

"I had maybe a bottle and a half."

"In a day?"

"Yes."

Christopher had short brown hair and large glasses. He touched his glasses with his hand and said, "That's no good, Hugo."

"What's not?"

"Drinking that much. No good will come from that."

"Easy for you to say. Drinking makes me feel better."

"Yeah? Well drinking a glass of wine a day is no big deal. A bottle and a half? While in grief? Big deal."

"Who are you to tell me that I shouldn't drink?"

"Well, of course I can't make you do anything. But last time I checked, you were paying me money to talk to you about your life, about what you are going through. That's why we're sitting here and talking. But you already knew that."

"Fair enough."

"So what I'm saying to you is this: if you and I are going to work together, if you are going to work through the grief process, because believe it or not that's what you are navigating through, then you need to cut down the drinking. I'd like it best if you cut it out altogether, but it's okay if you have a glass every now and then. There are a lot of blurred lines around drinking. What's responsible? What's not? It depends on the motivation behind using, body chemistry, and just plain who you ask."

"Okay."

"So, promise me you'll cut down on the drinking?"

Hugo looked at his own shoes. "Sure," he said, feeling like he had no other option.

"Cool," Christopher replied, "I think we're out of time."

5.

Nighttime was approaching and he had consumed two bottles of it over the course of the day. Just as the sun was setting, he passed out on the sofa.

November

I.

The ocean was infinite.

Staring out into a cloudy horizon, Hugo was filled with awe as he considered the sea. The sky was a milky, pearly gray, and the sand was a bright brown. In the background, there was the sound of the tide, that gentle respiration of the ocean, and Hugo could see from the porch of the cabin, faintly, the waves crashing into the sand, again and again pulverizing but never conquering it. An occasional seagull flew by, the sound of its call reverberating throughout. Despite what Hugo could see, the fact remained that visibility was actually quite low. The day was misty, clouds obscuring the view. In the air, there was the feeling of ambiguity itself, along with the sense of deep mystery.

As Hugo previously observed, people and their lives were like pieces of wood that drifted into the ocean and were at the mercy of what they encountered. Well, here was the ocean, and what a sight it was to behold. Hugo looked at the logs that rested on the sand, imagining smaller pieces of wood floating out on the waters. If Hugo's life was a piece of driftwood, then he knew that he had fallen off course lately. It took him a while, a couple weeks, to realize that he had truly been abusing alcohol, that he was oversleeping, in short, that he was depressed. Hitting Paul, his very best friend, was the one thing he would never want to do, to hurt him, but this had been precisely what he had done. Hugo hurt his own friend, and why? Because he had wanted something to drink? No, it went deeper than that. Hugo had been avoiding grief. Christopher used that word, and it stuck. Hugo was navigating the grieving process. He stared into the ocean for hours, allowing it to comfort him, to whisper sacred truths to him, and occasionally a smaller, but still present voice asserted that none of it really mattered. Death is supreme, this little voice of hollowness said.

Hugo and Paul had did not speak for a week after he hit him, leaving their plans of taking a trip up in the air. Then, one day while walking to the store, Hugo saw him. They made eye contact, and just as Paul was prepared to look away Hugo broke down and told him that he was sorry he had hurt him and that he needed him. Paul certainly kept his guard up, accepting the apology in a cold manner. Again Hugo had apologized, pleading for absolution, saying that in his heart Paul was his dear friend and that he was wrong to drink so much. Only therapy enabled him to realize the toll that drinking was taking on him.

A few days after their initial conversation, Paul forgave him and said that he was still willing to go on the trip to the coast with him. However, he had terms by which Hugo needed to abide.

"First," Paul said, "you need to promise me you won't touch a drop of alcohol during the trip. Second, you will only sleep at night. Third, you will stay in therapy."

Hugo's initial attendance was rather spotty, but he liked Christopher despite whatever he said otherwise. "I can do those things," Hugo replied with solemnity.

"The truth is this," Paul continued, "I love you like a brother. It wasn't the slap that worried me so much as the hurting person behind it. That's what concerned me."

Hugo had been anticipating the trip with excitement and trepidation. As the day in the middle of November approached, he packed his bag, making sure he brought his sunniest ties despite the gloomy weather outside. The rains had returned to Seattle. It was cold out, and consequently, the weather reflected Hugo's inner state. Nevertheless, in the midst of feeling hollow, desiring to drink and sleep, Hugo was optimistic, thinking that, just maybe, things were about to get much better for him. He was now receiving professional help. He was talking openly about his loss and affliction with the people close to him not in a histrionic way, but in a more candid, heartfelt one. Put differently, Hugo was feeling a lot of contrasting things. His heart and mind were all over the board. As always seemed to be the case, some days were easier than others. Some days were brutal, hard, unpredictable, a mess, and other days went smoothly, possessing little graces. One day Hugo would be breaking down while lying on the sofa. On another day, he was laughing until he couldn't breathe at something Paul said. What a day would develop into was never immediately apparent. Hugo was left to navigate his days like everyone, blindly. Clinging to the hobbies and people he had available to him, during those three weeks leading up to the trip he got back into the habit of going swimming, playing chess with Paul, and reading more literary classics. Everywhere in his house, her spirit dwelt, but he was feeling better equipped to commune with it, to not run away from it, to not panic. This was not always the case. Sometimes, when his heart began to beat quickly, or when he started to twitch or sweat, he would go and pour himself wine, but as Christopher said, it was difficult to draw a line and say where abuse began. On the whole, though, since becoming reconciled to Paul, Hugo was drinking much less, and this was a cause for celebration. The notion of not drinking a drop while on the coast certainly intimidated him, though.

Still, Hugo continued to stare at the sea, reflecting, thinking, feeling, simply occupying the same space as the waves, his heart at peace.

In therapy, he had realized a number of things, but the most important one was the larger trajectory of his own life since she had died. Hugo was more or less in denial during the initial months. He was not interested in talking about it. He genuinely believed that there was no point or function in having a discussion. Despite the efforts of his friends and family to discuss it, he was resistant. Thinking or talking about it had caused him immense suffering. Next, he was angry. Seething, intense, fiery anger had consumed him. He lashed out at people, was prone to panic attacks, and was rather on edge. Though he started to talk about his wife, the conversations were marked by intensity, bitterness, and other feelings that threatened to destroy the self. This was the story of his life during the spring and early summer. Third, and most recently, he was depressed. The easiest of the three to identify in himself, in depression he developed habits that had proven to be rather self-destructive. Similar to the denial phase, he saw no point in talking about her, but more universally, he saw no point at all in talking about or doing anything. Purpose and fulfillment eluded him as he wandered in darkness. He withdrew from the people close to him. This was precisely the point at which Christopher started to intervene. Hopefully, Hugo was through the worst of it. He could not fathom tolerating any more destruction in his life or the lives of others.

Staring at the horizon, Hugo was left to wonder, what came after depression?

Intellectually, he understood that the final step in the grief cycle, supposedly, was acceptance. He reviewed it all with Christopher. But what did acceptance look like? Such a concept seemed to rest beyond him. It was not attainable with the understanding that he had. Maybe it was just a matter of time. Lily said that time had a way of changing things, changing us. Well, Lily said a lot of things. Meanwhile, another thing Christopher said about grief was that it wasn't a linear line, but that rather it was more of a dynamic phenomenon, that people would go from being in denial, to angry, to depressed, to accepting, all within days, within minutes.

What was this word, "grief", and how was it capable of capturing what he felt, what he thought, what he saw?

Mesmerized by the ocean, Hugo was startled when Paul patted him on the back.

"How are you doing?"

"Oh, all right."

"Want to go and walk along the shore?"

"Sure."

"Let's go!"

Paul started to trot towards the water. Hugo followed after. Both men, while not young in a relative case, were still more than able to run short distances. They ran and they ran, but the water got no closer to them. It was the second, middle day of their trip. The first day, which was rainy and dark, comprised of playing chess and chatting. Today, which was supposed to be the nicest albeit still nasty day, was their opportunity to spend some time outside, they knew.

The sound of the waves crashing was growing louder. Eventually, it was a hushing sound that silenced everything else. The sky was bright, though the sun was securely hidden behind the clouds.

"This is probably a good place," Paul said.

They proceeded to walk together, at a slow, peaceful pace. With the exception of the houses that lined the edge of the sand, there really was no way to gain a sense of perspective. The sea was everything. They walked and they talked, often laughing.

"I'm so glad we made it out here," Paul cheered. "It has been nice to just get away from everything, don't you think?"

"I agree. I want to go swimming in the ocean sometime."

"Then go for it!"

"Maybe I will!"

"You sure talk a lot. Where's the action?"

"I'm waiting for the right moment," Hugo said, "and I think it's coming soon."

"Very well."

"Now, tell me something," Hugo began.

"What?"

"We have been out here a little more than a day. I can feel the way in which the ocean is a healing presence. What else leads to healing? What will enable me to be healed of my grief?"

Paul was walking at Hugo's side. "Well, I don't think it happens overnight. It's a process, a long and complicated one."

"I agree."

"One thing I think that does help bring healing is to remember."

"Remember?"

"Yes, to tell stories. Think of it as an exercise."

"Oh," Hugo said, "I see."

"So what stories can you tell me? What can you tell me about Sandra?"

"Hmm."

"We don't have to talk about it if you don't want to or don't feel ready."

Clearly feeling empowered by the state of things, Hugo had a desire to remember, to open up his mind towards what had happened in his life rather than evade it as was typically the case. Hugo wanted to go towards the memory, not away. He wanted to allow himself to feel the feelings, rather than numb himself. So he spoke, telling Paul what most immediately came to mind.

"Well, if you really want me to tell you a story, here goes. Sandra was born near San Diego. Because her father was in the armed forces, they moved numerous times, but they spent the bulk of her childhood living in Maskville, Indiana. She was the youngest of five children. Growing up in a firm Roman Catholic family, her parents raised her to be responsible and astute. Growing up, she was often teased by her siblings, as siblings will do, and she had a happy childhood. In particular, she had a very active mind. It was uncommon for her to wander into the woods and pretend that she was going on adventures. She would rescue a prince from a dragon, or else she would invent her own imaginary pet that possessed whatever superpowers she wanted it to have. Flying? Sure. Swimming long distances? You got it. She owned an active mind, but she had an even more analytical mind. She spent much of her time reading the classics, the experimental prose stylists who shaped her own abstract brain: Joyce, Woolf, and Faulkner in particular."

"I know you enjoyed reading them, too."

"Also she was athletic, playing soccer, basketball, and even swimming a little bit. Not only that, but she was musical as well, taking piano lessons for many years. Playing the piano is something she would do for much of our life to-gether. Anyway, I think it is fair to say that she was skeptical of her parents, skeptical of society, and skeptical of institutions such as the Catholic Church. Her mind was complex, capable of generating more ideas and thoughts than she could ever hope to convey at any given time. That was one of the great challenges she had had: expressing all the things she was thinking. Throughout her life, she wrote in a journal, where she reflected on her own experiences and processed the world she was living in.

"Tell me more."

"That world that she was living in expanded when her family and she moved to Edmonds, Washington. She was starting 11h grade. The move wasn't particularly challenging. Sandra had had plenty of friends in Maskville, and she saw there being no problem in making friends in a new place. In particular, she enjoyed how green and forested Western Washington is, for in its misty, green lushness she encountered a new headspace for herself. She went to Edmonds Middle School and then to Hillcrest High School. It was there that she and I met. We were both juniors when we were placed in the same couple of classes. Oh, what a magical time it was. I remember seeing her, her green eyes, her black hair, and beholding her sense of serenity. Above all else, Sandra emanated a sense of serenity, for she was truly at ease with the world and with life, no matter what a situation presented her with."

"It's true," Paul nodded slowly.

"In that regard, she and Janet are very similar people. While some would accuse her of being disorganized and scattered, I would say that Sandra wasn't. She was calm, relaxed, even passive. Also, she was highly thoughtful. When we met, it was not long before we started dating. I was drawn to her mind, and I'm not so sure what she saw in me. I think in me she saw someone who, like her, loved to learn and think. We were two thinkers.

Hugo continued, "Anyway, we dated in high school, and that was a fun, if silly, time for us. Who doesn't look back on high school relationships and smile just a little bit? Sandra was smart, but she didn't take school all that seriously. She loved to learn, but she didn't enjoy the monotonous grind of school. Consequently, when I got into UW, she had to settle for Seattle University, which was still an excellent school, if not quite as excellent as UW. It was sad to be away from her. We were going to two colleges located less than ten miles apart, but it had felt like we were entering two very different worlds. She went off to her school and I went to mine, us pledging our affection toward each other, stating that we wouldn't let distance get in the way of how much we cared for each other."

"That was a really hard time for you two."

"While she was at SU, she figured out rather quickly that she wanted to study journalism. What she was interested in doing was taking her analytical, critical mind, and putting it to use to investigate and write stories. It was a natural fit for her because she loved to chase after a good story, and her passion for social justice meant that she would be doing something she found to be fulfilling. I, on the other hand, went towards accounting. I possess a mind that believes in order and structure, and so the number balancing of accounting was natural for me. Throughout high school, I loved English and history, but during college I found my calling in mathematics. Mostly, I spent college goofing off, playing chess, and riding my bike to Sandra so we could go on dates. It was a fun time, but the distance remained a challenge. You didn't have technology the way you have it today. It was writing letters, or talking on the phone, or being together in person. Simple as that. There was none of this interacting on smartphones or with social media on the computer. But I'm distracting myself. We spent four years in college, well she actually took five years and double majored in Journalism along with English Literature, but we were living together during that final year of her schooling.

"She was so smart."

"Once we were reunited and living together, it was a joyous time. We went on many adventures through Seattle together. We would explore restaurants and bars together, walk around Green Lake, or explore Magnuson Park, for we

lived in a house right by that park. It was a time of maturation for us. Of course, we were not without our fights and
conflicts. At times her sense of serenity with the world was
more than I could handle, for I was not someone who felt at
ease with the world all the time. I, on the other hand, could
be rather uptight, on edge, and so we were not always com-
patible in that regard. Sometimes it seemed like she was
simply floating through life without a plan. I had usually
wanted there to be a plan in place. At times it felt like we
were trying to change each other, to make the other more
like us.

Still, Paul was nodding.

Hugo said, "There was one incident in particular that led
to a lot of arguing between us. We had planned a trip out to
the coast together, kind of like this, and I had wanted to have
things prepared in just the right way. She had wanted to
simply go, without any sort of agenda. We argued bitterly
over how to approach the trip. We went on the trip, and it
was a relative disaster. The car got a flat tire. We had no ho-
tel to stay in. Even once we finally arrived at the coast, we
were too upset to enjoy anything. We were too mad at each
other."

"Did you come here to Grayland?" Paul asked.

"No, Westport. Anyway, that trip, which was a few years
into our marriage, sort of served as a benchmark moment. It
was a moment when we had to confront how we were guiding ourselves in our marriage. From then on, we worked
hard to come together, to communicate more on what we
were doing and wanting to do. I suppose that while she was
alive I did, in fact, believe that the world, at times, was a
place that I could be at ease in."

"That's beautiful."

"A few years later and we had Adrian. Oh, you know that
she was positively born to be a mother. That gleam in her
eyes, she absolutely loved him with all her being from the
moment she first met him. Holding little Adrian in her
hands, she was a natural mother. Having a child really did
bring us together as a couple. We had many conversations

about the sort of child we wanted to raise. Some of the values I wanted to instill in him included a sense of hard work, personal responsibility, honesty, and integrity. I wanted to teach him that he could be any person in the world that he wanted to be, that he should expect great things out of life. As you know, I worked hard to get ahead in my career, and my hope was to create similar opportunities for my son. My wife wanted to teach him to be a caring, compassionate, and sensitive individual, someone who had a heart for the whole world, someone who was culturally aware, and finally someone who loved learning and being creative. In short, we wanted things for our son that were similar yet quite different."

"It makes sense to me that such a set of circumstances would arise."

"Then there came the conversations about religion. To put it one way, Sandra's faith was revitalized during college, particularly in the way that spirituality informed social change and personal transformation. She arrived at a place in which she felt loyal towards the Church's teaching and doctrine. I was never one who was all that enthusiastic about religion. When it comes to politics I am for big government and with religion I am anti-establishment. So you can imagine I was nervous when she had said she wanted to have our son be baptized in the Church and raised in the faith. But, being willing to oblige, I subjected my wishes to hers. After all, in the face of the spiritual answers that were promised to the problems facing the world, I didn't have much that could compete beyond citing the importance of working hard. So we started to go to mass weekly. We enrolled Adrian in special classes that taught theology when he was a few years older. We had him go to public school because I still championed the merits of public education despite whatever people said about schools in the city."

"The schools are great."

"Adrian had no problem making friends. He was outgoing enough, and it was not long before he was having play dates with other kids. He was a pretty strong student in school. After all, we spent hours reading to him, tutoring him in writing and math. During this time, when Adrian was young, I was still beginning to make progress at my company, and so I was working long hours. Sandra was not working, and so she was wholly available to our son. In some respects, it was a difficult time, because my job kept me separated from my family, but this is in no way a unique experience to me. I had work that was meaningful, and I was totally invested in it. But at the same time, what parent can bear to be away from his or her child, no matter how enjoyable work is? My being occupied with work, unfortunately, was not an anomaly but would prove to be the pattern for many of Adrian's younger years. As far as I was concerned, I was working to provide for my family, and so in that respect, I was being the best father I could be. Thankfully, I did work normal business office hours, and so I was always able to be there for dinner, to tuck my son into bed.

"They may seem like small things, but they are important."

"As is always the case, Adrian grew up much too fast and before we knew it he was off to high school. A member of the marching band, he proudly played his trumpet. Marching band proved to be a source of lasting friendships for him. He had fun marching and playing his instrument, but he also just really enjoyed hanging out with his friends. Was he the greatest musician in the world? No, but he had a good time of it. Additionally, he ran cross-country, where he was a moderately talented athlete. In short, Adrian had a very normal, ordinary high school experience. In the social hierarchy, he was somewhere in the middle, a member of the cool kids who happened to be in a band. It was around this time that Sandra obtained her first job working for a paper. She wrote a column and wrote investigative journalistic pieces. She had a great time digging up stories, using her analytical mind to solve problems and write about the most pressing issues facing our country and the world. Truth be told, it was a bit of a shift having her working. It meant that, between the busyness that we were all experiencing, there was a lot less time that we spent together as a family."

273

"Another difficult era."

"Working for the paper meant that Sandra at times had to work kooky hours, laboring into the late afternoon and sometimes even the evening, so it was harder for us to do something as simple as have a dinner together. Fortunately, Adrian had a good group of friends to spend his time with, who kept him out of any sort of trouble, not that he was drawn to it. At times, with all the working, it felt like Sandra and I became distant from each other, but we worked hard to still spend time together in the little ways that we were able to, even if it just meant having a cup of coffee together to start the day. To summarize, the high school years were a time of busyness, at times chaotic, but they proved to be a place where we all grew and matured a great deal."

"Tough times lead to maturation, my friend."

"Of course, at times there was the creeping doubt that I was actually not spending my time in the right way, that I was too bogged down in work. What I did during these moments of doubt is I reminded myself that I was working towards Adrian's future, and that it was through all the working that my son would be able to have the same opportunities that I had had. The high school years are a bit difficult for me to remember; at times, they just feel like a flash of work, but I must say I still look back on them fondly.

"Then Adrian went off to college. What a difficult goodbye it was to say! Sandra and I cried together for many nights after he initially left. You have to understand that our family was a little one, and so losing a member was devastating to our sense of fullness. Adrian, in a rather surprising move, went off to The Art Institute of Seattle. We were expecting him to go to a college like Western. His grades in high school were not spectacular, but we could have seen him going to Western and studying something like math. But instead, he went to an art school and decided to study photography. He proved to be a capable photographer in high school, taking pictures for his school projects, and even completing a number of personal projects. But to think that he was going off to study it as his major was hard to fathom!"

"That was rather surprising."

"I remember having conversations with him about it, trying to encourage him to transfer to another school. It wasn't that I disapproved of what he wanted to study, but I wanted his college experience to put him in a position to be maximally successful in life. What I wanted was what was best for him. I worked hard just to get by in my own life, and I chose a relatively safe field to enter into, so it made me anxious to think that my son was entering a hyper-competitive job market with a measly degree in photography. Sandra, on the other hand, held the creative arts in high esteem and believed that no matter what he chose to study he would be successful because that was the type of person he was. We never got into much in the way of an argument about this. We had mostly moved past the arguments of our early married years. She was content to pray for Adrian, believing that all would work out in his favor."

"She was certainly faithful."

"Adrian and I talked on the phone occasionally during these years, and I even came to visit him every now and then, but the truth is we didn't see as much of him during this time, which I suppose is to be expected. Unsurprisingly, he was quite successful in his classes. After all, he was a gifted photographer. He talked to me with such zeal and light in his eyes about working as an artist, as being someone who took photographs and had them in exhibitions for a living. Now, I like to listen to jazz, but that's about as far as my knowledge of art goes, that and reading. My son had a great deal of passion about what he was studying, and I needed to come around to accepting that. But something happened when he graduated. Somehow, he lost that light in his eyes. He wasn't able to find a job and ended up working at Java City instead. It was during the next twelve years that our relationship became strained, with us speaking less frequently. It was not a matter of us severing ties or anything like that. We just spoke less often. Still, Sandra prayed for him, believing that good things were in store for him. She believed that, even as a barista, he was still capable of doing good for the world and making a difference. She was content with him being a barista, and I was not.

"Now that's a tough spot to be in."

"What is there to say about those years? Sandra kept in close contact with Adrian, and I did not. Sandra worked hard for the paper, and I labored for my company. We continued to work on our marriage, growing closer with each passing year. I embraced her peaceful spontaneity, and she embraced my calculating nervousness. Really, our marriage was wonderful. We went on trips together. I went to mass with her, even though I was not interested in the ideology that was being espoused. I spent many nights just sitting with her, holding her close, cherishing her, delighting in her. She watched me tend to my garden. I went swimming, and she would go running on the treadmill during our trips to the gym. I know that my story is starting to collapse on itself a bit. I guess I just don't really know how to talk about the years leading up to it, to her illness."

"That's where things get...difficult."

"Right. We were happy together. Together, we were complete. That's why it was so devastating when it happened. It truly came out of nowhere. As I've told you before, and as you know, it was very sudden, and I wasn't prepared for it. I truly believed that she and I were going to be together forever. I believed that, but I was wrong. Anyway, last January she died, and I didn't know how to deal with it. Adrian and I were somewhat out of contact, but I suppose her leaving us brought us together. Now I feel very involved in Adrian's life. I suppose one of the greatest ways I can honor her memory is to believe in the dreams of Adrian in the way she always did. Even when it is hard for me to see how his plans are going to lead towards a successful life, I can channel her faith in him, and in that way, I am bringing her back to life, if only for a moment."

Paul was beaming. "That's beautiful!"

So she died in January and I just didn't know what to do. Who is ever ready to lose their spouse? It's like watching half of your world be destroyed. There are no words for it. Nothing is ever the same. I will never be the same. The reality I need to accept is that I am permanently changed as a result of losing my wife. Though I was never exactly chipper, I was cheerful enough before I lost her. But now all that's left is bitterness and cynicism. I don't believe that the world is a safe or inviting place. I believe the world is a dangerous and threatening place. I used to have energy and vitality, but now I am slow. I used to hardly drink, but now I have consumed enough of the stuff that I would be willing to hit my own friend. I used to be quiet and reserved, but now I have been willing to explode in anger at the people who love me most. What has happened to me? How can I salvage what's left of me? What is left of me? I feel haunted by these questions."

"I don't have the answers."

"It's true that there is so much uncertainty that surrounds death. When someone dies, it leads to many questions. What will happen to the household? The children? The finances? The future? That was the case for us when she died. At the time, I had liked to pretend that everything was perfectly certain, that there was no reason to think that anything in my life was going to change. But as I already said, that was not the case. Change came. Now I am repeating myself, but I don't really mind. Change came, but not all at once. The truth is that death is never a single isolated event, but rather, a constant, burning absence that is felt and experienced each and every day. When she died, I thought that that was it, that I would adapt and move forward with my life. I thought of it as a single transaction. But it's not like that. It's more of a steady series of transactions that take place irregularly, and that are irregular in amounts. Death is messy. It's difficult to talk about because it's so far removed from what we understand. Death is like the weather. Things can be perfectly sunny and nice one moment, and then become stormy and blustery the next, and then they can switch back again just as quickly. I can't pretend to be anything of an authority in the nature of death, even with all the experiences I've had in the last nine months. Death is just as distant from me as it was in the beginning, the only difference being how I relate to it. Anyway, I don't think I can keep talking. I've reached my limit. You wanted me to tell you a story, so I did just that. Now, I think I am indeed done. Is that all right?"

Paul, who had been walking at his friend's side and had said relatively little throughout the story beyond empathizing, replied, "Yes, my friend. That is perfectly all right. I think we should turn around and walk back towards the house."

The friends walked together, saying little. Hugo was glad he had agreed to go on this trip. When they made it back to the house, they played chess. After having dinner and reading for a while, they went to bed early. But before Hugo went to bed, he stepped outside, to be with the ocean one more time.

Staring into the nocturnal darkness alone, Hugo breathed in and out slowly and deeply. His eyes were open wide. This first year of living, of living in her absence, it was surely the year of oceans. He was being plunged into sea after sea, by oceans just like this one that he was looking at. Every season, every day, every moment existed as its own ocean, a cold, vast body of water to be explored and navigated. All Hugo was left with was a series of oceans to swim through. He was an able swimmer in a literal sense, but he doubted his abilities to swim through grief. Just like an actual ocean, the way through grief was frequently unclear. Floating through the icy water, in the dim light, it was difficult to see any way forward. Would he have what was required to make it? Would he ever wash up on a shore? Regardless of anything else, Hugo knew that he was in the middle of yet another ocean, that more of them were behind him and still more were before him.

2.

"A strike! Way to go, sweetheart!"

Martin gave Cassandra a high-five as she walked up from the lane. She was giddy with joy. Tossing the ball, she had watched as it bounced off one wall of the barriers and then the other, all the way down the lane, where it had collided with the pins. She looked at Martin in excitement and then turned to Hugo, who also offered her a high-five.

"Your turn, great-uncle Hugo."

Walking up the front of the lane, Hugo held the ball delicately. He looked down the lane, concentrating on the pins, and then released the ball from his grip. The ball traveled up through the lane, veering towards the right and striking a few pins. A bit annoyed, Hugo stood and waited for his ball to be ejected by the machine.

"Nice shot, big brother!"

Taking the ball in his hands once more, Hugo rolled it, which failed to hit any pins.

"It's okay," Hugo said to them. "I never was much of a bowler."

The mood was jovial as Martin drove Cassandra home to James' house. She gave Martin a hug, said goodbye to Hugo, and went inside.

"Now it's time to take you home, big brother."

They drove on the familiar roads, speeding along. The atmosphere was light and cheerful while Cassandra was in the car with them, but something had changed. Hugo's mind was full of visions of the sea, of waves crashing, seagulls soaring, the horizon expanding outwards beyond what the eye could see.

He felt like his head was clear, like he was seeing and experiencing things as they really were. In particular, he and Paul had had a very meaningful conversation on the second day, when Hugo opened up about his past in a way he hadn't in years. Being vulnerable was not something that he was versed in. Though Hugo presented himself as tough, cold, and intimidating, the reality, he found, was that he was sensitive, tender, and deeply caring. He cared about the people in his life passionately, though he often didn't know how to express it. Of course, he cared about his brother Martin, but feelings of resentment and jealousy were threatening to get in the way of their relationship. Hugo didn't know what to do other than be honest, which had been his approach during his stay in Grayland. Just be honest, he told himself.

Even when it's difficult, when you don't know what to say, just be honest. There he was, sitting in the passenger seat with his brother, feeling the tension of being with this person who in many ways viewed the world in a way that was antithetical to his own perspective.

"So, how was the trip?" Martin asked.

"It was good. It was a very nice time for me."

"Good to hear!"

Hugo thought carefully about his words before saying, "I am looking forward now."

"What do you mean?"

"What I mean is that I am focused on how I can make progress, how I can continue to improve myself. I know that losing Sandra was devastating, but I am beginning to envision a life for myself where I can live without her, as hard as that is to imagine."

"That is so very good to hear. I know it has not been easy for you to adjust your life to living without her, but I knew you were capable of it."

"It's not easy, though."

"No, it's not. It is very difficult. It is very difficult."

"Do you think you know anything about difficulty?" Hugo challenged.

"Well, I wasn't born yesterday. Surely I am acquainted with—"

"You don't know anything about suffering," Hugo proclaimed.

"Big brother, I have been—"

"Enough. I don't need to hear it. I have lost so much. I have lost everything: my job, my hope of a grandchild, and my wife. What have you lost? You are stuck in the dilemma of being able to choose whether or not you continue to work. You have a granddaughter who is precious, adorable, and precocious. You also have your wife, who is lovely and great to you. You have everything, and I have nothing." Hugo knew none of what he was saying to his brother was new, but still, he said it.

"Big brother, do you think I actively chose for things to be the way they are?"

"No, but you bask in it. You bask in it, and then you act like you understand my life. You do not understand my life. It's easy to be positive and cheerful when nothing bad has happened to you."

"Do you think I felt nothing when we lost Mom?"

"Sure you lost your mom, you and everyone who has lived to be our age. Losing a parent is part of being a human being. Tell me about one loss you have experienced that compares to the losses I have endured. Just one loss!"

"Big brother, losing people is not a contest where one keeps track of points. Losing people is—"

"Don't begin to tell me about what losing people is, because you are in no way an authority to speak to that. I am not even an authority to speak to about losing, and I have been through it. I have personally, intimately experienced loss in all of its raw ugliness. What have you been through? Nothing!"

"But don't—"

"Stop talking. I don't want to hear about it. I am tired of hearing about your gospel of positivity. I have spent the last sixty years in your positive shadow. People have always labeled you as the positive one and me as the negative one, even within our own family. How do you think that made me feel? I lost my wife, and then you came in and tried to cheer me up, like there was a way for me to feel better about it. You told me I would meet her in heaven. Well, what if I told you I wasn't in a position to believe in such a thing? But I understand why you believe in heaven. It's easy for you to believe in heaven because only good things have happened to you. You already live in heaven."

"Big brother..."

"What?"

"I, I don't know where to begin. I find your words to be quite troubling. You don't think it was difficult for everyone else in your family to watch you lose her? You don't think it didn't have an effect on us?"

"Not in the way it had an effect on me, that's for sure."

281

"Hugo," Martin said, directly addressing him, "it broke our hearts when Sandra died. We didn't know how to explain it to Cassandra. Do you really think it didn't hurt us? In the last year, do you think we haven't been hurt watching you struggle? Do you think you are invisible? We invited you to family functions, to come to our trip to Chelan, and you were distant from us. You were clearly hurting, and we didn't know what to say to you. All we wanted was for you to feel our love. But it felt like you rejected our love. Do you know how much that hurt us, how much of a loss that was? All we wanted to do was be there for you, but it has felt like all throughout this process you have rejected us. So where does that leave us? It means that we feel like we have lost Hugo. In the blackness of grief, we have lost Hugo, and we have been unable to reclaim him. That means that we have failed you, that it is our fault."

Hugo said, "All you have done is made it into being about you. I am the one who lost someone. You are just spectators. Yet am I supposed to pity you? How can you be so selfish? All this time I have been hurting in ways that I can't put into words, and yet you throw a pity party just because I haven't always been interested in having cheerful conversations with you. Couldn't you see that I was on a journey with grief, and that I needed to take that journey alone, that I needed space? It wasn't about you. You weren't a part of the equation. All that was happening was I was figuring out how to deal with the loss of her."

Martin was breathing deeply. "I know it may feel like we aren't a part of the equation, but death always affects the community, the larger family. Did we feel grief on the same level as you? No. But did we feel something? Yes, we certainly did. Nobody has to be selfish. You felt something very deep and profound, but we also felt something, too. It doesn't have to be a contest of who lost the most, because that was obviously you. All we want to do is be here to support you. You said you were thinking about living a new life, a life without her. Well, what we hope and pray is that we can be a part of that."

"I appreciate that. But tell me something. Why do you think you were allowed to keep so much in your life, while so much was taken from me?"

"I don't know the answer to that, big brother. If I could switch places with you to alleviate your suffering, you know that I would."

"Bullshit! There is no way you would trade your luxurious life for mine. Who would ever trade what they have to be me?"

"I am not lying when I said that, Hugo. It's the truth."

"It's a lie. You are lying to me just to try and make me feel better. What kind of sorry sap do you think I am?"

"It's not a lie!"

"Whatever. I'm not interested in arguing like a child with my little brother. You know," Hugo said, "the truth is we never fought a lot throughout the last sixty years. That was because I always felt inferior to you. I felt like I had an inferior life because I wasn't so positive like you. You went to church. You spent your free time volunteering. You donated money and raised your kids to be religious. I did none of those things. Sure, we raised Adrian in the Catholic Church, but I didn't care about his spiritual development, not like you did with James or Cassandra. You were always doing special things as a family. You sent out a flashy Christmas card every year. You were always going on trips and doing activities together. We were involved as a family, too. But we couldn't compete with you. There was no hope for that."

"You think it was a contest? Who is being childish now?" Martin asked.

"That's it," Hugo roared. "I can no longer continue to have this conversation. No good will come of it."

"But we need to—"

"No. That's enough. I am finished."

They were passing over the lake as Hugo said this. In the bleak darkness, the two brothers sat, festering in their own thoughts and feelings. Hugo was so angry he knew that he would only say hurtful things if the conversation had continued. Selfish, Hugo thought, he is being so selfish. So they had sat in silence. The tension hardly bearable, Hugo was pleased to get out of the car when it pulled up to his house. He said a terse goodbye. He went inside and went to bed.

3.

Sitting in the study, loading the bag with books, Hugo sighed. He was gazing at the classics that had belonged to her. Some of the books he had liked and wanted to keep, but others did not interest him. These were the volumes that he put in the bag. It was not long before the bag was full.

Hugo rose from where he had been sitting and walked upstairs, into his bedroom. He had known that this was going to be the most difficult part of the process.

Opening the door of the closet, he looked at her clothes.

At his feet were two big grocery bags. He proceeded to walk through the spacious closet, taking every article of clothing that had belonged to her, and stowed them in the bags. He grabbed the clothes and put them in the bags rapidly, as though the clothes, which still smelled of her, were contaminated and might make him ill. Steadily he made progress through the closet. He grabbed blouses, dresses, sweaters, socks, pants, and other things. Holding the clothes in armfuls, he allowed the cloth hangers to fall on the floor. It was not long before the two bags were full, and still, there were clothes to gather. Downstairs he walked, where he opened the door of the other closet and grabbed two more bags. Arriving upstairs once more, the blood pumping in his temple, he continued to gather clothes.

Fifteen minutes later, he had six bags filled to the brim. How was he going to get all of this to the thrift store? Certainly, he didn't want to make multiple trips. He stepped outside and knocked on Paul's door. Ever since they had gone on the trip together, despite whatever had happened in the past, the two friends felt closer than ever. Patiently Hugo waited, hoping that his friend would be available to help him carry the bags to the store. There was no response, and so he turned around and walked into his backyard, to the shed. Inside, he found what he was looking for, which was an old, rusty wagon. He stepped around several pots of plants and looked for the handle of the wagon, but he was unable to find it in the dim light. Lifting the wagon into the air, dust fell out of it, and as he stood up he banged his head on a wooden shelf. Cursing to himself, he took a step back, gripping the wagon in two hands. Having made his way out of the shed, he lowered the wagon and finally grabbed the handle. He pulled it around the side of the house and left it in front of the door. Then he went inside and proceeded to load the bags of clothes onto the wagon.

A part of him felt like a child as he pulled the wagon towards the thrift store. However, he didn't care, for he was being pragmatic. There was no way that he was interested in making multiple trips to the store, and since Paul was unavailable, this was his only option. He had been thinking about doing this for a while. The clothes and books that belonged to her had haunted him each and every time he opened the closet or the study. But more so than being haunted, what Hugo wanted was to cleanse a part of his life of her, to move on, to make peace with her ghost. It seemed simple. There was no need for her clothes or books to be around. For months, he had experienced a wide variety of feelings whenever he had gone into the closet or the study. Christopher talked about working on acceptance, and suggested that cleaning out the rooms was a good start.

Though it might have seemed like a small gesture, taking the clothes and books to the thrift store felt like overcoming a monumental challenge for Hugo. Christopher, additionally, suggested visiting the grave as a part of Hugo's acceptance work, to which he replied that he was incapable of doing such a thing. Christopher said that this perspective may change with time, but Hugo had disagreed, stating that he didn't think he would ever manage to do it.

Walking slowly down the street, the wagon bumped with the cracks in the sidewalk. People, riding bikes and walking, passed by him. The day was clear and crisp. Fallen leaves still remained on the ground, the remnants of autumn. Walking past the liquor store, Hugo felt the urge to drink, wishing that he could escape his situation. He turned around, looking at the clothes and books, desiring to be rid of them. But he knew that this was his cross to carry, that he needed to travel with them all the way to the thrift store and that there was no other option.

In fact, he hadn't touched a drop of alcohol since he went to the coast. Something about that trip was sobering in a very real, transformative way. Hugo talked to Christopher about it, and he was encouraging, citing the importance of going on adventures and embracing change. Though Hugo hadn't had anything to drink in the last few weeks, this was not to say that he wasn't without the urge to drink. The urge was real. But with the help of the ocean, which never left Hugo's consciousness for long, he was able to overcome any need to drink, at least for the time being.

Approaching the thrift store, Hugo felt the strain of pulling the wagon. He entered the store and was struck by the sheer volume of stuff present. There were racks of clothes, shoes in the corner, a bookshelf, and fitting rooms on the sidewall. The store was bustling with customers who were shopping. At first disoriented, Hugo was unsure as to where he was supposed to go. A woman standing at a counter waved at him, and so he walked over to her with the wagon.

"Hello there," she said.

"Hi."

"What can I help you with?"

"Just want to drop off this stuff."

"Sure thing."

He left the bags at the desk, turned around and left the store as quickly as he entered.

On Hugo's mind were the upcoming holidays. Already he had arranged to celebrate Thanksgiving with Paul. Currently, he was not really speaking with Martin, though he imagined this would change before the Christmas season. Thanksgiving for the Larson family was a low-key affair. Since this was the first year without her there to celebrate it with Hugo, he initially had not known how to approach the holiday. Normally, he could expect an invitation from Martin, and Martin had, in fact, called him several times, but each time he had let the phone ring. Consequently, Hugo made plans with Paul, and also talked to Adrian, who said he would be pleased to celebrate Thanksgiving with a group of his friends from school.

Hugo was dreading Christmas. He knew it was going to be a difficult time with her not here. He knew that all the little things, the Larson family traditions, were going to be difficult in her absence. The enmity between Hugo and his brother did not serve to help things, either. Christopher said that, though Christmas was likely going to be a difficult time, it also presented itself as an opportunity. Hugo liked the sound of this, but he was skeptical. Regardless, his focus was narrowed considerably; he was concentrating primarily on getting through Thanksgiving.

Before he knew it, he had arrived home. He walked around the side of the house and deposited the wagon in the shed. Pleased, he entered his house through the back door, but not before noticing that there was a pile of leaves he had raked the other day. Fall was certainly coming to an end. Soon the world would be getting colder. Well, not the world Janet lived in, but at least the temperature would be getting lower in Seattle. The city would slow down. The trees would become bare. The nights would be long and the days short. What this meant is that the world would be much the same as it had been right around when she had been the most ill, and when she had died. Hugo was in the process of completing a full rotation of the seasons.

Inside, he poured himself a glass of water and had a seat at the kitchen table. The phone started to ring. He picked up the receiver.

"Hello?"

"Hi, Dad."

"Hi, son. Everything okay?'

"Yeah, just wanted to check in."

"Okay. How are the new classes?"

"Good. I'm actually struggling a fair bit."

"Really? Why's that?"

"Lot's of homework. The classes are pretty challenging. The professors are demanding of us."

"Well, that's how work goes sometimes, my son. It's manageable, though, isn't it?"

"I think so. I was thinking about taking some time off."

"What? Here you are, quitting the second program in less than a year. How could you even consider doing such a thing?!" Hugo could feel the blood rushing to his head.

"I know, I know. It's just I've been feeling really discouraged. I put together a collage as an assignment in one of my classes and I didn't get a very good grade on it."

"What did you make the collage of?"

"Pictures of Puget Sound."

"Neat."

"I thought so too. But my professor was pretty critical of it. It really bummed me out. I put so much work into it, and then he just ripped it to shreds."

"Yes, but the fact remains that you shouldn't quit just because of one bad experience. Wouldn't you agree?"

"Yes, I agree. I know that photography is my passion, I just don't know if this is the right time for me to be pursuing it. I don't even know if it will translate into a job."

"Is that what you're really worried about?" Hugo asked.

"What?"

"Are you actually thinking about quitting because you don't know if you will be able to make money practicing it when you're done?"

"I...maybe...I don't know."

Hugo thought about the ways in which he had previously lashed out at his son. What was a more caring, compassionate way to engage with him? "Because you remember what we talked about. You need to follow your passion. You need to believe in what you care about. Let the career and the rest of that fall into place."

"Thanks, Dad. I needed someone to remind me of that."

"Sure thing."

"It's just tough, though," Adrian continued.

"I know it is, son, but you're tough, too."

"I'm gonna keep thinking about it."

"About staying in the program?"

"Yeah."

"Stay in the program."

"Okay, I think I will. Wanna meet up sometime before Thanksgiving?"

"Sure, sounds good," Hugo said. "Bye."

"Bye."

Just as Hugo was about to hang up the receiver, he heard Adrian say, "Dad, I love you."

"I love you too, son."

December

I.

It was a cold, dark night, and downtown had come to life, with throngs of people walking about. Streetlights and headlights from cars poured light into the shadowy, dusky darkness. Buildings were decorated with yellow, red, and green lights. The edifices were like walls that protected the people from the all-encompassing night.

In the center of the street, on Union Street between Fourth and Fifth Avenue, stood the tree. It was a glorious sight to behold. Standing tall, proud, it was massive in size, and was decorated in an elegant way. Covered in ornaments, the tree contained large silver and gold balls that further reflected all of the light. On top, at the very tip, there was a star that evoked the way in which the tree seemed to reach for the heavens, towards the very cosmos. A crowd of people was gathered at the bottom. People were passing out song sheets, and were proceeding to sing "Oh, Christmas Tree".

Hugo stood with Paul and Kim Schaefer. Though his companions were singing with loud, enthusiastic voices, Hugo was merely lip-synching the words. Normally, Hugo had been excited to bring home a Christmas tree, to partake in all the traditions and gatherings that the holiday season entailed.

Christmas took place during the darkest time of the year, and it presented itself as a triumph of light, of human kindness and warmth, in overcoming the oppressive night. People, even those who normally never talked, came together to commemorate how magical indeed the world could be. For many, the holidays were a deeply spiritual time, filled with contemplation, repentance, and joy. Hugo was more concerned with the capacity of the holidays to bring people together. This was funny, for most of the year Hugo had been participating in an exercise in how to alienate himself from other people, and now he decided he was interested in coming closer. Despite whatever interest he had in being close to others, though, the fact remained that the first week of December was coming to an end and he still hadn't talked to his brother or to anyone on that side of the family.

Hugo stood close to Paul and Kim, observing the splendor that was unfolding before him. The sonorous sounds of people's voices filled the empty spaces of downtown. Traffic was a nightmare, with people walking across street intersections in large droves. Coming to the tree lighting festival was one of many traditions Hugo and his family possessed. Each and every year, he, Sandra, and Adrian would come to watch the tree come up, to sing songs, to bask in the spirit of the season. Such a tradition was something they had held onto dearly. Now things were different. In the back of Hugo's mind, he was thinking about how he was going to navigate the holidays without her. Thanksgiving had been easy enough. He enjoyed dining with Paul. But Christmas, he knew, was a bigger, more complex affair. It was a holiday that lasted multiple days and had weeks of anticipation leading up to it. Here he was, completing his first challenge: getting through the tree ceremony with his new, makeshift family.

The other week Paul hosted a get together for the neighborhood, and while there, Hugo got into a conversation with Kim:

"The apple tree looks bare," Hugo said.

"Yes, indeed it is."

"Oh well."

"Tell me something," Kim spoke. "What are you doing on Wednesday night?"

"Oh, um, I'm busy."

"Because there is the tree lighting ceremony, and I go every year. Would you like to accompany me?"

"I, well sure," Hugo said, "that would be nice."

"Great! I'll see you at seven."

So they had gone.

Thirty minutes later and Kim suggested they head back to Wedgwood, saying that traffic was only going to get worse and worse. They walked the few blocks, past crowds of people, and piled into Paul's car. A deft driver, Paul moved through the city blocks unfazed by all that was going on around him. Before long, they were back on the freeway, headed home. Turning around to look at the view, Hugo saw the buildings of downtown, which were like illuminated statues standing in the wake of the onslaught of night.

The world truly was dim. Looking up through the sunroof of the car, Hugo was unable to discern a single star in the night sky. Where were all the other worlds that rested in the cosmos, that typically shone their brilliant light down on the earth as a form of blessing? Hugo thought about the idea that this world was the only planetary body in all of space that possessed life, that it was just a single floating orb that moved around the sun with no clear purpose or meaning behind it. He thought about the missions that NASA and other organizations had embarked on, to explore Mars, to learn more about the other planets in the solar system. The Milky Way was only one of a seemingly infinite number of galaxies in the universe. The end of the universe was unknown, or even unknowable altogether. How could the parameters of the universe be unknown?

When they arrived back in Wedgwood, Kim asked if they would be interested in coming in for tea. The truth was that Hugo felt rather tired, but he knew that his opportunities to spend time with this woman were precious and rare, so he obliged. They stepped inside of her house, which was small and certainly lived-in. On the wall of the main hallway, she had a collection of clocks, all ticking and tocking to slightly different rhythms. The tearoom, as she referred to it, was a small room with a fold-up table, several chairs, and a big teapot. Paul and Hugo had a seat.

"Would you be interested in 'Transcendent White' or 'Peaceful Black'?" Kim asked, holding two cases of tea.

The two friends looked at each other. "We'll take the transcendent one," Paul replied.

Though she was old, Kim moved with surprising sprightliness, going from one room of the house to another in a hurry, pouring the water and preparing the tea. Hugo, in fact, was a neutral fan when it came to tea, but these days he was feeling more eager to please others.

Soon, she had poured the water and place the cozy on the teapot. "It will only be a few minutes," she said.

"Wonderful," Paul said. "Thank you so very much for having us over like this. We really appreciate it."

"Oh," Kim said beaming. "It's the least I can do after all those gatherings you've invited me to at your home. You have been nothing but a delightful host."

"Well, thank you," Paul blushed.

"So," she continued, "are you two feeling excited about the holidays?"

"I certainly am," Paul said. "Christmas is the best time of the year, isn't it?"

"And what about you?" Kim asked, looking at Hugo.

Part of Hugo wanted to shrug the question away, to act like he didn't care one way or the other, but he knew he was with friends, and that the best approach to take was to be honest.

"I am actually dreading it quite a bit," he said.

"And why is that?"

"Well, you may or may not know that this is my first Christmas without my wife."

"You poor thing! Here, have a cup of tea. I think it's ready." She grabbed the mug resting before him and filled it with some transcendent tea. "Going through the holidays without your wife, what a terrible thing to have to go through. I remember my first Christmas without John, but you see, I don't talk about that. How about that tree display?"

Hugo burned his tongue as he had his first sip of tea. Strangely, in Kim, he was seeing himself. What he saw in her was someone who was unwilling to confront the effects of death because it was difficult and painful to do so. This very much was how Hugo had acted in the first few months after she died. But how long had Kim lived without her husband? Surely she had had time to process and work through it? Maybe not. That was when Hugo was filled with horror because he realized that not everyone actually ever embarks on the grief journey. Hugo was fortunate, lucky that he was able to navigate all the feelings and sensations of grief that he had, all the thoughts and memories because it allowed him to make progress. Kim, on the other hand, it seemed, was still on day one, because she had been unwilling to ever begin the journey. Hugo was filled with sadness and regret, looking at Kim through new eyes, thinking about all the apples that fell from her tree, how full of life she was and yet how drowning in death she was, all at the same time. Hugo identified with her. He felt like he understood where she was coming from.

It was then that Hugo realized that it was a result of his community and the tools at his side that he was able to navigate the grief process as far as he had. Truly he was fortunate.

"The tree display was absolutely marvelous," Paul beamed. "It was really lovely."

"What are some other Christmas traditions you have?" Kim asked.

"Well," Hugo said, "we like to put up our Christmas tree the day after the tree ceremony. We like to go caroling later in the week. We also usually have brunch at the Wandering Goose sometime before Christmas. I spend Christmas day with my family, and I usually give my brother a call so that we can go over and visit his family later in the day. Mind you, this is all how things were when my wife was with me. She died last January. I don't know which traditions are going to remain this year and which ones are going to disappear. I just don't know."

"Oh, Hugo," Kim exclaimed, filling up his cup with more tea. "You feel free to follow your traditions as you see fit. You don't have to go to the Wandering Goose if you don't want to."

"Thanks."

"Now would anyone care for some wine? What better way to celebrate the season than with some wine?"

"No, thanks," Paul answered

Hugo said, "Sure, I'll take some."

Kim returned with a bottle of chardonnay, and poured a glass for herself and then him.

"I find that a little wine can take the edge off the holiday blues," she said.

Hugo looked around the tearoom, realizing that there were no pictures of her husband to be seen.

He had a sip of the wine, but it seemed to have no effect on him.

"Just keep sipping it. It will do good for your soul," she said.

They stayed only a little while longer, and then the two friends walked home. Hugo said goodbye to his friend, entered his home, and poured himself a glass of pinot grigio. He stared out through the back window of the kitchen, into the winter bleakness, and sighed.

2.

"Life is good," Hugo began. "I can't complain."

"Good to hear, Hugo," Christopher responded.

"Did I mention that I took all of Sandra's clothes to the thrift store the other day?"

"No, you did not. Tell me about that."

"Well, it was a strange experience. I went into the closet, gathered all the stuff, put it into bags, and took it to the store. Funny, it felt like I was ridding myself of a part of her by taking away those clothes."

"Often there are many small things in life that remind us of the ones we lost. You get rid of anything else?"

"Books."

"Well, I consider it progress that you got rid of those clothes and books. I'm sure it wasn't easy for you. That took courage."

"I don't really feel courageous."

"Why not?"

"All I did was take some clothes to the thrift store. What's the big deal? Anyone could have done what I did."

"Oh, not everyone," Christopher corrected. "Many people hold onto the things that they have from lost ones. People hoard and hold onto things for years."

"Besides, there are other things that I am afraid of."

"What are you afraid of?"

"Well, there's visiting the grave."

"And why are you afraid of visiting the grave?"

Hugo paused, trying to form his words. Out of habit, he looked down at his tie, which had rainbows on it. "I don't know, I just am."

"Okay."

"There are so many emotions. I just can't imagine standing in a cemetery and looking down at her name written on the ground. The reality of it all, of her death, I just can't imagine looking at her name and being there. The whole thing feels really unreal to me."

"I get that. Sometimes to protect ourselves we put up little mental shields, and that can cause things to start to feel unreal. Simple as that."

Hugo liked Christopher. He thought he was at times a bit too matter-of-fact in his delivery, and he was quite direct, but this was what Hugo responded to, for Hugo was direct as well. Now that Hugo had been seeing Christopher for a few months, a relationship was beginning to form between them. Hugo felt like he could trust his counselor, and he sensed that Christopher, in turn, took interest in him.

"Do you think I should visit the grave?" Hugo pondered.

Christopher paused. "I don't think you have to, but it could be really good for you. It could lead to a lot of healing. That being said, you need to do what you feel comfortable and capable of, and I don't want to force you into doing something that you might not be ready to do."

"When do you think I will be ready to go?"

"For all I know, you already are ready to go. I think that no matter what it's going to feel like a challenging stretch to make it to the cemetery. It will push you and make demands of you. But that's good. It's all part of the grieving process."

"The last step of the grieving process is acceptance, right?" Hugo confirmed.

"I don't know if I would say it's the last step, but it is the supreme step. Grief does not proceed in a linear manner. Know what I mean?"

"I do."

"Good. It sounds like you are living your life in a very accepting fashion."

"You think?"

"Yeah!"

"Well, I guess so. I got rid of those clothes and books. My son is doing well in his program, and I feel at peace with his career moves even though he is not making the most money or earning the most respect from his field. I feel at peace with my brother, at least I do most of the time. I was nervous to go on a trip to the coast with my friend Paul, but I accepted the situation and went, and it was great!"

"See? Acceptance. What part of your relationship with your brother do you think you do not feel at peace with?"

"Oh, it's nothing. I'm at peace with him."

"You sure?" Christopher looked skeptical.

"Yes, and if there are things that I'm not at peace with, then I will accept that lack of peace and move forward."

"Tell me more about your brother, Hugo."

"Well, there's not a whole lot to tell. He's a teacher, thinking about retiring. He is married, has a son who is married, and an adorable granddaughter."

"Sounds like a great life."

"It is pretty great."

"Tell me something. Do you compare your life to his?"

"A little bit. But I'm working on it. I know it's not healthy."

"Remember: don't compare yourself to others, celebrate yourself."

"Easier said than done," Hugo said.

"Sure."

Hugo looked out the window. He rested a hand under his chin. It took Christopher a moment to get his attention again.

"There's also my friend, Lily."

"Tell me about her."

"She runs the bar near where I live. I like to go and watch soccer games there. Anyway, she lost her husband a long time ago and she has been there to support me."

"Excellent."

"But we're just, you know, friends. Nothing romantic going on."

"Hugo, you lost your wife less than a year ago. I wouldn't expect there to be anything romantic going on. If you were dating, that would potentially be okay, but since you're not, there's no issue."

"Yeah, I get it."

"Well, it sounds like your life is going really well!" Christopher said, smiling. "How are you feeling about the holidays?"

"Okay, I will be fine. I can't say I'm all that excited about getting through Christmas, but it should be all right. I'll probably spend it with my friend Paul or something."

"You know, the holidays can be a really challenging time for families in the best of times, so it would make sense to me if you were struggling. You know you can talk to me about it if you are having a tough time."

Hugo looked surprised. "I mean, the holidays are not amazing, but I'm doing fine, really. I am living a life of acceptance and I am making my way through the grief process. I am making progress. I have good relationships with the people I care about. Like I said before, I really can't complain."

"Nice," Christopher said while standing up. "We're out of time."

3.

The mall was full to the brim with masses of people, hoards of shoppers eager to purchase their goods. Hugo walked at the side of Adrian, past a café that had a line of people winding around the corner. People moved with energy, carrying bags that contained toys, clothes, and other material things. All of it, Hugo thought, was a vanity. Of course, Hugo appreciated the capacity for Christmas to bring people together, but this was not what he had in mind, the incessant need to purchase, always buying more at whatever cost. Christmas was about people being together, not sharing in material goods, but simply being together.

Unfortunately, Hugo was not above cultural tradition, and so here he was, like everyone else, at the mall, a week before Christmas. On his list of gifts left to purchase there was only Paul. What he was thinking of buying him was a glass chess set, available only at a special store for games. Unlike the last time Hugo was at the mall, this time he knew where they were headed, and so they walked at a brisk pace, for he wanted to be out of the mall as soon as possible. He was hoping for a brief trip, with no complications, no errors, just getting in and getting out.

"Don't you like this time of year?" Adrian asked. "Everything is so...full of energy."

"It's okay."

"Come on, Dad. Where's your Christmas spirit?"

"It left when all the shoppers arrived."

They walked past a group of people who were moving slowly. Hanging from the ceiling were red and green decorations, which served to dress up the mall nicely. Virtually every store had lines of people extending far out. This is madness, Hugo thought to himself.

Here were so many people busy going about, purchasing presents for loved ones, when the reality remained that people every day in the world were living and dying. Hugo thought about what he had lost. This year, he had one less person to purchase a gift for. Of course, this gift had been the most special one that he even bought. People were pre-occupied with buying the latest and greatest thing, whether it was a computer or a phone or a video game, and the real present, which was people themselves, remained overshadowed by consumerism. Hugo thought about Sandra, wishing he had cherished her more, wishing he hadn't taken all those Christmases together for granted. He wished that, just for a moment, he could go back and live in one of those Christmases again. He knew such thinking was futile, but he did it anyway. The reality stood that there was no going back. Nothing ever stays the same, he thought. Everything is always changing. As they were walking through the mall he longed desperately to be able to walk into one of the stores and bump into Sandra.

"Where do we go next?" Adrian inquired. It seemed as though he was doing his very best to have a good attitude, which only made Hugo more negative.

"This way," he said abruptly, taking a turn into the store.

Inside, they were greeted by all sorts of board games, which sat out on tables and formed towers of boxes. Hugo scanned each tower of boxes rapidly and then moved over to a shelf that contained even more games.

"May I help you?" an attendant with glasses asked.

"No, we are perfectly well off, thanks."

Still, Hugo was looking. Adrian, too, was searching, but he seemed to be interested in each and every game he came across.

"This one looks fun," he would say occasionally, pointing at a box.

"There is only one game to play," Hugo declared, "and that is chess. That is what we are here for."

"Yes, but other games are fun too, don't you think?"

"No, I find no other games to be enjoyable except for chess."

"Gotcha."

Chess, of course, was a great passion of Hugo's. Right now he was thinking about the last game he had played against Paul, which had been only a few days ago. Hugo had won magnificently, albeit closely. In the game, it had come down to Hugo managing to get a pawn across the board so that he could reclaim his queen. This redemption had enabled him to go on the offensive and win. Between Paul and him, Hugo estimated that they both won half the time. The two of them were very comparable players, though Hugo had been playing longer.

In Hugo's thinking, it should be easy to find a chess set. After all, it was the supreme board game, the definitive classic.

"Excuse me," Adrian said to the attendant.

"Yes?"

"We are looking for your chess sets."

"Oh, I'm terribly sorry. We don't carry any chess sets."

It was then that Hugo realized they had entered the wrong store.

Enraged, Hugo thought about asking the attendant how, in good conscience, this store could purport to be a game store when it was lacking the only game that really mattered. Hugo considered lashing out until a chess set magically appeared, but he restrained himself. He felt far too drained emotionally from getting through the season to engage in such a battle. Instead, he looked at his son.

"Let's go," he said.

"Dad, this game looks pretty cool." In Adrian's hands, he held a game called "Star Avengers."

Hugo walked over and read the description. Apparently, the game involved navigating space in an aircraft and participating in intergalactic warfare with aliens.

"Let's go," Hugo repeated himself. "I want us to be on our way."

The father and son walked out of the store, back into the crowd of people. Somehow, it seemed as though there were now more people out than there had been before. The mall was reaching a critical mass of people.

"Where do we go?" Adrian asked with concern.

Hugo looked up at the sign of the store and realized that, indeed, it was the wrong store.

"We need to find a map," he said.

Nearby there was one of the mall maps. Hugo scrambled over to it, maneuvering around a man who was staring at his phone, and inspected it. He realized that the store they were looking for was located on the other side of the mall. He turned to his son.

"Let's go," he said yet again.

Nearly running, Adrian struggled to keep up with his father. Over the loudspeakers, there was holiday music, peaceful and tranquil, playing.

"Where are we heading?" Adrian wondered.

"I'll show you."

"Okay."

"How are classes?" Hugo asked, changing the subject.

"They're okay," Adrian answered after a pause.

"You still sticking with the program?"

"Uh-huh."

Hugo looked down at his tie, which had teddy bears on it, stroked his mustache, and then asked, "Are you finding your classes to still be challenging?"

"I am. We are moving into the end of the term, and things are really ramping up."

"When is that?"

"The term ends in January."

"I see. When in January?"

"Don't know. I think towards the end of the month."

"Got it. What do they have you doing for the end of the term? What kind of projects are you working on?"

"We are making an exhibition." Adrian seemed nervous.

"Neat!"

"Yes," Adrian continued. "We will be having a portfolio of photos, and then we will display them at a gallery and allow people like you to come and look at them."

"Sounds like a cool opportunity. Do you know what you are going to focus your portfolio on?"

"I'm not sure yet," Adrian replied.

By now, they had reached the other edge of the mall, the game store they were seeking being only a bit farther off. They entered it, which looked strangely similar to the first store they had visited, and continued looking through games. Adrian got the attention of the attendant and was pointed in the direction of the chess sets. Reluctant to go due to the fact that an attendant had been involved, Hugo walked over and surveyed the different types of sets they had.

A part of what excited Hugo about getting this gift was the fact that he would be able to play on the set, that he would reap the benefits of the gift himself. Was this selfish? Perhaps, but Hugo was not concerned over the matter.

There were sets made of aged wood, others that were plastic, and finally, there it was, the glass set Hugo had been seeking. He lifted the box and held it in his hands, thinking about the incredible weight of the pieces, and looked at his son, smiling.

"Now this," he said, "is a game."

Walking over to the counter to purchase the game, Hugo was surprised by the staggering cost, though going into it he had known that it would be expensive. Fiscally conservative, Hugo had developed a reputation for the austere manner in which he managed his funds. Never did he pay more at the store than he felt was necessary, and he was always sure to balance his checkbook. Such practices, of course, accompanied the territory of being an accountant. Nothing less was expected of him.

Though it bothered him to pay so much for a game, even for chess, he still abided by the situation and paid for it, trusting that over time he would gain much enjoyment from the game, from holding the small, ornate pieces in his hands, and from looking at them while surveying the playing field.

The two men walked out of the store. Mall fatigue, a very real and serious condition, was descending upon Hugo, who could hardly bear the thought of going into another store. Fortunately for him, there was no need to shop anywhere else, and so they were now free to leave.

"Let's get out of here," Hugo muttered under his breath.

As they were walking, Adrian appeared to be wanting to say something, for he kept opening his mouth and breathing quickly, but each time he restrained himself.

Hugo looked at Adrian and asked, "You okay?"

There was a pause and then he answered, "I gotta be honest. I think I'm going to quit the program, Dad."

"How could you even possibly think of doing such a thing?! Do you have any idea how much I've done for you? I've been here for you, I've advised you in the ways that I know are good, and you have disappointed me again and again. How can you give up so easily?"

"I haven't given up easily—"

"Here it is, almost the end of the term, when you are putting together your portfolio, and you choose to quit. First, you quit the business program, and now it's this. Are you going to quit everything except for being a barista? Is that all you are, a quitter?"

"Dad, I tried my best. It was just too tough for me."

"What is too tough about it?"

"The professor, the way he grades, the assignments, and I just don't feel like my heart is in it anymore. I don't know what happened to my passion for photography, but it is gone. Somewhere along the way, I lost it. I'm sorry."

Hugo turned and looked at him. "You have let me down, son."

They stepped outside of the mall and into the parking lot. Dark, gray, and sinister, small flakes of snow were falling from the sky. Night was approaching. The days were getting darker earlier to such a degree that it frightened Hugo.

"I'm going to quit, Dad, and that's that."

Looking at his son again, Hugo sighed. They got into Adrian's car and drove off, towards Wedgwood.

"Can you respect the decision I've made?" Adrian asked at one point.

Staring out the window, not wanting to look at his son, Hugo replied, "No, I cannot respect your decision. You are my son. I love and cherish you, but what you have got to understand is that in life you must be willing to work hard, to strive. Good things never come about easily, not without some hard work. The truth is I cannot respect your decision precisely because you have let me down. It was one thing for you to quit the business program because it was hard, but this is another thing entirely."

"I understand," Adrian sighed.

The car eventually wound up the Mason Street, coming to a halt in front of Hugo's home. He looked at his son one more time, said goodbye, and got out of the car.

4.

It happened simply enough. He went to the Blue Hen to watch his team play when she came over to talk to him. Describing their holiday plans, she mentioned that she was throwing a party to celebrate the holidays, and she invited him.

"Bring a guest with you, if you like," she said. "Hope to see you there."

The primary candidate to accompany him to the party was Paul. They had talked about it, and agreed that it might be a fun way to spend one of the days leading up to Christmas.

They arrived at her place at 6:00 pm sharp. Always punctual, Hugo desired to not appear rude by not being on time. Paul, on the other hand, was indifferent and fine with arriving at any time. The two friends agreed that they did not intend to stay long. Rather, they wanted to show up, make their presence be felt, and then head out shortly thereafter.

Answering the door was Lily, who smiled at Hugo and his friend, saying, "You made it."

They stepped inside. Her house was not lavish by any means, but was nice, clean, and cozy. Hanging from the wall were photos of her daughters and even her late husband, who all had blonde hair. A few guests were present, sipping beverages and making conversation.

"Can I get you anything to drink?"

Paul took a beer and Hugo a glass of wine. It was Hugo's first alcoholic beverage in a week. Simply put, he hadn't had any reason to drink. Since he had been out and about so much, the opportunity hadn't presented itself.

Hugo stood by Paul, the two of them mainly talking to each other and to no one else. Guests were steadily entering the party. Then, Paul turned to Hugo and asked with disbelief, "Is that Gabe?"

Nearby stood a man with short blonde hair, who turned around and said, "Paul!"

The two men walked up and embraced.

"This is an old co-worker of mine," Paul said. "We worked together for fifteen years."

"Or was it twenty?"

"No matter. It was a long enough time."

The two of them laughed, and proceeded to chat, leaving Hugo on his own.

Lily walked up to Hugo and smiled, saying, "I'm glad you were able to make it tonight."

"Me too. Thanks for inviting us."

"Are you enjoying the holiday season?"

"Well enough."

"What's that mean?"

"The holidays are the holidays. I appreciate a nice quiet day or two to spend with my family. But as you know, this year is different."

"I do know," she answered. "How have you been getting along?"

Hugo took a sip of his wine. "Of course I miss her more than I can say, but life goes on, right? Doesn't time heal all?"

"Well, yes and no. I don't really think the pain of losing someone so close to you will ever quite go away. "

Then Hugo broke down. Tears were forming in his eyes. "I haven't been doing that great, Lily," he whispered.

"I get that."

"There are just so many things that remind me of her. Like the gift I got her last year. Last year I got her a bracelet made with diamonds. It was the most beautiful thing. I knew her time with me was short then, so the whole holiday season was colored by that. But you should have seen the way her eyes lit up when she opened that present. She was so happy!

Of course diamonds are just a material thing, but still. It was a great gift. Now, this year, I have the diamond bracelet, and it is just sitting in the closet of my bedroom. I have nothing I can do with it. That's just one example of how this year is different than every other year: I can't buy her a present."

"How else is it different?"

"Well, we used to have a tree celebration. When Adrian was younger, we would always go off to the tree farm together. I would buy a tree and carry it onto the car. We would take the tree home and I would put it up. Then we would walk around it, decorating it, playing music in the background, and I would go and cook a big roast for us to eat in front of the tree. It was our own way of celebrating the season." Hugo had wiped his eyes several times, and he no longer had tears in them.

"That sounds like a lovely tradition. Anything else?"

"There's a bunch of other little things that make the holidays tough for me. Where do I begin?"

"Fair enough."

"We used to go caroling. Every year, a week or two before Christmas, we would dress up and go with some family friends to carol. Paul, the guy I brought here with me tonight, would come along with us and some other people in the neighborhood to carol. We would walk through the streets and sing songs. You should have seen how excited Adrian got when he was singing. It was the most spectacular thing! It might be cold and snowy out, and Adrian would have on his red hat, and his cheeks would get red from the cold. We would sing until we lost our voices. It was the grandest time."

"Wow, Hugo. It sounds like you had a lot of things in your family that made the holidays special for you," she said with sincerity. "Me, I just have this party mainly. Every year, Sebastian and I would throw it as a way to bring together all of the people who are important to us. I guess you have become a member of that company now!"

"That's great news. I guess what I'm trying to say to you is that I don't really know how to get through the holidays when so much of what made them great is gone. It just hurts.

It makes me feel bitter. The truth is a part of me is just waiting for the New Year to come and pass so I can get on with the next big challenge."

"Looking at one year since you lost her, huh?"

"Exactly, that might be one of the things I am dreading most of all. Part of me feels like I need to visit her grave, at least that's what my shrink says, but I just don't feel ready."

"It's okay if you don't feel ready. You can take your time."

"I can and I can't. I feel like I need to move along in this grief process as quickly as I can."

"No need to rush it. The whole thing is beyond your control, anyway. Why try and force it?"

"Is it beyond my control? I never thought about that. Tell me, what can I do to get through the holidays?"

"Well, I think you are already doing precisely what you need to be doing."

"Which is what?"

"You are taking time to remember. You have told me stories about how you used to spend your holidays with your family. Not only that, but you are being pro-social, going out and doing things, like coming to my party." Still, she was smiling.

"My son and I got into a big fight a few days ago," he said suddenly.

"What about?"

"You see, he was first enrolled in this accelerated business program— I don't even really know what it was. He quit the program, saying it was too hard. Then he enrolled in a photography program, one that follows a more normal calendar, and now he says he is quitting that. I just can't stand so much quitting. Why can't he stick with anything?"

"I don't know, Hugo."

"Anyway, we got into a pretty big fight, and we haven't talked since then. It has made things kind of weird."

"Have you thought about the fact that your son is doing the very best he can, the very best way he knows how?" she asked.

"I don't know about that. If that were the case, then why does he keep quitting?"

"Clearly he is struggling. What I think he needs more than anything is for his father to show love, support, and compassion to him. He needs his dad in his life, and to feel supported by him. Don't forget that he has lost his mother. That must be really hard on him."

But Hugo was too preoccupied with his own grief to fathom that of another.

Lily, continued, "Do you think— what is your son's name?"

"Adrian."

"Right, do you think Adrian likes being in this situation, where he keeps trying things and finding that he is unsuccessful? No, it must be awful for him. If I were you, I would give him a call, talk to him, just show him that you love him."

"Easier said than done. The truth is that I just feel really angry, and I don't really feel ready to talk to him. I need more time. The emotions are still very real, but thanks anyway."

"Sure thing."

"Also, I am not talking to my brother, Martin." Hugo was fully opening up now.

"Oh."

"My family is rather fractured right now, during the time of the year when families are supposed to be the very closest. Why is that?"

"I don't know. I can't say I have all the answers. In fact, I can't say I have many of the answers at all, but I am always happy to listen."

"I stopped talking to my brother because I was so angry at him. Throughout my life, there has been this steady accumulation of anger towards him, and it finally came out. It was all unleashed in one crashing wave."

"What do you think you are mad at him about?"

"Maybe it's not anger. I feel jealousy, resentment, bitterness. He has so much, and I have so little. It makes me feel like the world has set me up from the beginning for failure, while he has been set up for success. Then the world blames me for being so negative. It's not fair!"

"I see."

"It makes me mad, and it hurts me to hold up my life against his and see that he has all these things I wish I had. Then he goes and tries to involve me in his life. He tries to evangelize me with promises of heaven and salvation. He tries to get me to go to church with him. But I always find a way out."

"What makes you think there isn't heaven and salvation?"

"Are you religious, too?"

"Not particularly," she said. "I just like to pick your brain a little bit. Why can't those things be real? Aren't they comforting to think about?"

"Yes, but being comforting doesn't make something true. If you want to think rationally about the whole business, then here goes. We are organisms, and what is observable about us is that we live, reproduce, and die. Really, that is all we can say for sure about us as a species. Spirituality, organized religion, they all have evolutionary provisions in them that make them advantageous to an organism. It is advantageous, I suppose, to live as though heaven is real, because that means you live without fear, you live life fully. But like I said, just because something is advantageous to believe in doesn't mean it possesses a positive truth value."

"Okay. But do you find the idea of believing in heaven comforting? Does it comfort you to think that one day you will be reunited with her again?"

"Well, according to Church teaching I am going anywhere but to heaven."

"Why is that?"

"Because I don't believe. I don't believe that Jesus saved me, or that God can make a difference in my life. Most of my life I have not believed those things. Most of my life I was more preoccupied with things like my career and my family. I was too busy to think about spiritual things. Then my wife becomes horribly ill and I'm supposed to surrender to a system of belief? The whole matter feels like an exercise in weakness. I don't want to appear weak by giving into belief. Plus, if I spent the majority of my life not believing, wouldn't it seem rather cheap for me to suddenly become interested in the divine? Isn't that selfish? Isn't that wrong?"

Lily said, "Let me ask you a question since we are talking about spirituality. Do you think that it is ever too late for a soul to become united with God?"

"Do you?" Hugo challenged.

"Why, who cares what I think? I'm just asking you, because I can tell that you are really hurting a great deal. You are hurting, aren't you?"

"Of course I am! I lost my wife and I am getting through the holidays without her, and half of my family won't talk to me!"

"Now, to be fair, it sounded like you were the one not talking to them. Not talking in families is always mutual."

"Fine, whatever. To answer your original question, I do feel like it is too late for me. I'm sixty-seven years old. I've spent the majority of my life working to build something that would last, and the reality is that none of it is going to. All of it is going to erode away, to decay, leaving me with nothing, and then soon I will erode away as well."

"Don't you think it's possible that not everything will be gone?"

"What do you mean?"

"Well," Lily began, "Though it appears that everything is eroding, all the time new things are being created. There is a cycle of life and death, and we are all a part of it. You are a part of the universe. You may die one day, but you live on through Adrian, and for all we know you may live on in another form as well."

"I don't know about that. That sounds like some Eastern stuff to me. Sure, I live through Adrian, but one day he too will die, and then there will really be nothing for me to live through. Besides, I am not a part of the universe; I am just me."

"That's one way to view things."

"If I was an adherent of any religion, and I'm not, it would be Christianity...Catholicism. So, speaking to that tradition, how can I even begin to approach God when I don't believe in him? What would I say?"

"Maybe, 'hello'?"

Hugo laughed. "Sure, I'll go and say hello to God, and then I'll ask him why he took my wife from me, or why he made my son into such a disappointment, or why he put my brother in my life as a way to flaunt all of the things I don't have, or why God made me so I like wine so much."

"Like wine so much?"

"Yes, I like wine, but bad things happen to me when I drink it. When I got drunk a few months ago, I hit my friend Paul."

"Hugo...."

"Aren't you sympathetic!" Hugo quipped.

"Hey, I'm just trying to be there for you in the ways that I can. That's all I've ever wanted to do, because the truth is that I have always seen myself in you."

"Really?" Hugo's interest was piqued.

"Yes, I lost my husband, and you your wife. Ever since I first met you at the bar I felt like we were kindred spirits. I felt a connection to you."

"Well that's all nice and everything, but it's not going to bring Sandra back, and it's not going to bring Sebastian back."

Lily tilted her head to look around the room and then said, "I need to go and catch someone before they leave. Listen, would you be interested in grabbing a coffee together sometime, just you and me?"

"What do you mean just you and me?"

"You know, to go deeper into this conversation. I've really enjoyed getting to know you in the past year, and I'd like to continue to learn more about you." Her cheeks were turning red. "I like spending time with you."

Hugo was taken aback. "No, I would not like to get a coffee with you. I thought you were being my friend to support me, not because you had a crush on me," he snapped. "Now, I think it is time that I got to be going."

Hugo went and pulled Paul away from Gabe, saying that it was certainly time to go. Paul was interested in staying and connecting with his old friend, but his loyalty to Hugo was greater, and so they left.

Many thoughts were traveling through Hugo's mind as they were driving back to Wedgwood. Who was this Lily, who owned the bar he so liked to visit? Was he attracted to her? Of course not! His devotion was directed towards Sandra, and since she was gone now, there was no one on the earth for him to be devoted to. Going out for a cup of coffee with another woman was the greatest form of betrayal conceivable. How could Lily have asked him out like that? The whole gesture felt to him like a mammoth affront. It was an insult to his grief that she would go and investigate his spiritual convictions and then turn around and ask him on a date. All throughout this past year of grief, he had never even considered dating or remarrying, and he certainly wasn't considering it now. The fact of the matter was that Hugo held romantic notions about love. There was only one love of his life, and no one else would ever compare.

"Lily asked me out," he said to Paul.

"Really? What did you say?"

"What did I say? What do you mean? I said no!"

"Sorry, I was just asking."

"How could that even be a question that came across your mind?'

"I don't know, I just thought it was possible that you might, you know—"

"No, it was and is not possible. What Sandra and I had is undying love. She will always be the only woman that I ever love. Simple as that."

"Understood."

"Well, at least you had a nice time at the party."

"I did. Did you not?"

"I was having an all right enough time until she popped that question on me, that is."

"I see. Well, at least we gave the party a try."

"At least we did."

The two friends said little more for the remainder of the car ride.

5.

It was Christmas Day, and he was alone.

Paul was spending the day with his mother and her extended family, leaving Hugo to be by himself. Still, he was not talking to Adrian or Martin, and now Lily was added to that list, not that he had talked to her all that often. Hugo sat on his couch, watching a Christmas special on the television.

Hugo had in his possession a single bottle of wine, though he knew that the liquor store would be open too for all the other hopeless people living in this city. Initially, he rejected the urge, but it seemed to keep coming back with more and more force. Looking around his living room, he realized that this year he hadn't bothered to decorate it in any way. Desperately, he had set up a fake Christmas tree. But there were no presents beneath it. There was no one, just him. Loneliness, like a specter, was floating through the air, filling in the corners of the rooms of the house with a gloom that was cast down violently.

He rose from his seat on the couch and walked into the kitchen towards the bottle of chardonnay. But as he was moving, he reconsidered the matter, turned around, and walked back into the living room, taking up his place on the sofa. He thought about how, previously, he had worked hard to keep the house full of fresh flowers, and how that habit had been in decline. No way to blot out the real odors, he thought to himself. Lying down on the sofa, he closed his eyes and drifted away from reality for a while.

Waking up in a cool sweat, he looked around the room, rising from the sofa quickly. He looked at the clock and realized that two hours had passed by. Then he turned to stare at the television, which was still playing a Christmas special. He reached for the remote and turned the television off. With the remaining energy he had, he managed to get up off of the sofa and walk into the kitchen.

Now he was in a different room, but what good did it do? Should he go over and sit at the kitchen table? He went up to the bottle of wine and poured himself a glass. Next, he had a seat and proceeded to sip his drink. The wine was having no effect, for as he continued to drink he still felt the same things. So he began to drink more quickly, finishing his first glass in minutes, and pouring the next one at once. He sighed, looking out the back window, into the backyard, at the solitary tree that stood so mightily. He wished he could be like this tree, to carry his weight with strength and grace, but he knew he was more like one of the nearby bushes, a pathetic little shrub.

The phone was ringing. Startled, he thought about answering, but then decided not to, not wanting to chat with whoever wanted to talk to him. The truth was he didn't want to talk to anyone in all of the world. He felt abandoned. He felt abandoned by Paul, who had had other plans for Christmas, by Adrian who had been a disappointment, by Martin who was likely off with his own giant, prosperous family, celebrating the holiday in style, and by Lily, who he had thought had cared about him in a genuine, human way, but had only cared because she was attracted to him.

But worst of all, Hugo felt abandoned by Sandra this Christmas. Where had she gone?

Feeling the bitterness swell, Hugo drank his wine, reveling in it. Glass after glass of it passed through his lips. This was the only thing he had, the only one who hadn't abandoned him, this glass bottle, which was rapidly being depleted. Somehow energized by the drinking, Hugo rose from where he was sitting and walked back into the living room. He opened the front door of the house and stepped outside.

The air was crisp, cool, and moist with precipitation. Knowing that he would need something more to drink, he walked towards the liquor store. He hadn't eaten a thing all day, and so the wine went straight to him. Neither did he have any plan for what he was going to eat. His pantry was practically empty, but he didn't mind. All he wanted was to drink, not eat. Ambling past Kim Schaeffer's house, he thought about how pitiful and yet how right she had been to avoid talking about her dead husband. To be so reticent was a sign of weakness, but there was something pragmatic about it. Death remained the great absorber, and so simply not talking about it seemed to be the best approach to take.

Passing along Mason Street, he was approaching the liquor store. He entered and once more did his best to appear sober, something he was rather gifted at doing. He purchased two bottles and had them stuffed into a large paper bag. As he exited the store he was almost laughing to himself with glee, thinking about the company he had with him now. He wasn't alone anymore; he had these drinks to spend time with. Who needed friends or family? The only person Hugo needed was himself, he decided. He was smiling, but after a few steps his grin faded and he lowered the paper bag down to his side.

Outside it was cold, the wind carrying with it a stinging sensation that made Hugo's hands turn red. It was beginning to get dark, the rays of light from the horizon bending with the setting, hidden sun. Few people were out walking on the streets, and they were all in groups, often families that were talking and laughing excitedly. Thinking it might be best to take a different route home, completing the loop, Hugo took a turn in the opposite direction when he left the liquor store.

It was a soft, subtle sound at first, but it grew increasingly loud until it was a full swell, like a flower in bloom, the sound of people singing. Initially confused, Hugo wondered what it was, but then he saw the building not far off in the distance. He was walking towards it. It was a big, old wooden building with a bell tower and a sign that read: St. James Cathedral.

Curiously, the door to the church was wide open. You know what would be really funny, thought Hugo, is if I were to step inside.

The air was warm and still inside. The sanctuary space was vacuous, gigantic, filled with stained glass windows and long pew seats. Space had been reduced to standing room only, people lining the walls of the room, standing under the holy, radiant light of the windows. The people were singing, likely a Christmas psalm sung by the Church for millennia.

The sound of the singing was tranquil, repetitive, deeply calming. Though there were many voices, they seemed to move in unison, men, women, and children all together. In the background, there was the occasional sound of a baby crying. In the front of the sanctuary, there was the priest, who stood facing the masses of people. It was an interesting juxtaposition to compare this crowd with the ones from the day of shopping at the mall, for they felt very different.

Something stirred in Hugo. He stood at the doorway, a beard forming on his face from days without shaving, filthy from not bathing, clutching the bag of secret wine, and he at once apprehended he was in the presence of the divine.

A voice seemed to be speaking to Hugo. Be at ease, it spoke, open your heart to God. Bask in the reality of God.

Where is such a voice coming from? Hugo wondered. Am I that intoxicated?

Hugo dismissed this message and once more looked around the church. He saw the cross at the front of the sanctuary, from which Jesus hung. He thought about all the stories he had been told about the gospel, about the pain, suffering, and loneliness that had gone into Jesus bearing the cross. He imagined Jesus in the garden, praying that the cup would be taken from him. Hugo's mother told him these stories when he was young, and they left a distinct impression on him. Hugo looked at Jesus for a long time. He started to feel the onset of panic. He sensed that he didn't belong in the church, that he had taken a wrong turn, that the Christian story with its message of restoration, joy, and redemption was not for him. He left the church.

Walking quickly back home, it was snowing. Soft, delicate flakes of snow fell on his head and on the ground around his feet. To his amazement, the snow was actually sticking. The wind was cruel as it blew directly in his face. He clutched the bag, breathing heavily, weak and pathetic. In that moment, he felt utterly unloved by the world and the people in it. He was left with this grief and was destined to spend eternity wandering the dark surface of the earth, searching for something to last but unable to find it. Such was his fate.

To his right, there was a park. Tired, he brushed off a bench, which was readily collecting deposits of snow, and then had a seat. Not minding that snow was falling on him, he pulled out one of the bottles and proceeded to drink from it. The taste was so bitter he grimaced. All was dark except for a nearby street sign. Hugo laughed to himself, thinking that he rather resembled a person who lived on the street.

When he was a child, Hugo had been told that there was a God who loved him, but somewhere along the line, he lost faith in this. He didn't believe that there was a loving deity watching over him because his life was emptiness. What he felt was forgotten. It would have been too disharmonious for him to believe in the love of God and continue to live the life set before him. Moreover, he couldn't comprehend how such a God would enable so much suffering and pain to happen in the world. Hugo knew he wasn't the first person to think this. A lot of Hugo's faith in God was shaken when he lost his mother. Ten years earlier she had died, and the pain had been so monumental, so intense, that he initially did not know how to cope. He and Martin had been very close to each other during that time, helping one another grieve. But what Hugo realized now was that he had never really grieved the loss of his mother, not fully, and now he was failing to grieve the loss of his wife. Feelings of inadequacy and worthlessness washed over Hugo, who began to cry. Tears fell in the snow, and still, he continued to sip from the red wine. He drank mindlessly, with little regard for how it made him feel. Eventually, he lost consciousness, passing out just as the snow stopped falling.

January

I.

Surprisingly, he left the store with only one new tie. It was vibrant, purple, with cats all the way across it. Hugo enjoyed visiting this store, which sold ties of all sorts and descriptions, every once in a while when he felt a need to add to his collection. Though he already owned a lot of ties, he still enjoyed the pleasure of buying one, that joy at having something new to wear and show to others.

He stepped out of the store and walked up the street towards the bus stop. To his left, there was the Sound, which was pristine in its beauty, the water lapping gently, cupped around the edge by the peninsula on the other side, which was rich green. Walking past a café and then a restaurant, Hugo was thinking. Christmas proved to be a miserable affair. As he remembered it, he woke up lying on a park bench in the freezing cold. By his own estimation he was not unconscious long, but still, his head ached from all the wine he had had. He scrambled back to his home in the cold night, pitiful and unknown. The remainder of the night he spent sleeping in his bed, huddled beneath the covers.

Now the holiday season had passed, the New Year having arrived only a few days before. Still, Hugo was not speaking to the people in his life, and this bothered him. He felt like he needed to achieve reconciliation, but he didn't know how to go about it. Left to live a solitary life, he was continuing to go about the things that he enjoyed doing, taking a trip to Ballard to visit the specialty tie store being just one such example.

Having reached his bus stop, he stood and waited. In the air, there was a dry, crisp coolness that was refreshing and yet also bothersome. The day was overcast, the sun occasionally poking through the clouds but never for long. People were walking by in thick jackets, their breath visible. Nearby where Hugo stood there was a restaurant that was full of people. He stood at the stop, looking down at the timetable and feeling mystified, for the bus should have arrived by now, but where was it? It was not rare for him to become irritated by a late bus. Willingly forfeiting his own driving privileges was a choice he made, and for the most part, he was pleased by not having to drive, but with it came consequences such as often having to wait. A few more minutes passed, and still the bus had not arrived. Again and again, he turned his head, looking for it, expecting to see it come around the bend at any moment.

Then an idea came to him. What if he walked down to the beach and spent a little time there? Not on any specific schedule, not having anything or anyone waiting for him at home, he decided to cross the street, moving towards the nearby staircase that would lead closer to the water.

He reached the stairs and made his way down slowly. There were many of them to traverse, nestled within the coverage of trees. He walked down, using the hand railing, making progress. In his hand, he held the bag that contained the tie he purchased. Currently, he was wearing a tie with sailboats on it, which seemed appropriate given what he was doing. Once he reached the bottom of a set of stairs, there would be a flat stretch to move across before the next set. Blanketed in trees, he looked as though he was swallowed in a forest.

Finally, he reached the bottom, where there was a small bridge that went over the railway tracks. Metal netting was in place around the bridge to make it safer, for it was exceptionally high up. He walked across the bridge, brushing the metal netting with his hand. Before him, there was the shore. Stepping down the last set of stairs, he was now moving across sand. Of course, the sand to be found anywhere in this city was rocky, rough, and hardly eligible to be considered sand at all, but it was the best thing that was available. He hopped onto a log and nearly slipped in the process. For a moment he stood and simply stared at the water.

On the other side was West Seattle, that curious peninsula of beach communities and eclecticisms. The waves in the water rolled gently. A seagull flew by, making its presence known. Stretching out far, the water was vast, and it inspired Hugo. Sure, Puget Sound did not technically count as an ocean, though it was ocean water. It was an estuary, a place of great mystery. Compared with the pure, uninterrupted ocean of Grayland, Puget Sound was something else entirely, but there was something special about it, for it was the lungs of Seattle itself. The city rested on the Sound, and it gained its life and energy from this water. This water was spiritual.

Then, while looking at the water, the Sound spoke to Hugo, telling him things.

Standing on the log and beholding the Sound, Hugo became aware of two things. This life he had been living, being solitary, drinking, sleeping too much, again he saw that clearly, it was not working. Changes needed to be made. Next, if all of human life and creation were represented by the ocean, then Hugo needed to allow himself to dissolve into it, to take all of his loss and uncertainty and return it to that body. Loss was best handled communally, with other people, and so it was imperative that Hugo get back into contact with the people in his life. Though he and Paul were not estranged in any way, he still needed to go to him and confess his drinking habits. Just as each droplet of water came together to form the sea, Hugo knew he needed to go and join together with his brother and be reconciled. Further, he needed to be accepting of his son's situation and let him know just how much he loved him. Hugo didn't know what to do as regarded Lily, but he realized he cared about her as a friend far too much to allow things to end as they had.

All of this dawned on him as he looked at the sea. It was clear that a lot was being asked of him. Where was he even to begin?

And then he knew precisely what he needed to do. There was one challenge, one objective confronting him that, he knew, would enable him to bring all of these people back into his life. But what he was wondering was if he was capable of doing what he knew he positively needed to do. Looking at the sand for a moment, and then turning to look back at the bridge and the railway tracks, Hugo sighed with discouragement.

2.

It was a sunny day, which was refreshing given the time of year.

Hugo closed his door and locked up. Then he stepped out onto the street and began to walk towards the store. It was not his preference to buy flowers, but given the season, he was left without another option. As he was turning right, he heard a voice call from behind.

"Hey, neighbor."

"Hi, Paul."

"You off to get those flowers?"

"Yup."

"Great. Well, I guess I'll see you in thirty?"

"Sounds good to me. I'll come over, and then we can walk together."

Continuing on his way, Hugo felt dread. Thinking about what he was going to do today was more than he could handle, so he did his best not to think. He allowed one foot to follow after another as he made his way. Crossing an intersection, he continued walking. The air was still cool and crisp, and the days were proving to be brutally short. Winter, he knew, was a time of death in the world. The natural world seemed to come to a halt.

Now he was on the main stretch of Mason Street, and he made the familiar turn towards the grocery store. There were no items he needed except for the flowers. Before him the store stood, looming like a menacing source of darkness. Entering, he went towards the floral department. What type of flowers to get? What would be fitting given the circumstances? Deciding that there was no other option, he purchased a bouquet of roses. Nearly a year ago he had bought tulips for his home, but now it seemed that roses were what he should get. He knew these flowers, with the sense of grandeur they evoked, were more than appropriate. He held them in his hands and went to the checkout stand. The cashier complimented his argyle tie, which Sandra had purchased for him the Christmas before.

Having made his purchase, he walked back towards his home. The walk back, it seemed, was much longer and colder. Over and over Hugo's mind returned to what was before him, and he apprehended feelings of panic and fear. His heart rate picked up considerably. But, remembering what the sea told him, he continued on his way. The Sound was a comforting force for him, promising him protection and safety as he embarked on the task at hand. It was not long before he was heading up towards Paul's home.

A few days before, Hugo went to Paul and told him about how he had spent his Christmas.

"I drank and I drank," he had said. "I wandered into a park and drank until everything went black." Hugo locked his eyes on Paul's.

"Christmas must have been horrible for you," Paul replied. "I could see how you would have been led down that path. You must have been so alone. I'm sorry I wasn't around during Christmas to be with you. Feel no need to apologize to me. I love and respect you just as you are."

"What's so strange about it all," Hugo said, "is how successful I was at avoiding alcohol while we were in Grayland. Anyway I would like for you to be a source of accountability for me, to hold me to a higher standard."

"Okay, well first things first. We need to pour out all the wine you have."

"Are you sure?!"

"Yes, and you need to tell me about any alcohol you consume."

"But—"

"Do you agree to those terms?"

"Hugo nodded."

"Good. I think you're going to make a lot of progress by doing this."

It was funny, for most of what Hugo had realized days earlier, all the insight about drinking and oversleeping, he had gained when he was in Grayland back in November if only to go and lose it. It seemed as though he was learning the same lessons again and again. Still, progress was being made. He was stumbling to the ground and then getting back up on his feet, getting stronger and more aware each time.

Knocking on Paul's door, Hugo stood and waited, anxious.

"Hello, again," Paul said. "You ready?"

"What time is it?"

Paul looked at his watch. "A bit past one. What time is everyone meeting there?"

"Two."

"Well," Paul spoke, "I guess we have time for a game of chess."

They went inside and set up the board. The new set was looking very nice. Feeling competitive, Hugo was focused as he played, being more bold than usual in his approach. They played for half an hour, but the game was not resolved, so they decided to leave the game out and finish it another time. They had somewhere they needed to be. They stepped outside Paul's house and began to walk.

"How are you feeling?" Paul asked.

"I am feeling quite nervous, but I am glad you are here."

"It is understandable for you to feel that way."

They passed through the empty field and continued on their way. Before long, they were standing outside the cemetery.

Feeling a sharp ache in his chest, Hugo stood with his friend. They chatted about chess and then about what they had been up to the past few days. Anything that could take Hugo's mind off of what they were doing was a good thing. Where was everyone else? Hugo and Paul were not all that early, so it seemed only right that the others appeared soon. A few minutes later and a car pulled up to the lot. Out stepped Lily.

"Hi, Hugo," she said. "How are you?"

"Doing all right."

"Thanks for inviting me," she said. "It means a lot to me."

"Sure thing."

They stood in front of the entrance to the cemetery and talked about one thing and then another. Death, Hugo observed, had a funny way of causing people to talk, to talk about anything at all to break the overwhelming silence that it incited. There was something inherently unsettling and uncomfortable about being near a cemetery, at least for the living.

Then Martin's car appeared.

"Hi, big brother."

"Hey."

Hugo and Paul introduced Lily to Martin.

"Are we waiting for anyone else?" Martin asked.

"Yes, there is one more person," Paul replied.

As he said this, Adrian drove up and parked next to Martin. He climbed out of his car. His hair appeared messy, and he seemed to be in a hurry as he joined the others. They all stood and chatted for a few minutes more before Hugo addressed them.

"Hello, everyone. Thank you for coming today. I know that the last few months have not been the easiest for me. I know I have been unfair and unkind to each of you in different ways. But the truth is, a few days ago I realized something very important. I have spent most of this year trying to deal with a loss on my own. I wanted to be strong and independent because I have spent the majority of my life living that way. But the reality is that loss is best handled in a community, as my brother Martin told me earlier this year.

Adrian, my dear son, I love you more than I can say. I can't begin to convey to you how sorry I am that you lost your mother in the sudden, horrendous way you did. I want you and I to come together and grieve the loss of Mom as a family. Paul, you have watched our family grow up in this neighborhood for years. You knew Sandra as a friend, and you were like family to us as well. It means a lot to me to have you here with us. Martin, you were always so kind to Sandra, so brimming with positivity when you spoke about her to me. You have known her since you were a child, and even then you approved of us as a couple. Thank you for that. You have made a strong effort to bring your family close to mine, uniting us all as a one. I was not always the most receptive of those efforts, but I know my wife appreciated them. Now that she is gone, I don't want anything to stand in the way of Adrian and I being a part of your family. Not even traffic along 520 and I-90 can separate us from each other! And then there is you, Lily. You never knew Sandra. Yet you were compassionate towards me. I have always liked going to your bar, and you feel like an old friend. You, who lost someone you held very closely, saw yourself in me. Thank you for all the conversations we had, about how you yourself navigated grief, and how you knew, at the end of the day, that grief was my journey to take alone. But that's just the thing. Grief is a journey I take by myself, but at the same time, today I am choosing to take it with all of you. I spent my fair share of time wallowing in grief by myself, getting drunk, wandering off by myself, cutting off my relationships and trying to hide from the love that each of you offers me. Not anymore. I have invited each of you to be here with me today as I do something I didn't think I would ever be able to do, to visit her grave. Honestly, I'm a bit of a mess. I feel shaky, and I think I could throw up right now, but here we are. I know that I couldn't make it to the grave by myself, but with all of you here with me I know there's no limit to what we can do! So, without any more waiting, because I don't know if I could handle that, I say it's time that we got ready to head inside. As you know, I love gardening, but today I decided to just purchase some flowers to bring to her grave.

These roses may not come from my own garden, but they are still imbued with love, the love that we all together bring, and I think there is something truly special in that, something lasting. Um, so as we get ready to head inside, is there anything you would like to say to me?"

Paul cleared his throat and said, "Well, I'd just like to say on behalf of all of us how much it means to us that you invited us to come here and share this day with you. We know how difficult it is for you to be here at this cemetery; it would be difficult for anyone. Also, we know how challenging the last year or so has been, but all told, I'd say you have done a spectacular job of getting through it. Loss is not an easy thing to talk about, so I won't say much more, but what I will say is that we love you dearly and I consider you to be my brother. Thank you for inviting us here."

Hugo smiled at his friend and then looked around at the other guests. "Well, should we go inside?"

They walked past the open gates and entered the cemetery. Inside, the mood was strangely tranquil, practically idyllic. There was a large field with an occasional tree, and lining the grassy patches were tombstones, which from afar sat plainly like little pebbles. Nearby there was a building that must have been the main office of the cemetery. Adrian stepped towards this office, saying, "We might as well ask where the grave is located."

Not wanting to contradict his son, Hugo relented, saying, "Sure, let's do that."

The group entered the office. Inside, they spoke to a calm man who told them where they could find the grave of Sandra Larson. Apparently, it was located in the southwest corner of the cemetery.

Leaving the office, they proceeded to walk through the cemetery together. Hugo, with Adrian, led the way, Paul and Martin following closely behind, and then lastly there was Lily. In a sense, they were an odd group of people to be together, but the reality was that they were a mixture of friends and family, bound together by one thing, or by the absence of a person. It was this loss that brought them together, that and the different connections they had all formed with Hugo.

Stretching, rolling, the cemetery went on and on, with there being no sign of the end. They would walk past one series of tombstones only to realize that there was still farther to go. Adrian, who talked to the man in the office, received and internalized detailed instructions about how to find the grave, and he was guiding his father and everyone else onward.

Hugo and Adrian had talked little about Sandra's death. Though it was a loss that they shared, it was simply too unpleasant to bring up, and so they had not talked about it. Of course, Hugo was resistant towards talking for a long while, leaving Adrian, who was not as emotionally resilient, on his own. He had proceeded in his life the only way he knew how, working as a barista and going about the little niceties of daily life. Navigating the business program and then the photography program had kept him plenty busy, but still, he needed to process grief just as much as his father. Sensitive, while not prone to deep or reflective thought, Adrian did not have much of a conception around death. He was very close to his mother all the way up until her passing, but when she left, he moved on the best way he knew how to.

"It is a beautiful day," Adrian said to his father.

"It sure is."

"You okay, Dad?"

"I'm fine."

"If you find today to be difficult, I understand. I know how it feels."

For the first time, those five words meant something to Hugo, who so easily believed that he was going through his life and experiences alone. Hugo reached out an arm and patted Adrian on the shoulder.

"Love you, son."

Now they were approaching the other end of the cemetery, for a metal fence was visible. On the other side of it, there was a golf course, peaceful and well maintained. It was strange, Hugo thought to himself, that people would be capable of occupying themselves with something like golf when, just over the fence, there were the houses of the dead. Something as unassuming and everyday as golf was juxtaposed with the cemetery, which was of an infinite gravity, an infinite solemnity. Hugo imagined old men like himself, likely rich, who played golf every weekend together, thinking of little, watching the clouds rolling by as the day wore on. Meanwhile, across the other side of the fence, there were those who bore heavy burdens, who came to honor the memory of lost ones, filled with questions and doubts.

Having reached the fence, Adrian guided the group towards the left, to the southwest corner. Onward they continued to go, in the still and quiet air of a sunny day in January. It seemed as though the entire city was in a restful, pensive state. The whole world had come to a temporary halt just for Hugo and his group. What was he to think of this group as? It was a mixture of friends and family. No, it was all family, no matter how it was considered.

"We're really close now," Adrian said, who walked a few steps ahead of everyone else and looked down to examine the graves. The graves here did not stand up in the air like tombstones but were like little monuments that rested on the grassy ground.

Adrian was looking at one grave and then another, whispering the names to himself as he read them. The rest of the group, at this time, was standing still. No one seemed to feel a need to speak. Paul walked up to Hugo, looking at him, and smiled.

"Here it is," Adrian pointed in a quiet voice. Adrian took a few steps back to join the others.

Most of the group stayed still, and only Hugo stepped forward. Turning his head to look down, Hugo was trying to prepare himself for it, for the moment when he saw it, but he knew he wasn't ready. He knew he wasn't ready, and that the moment was going to happen anyway.

He looked down at the grave and beheld both death and life.

There it was, written in stone: Sandra Larson, with the years of her life, and a space next to her name. Hugo looked around, at the many tombstones of the cemetery, and his heart rate spiked. Then, imagining the sea, he calmed down.

In his mind, he pictured a captain of a sinking ship. The captain was given a choice, either to fight and resist the on-coming tide of oblivion or to stare forward and embrace his fate. Death remained indifferent to the reaction of the one dying. As Hugo thought of this made-up captain, he decided to choose being calm and accepting. He stared at the grave and did not look away for a while.

He had expected when this moment came to begin crying. No tears, though, were coming. He looked at the name, etched into stone, and thought about all that it could not capture, the human life, the warm presence that had been, and the utter failure of the grave. After all, it was nothing more than a stone. The reality was that not even here, in this place of all the places in the world, could she be found. The one place that was supposed to hold on to her memory more than anywhere else on earth had no stronger, no more real claim to her than anywhere else. All this time Hugo had been filled with dread, thinking about coming to the grave, but as he stood there, in the company of people who loved him, he felt hardly a thing at all.

He continued to look at the stone. He thought about the funeral when she had been brought here for the first time. On that day, Hugo was a stoic mess. Though no emotions were externalized, on the inside he was a wreck. Vividly, he remembered putting an arm around Adrian and listening as the priest recited a prayer and then the body was lowered. On that day, like today, Hugo was in the company of people he knew and loved, but something felt different about today. Looking into the stone surface, he envisioned her face, those green eyes, black hair, the little wrinkles, and he felt as though he was communing with her through the doorway of life itself. There is so much I want to say to you, he thought, but right now, for the time being, I just want you to know how much I love you. My love extends beyond this world, to you, wherever you may be.

Then Hugo began to cry.

Tears fell from him and landed on the stone surface. He sobbed and breathed deeply, completely surrendering himself to the moment. With a turn of his head, he looked up to see the others standing not far off, not watching him. He cried and he cried. It was as though a year of feelings and thoughts were being unloaded all at once.

Gently, gingerly, he lowered the flowers down on the grave, placing them just below the name. At that instance, several petals from the flowers fell off, landing on her name. He knew the name, the etching in stone, was just a representation, that it was not Sandra herself, but still, he had a need to honor it, to honor her, and so he reached down with his hand and picked up the petals. He held the petals in his hand, looking at them and thinking about how gentle they were, and it made him think about how gentle she had been. Wiping tears from his face, he continued to look at the grave, allowing what feelings and thoughts would come to come.

He accepted the fact that she had lived and died, that they had shared together a son and many years of happiness and unhappiness. Letting go of her, he said goodbye. Staring at the stone, which was his own reflection, he told her he loved her and said goodbye.

Then he was seized by the feeling of a reunion.

Could I really be in her presence again? he wondered. He envisioned those green eyes, brighter than the cemetery grass, and felt her presence.

`Brimming and overflowing with life, an inner part of Hugo cried out, longing for what had been lost, believing that it could be reclaimed. Hugo thought about God, the idea of God, and then more specifically the Christian message. Was it possible that, after all, everything was not lost forever, but that instead there was hope?

He wondered: Could it be?

On the one hand, there was too much destruction to be reckoned with for Jesus to be considered. Religion made people feel good about themselves, but it had no place in the mind of a rational, thinking person who considered all the suffering in the world. What Hugo lost had been devastatingly monumental, going beyond words or description. What he lost, as far as he knew, was permanent, eternal. What he lost had been undue and wrongful, and so how was he to reconcile this with God? Hugo didn't feel close to God. He felt like he had wandered up those starry shores of the lost too far to be reached by Him.

A voice in his mind screamed *I don't want to believe! The pain is more than I can bear. I am falling apart. I have been through so much, too much, to ever consider coming back to God. I have been hurt with a wound that will not leave. Not ever.*

Hugo looked up at the flowers that lined the edge of the cemetery, swaying gently in the breeze. Another voice spoke inside him, saying, *There is healing and comfort for you. You and her will be together again. Just believe. Come to Him.*

The first voice countered, *If you believe you will be hurt again. You will be destroyed.*

Then he felt a hand on his shoulder. "You okay, big brother?"

3.

He was sitting on the bus, looking out the window, smiling to himself. He had been looking forward to this day for all of the last week.

Watching the buildings of the city grow in size, he thought about how dark and blue the buildings of Seattle were. It seemed that the skyline itself directly reflected the oceanic, maritime conditions of the environment, of the water and the sky on a cloudy day. All of it was beautiful to Hugo, who was still smiling. The city bus moved sluggishly along, merging from one lane to another.

Since that day at the cemetery, it seemed as though everything had changed and nothing had changed, as empty as that thought seemed to be. First, Hugo went two weeks without touching alcohol. Second, he was in regular contact with all the people in his life. This was particularly significant, he noted, because it would have been really unfortunate to have to go and find a new bar that showed the soccer games. After the cemetery, he talked to Lily, and while she admitted that, yes, she had had a crush on him, she also confessed that she had had more than her fair share of crushes in her life, that she was understanding of Hugo's state, and that she would be pleased to move past her crush towards a state of friendship. This was agreeable to Hugo, who didn't want to lose her friendship so easily. Third, Hugo felt as though, somehow, some of the heaviness of loss was lifted from him. The reality was that the loss was still there, and that it would always be there, but for the first time in quite a while it felt lighter. In short, he felt more at peace with the passing of Sandra. Still, he missed and longed for her, but there was an acceptance present in him that hadn't been there before. With the acceptance there came a sensation of joy, that he was being present in his own life for the first time in a year. He still had questions, but he felt more content with not having the answers to them.

Despite all of these changes and developments in Hugo's life, it remained that his life resembled the way it always had since that previous January. Hugo liked to play chess with Paul, go swimming, watch soccer at the Blue Hen where he chatted with Lily, spend time with Martin's family, and be involved in Adrian's life in the ways he was able to, and he did precisely all these things with the same vigor he ever did them. In a sense, the underlying conditions of his life changed little, if at all. Hugo kept smiling.

Being involved in Adrian's life was the motivator for Hugo's riding the bus today. He was on his way downtown, to Adrian's photo exhibition, which promised to be an enjoyable time. To maintain a sense of surprise, Adrian had not told his father what the theme was of his exhibition, leaving Hugo to wonder.

The bus came to a stop at the corner of Pine Street and 9th Street, and he got off. Four blocks of walking separated him from the exhibition, and he was pleased to walk across them despite the cloudy, dark, and rainy day. Plenty of people were out walking about. As always, he looked both ways before he crossed the street, being extra cautious. What impressed him about strolling down here was the sheer size of some of the buildings.

Crossing 5th Street, he continued on. He knew what corner his destination was at, but he wasn't positive where he needed to go in the building. Now he saw the front doorway. Heading inside, he asked at the front desk where the photography exhibition was being held, to which he heard that it was on the seventh floor. Walking into the elevator, he hit the button for the seventh floor and felt the sensation of going up. He couldn't remember the last time he was in an elevator, but it reminded him of going up the Space Needle, which caused him to feel bittersweet as he remembered.

The door of the elevator opened and Hugo was astonished by the volume of pictures that were hanging from the wall, with the name of the school in the middle. He kept walking through the main corridor. On the sides there were open spaces where people showcased their exhibitions. People were walking in and out of these spaces, admiring the displays and taking their own pictures. Hugo looked into one room and saw a collection of photographs of dogs. Another room had pictures of boats and the sea. Still another room had pictures of the Space Needle, taken at different times and from different angles. The look of pride and accomplishment in the faces of these people was encouraging to see. Hugo continued to wonder what Adrian had based his own exhibition on.

Finally, near the back of the corridor, Hugo turned and saw Adrian standing in a space all by himself. Looking at the photos that hung up, it was not immediately clear to Hugo what the unifying theme was, but after a moment it became clear to him.

"It's beautiful," Hugo said in awe, who felt weak in the knees as he thought about it.

"It's called 'Places of My Mother.'"

True to the name, hanging on the wall, in tiny frames, were pictures of all the places Sandra had loved and cared about. There was a picture of Mercer Street Diner, a picture of Alki Beach in West Seattle, one of Wedgwood, and another of the Space Needle. What united the pictures was how subtle they were. None of them were taken from obvious angles or relied on having a lot of action in the picture. Rather, the photographs were somber, elegant, and in Hugo's mind highly thoughtful.

Hugo traced the outline of the exhibition with the tip of his finger, looking at the photographs longingly, then back at his son. He smiled.

"It's beautiful," Hugo repeated. "She would have been so proud of you, son!"

The father and son hugged.

"Has anyone else come to see your exhibition?" Hugo asked.

"A few people, but you're the first person I've known."

"Well, I think you have the best display in the whole damn building."

"Thanks, Dad."

Hugo stayed a while and looked at all the photographs closely. For each photograph, he was able to identify the place, as well as why it had been significant to her.

"I wanted to get photos of Maskville, but I wasn't prepared to go on a flight," Adrian reasoned.

"Makes sense."

"So I stuck with photos from around the area. I made out a list of the places and then visited them."

"I'm sure it must have been a very rich experience for you."

"It was."

"How long did it take you to get all of this together?" Hugo was looking at a photo of Seattle University's campus as he asked this.

"About a week. We were given a pretty tight schedule to work on."

"I'll say. How about we head out of here?"

"I have to stay another half-hour, but sure we can leave then."

So they stayed and looked over the photographs several times, mesmerized by them. Eventually, he wandered into other rooms to check out some of the exhibitions on display. Of course, none of them were as good or compelling as Adrian's. Hugo had never really taken the time to acknowledge it, but Adrian was truly a talented photographer.

Riding home in Adrian's car, Hugo asked, "So what's next?"

"Well, I still have a year and a half left of the program."

"And the difficulty of the program, the challenge, you've worked that out? No more flip-flopping about whether or not you're going to stick with it?"

"I am going to stick with it, no matter what. Honestly, I got pretty stuck when they announced the exhibition. I didn't know what to base my display on, but then it just came to me."

"It was fantastic!" Hugo paused and thought about his words. "Now, son, I know I haven't done the best job of, you know, being emotionally present with you, but I want to change that!"

"I would like that."

"So tell me, then, since I never really bothered to ask you: how has the last year been for you without your mother?"

"I appreciate you asking," Adrian replied. "The truth is it has been really tough for me. I never felt like I could bring it up with you, and I didn't know how you were doing with the whole thing. So I just felt alone in it all."

"Yeah. I understand that, the feeling alone."

"I know you knew her for a long time, and so it must have been tough to think about her being gone, but she was my mother, and I really needed someone to talk to about it. I would have seen a therapist if I could have afforded it."

"Oh, Adrian..."

"Anyway, I felt misguided. I was thirty-three years old and all I had to show for myself was my barista job, so basically, I had nothing. I wanted to make you proud, but I also wanted to deal with the pain I was feeling. Also, my girlfriend broke up with me right around that time."

Hugo became aware that, evidently, he had not read all the letters that his son had sent him.

"What kind of pain did you feel?" Hugo asked.

Adrian looked at the ground. "I felt really angry, and sad, and afraid. What happens after we die? I don't know, and I choose not to think about it. I felt down sometimes, too, like depressed. Like I said, I wanted to get help, but I didn't know where to go. I also wanted to shake things up with my career, and I wanted to connect with you, so I signed up for that business program, even though I had no interest in it." He made a fist with his left hand. "That was a mistake. Then we had some conversations and I decided to follow my passion, but that proved to be challenging. Finally, I did my best to stick with the program, and I found a way to connect my passion to the pain I was feeling, and that was really cool."

"That is really cool," Hugo affirmed. "I guess I was I was so preoccupied with my own suffering that I was unable to connect with you. It was selfish of me. I apologize. You know you didn't need to do that business program to earn my approval. You already have my approval, as long as you follow your passion."

"Thanks, Dad."

Driving home, they continued to chat, to connect, and they began to talk about their shared loss, remembering her together, and in a sense, invoking her life again.

4.

He was in his bedroom, walking towards his closet. Opening the drawer of the dresser, he pulled out the frame that had contained the picture of them together. In Hugo's hand, he held a new picture, which he placed in the frame. The picture was of Adrian, Lily, Martin, Paul and him in front of Hugo's house after the trip to the cemetery. The group was standing outside, chatting, when a couple walking a dog came by. Adrian asked the girl to take the photo of the group, citing that it was important that they were all together for this day, and that it should be remembered.

Hugo looked at the photo, at the faces of the people in it who meant so much to him. He smiled.

5.

The sounds of the singing were heavenly, uplifting, and transcendent. Hugo stood next to his brother, who was next to the rest of the family. They were at Saint James Cathedral. Singing a hymn for the first time in a long while, it was refreshing and revitalizing to Hugo, like a splash of cold water on the face. So they sang songs about God coming and making Himself present, about forgiveness and grace, and a part of Hugo, his heart, started to truly open itself to the possibility, the mere chance, that the promises of God were in fact true.

Then the priest came forward. He delivered a brief message about the way in which the believer must always eventually contend with doubt. According to the priest, doubt was a way for the believer to navigate faith in a more meaningful manner, to sharpen faith. Doubt was real, and it had the capacity to drown the believer, but more often than not, said the priest, God used doubt and challenging situations to make Himself known.

Of course, Hugo felt like a wreck as he heard this message. He considered his own doubt, how he had wandered far from the religious path that had been set before him by his mother, and he started to blame himself for his own shortcomings of belief. But there was another voice that said that all was well, that it was not too late to return to faith. Doubt being used by God to sharpen faith was a nice enough idea, but why did Hugo have to lose what was most important to him in order to grow in faith? Certainly, the bulk of the last year showed a man scarred by doubt, not built up by faith. It all seemed so very cruel and unthinkable to Hugo, but still, the voice continued to speak to him, calling him to come home to God. As hard as Hugo tried to resist, he could not push away this voice, for it came from deep within. His mind was racing with many, often opposing, thoughts as he sat in the church pew.

Reconciliation between Hugo and Martin had been relatively straightforward. When he called Martin to invite him to come to the cemetery with him, Hugo offered a sincere apology for how he acted all those weeks earlier. Moreover, he apologized for being out of contact, for being absent during Christmas, and vowed that he would never act in such a way again. Martin was quick and gleeful in forgiving his brother.

They left church and Hugo continued to dwell in the uncertainty that he felt. They got into Martin's van and sped along towards Alki, where they planned to spend some time walking along the beach. As usual, the traffic was a mess, and it took them a while to cross the West Seattle Bridge, but Hugo didn't mind. He was pleased to look at the views of downtown from this southern angle. The city, it seemed, was leaning on the edge of the sea, breathing in the oceanic, salty air.

Finally, they reached Alki, where Martin had no trouble finding a parking space. It was yet another cold, cloudy day. They got out of the car and proceeded to walk. Before them, there was the expanse of sand, the tide little more than some gentle, rolling series of waves. There were some people out playing volleyball, which seemed preposterous to Hugo, but there they were still. Along the stretch of the path there were people riding bikes, restaurants and cafes and trees, pretty in their bareness.

"So what did you think of the mass, big brother?" Martin asked.

Hugo scratched his head. "It was nice. I don't know what to think about it beyond that."

"That's okay. You don't have to have all the answers figured out. I know I don't!" Martin grinned.

Hugo was gazing up at the water, the look on his face troubled. "It was a nice service," he said, "but I just don't know if I believe. I have so many questions to ask God, and it goes beyond the loss of Sandra, you know. I have spent such a large chunk of my life not believing, so it feels like I have too much momentum to make a change in my beliefs at this point. Does that make sense? Part of me doesn't feel like God would want anything to do with me because I spent so much time not wanting anything to do with Him."

"That makes sense to me, big brother. That makes sense."

"So, what do you have to say about the matter?" Hugo asked. He was expecting his brother to attempt to deliver the perfect case for why he should, in fact, begin to believe. However, Martin was quiet, not saying anything, instead content to look up at the water and then down at his own feet as he walked.

"Like I said earlier, I don't have the answers," Martin said, smiling.

On and on they walked. James, Barbara, Patricia, and Cassandra all walked together in a group in front of the two brothers, who trailed behind, walking in a more leisurely manner.

"We're reaching the peninsula now," Martin gestured.

"Let's go out there, Daddy!" Cassandra exclaimed.

"Sure thing," James said.

The family walked out towards the water. Nearby there was a tree with a rope tied to it. They stood and surveyed the view of downtown on the other side of the water.

"Beautiful," Patricia exclaimed.

"Sure is," Barbara added.

While the family admired the view, Martin and Hugo stayed back. Martin turned to Hugo. "You've been through a hell of a year," he said.

Astonished, Hugo nodded slowly.

"And the truth is," Martin continued, "I have no idea what it's been like for you. I have no idea what it's been like to be you."

"I appreciate that, Martin."

The two brothers stood before the sea, unfathomable in its vastness. In the ocean, Hugo thought, there were all the answers that a man could ever need. The answers rested just beyond reach.

Hugo broke the silence and said, "I am still on a path towards healing. I am still learning to live in her absence each and every day. I am inclined to think that I learn new things each and every day. One of the most important things I learned of all is that the ocean is one of the greatest pieces of evidence that a God exists."

"Tell me about it!"

"I can't," Hugo said. "I can't put into words what I feel when I look at the sea, but something amazing happens. That's all I can say."

"I understand, big brother. I understand."

The two brothers stood and stared at the Sound for a while. Eventually, Martin said, "I am always praying."

"What are you praying?"

Martin looked away from the view and said, "I am praying that God will reach you, that He will make his love known to you, that you will know the love your family and friends have for you, because it's there."

"I know it's there."

Martin turned to face his brother. "What do you see when you look at this view?"

Hugo paused, and then said, "Put simply, I see all of last year distilled into the water. Everything, the people, the feelings, the memories, it's all there." Hugo's face looked peaceful.

For a long time, the two brothers stood before the water. Again and again, the water lapped against the sandy shore. From the endless sea, the water emerged as a wave, which crashed into the shore and broke up into droplets of water, which were then absorbed back into the sea.

Hugo looked at his brother. "This is my form of prayer."

"What is?"

"Just being with the sea."

"I think you're on your way," Martin said.

"What do you mean?"

"I'm inclined to believe God will reach you one day. What I mean is that you are on your way towards Him."

Again Hugo sighed. "I don't really want to go into that, to be honest. I just want to enjoy this moment. I told you earlier how I feel about the matter. Part of me wants to believe, but part of me is resolute in believing what I have always believed."

"Makes sense."

"I'm just not ready," Hugo said, his eyes not wavering from the water. "I'm not ready to fully commit to believing in a loving God. I haven't ruled it out fully, but here today, here right now, I'm just not ready."

"I understand, big brother. I honor that."

Hugo grabbed his brother in an embrace. "One thing I do know is how much I love you. I love you all, though I don't always do the best job of showing it. Please forgive me for being so heartless at times."

"I will always love you, big brother."

The two brothers, standing among the waves, filled with love, looked at the water.

"I'm gonna go get the others," Martin said, walking out towards the peninsula.

Standing alone before the sea, Hugo felt that he was being absorbed into it. Content, at ease, knowing peace, he stood solemnly.

"Maybe someday," Hugo said softly. "Maybe."

If you enjoyed this book, please consider leaving a review or a rating online.

For author news, new titles, and discount offers, subscribe to the Sulis International mailing list: https://goo.gl/2SVDju

ABOUT THE AUTHOR

Sean T. Anderson is a writer living in Seattle. A graduate of the University of Washington, he enjoys running, meditating, and being in nature. *The Year of Oceans* is his fourth novel.

87582202R00211

Made in the USA
Lexington, KY
26 April 2018